Born in Manchester of an Antrim father and a Mayo mother, DJ Kelly is a former UK government servant, turned researcher, genealogist, novelist and short-story writer. Having spent time in 20 countries across 4 continents, she now enjoys early retirement in Buckinghamshire, England, and this is her first full length novel to be published.

TITANIC PRESS

A WISTFUL EYE

The Tragedy of a Titanic Shipwright

DJ Kelly

Published by FeedARead.com – funded by The Arts Council

This book is lovingly dedicated to my father, David Kelly, late of Carrickfergus and Manchester, maintenance engineer, storyteller, joker and armchair adventurer, who taught me to read when I was three years old.

Acknowledgements

I should like to express my deep gratitude to my cousins Mary Downs (Australia), Jane Potter (Belfast), Gill Patterson (London) and Jean Ware (Dorset) for their unstinting assistance with my family history research; to my uncle 'just' Jim Kelly (late of Carrickfergus), for his ninety-two years of personal memories; to David Huddlestone at the Public Records Office of Northern Ireland; Dr Gregory O'Connor at National Archive of Ireland; David McVeigh at Harland & Wolff, and to my husband Terry and daughter Amy for their support, encouragement and indulgence.

CONTENTS

Part One – **THE YARDS**

The spring of nineteen ten was a long time coming to Northern Ireland. Winter had been slow to relinquish its iron grip on the land and reluctant daffodils were still in the green out around the fine gardens of the suburbs. In the crowded working class districts of Belfast however, there were few flowers to herald the changing of the seasons. Here, it was the gradually increasing daylight and the lessening of evening chills which were interpreted as a precursor of spring. As March gusted into April, the trees along Duncairn Gardens grudgingly opened their pink and white blossom, lifting the spirits of passers-by and providing free confetti for weddings at the church of St Barnabas.

The middle-aged couple trundled the hired handcart, laden with their furniture and cooking utensils, past the church and over the New Lodge Road, leaving early morning tracks in the damp, petal-strewn pavements. They had been up since early on, unable to sleep for the prospect of all they had to do for their latest house move. William Henry Kelly had taken the Saturday off work. He would make several more trips between their old house in Collyer Street and the newly rented little house in Shandon Street, before their modest possessions were all installed. His wife Belle now helped him unload the larger items, such as the dismantled bedstead and mattress, and manoeuvre them up the stairs of the new house, before she set about hanging their net curtains in the front windows, for privacy from their as yet unacquainted neighbours. Next, she lit a fire ready to boil the kettle, whenever it would appear off the cart, for a welcome cup of tea at the end of their labours.

The new house was not new at all, of course. There *were* no new houses in the New Lodge area, contrary to what the name might suggest, and nor were there any in Tiger's Bay, whence they had come. Of course, there weren't any Tigers there either. Belfast was a place of contradictions, right enough. Sailortown, however, where the couple had started their married life more than thirty years earlier, was indeed home to sailors, and their families, as well as to those who supported the city's great maritime tradition - the shipwrights, the ropemakers, the engine makers, the dockers and carters. All Belfast's working class neighbourhoods shared a dowdy and close-knit character. William Henry thought that maybe the people did too. One little street looked much like the next and one working class family looked much like another. The little red-brick dwellings had been hastily constructed, to a mean specification, almost a century earlier, to accommodate the many workers needed to support Belfast's rapidly developing industries. On slob lands, where once the curlew swooped and the oyster-catcher stooped, slate-roofed terraces had sprouted and had spread upwards in tightly packed rows, radiating outwards from the docks, around the shipyards, factories and warehouses. Where purple sea fog had once rolled in unimpeded, now grey smoke curled skywards from chimneys, both tall and small.

These industries, blooming like fungus around the swampy mouth of the Lagan, had drawn in from the Antrim countryside able-bodied men in their thousands. Men of agriculture had turned their calloused hands from the plough to the hammer and the bill-hook, and were now building ships and man-handling cargoes. Women too, who once had planted potatoes or herded cattle, now were spinning flax, twisting out ropes, and rolling tobacco. It was not only their occupations which many of the countrymen had changed when they came to Belfast however. Many of these men and their families had only survived a decade of famine by exchanging their Catholic beliefs for Protestant soup. This had been a few years before William Henry was born, of course and, though it was something the old folks still spoke of, it was a subject upon which William Henry's father had remained silent.

Belfast had been a town back then, not a city, and one which had been built *by* Protestants *for* Protestants. The forty thousand or so Catholics who had sought relief there from the starvation of the countryside had found no housing, jobs or schools waiting for *them*. The city's one Catholic church could offer little succour for the starving, and indeed could not even accommodate a fraction of them at Sunday mass, and they had worshipped on their knees in the streets around the church, praying for their survival. The town had offered them two choices – adapt or die. Most had adapted. William Henry's own father had been fortunate enough to have a post as head gardener on an estate in rural Antrim and so had not been as dependent upon the potato crop for sustenance as had his neighbours. In the eighteen fifties however, he too had been lured by the prospect of a better salary and improved prospects for his children, and he had migrated to Belfast with his wife and two young sons, William Henry and Patrick.

James Hodges Kelly's plainly Irish surname had raised a few eyebrows at first but, of course, it was a surname also found in Scotland, whence many of the Belfast Protestants had originated. William Henry did not know for certain how his father had come to have the middle name Hodges, which was English and therefore Protestant-sounding. He had asked, but had simply been told it was an old family name of long standing. Anywhere else in the world, this might not matter, but in Belfast it mattered a great deal. His father had once mumbled something about a tradition whereby boys in the family were named either James Hodges or William Henry. He did not seem to know how far back the tradition ran however.

William Henry would have liked to get to the bottom of this family custom, as he took a keen interest in history and also in politics – so far as his education and means would allow. He had noticed there were a number of men named Hodges who were eminent in scientific and medical fields in Belfast. He wondered if he shared a common ancestry with them or whether it was simply the case that his father had adopted this less Catholic-sounding name. Whatever the case, William Henry had ensured he continued the family tradition by naming his own firstborn son James Hodges Kelly and his younger son William Henry, after himself. The Hodges name had obviously been lucky for his father who, on quitting his gardening job, found no

2

difficulty in being recruited as a gardener for the Belfast Corporation, in the city's Botanical Gardens. William Henry and Patrick had benefited from a more modern, if still modest, learning at one of Belfast's Protestant church schools, as had their subsequent Belfast-born siblings.

It was a bit of a struggle manoeuvring the handcart up and down the high pavements as they crossed over Duncairn Gardens by the Presbyterian Church, and for a moment, William Henry thought he had lost control of the load, but passers-by were quick to assist. One kind young man even helped them push the cart all the way down Edlingham Street and across the New Lodge Road, since he assured them he was going that way himself anyway.

"Much obliged t'ye son," William Henry beamed at the youth who wished them well.

A few blocks along the New Lodge was William Henry's old school. Learning will set you free – or so William Henry's teacher had told him forty odd years ago. Quite how it would set him free, William Henry had still to learn. He had needed little learning for his work in the shipyards. However, it was his capacity for hard work and his accumulated experience that had ensured he kept his job there. Since leaving school, William Henry had made an honest if hard living with Messrs Harland and Wolff. As a youth, in his early service at their Queen's Island shipyard, he had been employed in processing Scandinavian pine giants into masts for sailing ships. Although short of stature, he had developed brawn at his trade. Next, he had been apprenticed as a caulker, making water tight the wooden trading vessels, which sailed under canvas out of the Belfast Lough to all corners of the globe. Armed with a caulker's knife, a wooden mallet and caulker's irons, he had laboriously applied the oakum and tarry sealant to the gaps between the wooden ships' timbers. The hot tar had burned away the skin on the tips of his fingers, until he no longer felt its heat.

He had laboured hard all his life, for such was his birthright. As a man with a strong work ethic and a keen sense of being part of the greatness of industrial Belfast, he had kept his shoulder to the wheel and his head down, in all weathers. Weather was a crucial factor in the shipyards, one which determined how the working day would go, whether pleasantly, passably or badly. Working out of doors, up on the staging, through the long Belfast winters, exposed to the winds which blew in up the Lough from the Atlantic and to the cruel sleet which vented sideways off the top of the Mournes, was a truly miserable experience. Moreover, the constant wind and the damp penetrated William Henry's inadequate clothing, sending rheumatic chills deep into his bones. As he sat by the fire of an evening, watching his damp clothes steam dry on the rackety wooden clothes maiden, the pain would begin to grip him. The many hours of standing at his work had stiffened his joints and patterned his legs with varicose veins, and the clamping of the short, solid caulker's knife between his teeth had worn away his lower front incisors, to a degree that they stung him with both the heat and the cold.

Bronchitis was another unwelcome reward for his outdoor labours and, as Belle would often complain, his chest wheezed and whistled like a banshee. His work enabled him to put food on his family's table however, and sure didn't everyone in Belfast fall victim to infections and skin ailments from time to time? However, he comforted himself with the thought that he was no worse off than his fellow workers,

3

and at least he was in permanent employment. He could afford to feed and clothe his family and keep a rented roof over their heads. That the casual dock labourers - Catholics for the most part - endured even worse working conditions and received pay which was inconstant did not console him. The conviction that his work was important had sustained him through the years, as had the hope that his own children and grandchildren would fare better than he.

By midday, the house was pretty much straight. Since William Henry and Belle did not own much in the way of furniture, everything fitted in pretty well. William Henry was upstairs, reassembling their iron bedstead, hammering it together with a half brick found out in the yard, when there was a knock at the front door. Their youngest son, eighteen year old William Henry junior - known to all as Billy to avoid confusion – did not await admission but let himself in through the unlocked front door. He carried a newspaper parcel under his coat and an unwrapped loaf of bread under his arm. He placed these down on the small kitchen table and produced a packet of butter from his jacket pocket.

"Fish an' chips!" he announced, "an' I brought ye a baker's loaf an' some Irish creamery butter to go with it."

Fish and chips was only an occasional indulgence for the couple, and most Belfast working folks had taken to buying imported Danish butter these days, for it was a good deal cheaper than, if inferior to, the home produced butter. Thus the meal was a special treat and a most welcome gesture.

"Ah, God love ye, son!" Belle kissed her boy's cheek. "Sit ye down and I'll find the forks. Wim Henery," she called up the stairs, for *Wim Henery* was what she called her husband, partly out of fondness and partly in jest, for he loftily insisted on both his names being used. If his workmates thought him odd for this, they did not remark upon it.

"Wim Henery," Belle called again, with more urgency, "woor Billy's brought us round fish an' chips. C'mon down and get it while it's hot."

William Henry's boots came clattering down the bare, wooden stairs and he patted the youth warmly on the back. The two kitchen chairs were cleared of pots, plates and linens, and the fireside stool was drawn up to the table. The three sat down to eat their lunch, straight out of its newspaper wrappings, before the now crackling fire. Belle cut and buttered thick slices of bread and poured their tea. William Henry tipped some of his into a saucer and blew on it. He sipped at it, even though it was still hot enough to irritate his sensitive broken teeth, for his exertions had given him a thirst. Food and warmth soon cheered the couple, as did Billy's news and gossip, hot from the customers at the *Glenalina Gentlemen's Hair Saloon* where he worked. Billy had served his apprenticeship at the barber's shop and he was now earning a modest wage as a fully fledged hairdresser. William Henry was secretly pleased that his youngest son would not have to blister his hands to make a living, but of course never in a million years would he admit this. Young Billy would never know his father was proud of him. Instead, William Henry would tease him about the effete nature of his employment.

"Did ye have any interestin' heads in yer hands this week then, son?" William Henry asked.

4

"Ach, just the usual crowd, from local businesses, some passin' trade, an' all," Billy informed him, "but we do more business in early evenin' when the yards closes and the squads calls in on the way home. Saturdays, after the yards shuts fer the week, is best though, as they queue down the road. There's one toff always calls in of a Saturday mornin', has his hair and moustache trimmed, has a shave and a wee dab of bay rum, then says 'I'm off now for an appointment with my accountant', and he saunters just a few doors down as far as the bookies. It's his *turf* accountant he's seein'."

"I wonder you don't cut his hair in the bookies' shop, for all the time you spend in there yourself," said his mother reprovingly.

"Ach, don't be naggin' the boy now, Belle," William Henry chided, "sure, we see little enough of him these days as it is. Don't you be drivin' him away."

"*Me* drive him away, well, Wim Henery ...?" Belle began to challenge him.

"What's the talk about this comet in the sky, then?" William Henry asked, changing the subject briskly and gesticulating ceilingwards with a chip impaled upon his fork.

"Aye, *Halley's* comet, it's called," Billy enthused, "it only comes around somethin' like every seventy five years or so, and the papers say we might get a good view of it tha night, that's if the clouds lifts. 'Trouble is it's hard to see the night sky from here in the city, what with all the street lights, so a bunch of us is going up tha Cave Hill to have a look from there. Do yez want to come along?"

"Not me," declared Belle, "for its comin' is said to be bad luck, isn't it?"

"Ach it's just a shower of meteorites - all rocks an' stuff that goes roun' the earth and keeps comin' roun' this way once in every lifetime, so why would it be unlucky?" Billy asked.

"Well now," began his father, "I heard that the earth's goin' to be passin' through a cloud of poison gases that the comet's trailin' behin' itself. That can't be good for a start. And I'm mebbe not as superstitious as your mother and the rest of the folks around here, but I've been readin' in the papers that the comet has always been considered to be an ill omen. According to the *Telegraph*, it first got a mention in the *Annals of Ulster* as bein' seen back in nine hunnert and twelve, and that was a dark and rainy year when the crops failed. Loads of people starved to death, so they did. And then, when the comet was seen again in ten sixty six, sure it certainly wasn't lucky for auld King Harold, was it?"

"Mebbe not," grinned Billy, "but it was more than lucky for William the Conqueror, wasn't it?"

"Then," William Henry continued, ignoring his son's logic, "they say that when it appeared back in the twelve hunnerts, that there Genghis Khan gets up aff his hunkers and sets about conquerin' Asia, so he does. Serious stuff, eh? Here's another strange thing though, that American writer, Mark Twain – d'ye mind I used to read you weans his Huckleberry Finn stories? – well, he was born at the time of the comet's last appearance in the eighteen thirties, and he's predictin' that the comet has now come back to take him. He's convinced he's gonnae die any day now."

Belle shivered and rose to clear the table, "ach that's horrible, fancy knowin' when you're goin' to die. I wouldn't want to know."

5

"Ach, why would *you* be thinking of dyin', ya daft aul hen ya, sure you're only forty nine?" her husband chided, "but Mark Twain must be seventy five now, so it's a safe bet he's not got long to go anyway. 'Course, he's probably sayin' all this just to get in the papers. There's mebbe more Americans will rush out and buy his books if they think he's about to die. It's just a publicity gimmick, that's all it is."

"Anyway, I thought we already seen the comet, back in January or February, wasn't it?" Belle asked.

"Ah," said William Henry, "that was a different comet, so it was. They weren't expectin' that one, and it didn't have a name. It took them 'stronomers by surprise."

"So, did anythin' bad happen when *that* comet came?" Belle asked.

The two men thought for a minute, then William Henry spoke; "Well, the nationalists gained eighty two seats in parliament at the February elections, and that meant the Home Rule Bill came up again. That was pretty bad news for us. We wuz hopin' the bill had gone away."

"Oh aye," added Billy, "and then Driscoll, the British featherweight champion, lost in his bid for the world title at Cardiff, and I lost a packet at the bookies. It was an outrageous decision, so it was, for he should have won against that Yank!"

"I'll tell you who you might see up the Cave Hill thanight," said William Henry, "and that's Thomas Andrews, one of the managin' directors of Harland and Wolff, for he's takin' his good lady and their wee daughter up there to see the comet."

"How d'ye know that?" Billy asked, impressed that his father should be acquainted with such a notable figure in the management of the shipyards.

"He told me so himself, for he was down last week lookin' over the Titanic, him and his uncle, Alick Carlisle, who's head o' the design department," his father smiled, "and, see, Andrews may be nephew to Lord Pirrie who owns the yards, but he served his time as an apprentice from sixteen just like the rest of us. He's awful well educated too, so he is, but he's a very easy manner with the shipwrights. He comes down and talks to us often, like we wuz his equals and asks us our opinion of the design. A lovely fellah althagether, so he is. No airs nor graces at all."

"Ach never mind themmins," Belle came and ran a hand through her son's hair, "how's things with you, son? Is your new landlady feedin' ye alright?"

Billy promised her he was being well looked after, but Belle was not reassured. Billy had been the last of their five children still living at home and had moved out just a week ago. Only a few months before that, his twenty year old sister, wee Belle, had also left to live with her married sister Jane over in Upper Canning Street. Wee Belle had said it was because of Jane's illness, so she could help with looking after Jane's baby girl, and in truth Jane's house was nearer to the linen mill where wee Belle worked, but her mother knew it was she and William Henry had driven their children away.

Belle swept back a few stray strands of her generous dark hair. A few soft, feathery tendrils framed her still fine features, though more than a glint of silver might be glimpsed at her temples. She was still a fine looking woman, William Henry reflected, as he glanced across at her. He could still glimpse the young girl whose ready smile and musical laughter had first bewitched him over three decades before. These days however, she smiled less often than she used to, and nor did she

6

sing as once she did. He would often do his best to make her laugh, and sometimes he succeeded, though these days, whenever she did laugh, she would first raise her hand to her mouth. Her looks were marred only by the absence of a front tooth. It was widely believed that a woman lost one tooth for every child she bore. 'A gnasher for a smasher' Belle's own, toothless mother used to say. Belle, having had six children but lost only one tooth, would say she had got off lightly. She thought it just as well that she had little to smile about these days, as she was still embarrassed about the gap. She now caught her husband's admiring glance however and blushed. 'Silly old fool' she thought, and set about tidying the table. She smoothed out the sheets of the chip shop's *Belfast Telegraph*. She would read them later and then they would be cut up into squares and hung out in the toilet down the yard, for further practical purposes.

Billy quaffed the last of his tea and put his coat on. As she saw her son prepare to return to his work, Belle felt a bitter stab of regret that her children were now all flown from her nest, and that it was just she and William Henry remaining.

"Cheerio son," William Henry called after him, "an' if I don't see ye through tha week, I'll see ye through tha windy!"

Belle stood at the door and watched her youngest as he headed off down the street. She reflected that, ever since his birth - was it really eighteen years ago now? - she had experienced a darkness which turned up on her horizon every so often. Being unable either to see or understand it, she could only interpret it as an unremitting black cloud. All her life's heartache and bad experiences were bound up within that cloud. When it came, it brought out in her the resentment she felt at her life. It stirred up recollections of the many arguments and, worst of all, the memory of the first of the two little girls who had been named Isabella, after her own mother. That beautiful, curly-haired infant - their first wee Belle - had lived just long enough to develop into a sweet-natured child with her father's blue-grey eyes. Her two older sisters had adored playing with her. Tragically however, she had died just two weeks before wee Jimmy was born.

As Belle now put the butter and milk away in the press, she again recalled her lost little girl. Seeing the infant waste away, had broken Belle's heart. She had given up breastfeeding little Belle of course. She had no choice, as she had another baby on the way back then, but her little girl had been weaned on the best infant food in Belfast. Everyone swore by evaporated milk as a weaning food. It came sealed in a tin, all nice and hygienic, which the grocer would open for you with his tin opener. Left in the tin on a cool windowsill, it would stay fresh for days. She did not know why little Belle had failed to thrive on this but had suffered all manner of stomach ache and digestive complaints. She had not been able to keep the milk down. *Marasmus* was the diagnosis of the doctor at the workhouse hospital, for all that that meant to Belle. She had entrusted her daughter to the hospital's care for the last days of her life, but to no avail. William Henry and his brother Patrick had walked in silence up the hill in the City Cemetery, carrying between them the little white coffin. They had lain wee Belle to rest in the family plot which William Henry had purchased in anticipation of the day when they would join their little girl. From that spot, there was a clear view of the beautiful hill nearby. Belle comforted herself with the thought that, if wee Belle's spirit was playing here, she would be happy. Still,

7

God had blessed them with three more healthy children and all five were now grown. Happily, the second wee Belle and her siblings enjoyed better health, a fact for which her mother thanked God each and every day.

Belle and William Henry's elder son, Jimmy, was away at sea with the Royal Navy's China Fleet; elder daughters Jane and Alice were married and settled in their own homes nearby and wee Belle was working as a stitcher in the linen mill. Billy had aspirations of one day running his own hairdressing establishment. With all her children raised to adulthood, Belle should have been able now to sit back in peaceful contentment, but no, for the black cloud would re-appear every now and again. Just when she thought perhaps things were brightening up, it would hover above her and release all its pent-up misery upon her, like the cold, Belfast rain. Her only escape from it was the insensibility offered by drink. She did not drink *every* day, as her husband did. It was enough that he spent so much of their income on drink without both of them doing so. However, on those days when the dark mood came upon her, she felt it necessary to seek relief in the same medicine which appeared to drive away William Henry's woes and discomforts – "sauce for the gander is sauce for the goose" she would say.

Belle stoked up the fire. The glow from the hearth filled the void in the room left by Billy's departure and made her feel a little cheerier. William Henry chided her for being so profligate with the fuel, when there would be just the two of them at home on this mild spring afternoon. He did not understand the importance to her of warmth and light, and indeed she had not the words to explain it. Whilst the children were still young, Belle had been busy enough to ignore her depressive feelings - mostly. However, now that the children had all left home and William Henry was out of the house for ten hours or more each day, it would not take her long to tend this small and empty house. Now she feared she would have too much time to reflect, to dwell on her loneliness. She gazed around the little kitchen, which was indeed tiny but which nonetheless accommodated their little wooden table and two chairs and a little sofa. The iron range was the same as the one in their previous house and the tiny scullery, with its large sink, single, cold water tap and old iron mangle, was similarly appointed to the Collyer Street scullery. Their former house had boasted a larger front parlour, which they had converted into a little grocery shop but Belle thought the Shandon Street parlour ample space for the two of them now. They would see out their declining years together comfortably enough in this little house.

Although she had enjoyed chatting with the locals who came into the Collyer Street shop for their messages, there were mornings when, William Henry having departed for the yards, her depression would not let her get out of bed. Unconcerned that customers were knocking, she would only rouse herself when prompted by hunger. A pot of tea might have cheered her, but she would have to light a fire to boil the water and somehow she could not raise the energy or enthusiasm for that. Staring into the blackness of the grate, its dead ashes awaiting removal to the earth closet down the yard, she would instead succumb to inertia. If there were liquor in the house, she would take a wee drink, just to chase the pain away. The relief that it brought would increase when she followed the one wee drink with another. Soon however, the tiredness would come upon her and she no longer felt like leaving her chair. She would scarcely notice the day passing and the arrival of evening.

On better days however, she would clear out the ashes, light a fire and do the weekly laundry and then use the washing water to swill over the floors. Her chores completed, she would take herself out to seek out the company of one of the neighbourhood women. Sometimes, she would invite one of them back for a cup of tea and a chat by the fireside. As the afternoon wore on, they would have a convivial drink of porter together, and then maybe another one or two. Drink was an escape, of sorts. It took her out of herself, made her feel calm and relaxed and helped her sleep. She would sometimes snooze in the afternoon, to pass the time until William Henry came home. Some days, the little bit of housework there was would be put off until the afternoon, and some days it would not be done at all. She usually tried to ensure there was a hot supper awaiting William Henry on his return from the yard, but some days, that did not happen. She felt though that, over the years, she had been a good wife to William Henry and that generally he had no cause for complaint, unless, of course, he had too much drink taken himself.

William Henry now poured himself another cup of tea. As he too looked around at the plain and dingy kitchen, he also thought of the bigger property they had left back in Collyer Street. He had put all their savings into buying the stock for their little shop, hoping it would keep Belle occupied and give her some sort of responsibility and a bit of company. He cared for Belle deeply, but he often wished relations between them were as good as they had been in the early days. He never understood why this was not so. He worked hard and brought home his pay - well most of it. The shop had not worked out as he had planned, however. He had not understood why sometimes Belle had not felt like opening the door to either customers or delivery men. Callers had knocked and knocked and then left. When he came home, the neighbours would tell him of the knocking and he would be embarassed. He would find the notes on the mat, advising of unsuccessful attempts to deliver goods, then he would find Belle herself indoors, half comatose, and he would lose his temper with her, not that it took much for him to lose his temper, especially if he had had his customary end of day drinks on the way home from the yards.

William Henry drank heavily of course. It was expected of a man to drink. For most working men these days life revolved around the public house. Nowhere was this truer than in Belfast, as it was the norm for the shipwrights to assemble at their chosen pub every pay day, so that each foreman could dole out the pay and bonuses to his team. It would be considered odd if a man turned up at the pub to collect his money and then left without standing his round. William Henry did not like to be thought odd. He knew his work mates already thought him a little strange for his love of reading and for his strong views, which he often expressed for their edification - with increased volubility after a drink or two. Then again, he could not be such a difficult man, for, if he were, surely he would have no mates at all. He could not help the passion he felt for the way the world was going. He had recently read a report in the *Belfast Newsletter* in which it was estimated the average British workman spent almost a third of his income on drink. He thought this terrible as, clearly he had some catching up to do. On the face of it, this seemed a damning statistic, but then again, beer provided energy for a working man. The pieces of bread and jam which William Henry took to his work to eat for breakfast and lunch certainly were not enough to provide a shipyard worker with the energy he needed for what was required of him. Unlike the managers in the yards, who sat down each day to a two course luncheon in the canteen, the tradesman had to eat his *piece* as he worked.

William Henry and Belle hoped that the house move and the brighter spring weather would invigorate them and drive some of the old cobwebs out of their life. The departure of their youngest son and daughter had made them seriously examine the way they lived their lives. In fact their children had given them an ultimatum. Unless they cut down on their drinking, the children would stay away. The couple had therefore agreed to sign the pledge. William Henry did not know if signing a bit of paper would actually firm up their resolve, but he had agreed not to visit the pub en route home each evening. He reasoned that, if he were home earlier, this would shorten Belle's lonely day and perhaps lift her gloom. There were no public houses or spirit grocers in Shandon Street, so temptation was not close at hand, and he hoped neither he nor Belle would be tempted to stray further afield in search of a drink. For her part, Belle felt that less time spent alone and the longer daylight hours might be just the tonic she needed. Shandon Street was quite a way from their old place, and there were no shipyard workers living here. They knew no-one in their new street, which was a good thing, for the gossip would not follow them. She hoped to make new acquaintances but, if ever she felt lonely, she would walk the seven blocks to where her daughters lived. It would be a fresh start.

Over the course of the next week, William Henry found himself waking up early each day and feeling unusually refreshed. He was a little sprightlier in his step now as he set off each morning for the Queen's Island. He was pleased to note that the days were getting a little longer and warmer. He also felt brighter in himself, having had a rare Saturday off for moving house, and a relaxed Sunday with a good lunch, followed by a night's sound sleep - achieved without the inducement of alcohol. Instead of calling in at the pub with his squad each evening after work, he would now bring home a newspaper and he and Belle would split it between them after they had eaten their evening meal, settling down to enjoy a quiet read. William Henry devoured the news and politics whilst Belle was an avid follower of the murder cases and criminal trials. She had an almost photographic memory when it came to famous murder cases. She could tell you who had murdered whom, and when, and how, and what the outcome of the case had been. She was quick to spot the news that one of William Henry's favourite authors, Mark Twain, had died the very day after Billy and his mates had gone to the Cave Hill to watch for the comet. She had been right about the comet bringing bad luck, and Twain had been correct in prophesying his own death. It seemed the comet had brought Twain into this world and it had indeed taken him away again.

The couple now agreed they did not need a drink in order to enjoy themselves, and instead they engaged in conversation and had a laugh at the day's events. William Henry was pleased to notice the little house was now clean and tidy each evening on his return. Washing would be drying on the maiden and supper bubbling in their old blackened pot over the fire. On the Tuesday evening, they walked along

10

to Upper Canning Street to visit their daughter Jane, her husband Walter and their baby granddaughter, Alice Evelyn. They were pleased to find Jane's health now improved. Wee Belle, was still lodging with Jane and Walter and she now hurried off down the road to fetch her other sister Alice and her husband Henry Anderson up to join them. Later on, Billy called in, with his new sweetheart, a slightly built and quiet young girl named Edith Walker.

The talk was all about William Henry's younger brother John, whose wife, thirty-one year old Lizzie, was expecting her eighth child any day. John Kelly, also worked at Harland and Wolff as a driller. Lizzie had given birth to seven girls, though the first born had died at only ten days old, and, naturally enough, they were hoping for a boy this time around. William Henry and Belle stayed until quite late, enjoying the company of their extended family, and Jane prepared tea and sandwiches for everyone. Later, on the walk home, William Henry declared that, walking out late at night with Belle, he was reminded of their courting days. On an impulse, fuelled by nothing stronger than tea, he pulled a handful of blue grape hyacinths from a garden and thrust them into Belle's hands, giving her a cuddle as he did so. His wife blushed and told him not to be so soft. He noticed the way the light from each streetlamp passed over her like a golden veil, illuminating her dark hair and casting gentle shadows over her still attractive profile. He savoured the thought that, after thirty years of marriage and six children, he still loved Belle very deeply. As they walked on, he sang to her the children's skipping song which always made her smile:

"She is handsome, she is pretty, she is the Belle of Belfast City, she goes a courtin' one, two three, please won't you tell me who is she?"

That night, the couple slept entwined in each other's arms, tired but contented, and not a cross word had passed between them.

On the Thursday, the prayers of John and Lizzie were answered, with the birth of a son. He was the latest family member to be named James Hodges Kelly, after his paternal grandfather. John had invited William Henry to join him that night in 'wettin' tha baby's head' down at the pub, but William Henry had made his excuses. Things were going well thus far for him and Belle and he wanted to avoid the over-indulgence that such a celebration would inevitably bring. He promised that he and Belle would be over on the weekend instead to see the new wean.

Friday came around at last, and William Henry set off for the yards at half past six in the morning with a plan forming in his head. Friday was pay day and he would collect his money from Johnnie at the pub after work but this time he would not linger. He would come home promptly and treat Belle to a hot supper from the local cook shop, then a night out at the pictures. Neither of them had ever been to the cinema before, but they had been talking about doing ever so since the *Star Picture Palace* had opened a couple of years earlier. The *Star* was Belfast's first purpose built cinema, and Billy had said it was beautiful inside, all plush seating and soft lighting. Now several more picture houses had opened up around the city, so William Henry thought it was time he and Belle went along to see what all the fuss was about. The *Star* was currently showing *Frankenstein*, an American film about a monster made up from bits of dead bodies. A couple of the men in the squad had been to see it and said it was very scary. Belle might take some persuasion, but he felt sure she would enjoy it, for all the corpses in it must surely warrant a good murder. Yes, Belle would like that.

Along his walk to work, William Henry fell in with other men from the yards, as they spilled out of their little houses, and he joined in with their conversation. Gradually, the various streams of men from the different little streets became a procession, and this in turn became a vast throng. There were some fifteen thousand men employed in the yards of Harland and Wolff and all the tradesmen and labourers wore similar garb of mismatched jackets, trousers, waistcoats and caps. For the past five years or more, William Henry had worn the same brown *duncher*, as the tradesman's cloth cap was called hereabouts. It was somewhat greasy and a little threadbare in places, but it sat comfortably enough on his head, so he saw no need to change it. Belle joked that, if they ever ran out of lard down at the chip shop, he could wring a pint or two of grease out of his *duncher* for them. He had his Sunday best cap at home, of course. If ever that became shabby, then it would be relegated to serve as his working cap and a new one bought for Sunday use. He also favoured white shirts, the kind with detachable collars, though he had no need of collars and studs in his work, so a cotton muffler sat knotted at the neck instead, to soak up the sweat of his labours and keep the draughts at bay.

As the large red brick walls of the shipyard came into view, a man wearing different headgear appeared at William Henry's side. John James Beasant was under foreman in William Henry's caulking squad. The foremen did not wear the cloth cap of the shipwright, but sported instead black bowlers, as their unofficial badge of office. In fact, amongst the men, the foremen were referred to as *the hats*. Johnnie lived in Spencer Street and had worked with William Henry for many a year. William Henry had a high regard for him and, since Johnnie's promotion, had taken to calling him, jokingly but respectfully, *Top Hat*. Johnnie in turn looked out for his old friend. Forty-nine year old Johnnie was also secretary of their union and, as such, was the champion of the men's employment rights and fought regular battles for fairness in their terms and conditions. Johnnie was an adoring father to eight children, and, although a regular worshipper with the Christian Bretheren, he would tolerate no talk of religious preference or prejudice in the squad. William Henry admired him for that.

William Henry did not normally have the pleasure of Johnnie's company on the way to work of a morning. It was normal for *the hats* to be at the yards ahead of their squads, to ensure that all the men turned up, had work assigned to them and were equipped with all the tools and supplies necessary to do the work. This Monday morning however, Johnnie was running a little late, which gave the two old friends an opportunity to talk as they made their way through the Queen's yard to the slips. Most of Johnnie's efforts these days went towards solving demarcation disputes. As new working methods and technologies were introduced, the delineation of work between the various trades had become blurred. None of the trades wished to cede any aspect of their work to another. It was common for one union to be locked into a dispute with another, each union battling to safeguard its respective members' interests. This struggle was made more difficult by the fact that the tradesmen on both sides of such a demarcation issue might both be represented by the same union. To add to Johnnie's difficulties, the unions were also fighting the war on another front - with the shipyard management.

"'Mornin' William Henry, how's it goin'?" Johnnie greeted him pleasantly.

"Aye fine, how's yerself, *Top Hat*?" his old friend asked.

"Gat to go till a meetin' this afternoon," Johnnie advised him, "on tha management's proposal to reduce squad sizes now that we have tha new technology up an' runnin'."

"Ach, we knew this would come, didn't we?" William Henry shook his head, "for it doesn't take a team of eight men to operate them new hydraulic rivetin' machines, no nor the pumps neither. But, sure for what little they pay us, throwing a couple of men off each squad isn't much of a savin'. Sure, it wouldn't keep Lord Pirrie in cigars, would it?"

"It's worse than that," Johnnie now looked grave, "for them machines can be operated by unskilled men, so they can. It'll be the skilled men gets laid aff and the cheaper labourers that'll be buildin' tha ships."

William Henry knew Johnnie was right to be worried. He knew what pressures motivated the yard bosses and he knew what threats faced the skilled tradesmen, for he and Johnnie had often discussed the subject. The shipyards of Scotland and the north east of England enjoyed the advantage of nearby sources of coal and iron. Belfast however was disadvantaged in having to import the raw materials for its ship building industry. Thus the Harland and Wolff yard and its neighbour and competitor, Workman Clark, faced even stiffer competition from the Scottish yards for contracts. Belfast imported her raw materials by sea via the Belfast Lough, and of course Belfast was not even a natural harbour, but had to be dredged of mud periodically, to keep the channels clear for the marine traffic. In hindsight, Belfast had not been the ideal location for shipyards at all. Its only asset was labour, and, as was the case the world over, manpower was cheap, easily sourced and expendable. Had the Belfast yards not been established, Ulstermen would have migrated to Scotland in search of work. It was a situation which always reminded William Henry of the old joke about the stranger seeking directions of an Irishman, whose response was "sure, I wouldn't have started from here".

"It's all about cost savin'," Johnnie continued, "and the best way of saving cost is to reduce tha size of tha workforce. More than half the men here now is fully skilled and them's who I represent. They've all served their apprenticeships and are fully trained. Then there's the semi-skilled, tha stagers and crane drivers, who niver gat any training at all and they earn only half what we do. They're in a union now, but they'll be cut back as well and replaced by the daily labourers who earn least of all. The labourers'll be desperate to take our jobs. There was a time when the unions would not let than happen but of course they're unionised now too, so the management is negotiatin' separately with *their* union."

"Ach, that'll be a black day for us when that happens," William Henry agreed, "for it's took us years to get a half decent wage as it is. Tha in-fightin' between tha unions can only work to tha management's advantage, Johnnie. It's a deliberate divide and rule strategy, so it is."

"Aye," Johnnie concurred, "that's exactly what it is, and I suppose the issue'll become even more serious for us if this latest Home Rule Bill gets passed. If tha nationalists gets self rule for Ireland, tha shipyards will be owned by tha new Irish state. God forgive me for sayin' so, but that means in Catholic hands, and all us Protestants will be shown the gates, so we will. We'll be outa here, right enough."

"Well Johnnie, if that day comes," William Henry said, "we won't just be driven out of the yards, we'll be driven out of Ireland itself. It'll be like sixteen forty one all over again. We'll be driven up inta tha hills to perish, or mebbe have ta swim to Scotland. I can't picture you in a kilt, Johnnie!"

Johnnie liked to discuss these issues with William Henry, for his old friend had been in the yards longer than he and he always had an informed opinion, which would bolster those arguments which Johnnie might later put to the management. He knew William Henry was right about the divisive policies of the management. It would be a difficult meeting later that day.

The men now divided to form queues at the long row of timekeeper's windows, for the important process of being signed in and allocated a *bourd*. This was a sort of wooden token, the equivalent of a timecard, which was uniquely numbered and recorded in the timekeeper's book as being assigned to each man. Each worker must keep his *bourd* with him throughout the working day, presenting it to the storekeeper pending the return of borrowed tools, and surrendering it at the end of the day, so that his hours worked might be recorded and his pay calculated accordingly. To lose one's *bourd* would mean no pay for that day's labour. Although a cumbersome system, it was currently the only conceivable means of reliably recording the presence of each individual within Belfast's biggest workforce. It required no fewer than three hundred timekeepers to ensure the prompt admission of the yard's workforce.

That the system was not *totally* reliable however was evidenced by those who frequently abused it. Sometimes, a man would be signed in, then leave his *bourd* with a workmate, whilst he slipped back out through the gates to spend the day elsewhere. His workmate would throw in both their *bourds* at the end of the day to ensure his absent friend was paid. It was not a custom of which William Henry approved, and nor would he take advantage of it himself. The previous Saturday, in order to move house, he had cleared his absence with Johnnie, and had forfeited a day's pay. Work was very important to William Henry, who frequently told his children that all a man needed to be happy was his health and his job. With those two advantages, everything else would come one's way. Work meant more to him than religion. In William Henry's philosophy, a man was only as good as the work he did. Being a tradesman gave a man status, and being a hard worker gave him a good reputation and enabled him to take pride in himself. William Henry expected to work until he died, and what better place to die than in the shipyard, surrounded by his comrades? Like the gunfighter heroes of the Wild West fiction he enjoyed reading, he aspired to dying with his boots on.

Whilst shuffling forward in the queue for the timekeeper's window, William Henry thought of the mob of poor wretches waiting outside the gates, hopeful of being selected for a day's casual and unskilled labour. The *hats* would select whatever unskilled men they needed, according to their own personal criteria, and admit them to the yard. The men not chosen would be turned away, to drown their sorrows in the nearest pub or, if penniless, to return home to explain to the woman of

14

the house why there would be no food on the table today. The selected men were paid an hourly rate, which, though significantly less than the wage of the skilled men, was acceptable. However, the unskilled men were lucky if they worked a full six day week. If they were Protestant and related to one of the regular tradesmen, or if they were prepared to buy the foreman's goodwill, with a drink or two at the end of the day, they could improve their chances of working six days a week. Most of the labourers were Catholic of course and more of them were turned away than were accepted for work.

A similar system of daily recruitment applied at the docks also, where the Catholics worked at the deep sea docks and there was a Protestant monopoly at the cross channel docks. The dockers too queued for work and looked like a pack of half-starved hounds, awaiting scraps from their master's table. Their work was difficult and dangerous. They ran up and down flimsy gangways and planks, carrying heavy loads, and all at breakneck speed, to a tumult of verbal abuse from a foul-mouthed foreman. William Henry knew this because his youngest brother, Hugh, had worked the docks for a time. Hugh Kelly had slowly lost much of his body weight, and the sight of this thin youth staggering home each evening, proud but exhausted, the shoulders of his jacket ripped open from the rough timbers he had to unload, had angered William Henry. It had been a relief when Hugh had snapped and hit his abusive foreman, thereby exiling himself from the docks for good. The daily engagement of labour was a process William Henry considered demeaning and inhuman. He cursed a system which made men plead and bribe for the right to work. He thought of these thin men in their thin clothing, the same clothing for winter and summer, and he thought to himself 'there but for the grace of God ...'. His thoughts were interrupted however as he was now jostled forward by the impatient men queuing behind him. He hated crowds and having to line up each morning to get to his own workplace, though at least his own employment was regular and secure. He was lucky to have been in regular employment all his adult life so far. Then again, he was a Protestant and this was a Protestant shipyard in a Protestant city – for now.

As the timekeeper's window came nearer, he reflected on the times in the past when, through his own folly, he had put his job at risk. On several occasions, his drunken exploits had landed him in a police cell for the night and he had missed half a day's work the following day whilst sobering up and endeavouring to pay his fine. Johnnie had always seen to it that his job would be waiting for him however. Then there was the time he had been charged with drunkenness and assaulting a policeman, though William Henry had no memory of having done so. Allegedly, he had been trying to pull up the newly planted saplings in Duncairn Gardens when one Constable Madden had appeared and had remonstrated with him. The constable said he had received a sharp smack in the chops for his trouble, though William Henry had absolutely no recollection of this. He had been sent down for seven days anyway. And of course, he had also served twelve weeks in the *Crumlin Road Gaol* some eighteen years back, over another issue of which had no memory whatsoever. He dismissed the painful recollection however as his turn came to collect his *bourd*.

William Henry now headed for the Arrol Gantry which was plainly visible on the skyline, and indeed could be seen from just about all of Belfast and its surrounding hills. The sight of the massive fretwork of steel, towering up above him, always inspired him. It was the tallest man-made structure in Belfast, and it cradled the developing frames of two magnificent ships. At the slipways, he met up with Hugh Hewitt, the caulkers' head foreman. Hughie, who lived over on Bryson Street, was another of William Henry's long-term friends. He had already started organising the various teams of caulkers and assigning them their tasks for the day. Some four thousand men had now assembled at slipways two and three, where the two latest, gargantuan ships stood, each in an advanced stage of construction. Against the vast bulk of the two ocean going ships, the surrounding timber staging seemed like a fragile assemblage of matchsticks, and the men like ants swarming all over it.

Earlier that month, the caulking squads, William Henry's amongst them, had finished making watertight the *Olympic*'s hull and had sealed the metalwork on her decks. The engineers had then moved in to fit her engines, and the caulkers had next turned their attentions to the hull of her junior sibling. Royal Mail steamer number 401, which was to be launched as *Titanic,* was the latest of the White Star Line's luxury class cruise ships purpose built for the Trans-Atlantic trade. *Titanic* was even bigger than her slightly senior sister. William Henry and his squad had worked on most of the *White Star Line*'s fleet and he could reel off most of the names from memory; *Cedric, Celtic, Baltic, Adriatic, Laurentic* and now he could add the *Olympic* and *Titanic* to his list. The most recent of their ships were named after mythical gods of the deep and the names always ended in '*ic*', whereas the names of the Cunard liners, mostly built in Glasgow, ended in '*ia*', for example *California* and *Lusitania*. William Henry had once read something about the Titans, who had fought a battle with another squad of gods, the Olympians, though he could not remember how the story had ended.

The *Titanic*'s keel had been laid just four months after that of her big sister and they had grown alongside each other. The central spine of *Titanic* was an impressive hollow, steel box girder, measuring five feet in depth, which was attached to the steel keel plate with a reinforcing solid steel bar. More steel girders ran parallel to the central spine and were linked with steel cross-members. The base of the hull was then plated with inch thick steel sheets, each measuring around six feet by thirty feet, to give the ship a double bottom section. This innovative safety feature would prevent water, in the unlikely event of it breaching the outer skin, from also breaching the inner skin. William Henry recalled however that, although the *Titanic*'s bilges were a full inch thick, those of the earlier White Star liners had in fact been two or even three inches thick, which he believed probably made them superior in terms of safety. He had the impression that new features were introduced with each new ship as a means of testing them out. However, he held the firm belief that the Harland and Wolff designers knew their onions.

The squads of caulkers progressed along behind the riveting squads and, like the caulkers, the riveters worked in pairs. The usual method involved a *holder-on* holding the white-hot rivet in place from one side whilst two *riveters* struck it, each in turn from the other side. They were backed up by the rest of the squad – the *rivet heater*, who would heat the rivets to a thousand degrees before tossing them, from a bucket, up to the *catcher*, who caught them in his bucket and passed them to the *holder-on*. The new White Star Line ships were only partly riveted in this traditional

16

way, however. The latest innovation applied was a new design of hydraulic riveting machine. This was a horseshoe-shaped machine, looking like a giant magnet, which was suspended from the gantry. It straddled the hull, hydraulically hammering in the rivets from both sides simultaneously. As Johnnie had pointed out, this machine could be operated by just two men, one to guide the machine into position and another to insert the hot rivets, and thus could easily make several men in each squad redundant. In fact, it did not need a five-year-trained riveter to operate the machine. It could be done by the unskilled labourers. Ironically however, it had not been foreseen that the machine would be far too bulky to be manoeuvred into the acute turn of the hulls at the bows, so here the manpower of the human riveting teams was still needed.

When the hull plates were riveted, they were inspected both by the foremen and by the *rivet counters*, who counted the number of rivets used, since this was the basis for calculating the bonuses. Any faulty or distorted rivets, which would then have to be removed and replaced, were noted and highlighted with a chalk circle by the counter. Sixpenny fines in respect of each defective rivet would be deducted from the bonus of the errant riveting squad. Once each riveted section of hull had been signed off, the caulking squads moved in immediately to carry out their processes to make each section watertight. They too used modern technology. The pneumatic gun, which pumped special putty into the joints, also had a chisel end which the caulkers used to force the edge of one plate against the next one, achieving a tight seal between the two. The work of the caulkers was examined in a similar fashion to that of the riveters who worked just up ahead of them. The foreman would run his pencil along the cut edges of each caulked plate. If the pencil ran smoothly, the seam was perfect. If, however, the pencil jumped off the plate at any point, that whole section would have to be undone and re-caulked, slowing the squad's progress and reducing their bonus. Riveters and caulkers worked in near perfect synchronicity. The whole process was meticulously planned and timed, each stage in the construction leading on to the next, so that no squad stood idle and no processes were held up for lack of materials. This planning alone was a major feat.

With first the iron-plated, and later steel-plated steamships taking over from wooden sailing vessels, William Henry had needed to learn new techniques for the use of more modern sealants, using the new hydraulic pressurised caulking tools. Harland and Wolff now built not only luxury liners for the White Star Line, but also dreadnoughts for the expanding British Navy. However, change did not occur overnight, and most of the vessels sailing the seas, whether pleasure craft or commercial schooners, were still wooden ones. Wooden ships, from elegant wooden-hulled motor yachts to sturdy cargo ships, were still being constructed and repaired at Harland and Wolff. The navy still commissioned wooden hulled launches and the passenger liners still required wooden lifeboats, so all of William Henry's skills, both traditional and modern, were in demand and he still carried his personal trusty caulker's knife with him. He wondered who would teach the unskilled men the techniques needed for repairing the older vessels, in addition to the easy skills for operating the modern machinery. There might still be a place for traditional tradesmen like himself in Pirrie's new world. William Henry had a depth of knowledge regarding the construction and waterproofing of wooden vessels, and he would not be too quick to impart that knowledge to others. The skilled tradesmen in the yards would not permit the erosion of their hard won elitism without a struggle.

Traditionally, the wooden ships were waterproofed below the waterline with pitch and oakum, and sometimes copper sheeting would be applied against the pitch, to deter barnacles from adhering to it and preventing marine creatures from boring into it. Copper had the special property of repelling pests - he recalled his own gardener father telling him that. Above the water line however, a cheaper form of waterproofing - white lead paint - was used. The white lead coating had to be replaced when it deteriorated, and this process was known as *paying* the hull. This involved William Henry chipping away the old white lead paint and pitch, stripping out the seams and joints with a metal seam raker, and packing fresh oakum and sealant into the seam. He would next hold his straight iron in place against the filler, whilst another caulker rammed home the iron using a sixteen inch, 'T' shaped hawsing mallet to compact the oakum and create a really solid seal. The caulkers worked in pairs on this task and, when the man wielding the mallet tired, they would swap roles. They would also stop every now and again, on the pretext of sharpening their tools by rubbing them down with an iron-oxide coated *crocus cloth*, but the main point of this was to give them an unofficial break, allowing them to catch their breath and straighten their aching backs. When all joints and seams were fully sealed, fresh white oxide paint and hot pitch would be applied to the upper and lower hull respectively.

The old lead paint would invariably be ossified and brittle and, as William Henry chipped away at it, he would become coated in sharp grey flakes and fine grey dust. Indeed by the end of a day's chipping, he would have a decidedly ghostly air about him. He didn't mind so much inhaling the dust, but he hated it when a sharp fleck of paint would lodge itself in his eye. He could not use his fingers to try to dislodge it as this would introduce further flecks and gritty dust. He would lose money if he took time out to go to *the minutes,* as the workers' toilets were called, to wash his hands, so he would soldier on and try to ignore the discomfort. Not even the circuitous route he took home, via the pub, would dislodge this whitish-grey matter from his clothes and boots, and Belle always complained that the dust found its way into every corner of the house. When her weans were at the crawling stage, they would be all the day playing in the paint dust, breathing it in and spreading it further around the kitchen. There would always be a fine layer of the dust on her table and it was the devil's own job to keep it out of their food. It made more work for her beating and washing their clothes free of it. The first Wee Belle had always been such a lively child, scampering about the house and leaving clouds of the paint dust behind her. That was how William Henry would picture his wee angel, her fair curls shedding a dust halo whenever she laughed. Nowadays, some folks claimed the white lead dust was dangerous and could send you mad, but William Henry had been working with it for many years, and he experienced no ill effects, and anyway didn't some say the same thing about electricity and were glad they did not have it in *their* homes?

William Henry still employed the old methods also when repairing the caissons - the watertight lock gates of the yard's dry docks and coffer dams. Belle preferred it when he worked with the hydraulics however, for she said her house was cleaner when he was so employed. With his mix of skills, traditional and modern, William Henry saw himself as a man who stood astride two ages – the old, slowly declining world of wood and sail and the new galloping era of steel and steam. He found that idea quite exciting, as it increased his sense of self worth. He was fiercely proud of his work and highly aware of its importance in the global trade of the twentieth century. He was also proud to call himself a Belfast man, especially since Belfast had been officially declared a City some four years since. Furthermore, there was a brand new City Hall under construction too, just in case any doubting Toms, Dicks or Harrys did not believe this to be the case. The colossal new liners were considered the pride of Belfast too. Although the shipyard workers earned no extra for working on them, they were nonetheless proud to boast that they had a hand in their creation. Even the families of the shipwrights were proud to be associated with their construction. All that is, except the doubting Belle.

Although he was tasked only with the sealing of the hull, William Henry loved to acquaint himself with the technical aspects of other parts of the construction process too. He had watched the riveters at their work alongside him and would listen with interest to the men of other trades discussing the work that they did on these monster ships. The design innovations interested him most of all. For instance, the double skin of *Titanic* included sixteen separate watertight compartments, with watertight doors controlled from the bridge. As Thomas Andrews himself had explained to the caulkers on one of his regular visits to the slips, if one of these compartments were breached in a collision, allowing water in, the others might be closed up immediately by command from the bridge. Moreover, the designer had informed his incredulous audience, such was the stability of the *Titanic*, that, in the extremely unlikely event of up to four of these compartments flooding, the ship would still remain afloat. As William Henry and Johnnie now walked along the nine hundred feet length of the structure towards their station, they remarked upon how disorientating an effect the steeply curved hull which rose up beside them had upon them. It was hard to tell whether it were ship or man which were not perpendicular. En route to the section they were to be working on today, they passed a foreman riveter with his hammer, chalk and notebook, undertaking his inspection of the previous day's work.

William Henry pointed out to Johnnie that there seemed to be very few chalk marks around the shining steel rivets along most of the hull, and yet there was a rash of them at the bow end. Johnnie stopped to discuss this with the riveter foreman, who was testing some of the bow rivets by striking them glancing sideways blows with his hammer. A head from one of the rivets suddenly sheared off and landed at William Henry's feet. He picked it up to examine it. Thinking the conversation between Johnnie and the foreman riveter might afford him the brief opportunity of a smoke, William Henry took out his pipe, pocketing the rivet head whilst he searched for a match.

"Though I hate to admit this, Johnnie," the foreman riveter was saying, "the hydraulic machine is doing a much better job of this than the riveters. Just look at the number of distortions here at the sharp end compared to those the machine's done further back!"

The two men speculated on why this might be so. Gazing up at the wall of neatly riveted steel towering above him and puffing thoughtfully on his pipe, William Henry reflected that he never felt anything less than elated at the sight of these Leviathans. Despite the prospect of the day's hard labour which lay ahead of him, he felt proud to be part of such a tangible achievement. He marvelled at the genius of the draughtsmen and design engineers, as each ship that was built had surpassed its predecessor, both for improvement in design features and for sheer size. Of course, Belle was wont to express her doubts about the ever increasing size of the ships, as she believed they flew in the face of God, and were tempting fate. Naturally, William Henry reproved her for her superstitious distrust of man's achievements. In his view, God made man in his own great image, and so man made great ships as a tribute to God. What could be wrong with that? No point in hiding your light under a bushel, he thought. If God gave man the ability to build something so great, then not to build it would be to turn one's back on God's gift.

Progress on the *Titanic*'s construction was proceeding in similar order to that of the *Olympic* over in slip 2, whose engines were now being installed. Once that was done, in around a year's time, the senior ship would be launched and would proceed to the fitting out wharf, where all sorts of luxurious furnishings and equipment would begin to arrive from Belfast's top manufacturers. Wee Belle and the other girls at the mill were already stitching some of the ninety thousand best linen damask napkins and the thirty-six thousand linen bed sheets which had been ordered for the two ships. William Henry gazed in awe at the various steel components which had been arriving daily at the slipways. The main anchors, each weighing fifteen and a half tons, had been transported there separately, each by a team of twenty horses. The whole of Belfast had come to a standstill to watch the spectacle of their arrival. Each link of the propeller chain allegedly weighed one hundred and seventy-five pounds, and, like most of the ship's components, had to be lifted into place by one of the many cranes on the gantry. The propellers for the engines had also arrived with some ceremony. Each was sixteen and a half feet in diameter and had four blades, made of valuable manganese bronze.

It tickled William Henry that additional dock police officers had been assigned to patrolling this area, in case someone with a Herculean physique should try to make off with one of these blades. It put him in mind of one of his brother Hugh's jokes, about the docker who was stopped by the dock police every night as he left the docks pushing his wheelbarrow, but the police search invariably found his barrow to be empty. When the docker eventually retired from the docks, having made a small fortune, an off duty dock policeman had asked him to confide unofficially what it was he had been smuggling out of the dockyard. "Wheelbarrows" had been his reply.

It seemed to William Henry that no expense had been spared and no refinement considered too grand for *Titanic* the latest ship of the line. Specialist engineers were installing Electric lifts for the passengers' ultimate convenience, whilst, in the carpenters' shop, men were busy carving and assembling the most elaborate interiors for the first class cabins and lounges. A delivery of black and white marble washbasins and decorative fireplaces had been crafted by Hamiltons, Belfast's monumental masons. Belle had thought this another ill omen, as she could not understand why a company which made headstones for the dead would be engaged to provide washbasins for the living, but William Henry had explained that Hamiltons were chosen because of the very fact that they were Belfast's finest craftsmen in marble. *Titanic* was to be a flagship – the most expensive and impressive ship the world had ever seen thus far - and he was extremely proud to be involved in her creation, no matter how much Belle might denounce this as sinful extravagance.

William Henry's pipe was now out and Johnnie had finished his conversation, so the two friends now joined their squad to begin caulking those sections of hull already completed by the riveters. Jim Thompson and the lads had the equipment prepared. The heavy equipment was suspended from the gantry on stout chains, so it did not require a great deal of strength to manoeuvre it. Little strength was required to operate it either, unlike the traditional mallet and caulking irons, since hydraulic pressure, and not human might, now pumped home the sealant. As Johnnie had remarked, even a couple of boys could manage it, and if he had worked that out, it would not have escaped the attention of the management who were still desperate to reduce production costs wherever possible. William Henry felt the mechanised caulking method, impressive though it was, did not allow scope for personal craftsmanship. Then again, he mused, if he had had this sort of machine to work with when he started out as a caulker, instead of working with the hot, tar-soaked oakum, he might still have his fingerprints. At the end of each phase, he would usually inspect the work, prior to Johnnie or Hughie Hewitt giving it the pencil test, for the foremen would be responsible for signing it off. William Henry had been looking forward to today however, for, whilst others in the squad continued the hydraulic caulking of the hull, he would be undertaking the final stage in the testing process on that section of the compartmented hull which they had completed caulking the previous day. This adjunct to the visual pencil test was always a satisfying stage in the construction for him, and it meant he could relax a little whilst measuring the success of the team's work. This stage alone required him to use his judgement,

William Henry found a convenient projection amongst the metalwork stacked along the slipway and used it to hang up his jacket, having first retrieved his breakfast packet and billy can from the pocket. He appointed one of the squad's smarter apprentices to operate the pump which would flood the sealed section of the hull with Lagan water. This was the time honoured method by which the integrity of the hull might be tested for, if the ship would keep water *in*, then logically she would also keep water *out*. Whilst the rest of the squad now commenced worked on the next section of the hull, William Henry directed the youngster to start drilling a drain hole in the lowermost part of the completed section and instructed him how to insert a tap, plugged with a screw-in bolt, around which a stout line was to be affixed. Once the hull had been flooded by the hydraulic pumps, subjected to twenty pounds pressure per square inch and checked over carefully for leaks, the bolt would be removed by tugging on the line, and the water allowed to drain away back into the Lagan. Should any leaks be found, William Henry would have to ensure these were re-caulked immediately.

It was a warm and slightly windy day as William Henry climbed up the staging to a narrow platform, some seventy feet above the ground, whence he might observe the water rising to the desired level. He set his piece and his billy securely on the platform beside him, for a dislodged billy can falling seventy feet could easily concuss a man below. He settled back as comfortably as he could and filled and lit his pipe again. He now had a great view of the Queen's Yard, and indeed of most of Belfast and the beautiful surrounding countryside, and what was more he would have several hours to enjoy it. Of course, he could still hear, from around the yards, the ear-splitting clangour of the riveters' hammers as they struck, each pair in unison, compacting rivet into steel plate and working with methodical precision. The riveting machines which were in use on slips two and three were no quieter than the traditional hammers. Indeed the sounds of riveting, both traditional and mechanical, might be heard all over the city. All the riveters became deaf at an early stage in their careers, of course, but so did those who worked in close proximity to them. William Henry had been losing his hearing gradually for some years now, but that could not be helped. It was an inevitable industrial injury. Perhaps because of this, he found it comparatively peaceful up on his chosen vantage point.

Keeping a watchful eye on the apprentice, who in turn kept his eye on the water level gauge, he reflected on some of the tricks the caulkers often played on the apprentices. A caulker in one of the other squads had given his apprentice a hand drill with a blunt old drill bit and had set him to drilling the drain hole in the flooded compartment. By the end of the second day of drilling, the poor boy had made no impression whatsoever in the steel hull and had burst into tears of frustration before someone had shown him how to sharpen the drill bit with a metal file. Once this was done, the task had then been accomplished within twenty minutes. On another occasion, no-one had warned an apprentice that he should retreat to a safe distance before withdrawing the bung from the drain hole, using the line which had been wound around it, and so he had knelt before the freshly drilled hole and had yanked out the bolt by hand. The deluge of water, released suddenly and under hydraulic pressure, had washed him clean over the quayside and into the Lagan.

William Henry did not hold with the practice of playing cruel jokes on the apprentices, amusing though they might be. He recalled several of those pranks which had been played on him all those years ago. These ranged from being sent to the stores to request a 'long stand' and being kept waiting for an hour or so until the penny dropped, to being instructed to sit on and stabilize a coil of rope which had a departing ship attached to the other end - with inevitable, watery consequences. The young apprentice was somebody's son after all, and a shipwright's son no less. William Henry's elder son Jimmy had started out as a boy rivet heater here in the yards. William Henry had been enormously proud to have his boy working alongside him for a couple of years. Jimmy had been hungry to see the world however, and had not been content to help build the ships, but had joined the navy in order to sail in them. William Henry hoped he would be safe at sea. Surely, he couldn't be worse off than here at Harland and Wolff? A couple of youngsters had been drowned or seriously injured because of childish japes here in the yards. William Henry believed it wasn't right. Things were dangerous enough in the yards without these silly shenannigans. According to Johnnie, around four hundred men and boys had been injured whilst working on the sister ships and the best part of a dozen had been killed so far.

William Henry himself had witnessed a number of fatalities over the years, and indeed it had been one such tragic incident which had made young Jimmy's mind up to leave. However William Henry had seen the most disturbing accident so far just a couple of months back, when two of the Olympic's plates, weighing around five tons or more, were being hoisted aloft by one of the ten ton cranes and had suddenly slipped out of the sling. They had crashed down, scattering the squads of platers and riveters working on the flimsy staging beneath and two of the helpers had been killed outright. One of them had been hurled thirty feet to his death and the other, Robert Kilpatrick, had died not ten feet from William Henry, his head clove in twain by one of the plates as it fell on him. William Henry had known Kilpatrick for some years and his death had been disturbing. The crane operator involved in the incident was untrained, and should not have been attempting to lift more than one plate at a time, but had done so in order to impress the *hats* and hopefully keep his job. This sort of accident convinced the shipwrights of the folly of employing untrained men, but of course the management were not so easily persuaded. William Henry had suffered nightmares for some time after witnessing that awful accident. The number of deaths on the two current ships caused little controversy in Belfast however, especially as, according to Johnnie, one death for every £100,000 spent on construction was considered the norm, in which case there might yet be more deaths. In any case, replacement labour was easily come by.

William Henry shook the awful images from his head and knocked his pipe out against the staging. He now took out his piece of bread and jam and, pouring some tea into the lid of his billy, he sat back to enjoy his breakfast. Food, no matter how modest, always tasted better in the fresh air, he thought. The sweet, milky tea, although no longer hot, refreshed and sustained him. His eyes narrowed in the reflected glare of the sun, as it now rose low over the Lagan water and he marvelled at the beauty of the green landscape which encircled the industrial city around him. Gulls were now circling and screeching overhead, so he guessed the fishing boats must be in harbour after a night spent out at sea. There were far worse jobs than shipbuilding, he mused.

A commotion along the slipway now caught his eye, and he observed a group of men, who instead of attending to their work, were having a bit of a fight. One leapt onto another's back, wrestling him to the ground and the rest piled on top. Nothing serious, he noted, just a bit of high spirits. The men here worked hard and they played hard. He noticed Johnnie gesticulating sternly at the group and they all returned to their tasks. However, he also saw Johnnie taking his *fines book* out of his breast pocket. Someone would lose a sixth, or possibly even a quarter of a day's pay for loafing. Johnnie was a stickler for health and safety. 'Good job somebody is' William Henry thought. Another thing of which William Henry did not approve was the foul language of the yards. He never stooped to using bad language himself - well, not when sober at least. In drink, so everyone told him, it was a different matter. He knew that many of his workmates considered him something of an oddity in this. Well, no matter, for everyone should have standards, even if they slipped now and again. Like Mark Twain, William Henry also believed that a man's character might be learned from the adjectives he used in conversation.

As enjoyable as his reverie was, it made the time pass all too quickly and William Henry's experienced eye now told him that the bulkhead compartment ought to be full to the top. Slipping the remains of his piece into his trouser pocket to have for lunch later on, and retrieving his billy, he carefully descended the staging, signalling to the apprentice to check the level. Next he examined the drain hole drilled in the hull by the youth, checking that the tap and bolt were firmly inserted and that the line was wound tightly around the bolt. Then, he and the apprentice set about checking the plated hull for leaks. He let the lad clamber up the staging to check the upper sections whilst he himself checked the lower areas. Once satisfied that all was watertight, he shouted for Johnnie to come over and re-check, as Johnnie would have to sign off this stage of the work. When Johnnie was satisfied that all was well, William Henry instructed the apprentice how to safely remove the bolt from the drain hole, by remaining well back, in an elevated position, and pulling on the line to gradually unscrew the bolt. When only loosened halfway however, the bolt ground to a halt and the lad began tugging somewhat over enthusiastically on the line, which snapped suddenly and came away in his hand.

The lad made to go forward to loosen the bolt manually, but William Henry stopped him and, picking up a lump hammer, clambered down himself. Signalling everyone to keep well back, he started to tap the bolt with the hammer, gently at first, then more positively, watching out for any signs that the bolt was about to give. Eyeing his nearest avenue of escape, William Henry gave the bolt one last almighty whack of the hammer, then leapt aside as nimbly as possible, just as the bolt flew out under the hydraulic pressure of thousands of gallons of water. William Henry almost cleared the path of the water, but the first flush just caught him as he leapt, soaking his trousers up to his thighs. The water was ice cold and caused him to catch his breath sharply. It meant he would now have to spend the rest of the day in damp trousers, but he thought at least he would cope better with this than would the lad. He did not even consider going home to change, of course, as he would be docked pay if he did so.

Slipping behind a huge anchor chain coiled up by the side of the slips, he stepped discreetly out of his woollen trousers and underpants and wrung them out as thoroughly as possible, before putting them back on again. Then, too late, he remembered the bread and jam in his trouser pocket. He turned out his pocket linings and scraped out the sodden pap which was to have been his lunch. One day, he mused, the management might install lockers so that the workers could keep a change of clothing, or maybe even, in a perfect world, there would be hot showers, and a canteen with hot meals. That would of course be the day that the Linfield players turned out in green shirts and the organ at St Joseph's Catholic Church played 'God Save The Queen'! He chuckled at the thought.

As it was, Harland and Wolff provided few toilet facilities. Those available to the shipwrights were located upstairs in one of the blocks and were referred to as *the minutes*, for each worker was allowed only seven minutes in the forenoon and seven minutes in the afternoon to visit the toilets. Moreover, a clerk positioned outside the toilets noted down the bourd number of each man and the times of his arrival and departure. A foreman asking for one of the men, would often be told "he's away *the minutes*". Predictably, many workmen preferred to urinate over the side of the quay as they worked, and would do whatever other urgent business they might have in any quiet corner between the stacks of scaffolding and plating. Still, conditions in the Queen's Yard were no different from those in any other Belfast work site and were perhaps a little better than some. For example, Harland and Wolff now maintained an ambulance, so that any casualties might be conveyed to hospital in rapid time. Johnnie Beasant had been partly responsible for that sensible innovation. William Henry would never have said so, of course, but an ambulance would have been very little help to poor souls with injuries like those of poor Robert Kilpatrick.

Johnnie, ever concerned for the welfare of his squad, enquired if William Henry would be alright working on in his damp clothes but the older man assured him he would manage until later on, when he might be able to air his trousers for a little while over the rivet heater's fire, whilst the boy heated the water to brew up their billy cans again. Sure it was no different to the soaking they all got on a rainy day in the yards anyway. There was no shelter to be had for the outdoor trades of course. He did not mention the fact that he now had no *piece* for his lunch, for he knew that, if he did, Johnnie would not hesitate to share his own food with his old friend. He determined that, if Johnnie later noticed he was not eating, he would say he had it eaten already. He would manage to hold out until the cook shop meal in the evening. The prospect of a decent roast dinner would keep him going.

"At least the weather isn't too bad tha day," William Henry remarked, "for it would be a different story entirely if we had a lazy wind."

"What's a lazy wind?" the apprentice asked.

"A lazy wind, son, is one which is too lazy to go roun' ye but goes straight through ye, flesh an' bones an' all. Just you wait till yer first winter here on the Queen's Island, when yer up on thon stagin' in a rainstorm with a howler blowing in off the Mournes. Then ye'll know what I mean," William Henry explained to the dismayed youth, who wished he had not asked.

As the afternoon wore on, William Henry's trousers did indeed dry out, eventually, but by then his knees and hips had started to ache and the cheerful optimism he had felt whilst sunning himself up on the staging now deserted him. He now had to use his arms to pull himself up and down the scaffolding and walkways, as he and the squad continued caulking the next completed section of hull, for his legs were now as stiff as scaffolding poles. The flooded compartment was still draining as the working day came to a close but the pump was now switched off for the night. It would be hours yet, maybe the following day, before it was empty. The remaining water would take longer to drain out, under the pressure of its own weight, than it had to fill up under the greater pressure of hydraulic pumps.

The introduction of hydraulics had certainly dragged the process of shipbuilding into the twentieth century. William Henry had avidly watched the progress on the building of the new and enormous Thompson dry dock, which had been built especially for the fitting out of the *Olympic* and *Titanic*. Five hundred men had been engaged in constructing the 'graving' dock - so named for its grave-like shape. Once finished, it would take ships up to around nine hundred feet in length, and its multi-million gallon capacity of water could be emptied out in less than three hours, again using hydraulic pumps. The construction of the dry dock had taken six years so far, which was twice as long as planned, mainly because the amount of earth which had been excavated had caused the adjacent Alexandra Dock to collapse. It was expected to be completed in a years' time however, ready for the fitting out and painting of first the *Olympic* and then the *Titanic*. William Henry had marvelled, not only at the mammoth construction, but at the vision of the yard's management in planning so far ahead for the advent of future giant ships. Belle's comments upon reading of the collapse of the graving dock had been predictably pessimistic, of course. Why, she had demanded, would they even think of calling it a *graving* dock? No wonder the earth had fallen into it. She had deemed its size yet another affront to God. Exasperated by her warnings of doom, William Henry had declared that he could not see God, but yet he could see the *Olympic* and *Titanic*, so maybe it was Harland and Wolff who were the gods?

William Henry's first job the next day would be to ensure the riveters returned to seal up the drain hole again. There was a strict order to these things and William Henry was charged with overseeing this final, but important stage before Hughie or Johnnie came to sign it off. He took a pride in ensuring that each of the hull's watertight compartments was indeed as watertight as possible. Of course, they could never be *entirely* watertight unless sealed on all sides, the top included, but this could not be achieved without cutting off access from one bulkhead to the next, as was the case with warships. An ideal design would ensure that, should one of the compartments be holed and flooded, water could not spill over the top into the next compartment, and so the ship would remain afloat. However, whilst it was feasible to have sailors running up one set of stairs and down another in order to proceed from one compartment to the next, one could not expect fare-paying passengers on a luxury liner to do likewise. There had to be easy access from one side of the liner to the other on all passenger decks. First and second class passengers wanted promenades and a variety of decks. They also wanted an easy, level walk from their cabins to the breakfast room, and, having dined well and consumed their fine wines and brandies of an evening, they would expect a direct route from the restaurants back to their beds. Thus the design of the watertight bulkheads on liners was different from that of warships, as the former were far less likely to suffer collision or damage than the latter.

Once the hull and the metal decks were fully caulked, the caulking squads would turn their attention next to *Titanic*'s sixteen lifeboats. Hughie had said that Mr Andrews' original design for *Titanic* had included twenty lifeboats, but that this number had exceeded the minimum recommendations of the British Board of Trade, and the Harland and Wolff management had decided to reduce the number. According to what Hughie had heard, Mr Ismay felt that too many lifeboats hanging from their enormous davits, would be off putting to passengers and would also restrict the amount of deck space available for leisure activities. That seemed an odd decision to William Henry. Surely, you either needed lifeboats for everyone or none at all. He bet Hughie that it was done to save money, for rumour had it that Ismay was 'as tight as a crab's arse'.

The publicity stated however that no item was too luxurious for *Titanic*'s passengers and that no expense would be spared in the décor and accoutrements. The idea was that these new luxury liners would feel like floating grand hotels. William Henry wondered what it would be like to travel on board *Titanic*. Wee Belle earned seven shillings and sixpence a week stitching the linen napkins for use by the *Titanic*'s passengers. However, she had calculated that, if she wished to purchase a dozen of these napkins from a Belfast shop, it would cost her a whole month's wages. William Henry couldn't imagine he would ever be dabbing *his* chin with anything so fine.

He now dabbed the accumulated sweat from his face with his grimy cotton muffler, and it was with much relief that he soon heard the single, long blast of the hooter signalling the end of the working day. He retrieved his jacket, checked his billy can was in the pocket and, still stiff and aching, made his way gingerly down the staging to join his team on the ground.

"That's us!" Johnnie declared.

The men who had drawn tools from the store set off quickly to return them as the vast swarm of working men began to snake its way towards the shipyard gates. The great procession of weary cap and jacket clad men and boys now funnelled towards towards the exits, filtering past the timekeepers' windows again. There was no patient queueing now as there had been at the start of the day however. Each man now took aim and deftly threw his *bourd* through the half open window. No man missed the window, as their day's pay depended on their *bourd* being handed in and recorded. However, some also managed not to miss hitting the hapless clerks too, either by accident or in a contemptuous gesture for the white collar brigade. The men of the shipyards, in their thousands, poured out of the gates and headed away from the Queen's Island. Some would go straight home to their tiny, terraced houses, but many would head instead for their preferred public houses, for shipbuilding was powerful thirsty work.

It was only half past five but the sun was setting behind cloud and the damp chill of evening was already moving in off the river. It had been a week now since William Henry had joined his fellow caulkers for a drink after work. In fact, it had been a week since William Henry had even tasted hard drink. He no longer accompanied them *every* night, as he would have done previously. This being a Friday and pay day however, he would make an exception. Johnnie would be handing out the men's pay and sharing out their bonuses in the pub, so naturally William Henry had to be there to collect. Once inside, it didn't seem right to be sitting in a pub, enjoying the banter and not have a drink in his hand. Sure, a quick pint wouldn't hurt, and indeed a wee whiskey chaser might stop his legs hurting.

The bright lights and the low glow from the fire in the hearth within soon raised William Henry's spirits. In the cheerful interior of the bar, Johnnie quickly dispensed the men's pay packets and doled out to each his share of the bonus which the squad had jointly earned. William Henry bought the first round, as he was going to be leaving shortly. Beers with whisky chasers were the order of the evening and the first great *swally* barely touched his parched throat as it went down. Soon, the conversation was flowing and a second round had appeared on the table. William Henry congratulated himself on being right about the soothing effects of the drink. He was no longer aware of the pain in his knees. He had even forgotten his hunger. He took out his pipe, filled and lit it and sat back, listening and nodding. He was a

27

thoughtful man, who didn't like to commit himself in any discussion until he had heard all the others' arguments and had assessed which way the tide of opinion was flowing. He determined to sip his drink slowly between pipes and thereby avoid over imbibing. The flinty, coconut aroma from his pipe soon dissipated into the blue haze of the bar's smoky taproom and the hubbub of the men's talk made the hands of the Guinness clock race.

The evening's main topic, and indeed that which was on everyone's lips in every Belfast pub these days, was the worrying spectre of Home Rule for Ireland. Welcomed and prayed for by the Catholic Nationalists, it was however a prospect which chilled the red, white and blue hearts of the Protestant Unionists. January of 1910 had seen the Liberals take power in the province with only a very small majority and the biggest worry amongst the Belfast Protestant community was the ever present possibility of being governed from Dublin. The Ulster Unionists had put their trust in the democratic process, confident that the British parliament would protect their community from what they anticipated would effectively be 'Rome Rule' but they had been shaken by the apathy and lack of support shown by the British electorate. The House of Lords' rejection of Lloyd George's so-called 'people's budget' had also dashed hopes of fair wages and improved living standards. The longer the parliamentary debate continued, the stronger grew the loyalists' fears that absorption of the province into an Irish Catholic state would mean the inevitable depletion of Ulster's wealth.

Johnnie Beasant's news from his meeting was not good. The management were steadfast in their resolve to reduce squad sizes. A timetable for this was now proposed. What Johnnie did not tell them however was that it would be down to foremen like himself to choose who would be let go.

Sam Elliott was holding forth; "I'm tellin' yez, it's the thin end of the wedge. We thought things couldn't get any worse than they wuz just before the nineteen-oh-seven General Strike but, sure, we've gained nothin'. We're just as badly off as we wuz before, so we are. What's more, things is set to get a whole lot worse if we're governed from Dublin. Government from Dublin will bring us down to tha ranks o' tha poorest o' the poor. If Dublin controls tha shipyards then who's goin' to invest in them, for Dublin has no money? And if Harlannanwulf takes its business to tha Scottish yards, then no-one will buy Belfast ships. We'll be finished."

Robbie Alexander cut in; "I think that, before that happens, tha Cathlicks'll run us outa tha yards. Whilst th'owners is Protestant, there'll be work in the yards for Protestant men, but if a Cathlick Dublin Government takes over, then naturally they'll want Cathlicks workin' in the yards."

"It's like as if tha British government *wants* to cut us adrift," added Jim Thompson, "don't they realise that it's tha Protestants who make the money for them here? Sure, all tha wealth that Belfast produces, and which pours into tha British pot, is produced by us. They don't seem to consider the fact that we're British too. If our fortunes gets lumped in with those of the Cathlicks, then before too long we'll be just as poor as the Cathlicks." The 'Ayes' of the group signified their accord with his view.

William Henry had been listening to the arguments and puffing contentedly on his pipe. Empty glasses were now piling up in front of him. He enjoyed the company of his fellow shipyard workers over a drink at the end of the long, hard day, not least because it was in the pubs that those political machinations which threatened to change their lives, were assessed and evaluated from a local perspective. Men came here for more than just the drink. If you didn't engage in the debate, you wouldn't be able to have an informed opinion, and if you didn't have an informed opinion, the politicians would ride roughshod over you. It was the duty of every working man to nail his colours to the mast and stand up for what he believed in. William Henry had no beef with the Catholics, far from it, especially since, though it was seldom mentioned in the present company, both his brother John and his sister Lottie had married Catholics. He did not know for certain, but had long suspected his own Kelly ancestors might have 'taken the soup' back in the days of the great hunger - a practice so common back in those desperate times as to have a metaphor ascribed to it.

The arrival in Belfast of William Henry's parents had coincided with the biggest Protestant revival the town had ever seen. William Henry's parents-in-law, the Gordons, had worshipped at the Berry Street Presbyterian church run by the charismatic, fundamentalist preacher Hugh Hanna, who delivered impassioned sermons to the community and stirred up riots. In fact, it was Hugh 'Roaring' Hanna himself who had married the Gordons and had baptised Belle. There was no doubting the Gordon's Ulster Scots ancestry. Back in those days, Catholics were converting en masse to Protestantism, even without the inducement of soup. Moreover, most of 'Roaring' Hanna's converts to Presbyterianism back then were female. William Henry thought this was a smart move on Hanna's part, since, in his opinion, it was mostly the women who maintained the faith in a household. Hanna's practice was to make house calls and preach loudly and passionately. It was said he frequently had women faint in the wake of his fervour. Those were feverish times altogether. William Henry had often wondered about this. His elder brother, Patrick Kelly, had been unable to secure work in the shipyards purely because of his name. No-one believed he had been named in honour of the patron saint of the *Protestant* church in which he had been baptized back in their village in rural Antrim. Patrick now worked as a flax dresser in Lindsay Thompson's linen mill over by the Crumlin Road and he lived in one of the poorer mill houses on Flax Street.

Jim Thompson was now on his feet and asking who wanted another drink. William Henry thrust his hand into his trouser pocket and pulled out a handful of coins which he pressed into Jim's hand.

"Take this, will ye?" he insisted, "for I wasn't intendin' to stay long, so let me pay for one more roun' before I go, c'mon now!"

Jim took the coins and was soon back with the drinks.

"What t' hell's this ye've give me, William Henry?" he laughed, slapping the rivet head on the table, "d'ye expect me to spend this, do ye?"

The men laughed at William Henry's mistake as he held the half-crown sized metal fragment aloft and squinted at it.

"For gawd's sake, would yez look at thon," he exclaimed, "it's a rivet head which gat knocked affa the hull of the *Titanic* thaday. What sort of steel is it that breaks wi' one wee tap of the foreman's hammer?"

Hughie took the rivet head from him and examined it closely. "Sure that niver cem affa tha *Titanic*," he declared, "for that's not steel but cast iron, and not very good iron at that. Look at the wee glassy spots in it. That's slag, so it is."

Johnnie Beasant now took the rivet head from him and also had a close look. "Is this the one ye picked up when you and I wuz talking with the foreman riveter?" he asked gravely. William Henry nodded.

"They're supposed to be using only steel rivets on the new ships," Johnnie advised, "so I hope this is the only dud and that it's got in by mistake, for one duff rivet by itself wuddna do any harm, but ye shouldn't mix steel and iron rivets or it'll create tension, so it will, and ye can't use shoddy iron like this on one inch steel plates."

"Aye, and ye can't use it to buy a roun' of drinks with neither!" Jim Thompson added, and the men roared again.

The conversation returned to the political situation again and the arguments continued to roll back and forth around the crowded taproom. William Henry's pipe was out. He looked into the blackness of its bowl and decided now was the time for him to chip in. He waited for a natural silence.

"D'yez actually think we *are* any better off than tha Cathlicks at the moment?" he asked. He used the stem of his empty pipe to gesticulate, "Ach, we might be in regular work and earning a shillin' or two a week more than tha Cathlicks, thanks to tha union, but sure we're livin' in tha same wee houses, in tha same wee streets as tha Cathlicks. Aren't we just as overcrowded and miserable as tha Catholics? Our weans gets tha same illnesses as tha Cathlick weans, and don't they die from them just the same? Sure, don't we all end up in tha same workhouse when we're too ill or too old to work? All of us here roun' this table went to school and got a learnin'. So did our fathers. We can all read and write pretty good, and yet we're all doing hard labour in tha shipyard and no prospect of anything better. So tell me now, will ye, *how* are *we* better aff?"

Pausing to quaff the foam off the fresh pint which Jim had placed before him, and wiping it from his unkempt moustache, he continued; "most of our ancestors came here some two hunnert years ago, driven outa Scotland, either by tha greedy landlords, failed harvests or religious persecution. We have persevered here in tha face of resentment from tha Cathlicks and in spite of repeated crop failure and famine and tha like. When the countryside couldn't support us, back in the eighteen forties and fifties, our fathers moved into tha toun, and we made Belfast tha great city it is today. And what has it got us?"

"Ach, yer head's cut!" exclaimed Hugh, "what are ye on about?"

"Out there," Willliam Henry gestured dramatically with his pipe towards the steamed up pub windows, "in that there shipyard, we're buildin' tha biggest ships tha world has ever seen. Why, when it's launched, th'*Olympic* will be tha largest moving object on God's earth. And, when her sister ship, tha *Titanic*, is finished, she'll be even bigger, so she will. There's thousands of Protestant men in Harland and Wolff are working on those two ships and those ships will make Belfast tha wonder of the world, so they will."

The others all agreed.

30

"So, tell me now, just tell me, *will* yez, why are *we* still livin' in tha crumblin' hovels of th'old houses, and why do so many of our children still die before they're five years old? Eh? I'm tellin' yez, those ships are not tha great wonder around here. Tha wonder is how we manage to build them so fine, livin' in squalor tha way we do."

"William Henry, ye're shoutin' now, so y'are," said Johnnie, gripping his arm and nodding reassuringly at the landlord, who was eyeing them with some disdain.

"Oh, Right," said William Henry, continuing, with just a slight reduction in volume, "but, look, I'm just tellin' ye, tha real enemy here isn't tha Cathlick, nor tha Pope, it's poverty, and it's here amongst us right now. An why are we poor? It's coz th'employers takes tha profit and gets rich whilst keeping down tha wages o' tha workin' man. D'yez mind tha dockers' strike three years back, when tha Cathlicks and Protestants of Belfast united against th'employers' federation? D'yez not mind how we all took up arms together? We supported the dockers. We, Protestants *and* Cathlicks, stood along them docks and saw the scabs they'd brought in to unload tha boats, and we let them have a taste o' tha Belfast steel. We knocked tha puddin's out of them with every nut, bolt and rivet in the yards. We even took th'eyes outa some of 'em with the auld *Belfast confetti,* so we did."

Indeed, they all remembered the dock strike, when Jim Larkin had come up from Dublin and had tried to unionise the dock workers. The shipyard workers had indeed joined in the fray and had brought with them the steel detritus of their trade, the discarded discs cut out of the sheet metal prior to insertion of the rivets. This waste product was known locally as *Belfast confetti* and found its way into many a shipyard dispute. William Henry continued;

"But sure it got us nowhere, for tha Shipping Federation won the day and tha men all hadda go back til work. Tha big mistake Larkin made wuz to encourage that settin' up of separate unions for Cathlicks and Protestants. That suited tha Federation fine. Divide an' rule, that's what they did. Tha dockers' pay is still poor, and ours is not much better. Nothin' changed since them days. Nothin' *will* change until we learn to put aside our differences. Tha Cathlicks isn't goin' ta go away and neither are we. We're all swimmin' in tha same swamp, so we are. Look at the conditions under which we're still working, unions or no unions – all respect to yerself, *Top Hat,*" he nodded to Johnnie, "and how many good men have died buildin' these two ships?"

William Henry's mates conceded he had a point,' and so he continued his diatribe;

"Sure, look at those two poor bastards in tha North Yard who were killt just a while back when thon hoist gev way and dropped tha bulkhead plates on them. What sort of chance did they have? What happens to *their* widows and weans? Yet still the Yards makes money for the owners and for their shareholders too, and most of that wealth goes to Westminster but precious little of it comes back here to be spent on safety or wages. D'yez *really* think we'd be any worse aff under Dublin rule, with Westminster cut out of tha picture? Could we possibly *be* any worse aff if that money from tha shipyards stayed here in Ireland?"

William Henry's voice had risen to a crescendo again, as it always did when drink fuelled his argument. He looked around at all his comrades' nodding, sombre

31

faces, and wondered if he had overdone the rhetoric again. "Well, whose for another drink, then?" he asked. But the men were all taking the Catholic landlord's disapproving looks as the signal that it was time they all went home to their suppers.

"Come on you, William Henry," said Johnnie Beasant, "an' I'll head a bit o' that way with ye. Let's away home now to the wee women. I thought you and Belle wuz goin' till tha pictures tha night anyway?"

William Henry suddenly remembered the evening's plans. He squinted up at the Guinness clock. Well, it was too late now for both supper and the pictures, and by now Belle would probably have started preparing an evening meal. In fact, if she had, she would probably have eaten it long since, and be wondering now where he was. Would she be wondering? Or would she guess he had been to the pub? Well, so much for his resolve to avoid the drink. He would have to go home and face her silent looks of reproval.

"Ach, hell roast ye, William Henry Kelly!" he cursed himself.

The two men continued along the homeward trail, until Johnnie had to cross the road. "See ye tha morra," he called out.

"All the best, *Top Hat*," William Henry Henry waved cheerily and headed, a little unsteadily, for Shandon Street. It was beginning to get dark and he could already see there was no light showing in his own house. His cheer instantly dissipated and his heart sank. That meant Belle was not home. And at this time of a Friday evening it meant she was likely to be out drinking somewhere. It looked as though they had both failed in their resolve. As he passed the first few houses in the street, he noticed the neat donkey-stoned steps. Through the net curtains he spied the flickering of flames from the neighbours' hearths. He also caught the aroma of something good cooking in someone's kitchen. It was not coming from his own kitchen, however.

He got out his door key and let himself into the cold, quiet house. He hated coming home to an empty house. This was as it had often been over in Collyer Street. He hated the fact that the children were no longer there. A house without a wee wife and a handful of children was not a home. The front door led from the street into a short hallway, with two doors leading off it, one to the little parlour, which he could see from the street was dark and empty. The other door led to the small kitchen and the tiny lean-to scullery beyond. As he had feared, there was no fire lit in the kitchen. The grate was as black and cheerless as the bowl of his pipe. He checked upstairs but Belle was not in either of the two tiny bedrooms and nor was she out in the little yard at the back. The back door was locked and Belle's coat was not hanging from the hook. No coat meant no Belle. No Belle meant no supper. No point staying home. He turned up the collar of his coat and went out again into the street.

He headed off back up the New Lodge Road to Upper Canning Street, where he called at his daughter Jane's house. It was Belle junior who answered the door.

"Hello darlin'," he kissed his daughter's cheek, "is yer mother here?" he asked.

"No father, I haven't seen her at all tha day, but come you in and have some supper, for I see you've already had a wee drink or two and you should put somethin' in your stummick," she urged.

32

"No thanks darlin', I won't, for I'd best call on your brother and see if your mother's there," William Henry said. Just then, his older daughter Jane appeared in the hallway, wiping her hands on a tea towel.

"Father, are y'all right? Come in and warm yourself a wee while" she bade him.

"No thanks, pet, I won't, for I'm waitin' on your mother coming home. Here's a wee something for the baby's moneybox though," he smiled and dug deep into his pockets to give her a handful of change.

As he kissed each of his daughters again and headed off, wee Belle called after him:

"Now, don't yez be arguing again. I know what yez are both like when ye've had a drink! I'll be 'round to see yez tha morrah."

William Henry waved goodbye and headed towards North Queen Street. He passed the top of Pinkerton Street, where he'd been living when he and Belle had got married. His mind flashed back to that day when the beautiful Isabella Gordon had become Mrs Belle Kelly, with the blessing of the minister at Newington Presbyterian church up on the Limestone Road. He remembered she had carried white lilies, and he had thought she was like a wee lily herself, small, pale and delicate and he had felt such a sense of responsibility for her. Then, the children had come along, and his sense of responsibility had increased greatly. At least he had always had work and could support them – just about.

Now he found himself at his youngest son's lodgings. The landlady answered the door and Billy was soon summoned. "What's wrong, father?" he asked.

"Oh, nothin's wrong, son, I just wondered if you'd seen your mother," William Henry asked, trying to sound cheerful so as not to worry his boy.

"Have you two fell out, again?" his son asked.

"Not at all," William Henry replied, "it's just that whenever I got home she wasn't there, and it's gettin' late now. There's no fire lit and no supper, so I wondered if she was over with you. I called at Jane's and she's not there."

"Did you try Alice's?" his son asked, "but if you don't find her, come back and we'll go and look together."

"Aye, son, I will," said William Henry, "and what about you, are you still alright in your new lodgin's?"

"Yes, father, I'm fine" said Billy, "Mrs Murphy does a good supper. I'm sure she could spare a plateful if you haven't eaten."

"That's all right son," said his father, "I'll meet up with your mother and we'll pick up something on tha way home."

"Maybe you should try Mrs Spence's house" Billy suggested, "d'ye mind it was Mrs Spence who was the one bringing drink into the house tha day you and Mother had tha big row, and I moved out."

William Henry bristled at the memory of coming home and finding not one, but *two* inebriated women in the house. Belle had started to insult him, then both women had laughed and he had been greatly embarrassed in front of Mrs Spence, so he had given Belle a slap. Nothing serious mind, just a wee smack, but Billy had come home right in the middle of it all and, well, William Henry knew it was wrong to expect your children to take sides. He had known it was wrong to slap Belle too, but sure a man couldn't be insulted in his own house, not when he's been out working

33

and only had a modest drink or two at the end of his long, hard day. A man had to establish himself as head of his household, otherwise there would be anarchy. For one thing, there would be no supper on the table ... just like now. He hated things not being right at home. He hated not having the children living at home, but, sure it was as much Belle's fault as his own, maybe more so. He supposed they weren't the only couple in Belfast to have a wee drink and a wee barney every now and again. He bade his son farewell and set off again. The lights were all out at his daughter Alice's house. He guessed they were all in bed already, so wouldn't disturb them. He headed back home again.

William Henry let himself into his house, but there was still no sign of Belle. By now, he was very hungry and realised he had eaten nothing since his breakfast piece that morning, so he picked up a china bowl and walked down the road to the cookshop. To his relief, it was still serving and so he bought himself a fourpenny dinner to take out. He had roast beef, with gravy, potatoes and peas. With his bowl well wrapped in newspaper, he popped into the public house at the corner and bought a half bottle of rum. At least he wouldn't have to dine alone, as he would have his old friend *Captain Morgan* to keep him company. The house was still cold, dark and quiet, but he saw no point in lighting a fire now, as it was almost bedtime. When Belle eventually came back and found the house cold and unwelcoming, as he had done, she might feel sufficiently guilty for her absence. He sat down at the small kitchen table, unwrapped his dinner and poured a large measure of rum to wash it down.

The dinner was good, and perhaps somewhat fancier that the stew Belle would have had for him. However, he would still have preferred to come home to a house filled with the aroma of home cooking after a long day's work.   Home cooking and a roaring fire made even the most depressing hovel seem homely. He had bought a large dinner, enough for two really, in the hope that Belle would be home to share it with him. He left a few slices of the beef still in the bowl, covered it with a tea towel and left the bowl on the drainer. His belly was full and his hunger sated, but he now began to feel lonely and resentful. He was angry at Belle, but he was also worried about her. He wanted her there now. He didn't like it when she wasn't home. He would not be able to rest until she came home. He resolved not to be cross when she did appear however, for he realised that he loved her so.

"She is handsome, she is pretty, she is the Belle of Belfast city :.." he began to chant to himself, but the song did not cheer him.

Her absence made him realise Belle was indeed the love of his life. Where was she though, he wondered? Was she safe? If he were any sort of husband, surely he would be scouring the streets looking for her? Hadn't they usually rubbed along well together, even though they each felt a certain degree of frustration at times. His own frustration stemmed from the fact that neither she nor their children understood his feelings of helplessness at not being able to give them all a better life, and a nicer home. He didn't have the words to express his helplessness at working six days a week for most of his life, yet never having been able to afford better than the tiny, two-bedroomed, rented house. When any of them had fallen sick, it had mattered not that Belfast had a new and reputable children's hospital, for it had to be the workhouse hospital for *his* babies. Belle had a right to expect more of life, and for

34

her babies not to die. Their children just did not understand that, as a man grew older his sense of the inequity of life, of life's missed opportunities and of what might have been, became more acute. Sitting down together in the evenings to a wee drink was their parents' relief from the disappointments of life. They had a parlour house now, which was but a small step up from the kitchen house, and now there were just the two of them in it. They were more reliant upon each other. Yet they still had a good laugh together, he and his Belle. And so what if occasionally the drink brought out the recriminations too? Whose business was that but their own? Hadn't the children always been loved and cared for to the best of his ability? Hadn't sacrifices always been made on their behalf?

William Henry was fifty-six now, and though seven years younger, Belle too had reached middle age. They had raised their family and had earned the right to a little self indulgence now, a little over-indulgence to chase away the reality. He hoped his children would not know the same frustration in life. William Henry drained his glass of rum and poured himself another. He decided he would go out searching for Belle again, in case she had fallen and hurt herself. Maybe he would just finish this drink first however and then go looking for her. He was, after all, so very tired now. The bottle was almost empty, and, so, still sitting at the little wooden kitchen table, he laid his head on his arm and closed his eyes, just for a minute or two ...

William Henry raised his head and looked around him. It was very dark and he guessed it must be the early hours of the morning. For a few moments, he could remember nothing. Why was he not in bed? What day was it? He worked out that it must be somewhere between Friday night and Saturday morning, so, in just a few hours, he would need to get washed, make a cup of tea and butter himself a *piece* before setting off to the yards. The faint moon's rays which had now found their way in via the small kitchen window, and which had awoken him, outlined the silhouette of the empty rum bottle in front of him. The house was still dark and silent, the kitchen gloomy and cold. He was thirsty and his hands were wet. He must have spilled the rum, for surely he could not have drunk it all. His throat was dry and furry, a not unfamiliar feeling.

He went over to the jawbox and ran his hands under the lone tap, then scooped the cool water into his mouth. It tasted of iron. That must be the beef, he thought. His head swayed and he knew the rum was the cause of his dizziness, but he also realised that his Belle had still not come home. Now he really *was* worried. He should visit his children. But of course he now remembered he had already done so. Where could she be at *this* hour of the morning? Stumbling around in the dark, and blundering into some stray kindling wood which he now kicked into the hearth, he managed to light the gas mantle. He wondered whether he should go to bed for a little while or stay up and await Belle's return. The kitchen chair on which he had slept was hard however, so he headed for the small couch, which would have been warm and cosy, had Belle been here to light the kitchen fire.

To his surprise, there was someone stretched out on it. He turned up the gaslight and saw it was Belle. His first feeling was of relief. He saw she still had her boots on, and so, very gently, he unlaced them and slipped them off her feet. He thought he ought to go and get a blanket to keep her warm, but, so relieved was he

35

that she was home, he bent down to kiss her forehead. He recoiled immediately however, for it was damp and cold to his lips. A sense of extreme foreboding came over him. He touched her hand. It too was cold and wet. He placed his hand on her forehead. It came away damp and sticky. At once, he rose to his feet and stepped back, frightened at the realisation. He turned up the gas mantle then knelt down beside her and held her wrist. He touched first her temple and then her cheeks in turn. There was no sign of life. There was no doubt about it. Belle was dead. William Henry fell back on his heels and screamed long and loud.

He tried to revive Belle. He rubbed and patted her hands. Then he half raised her head and shoulders and shook her lightly. How could she be dead? How could this happen? Who could have done this, and how, and when? How did this happen without his hearing it? Could he possibly have been so drunk that he heard nothing? He cursed himself. Had she walked in front of a cart or fallen under a van or something, and the driver had brought her back home and left her? Why didn't they wake him? William Henry took a clean, white pillowcase from the drying rack over the fireplace and wet it under the tap. He used it to clean Belle's face, for he could not bear to see her bloodstained features. She looked so peaceful in the soft glow of the gaslight, as if asleep. But yet there was no doubt she was dead. He held her to him, cradling her head to his chest and he cried out again.

He noticed a shaft of light streaking across the back yard wall outside. He had awoken the neighbours. He hardly knew his neighbours, for he and Belle had only moved into the little rented parlour house a few weeks earlier. He did not want to be with strangers. He wanted his family. He would fetch the children. He left the house and ran down the road, crying all the way and steadying himself with a hand on the wall at each corner. He got to Jane's house, and it was in darkness. He banged on the door and shouted for his daughters Jane and Belle. The baby started to cry and lights came on. It was some minutes before his daughters dressed and came to the door. At seeing their father in such distress, they too were alarmed. He blurted out the news that their mother was dead.

How and where, they wanted to know, but by now, having heard himself speak the words out loud, the full horror of his loss had hit William Henry and he could only cry and shout incoherently.

The girls left Jane's husband Walter to settle the disturbed baby and they set off with their distraught father to his house. En route, wee Belle took a detour and went off to Glenravel Street to seek assistance at the Police Barracks. Shortly after William Henry and Jane got to the house, wee Belle turned up with a constable, whom she had met on the way to the barracks. More light was shed on the scene and the constable confirmed that Belle was indeed dead. He started to take notes. He noted the bloodstains around the room, on the kitchen door frame, on the floor and on the nearby mangle, but none by either the front door or back door. One of the wooden kitchen chairs lay broken on the floor, a few splintered sticks from it lay in the hearth.

"It happened here in the kitchen," he opined, "this is where Mrs Kelly was attacked".

The constable took more notes. He noticed the bloodstains on William Henry's hands and clothing. William Henry saw the direction of his gaze and noticed the state of his own clothing.

"I tried to revive her," he explained. "Oh God!" he shouted, "my Belle is dead. You must catch whoever did this and hang them. You might as well hang me too, for I cannot live a minute without my Belle! I will hang myself!"

"Father!" Jane hushed him, "stop shoutin' now, do."

By now, the reality had hit Jane and Belle and both sisters were crying too. Shocked and incredulous, they did their best to answer the constable's questions. The constable went out front to talk to the little gaggle of neighbours who had gathered outside. Presently, another two constables arrived and one of them started taking statements. Everything seemed unreal to William Henry. He was searched and his pipe, spectacles and caulker's knife were taken by a policeman, who asked him to give an account of the evening's events. William Henry tried to be coherent and stick to the point, but somehow he could not. His mouth was dry.

Tears poured down his face and he could not help himself from shouting "somebody must have done this on Belle, for she couldn't have done it on herself! I can't live without my Belle! What am I going to do?"

He was inconsolable and eventually, two of the constables walked him down to the Glenravel Barracks where he was formally arrested on suspicion of the murder of his wife. He felt numb and confused as the police carried out their processes. All his clothes, barring his underwear, were taken away as evidence. He was given an old blanket and was placed in a cell, where he continued to cry and shout intermittently until daybreak, when eventually he lay back quietly on the iron cot.

It was around nine o'clock that Saturday morning when a police sergeant brought William Henry a cup of tea in his cell and explained he would shortly be given some breakfast. William Henry said he would be unable to eat.

"Do you know, my wife is dead?" he asked the constable.

"Aye, I do" the sergeant said softly.

"We wuz married upwards of thirty years," said William Henry, "what am I going to do without my Belle?"

"You feel bad now, Kelly, but things will get much worse, believe me. You should drink your tea now," the sergeant said, and he pulled the heavy cell door shut behind him.

Later in the day, Billy and Belle junior were allowed to visit their father. At the suggestion of the police, they had brought him some clothes. As he dressed, they pressed him to tell them what had happened, but William Henry had no recollection of anything after he had come home with his supper and the rum. He had not heard Belle come in and had not witnessed the events leading up to her death. He had spent the day tapping his aching head and racking his brains but had no idea at all what could have happened.

"Do the police have any clues?" he asked.

His son and daughter looked at one another and William Henry junior said, "Father, they think *you* did it."

William Henry was stunned. "How could they think that?" he asked, "things weren't always great between us, so they weren't, but you know I loved her and would never have killed her. Oh God, if they think I did it, then they won't be looking for the real killer."

Belle junior looked at Billy again then said, "the police spoke to our cousins, Lottie's son Sammy and Lena's boy Tommy. They saw mother out last night in Mackey Street. She had too much drink taken. She kept calling out for you and she fell over several times, so they brought her home at around one o'clock in the morning. They say you weren't in when they got here and they had to borrow a key from the neighbour, but that mother was alright, and was sleeping on tha couch when they left."

William Henry tried to take this in, "well, it must have been before ten o'clock when I got in. I'd seen you both, and could not find anyone in at our Alice's so I called in at tha cookshop and got myself some dinner and brought it back here to eat it. Somebody must have come in whilst I was asleep. I had drunk a lotta rum and I musta fell asleep."

"Are you sure you cannot remember what happened?" Billy asked, "for it would really help if you could remember something, anything. Did you go out again looking for Mother? Can you remember if she was here when you got back?"

William Henry slumped down on his bunk, his head in his hands. Why could he not remember?

"Don't worry father," said Belle junior, "they're holding a post mortem today, and first thing Monday morning you'll have a solicitor to take your statement. Billy will take time off from his work to go down the Queen's Island and see Johnnie Beasant to explain what's happened. Hopefully, they'll keep your job open until this all gets sorted out."

Then William Henry was alone again in his cell, for the rest of that day and all of the next with just his muddled thoughts. Did he or Belle have enemies? He knew he could be outspoken, and he had probably upset a few people in his time, including a few Catholics, and feelings were running high in Belfast at the moment, right enough, but surely no-one would do this to his beloved Belle? Who would kill a poor, honest wife and mother, who meant no harm to anyone but who meant the world to him?

It was in fact Monday afternoon when the solicitor came. Mr Graham introduced himself, explaining he had been waiting for details of the coroner's report before coming to the cell. He asked William Henry to give an account of the previous evening's events, whilst he took notes. When William Henry had finished, Mr Graham slowly read the coroner's report to himself. When he had finished, he looked at William Henry for a few seconds before he spoke.

"Did they tell you *how* your wife died?" he asked.

"No" said William Henry.

Mr Graham explained; "She was the victim of a violent attack - brutally beaten to death. Numerous ribs were broken, scalp slashed down to the bone, liver ruptured, defensive bruises to her arms and upper body. She might have survived the attack, had she been given timely medical attention. She was left to bleed slowly to death however. How do *you* think this happened?"

William Henry was shocked. He did not know what to say. He tried to take in what Mr Graham had said.

"Did *you* do it?" the solicitor asked.

"No, sir, no I didn't. I couldn't have. How could I, when I loved her so?" William Henry protested.

"Have you any idea then *who* did it?" Mr Graham pressed.

"No sir, no idea at all," William Henry answered, silent tears staring to roll down his cheeks.

"Was there anything stolen from the house?" the solicitor suggested.

"I don't believe so," said William Henry, "for we have nothing worth stealing. Belle and my children are my only precious things."

"And you heard nothing? Could somebody have come into the house? Would the door have been left open?" Mr Graham continued.

William Henry confessed he had been drunk and insensible and heard and saw nothing. Mr Graham asked if another family member could have killed Belle, the two nephews perhaps?

"Ach, they're just fifteen, for God's sake. Why would they, and how? They're good lads, the both of 'em," he protested.

"We seem to be running out of options," Mr Graham lamented. "We'll leave it there until I see all the witness depositions. I understand however that the neighbours claim to have heard a disturbance in the early hours. That may be helpful, or ... it may not," he said and he took his leave of William Henry.

Part Two – **THE CRUM**

Later that day, William Henry was formally charged with the murder of his wife and was taken under escort to the Crumlin Road Gaol – *The Crum* as it was known locally. His pipe, caulker's knife, small change and spectacles, still in the police envelope, were handed over to the prison reception officer, for safekeeping. William Henry was photographed and then taken to the medical officer's room where he was ordered to remove his outer clothes and wrap a blanket around his waist. He was weighed and had his height measured by a medical orderly then the Medical Officer came in to start the examination. Notes, dictated by the doctor, were taken down by the orderly as William Henry was checked over:

"Prisoner: William Henry Kelly; age: 56; height: five foot four inches; weight: one hundred and forty one pounds; hair: grey; eyes: grey; complexion: fair; varicose veins in both legs; lower two front teeth missing; birthmark on instep of right foot."

Standing before the Medical Officer, clad only the blanket and his woollen vest and underpants, and conscious that his undergarments had seen better days, William Henry felt thoroughly de-personalised. Being described in such intimate detail, and as if he were not there, was also humiliating. He was taken, wrapped in the stale-smelling blanket, to the prison barber who shaved off his moustache and ran the clippers over his head, leaving him with the regulation 'number one' haircut. Next, he was escorted to a cell, where, since he was a remand prisoner, a warder returned his own clothes to him. A short time later, the warder brought him some thin gruel in a tin mug, and also some bedding. He could not eat but he made up his bed and lay down. He spent another night wide awake, going over events in his head, but these were no clearer now than they had been on the awful night when someone had robbed him of his beloved Belle.

At six o'clock the next morning, his thoughts were disturbed by the arrival of a warder, accompanied by a prisoner who dispensed hot water, some for drinking and some for personal ablutions. William Henry was allowed to take out his toilet bucket and empty it in the toilets at the end of the landing. He was warned however that he was not to speak to or associate with the other prisoners. Free association was not permitted. He was aware of that, of course, for he had been here before. After washing and shaving himself with the communal razor, he returned to his cell, where more gruel was served to him, this time with a hunk of white bread. A large mug of tea was also dispensed and he was now assigned his own personal metal eating implements and instructed that he should clean them after every use with the piece of brickbat provided. He must also ensure his cell was kept clean. The gruel was a mixture of oats and maize and was quite the most disgusting thing he had ever tasted. He ate some of the bread, dunked in the tea to soften it. He then cleaned his tin mug with the water provided.

This done, he was marched out to be assigned work. Down in the prison yard, he was shown how to chop logs into regulation size small sticks for heating the prison boilers. He smiled to himself at this needless instruction, for he was a man who had turned whole trees into ship's masts in his younger days. He was given a small hatchet and worked with two other men under the supervision of a warder. He recognised one of the men as John Moss, a local man from Clonallen Street. William Henry remembered Belle reading aloud to him detail of Moss's trial some three or four months earlier. He had beaten his wife and had put her in the hospital, for which he received a six month sentence in *The Crum*. It had been his twenty-third conviction for wife beating. Moss tried to make eye contact and nodded at William Henry. William Henry did not acknowledge him however. He was glad the gaol forbade free association as he certainly did not want to associate with *that* type of a man.

At twelve thirty, William Henry and all the other prisoners were returned to their cells and the warders and prisoner orderlies came around again to serve them lunch. This was a thin, watery broth in which floated some four ounces of grey and indeterminate meat, an equal amount of overcooked vegetables and one whole pound of potatoes. William Henry sat facing the wall in his cell and tried to eat the food but he found swallowing difficult. It felt like there was a huge boulder lodged in his stomach, just below the gullet. At two o'clock, he was summoned down to the reception area to meet with his lawyer again.

"How are you, Mr Kelly?" his lawyer asked.

"I'm ..." William Henry began, but could not think what to say.

"Sit down Mr Kelly. We need to go over your recollection of the events of last Saturday evening" said Mr Graham, "Can you add anything to what you said the other night?"

William Henry did not like to admit he could not even remember what he had said previously. He simply shook his head.

"Have you ever been in trouble with the police before?" he asked.

William Henry looked down at his hands, at the shiny pads of his fingers, and shook his head.

"And how long have you worked for Harland and Wolff?" his lawyer asked.

"Thirty-six years" said William Henry, feeling a little more comfortable now, "I started out in the mast building yard and am now a caulker."

"And how long were you married?"

"Over thirty years, and we have five children, three daughters and two sons, all of them happy and well cared for," William Henry boasted.

"Tell me about them" Mr Graham urged.

"Well, two of the girls are married, that's Mrs Jane McBroom and Mrs Alice Anderson, and the third, Belle, lives with her sister Jane, helping to care for the baby. Belle also works at York Mill as a stitcher. My eldest son, James Hodges Kelly, is in the Royal Navy and the youngest, Billy, is working as an apprentice barber" William Henry said proudly. He perked up at the thought of his children.

Mr Graham took notes. "And what is your religion?"

"Protestant" replied William Henry.

"And your late wife, was she a Catholic?"

42

"No" said William Henry, surprised at the question.

"So, how were things between you?" Mr Graham asked.

"We loved each other," said William Henry, "she was everything to me. Ach, we'd argue from time to time, as all couples do, especially if we'd both had a drink. However, Belle was my partner in life. I love her. I mean ... I'll always love her. Have the police found her killer yet? Are they still looking for him?"

Mr Graham explained that, so far, William Henry was the only suspect. He went on to explain that all the physical evidence pointed to William Henry having killed his wife. There was blood all over his clothing and signs of a struggle in the room. Some long dark hairs matching those from his wife's head had been found adhering to his clothing and a leg from the broken kitchen chair appeared to have been the main weapon used against her.

"There's also a fair sized abrasion on your left cheek, Mr Kelly" he added. William Henry put his hand up to his cheek. Prisoners were not allowed mirrors and there were none in the toilet area at the end of his landing. He had not seen his own appearance since he had been admitted to the prison. His cheek had felt a little tender but he had thought that was from the prison barber's attempts to dehumanise him.

"The neighbours have given statements that they heard you both arguing loudly very late on Saturday night. They have also told police you fought frequently."

William Henry sighed and his shoulders sank noticeably. "Belle .., well, Belle had taken to the drink over the past few years. She would go out drinking during the day when I was at work. I made arrangements for her to have several different jobs, but she lost them all because of her drinking. Things was difficult for me, but I still loved her, and there's no way in this world I would ever hurt her."

Mr Graham looked over his notes. "The statement you made to the police does not help your case greatly" he said.

William Henry looked surprised, "What statement? The police didn't interview me yet."

"Yes, they did," said Mr Graham, "they recorded in writing everything you said at the house and again at the police station."

William Henry was shocked. "But I don't remember what I said. I had been drinking a bit myself," he recalled.

"Apparently, you were shouting very loudly and made statements to the effect that you would kill yourself within twenty-four hours, so there was no point in a trial nor in the authorities bothering to hang you. You didn't exactly confess to killing your wife, Mr Kelly, but your statements to the police thus far might be construed as expressing guilt. We might be able to have those discounted as you were under the influence of drink, but, if you decide to give evidence in court yourself, then those initial statements may still be read out in court. It would be best therefore if you said nothing more to the police, nor indeed in court. Can you manage that?" William Henry nodded.

"I have spoken with your nephews, Samuel Condit and Thomas Patterson," Mr Graham continued, "and they have also made statements to the effect that they saw your wife Belle late that evening, rather worse the wear for drink and wandering around Duncairn Gardens. In fact, she was most unsteady on her feet and they were

43

concerned for her welfare, so they accompanied her towards home, though she fell down two or three times. Some of her injuries may have been sustained when she fell. We'll have to see what the pathologist says in court. The boys say your house was empty when they got there and your wife was still demanding drink but they could find none in the house. They gave her some roast beef they found in the kitchen and then she insisted they go out and buy her a glass of rum from the public house. After the rum and the beef, she lay down to sleep and they left."

"That would be the beef I brought in after I came home and found no food in the house" said William Henry. "That proves I was there and then I must have left again before she got back with Sammy and Tommy. If they say I was not there when they brought her home so I must have went out again and had a few more drinks myself. Then I must have came home and fell asleep, not noticing she was dead."

Mr Graham looked grave, "it could also be that you came back after the boys had left, that an argument broke out and you killed her. At least that's how the police may present the case. We will have to see what statements the neighbours will make. It will be helpful if your memory returns. Perhaps you'll let me know if anything comes back to you, anything at all? We'll speak again before your trial."

After several days of chopping wood and sitting alone in his cell to eat his meals, and, of course the long hours of thinking, when he would slap his hands against his forehead to try to prompt the return of his absent memory, but without any inspiration as to what had happened, William Henry found himself supervised at his labours by a different warder. A soulless and dour individual, Warder O'Hagan seemed to take an instant dislike to William Henry and to John Moss.

"Choppin' sticks, is it?" he sneered, "I think we'll get you men on something more suitable tha day, some proper men's work."

Leaving the third remand prisoner in the wood yard, O'Hagan took William Henry and John Moss back to their cells. William Henry sat in his cell, awaiting the warder's return, lamenting the loss of his fresh air occupation, and wondering what sort of cell-based activity could be 'more manly' than wood chopping.

His curiosity was soon satisfied. O'Hagan and another warder appeared with a rough wooden stool, which resembled the seat end of a spinning wheel, except that, where the wheel part would normally have been, there was a strange hook device. Soon, a large heap of rope ends were dragged in on a canvas sheet and O'Hagan explained the task to be done. The rope ends were black and pungent with a tarry substance. In fact, because of the coating of tar, they were rock hard, like constables' truncheons.

"You're going to be tow-pickin'" O'Hagan explained, "these rope ends has to be worked over and over against the hook, to be softened and teased out and worked into the softest, most absorbent threads possible, for use as oakum. I'm sure you're familiar with oakum, Kelly, what with you being a caulker in the Protestant shipyard, and all!"

O'Hagan grinned derisively, "the finished oakum is sent over to the yards for them Protestant bastards to use to caulk their ships. The finer the oakum, the easier it is on the caulker's Protestant hands. You leave too much hard tar on the fibres and your Protestant bastard friends' fingers will bleed and it won't be absorbent enough

44

to be any use, so your ships will let in water and the Protestant passengers will drown. You have to pick at least four and a half pounds of oakum a day or you'll be up before the Governor. So remember, if you don't do the job properly, them Protestant bastard fellow workers of yours will suffer. So, now you know where the oakum came from that you used to use. Ironic, isn't it?"

O'Hagan relaxed back against the cell doorframe, arms folded, grinning savagely. William Henry noticed the heavy truncheon hanging from his belt. 'If it wuz just you and me, out in the yard, and no truncheon ...' he thought, but he held his tongue.

"Life's just a great big inter-dependant circle, isn't it? Just like them Buddhists believe. Except you're not a Buddhist, are you, Kelly? You're a Protestant bastard!" He laughed.

The door was slammed with even greater force than usual. As O'Hagan's forced laughter continued down the landing, William Henry set to work at his new task. He was no stranger to religious prejudice of course, but nevertheless he was taken aback by O'Hagan's attitude. He hadn't even known whether John Moss was a Catholic or a Protestant. People didn't always know just from looking at a man on which side of the religious divide he stood. His name might suggest his religion, for, generally, those with Irish names were Catholics and those with Scots or English names were likely to be Protestants, but not always. He himself was an example of that. A more likely give away perhaps was a man's occupation. There were comparatively few Catholics employed in the shipyards, for example.

William Henry's occupation had tagged him as a Protestant. It was ironic really, as he had a sister-in-law and brother-in-law who were Catholic and it had made not a jot of difference to the Kelly family. Nowadays though, things were getting tricky in Belfast and sectarian attacks were starting off again. It always seemed to happen when that old demon poverty broke out of its box. When people felt their jobs and livelihoods were under threat then, predictably, they worried that folks of the alternative religious persuasion were, or might become, somehow better off or more privileged. O'Hagan clearly felt threatened by Protestants and so had a down on the Protestant prisoners. William Henry knew he would have to roll with the punches and keep his old, grey Protestant head down.

April warmed into May, and a cheerful sun pierced the Belfast gloom, finding its way even into some of the more accessible corners of The Crum. William Henry had managed to persevere with the tow picking for six weeks or so. Broken nails and blisters were no strangers to him, and his finger tips were pitch hardened from the caulking, but nevertheless, they now bled and had become stiff under the relentless repetition of twisting, unpicking, teasing and pulling the tarred rope. He had eventually summoned up the indignation and frustration to ask to see the Medical Officer. The MO had been shocked at the state of the fifty-six year old's hands and had issued a written recommendation for him to undertake lighter work. For William Henry however, persevering with the tow picking for this long had been a matter of honour. It seemed John Moss also had withstood the rigours of the oakum picking, perhaps thinking it a fitting punishment for a persistent wife beater. William Henry found himself back in front of the prison's Discipline Officer, to learn what he would do next for his labour.

He was sent next to the tailoring shop, where he was taught how to cut out and stitch the rough woollen suits for the prison's convicted inmates and, when demand for these slowed, there were mailbags to be stitched or canvas mats to be run up, for as everyone knows, the devil makes work for idle hands - even the rough, calloused hands of a skilled Belfast shipyard worker. In the evenings, William Henry would return to his cell and await the arrival of the orderly with the huge bucket out of which he would dole into each prisoner's tin mug a ladleful of *skilly*, the watery, faintly meat-flavoured gruel, which was supper. William Henry would mostly toy with the revolting, oily liquid and would use it to moisten his hunk of bread, which was all he could eat of the meal. *Skilly*, he mused, from the Irish word *skilleegalee*, meaning fanciful. He supposed one were meant to fancy there might be some goodness in this grey, greasy concoction.

As a remand prisoner, William Henry was allowed to purchase one newspaper a week from his nominal prison earnings – no money ever appeared, but credit was added to his 'account'. He could also borrow books from the prison library, though there was a very poor selection of reading matter in *The Crum*. He was not allowed to keep letters, photographs or any other personal belongings or mementoes in his cell, though his spectacles had been returned to him, so he had little to occupy himself in the evenings. One thing he managed to do, which did not seem to breach the prison rules on associating with other prisoners, was to swap his newspaper with other prisoners, so he would read different accounts of the same stories in the various papers. To his surprise, he now learned that King Edward had passed away on the sixth of May. The king's son, young Prince George, was now to be their new monarch. William Henry expected the coronation would be celebrated in Belfast. He wondered if he would be released in time to see all the celebrations. This news was soon eclipsed by something of a far more scandalous nature however. William Henry, and doubtless all the other remand prisoners, had also been keeping up with the press reporting on the case of another man who, it was alleged, had murdered his wife.

Doctor Hawley Harvey Crippen, an American working in London as a purveyor of patent medicines, was being sought by police for poisoning his hard-drinking and verbally abusive wife and had debunked with his younger mistress. Physical descriptions of the pair had appeared in the newspapers and the authorities, on both sides of the Atlantic, were on alert for them. The public's imagination had been gripped by the case. William Henry read that Crippen's missing actress wife had been born with the name Kunigunde Mackamotzi, but used the stage name Belle Elmore. The irony of William Henry being in prison for the alleged murder of his wife - also named Belle - had not been lost on sadistic warder O'Hagan. William Henry dreaded O'Hagan being on duty, as he would never pass William Henry's cell without passing some comment.

"I suppose ye beat *your* wife to death because you couldn't afford the poison!" he baited William Henry, "and did ye do it because you were planning to run off with *your* lady typist?"

"Oh no, Mr O'Hagan" retorted William Henry drily, "it was because she bought a green coat."

46

At night, William Henry still slept fitfully. Sometimes, he lay awake into the small hours, listening to the numerous snores and occasional moans of his fellow prisoners. Prisoners were not allowed to share cells. All the cells were for single occupation only. William Henry understood this was an important stipulation of the prison reforms which had been introduced in the previous century, and though there were many men on his landing, and he could hear their every sigh and intimate bodily function, ironically he was not allowed to communicate with them. Increasingly he felt the loneliness as well as the continuing sadness over the loss of his Belle. He missed the laugh and the chat he and Belle would have together most evenings, whether or not they had a wee drink. They would talk over the day's events at the shipyard or discuss what the weans had done or said. Those days would never return, however.

He reflected upon how he and Belle would enjoy the simple pleasure of reading the evening newspaper. William Henry would read every page. He thought it important to be informed of current affairs, especially these days, with the way of life of the Irish Protestant under threat. So long as you kept yourself informed, he would tell Belle, those in power couldn't hoodwink you. Belle had loved to read all the news about what was happening in their community - the crimes, scandals, local events, births, deaths and marriages. After thirty years together, they had still enjoyed each other's company. Now however, he wondered if he weren't better off here in the gaol than sitting at home in the empty kitchen, looking into a cold, empty hearth. Another of his remembered quotations from Twain now came into his head: 'Grief can take care of itself, but to get the full value of a joy, you must have someone to share it with.' He imagined there would be little joy in his life from now on.

From the start of his incarceration, William Henry found himself having bad dreams. It would be the usual sorts of nightmares to which he had always been prone but with an added dimension. He would be falling from the shipyard gantry, in slow motion, hurtling towards the ground and vaguely aware of the far off hills, of the grey, wet slate roofs of the Belfast houses and of the massive, scaffold-clad ships in various stages of construction around him. Then, as his descent hurtled towards a predictable conclusion, he now saw immediately beneath him on the ground, the bloody and battered body of Belle. Before hitting the ground, he would awake with a start and cry out. Sometimes, in his dreams he saw again the thin, hollow-eyed face and wasted body of his deceased infant daughter, his first wee Belle, lying in her tiny child's white coffin. She would open her eyes and extend two pale bony arms to him and cry, feebly and pitiably for her mother. The tiny, spidery arms would push William Henry aside as she would not be consoled by him but wanted only her mother, whom, to his extreme frustration, he could not produce.

Other nightmares involved William Henry entering his house and seeing his wife struggling with a monstrous assailant. He would race forward to tackle the man and a fierce struggle would ensue. He would drag the attacker over to the jaw box and push him backwards over it, in order to see his evil face in the moonlight streaming in at the small kitchen window. To his horror, he would see that the man in his grip was in fact himself. Always, during those narrow hours of semi-consciousness, between sleep and wakefulness, he would have disturbing flashbacks to the night of Belle's death. He sometimes found himself holding her delicate, soft throat in his strong hand and shaking and squeezing the life out of her. He heard her calling out to him; "Wim Henery, stop, you're chokin' me!" At other times, his nightmare started off with him chopping sticks vigorously out in the prison wood yard, then the hatchet turned into a wooden chair leg and he was bringing it down repeatedly on Belle's dark hair, as blood sprayed from her scalp in a fine arc around their kitchen, drenching his face and hands.

Sometimes, he would be awoken by a prisoner shouting, and, as he came to and sat up in indignation at the disturbance, he would realise that in fact *he* was the prisoner doing the shouting and that he had been crying out profanities, and cursing his wife in the foulest terms. He worried that others would have heard him. The nightmares now seemed to intrude into his waking hours too. When carrying out the fortnightly stripping of his bedding, he would hold aloft the coarse mattress, then would pummel it hard, as per the warder's instructions, to break up the lumps in the coarse coconut fibres within and redistribute them, making it more comfortable and knocking out the accumulated dust. In doing this however, he would have a sudden vision of holding his beloved Belle by the throat and pummelling *her* with all his strength in her soft belly. This was the same warm belly which had borne his beloved children, and he was pounding the life out of it. He would stop sharply and recoil in disbelief. Clearly, he reasoned, he was still suffering from shock. Maybe when the police had found Belle's killer these awful nightmares would stop.

The weeks in *The Crum* turned into months however. By the time the date of his trial was announced, he began to wonder if it just might be possible that he himself had indeed beaten the life out of the woman he loved. Images seemed to be forming in his head in small, awful pieces of a bigger, painful picture. He was unsure whether these were recollections or just gruesome imaginings. He felt as though someone were showing him little snapshots of the past. How cruel for the reality of his deed, if such it were, to be presented to him in small doses like this, and almost daily now. His lawyer came to see him for final instruction before the big day. Mr Graham looked visibly shocked when he saw the prisoner.

"Are you alright, Mr Kelly?" he asked, for William Henry had lost weight and had a most pale and haunted look about him.

"Ach well, the food in here is disgustin', so it is, and I haven't been sleeping very well. And sure I must look as white as a haddock without the auld moustache. They don't allow us scissors to trim them properly or a mirror for grooming, so there's no point in having whiskers. Sure, I doubt my own wife would know me ..." he broke off.

"There's a few things I need to go over with you," Mr Graham continued. "It's probably still best if you say nothing in court. Others will speak on your behalf, your children for example and perhaps your minister and your foreman from Harland and Wolff. However, I have concerns about one witness whose testimony may be less than helpful. Do you recall meeting a Mr William Robinson on the night of your wife's death?"

William Henry looked blank. Robinson? He had friends in the shipyard named Robinson, for it was a fairly common name in Belfast, but not a William. The name rang no immediate bells. But, wait, there had been a Billy Robinson who had worked in the shipyard but had left about a year ago to work in a hotel restaurant. He had not been popular and he had had a few fights with some of his fellow workers. William Henry had had some sort of run in with Billy Robinson, he recalled. Yes, it was coming back to him now. He remembered something of the disagreement, yes of course he did. It had been thought that Robinson was one of those depraved types of fellow who sought out the company of men and didn't like women. He had never married or been seen courting girls but was always hanging out with the apprentices in the yards, especially the younger ones. He was always offering to buy drinks or cigarettes for the young boys who worked in the yard, even after a few of the other men suggested this was inappropriate.

William Henry now recalled something of a few bad words exchanged between them, when he had a few drinks in him and had told Robinson what he thought of him and his kind. Robinson had not taken kindly to William Henry's loudly expressed opinions. William Henry had thought at first that Robinson was just a bit of a *Mary Anne*, but later on it was strongly suspected he was a potential child molester. William Henry had heard that some wee boy's mother had accused him of interfering with her son and she and a few other local women had sorted him out. A bruised Robinson had kept a low profile on the streets after that and, soon after, he had left Harland and Wolff for a job more suited to his temperament, and one in which, some thought, he was less of a danger to young boys. There were a few like Robinson in *The Crum*, but they had their own landing and were kept away from the general prison population.

"Robinson says he bumped into you in the New Lodge Road on your way home from work that night, and that you and he had a conversation, during which ..." Mr Graham scanned the copy deposition he had with him, "... you mentioned having a wife who was addicted to drink and said you had a plan to knife her. He said you had been drinking heavily yourself."

William Henry was shocked, "I had had a few beers on my way home, it is true, but I was not drunk, and yet I have no recollection of meeting Robinson, let alone having a conversation with him. I haven't laid eyes on him since he left the yards, in fact. For I heard he works in the dining room of a big hotel, and, sure, I would not have the money to frequent that sort of establishment."

"Do you have any idea why he would say this?" the solicitor asked.

"No, none," said William Henry, "except that a few of us, especially me, mebbe prompted his decision to leave the yards, on account of us being uneasy at his behaviour around the boys working there."

"Do you know if he has any criminal convictions, then?" Mr Graham asked.

"I don't believe so," William Henry shook his head, "for everybody around here knows everybody else's business and, if so, then somebody would have heard it."

"Well, hopefully, we should be able to discredit his testimony. There's another point, Mr Kelly," Mr Graham continued, "When we first met, you told me you had never been in trouble with the police previously yourself, however, the police officer who arrested you has advised me that you and he are well acquainted and that, in fact, you have a number of previous convictions, is that so?"

William Henry had a sudden cowardly urge of self preservation, "Not me," he said, "but sure, there's an awful lot of Kellys in Belfast."

Mr Graham looked William Henry in the eye for a second or two before he again spoke; "I hope that's the case, Mr Kelly, for there's also an awful lot of wife beaters and killers in Belfast these days, and the judges don't like it. In fact, they've been handing out some pretty stiff sentences just lately. I must remind you that you are charged with murder, and that is a capital offence. You could receive the death sentence. This is what the public demands these days and judges do so hate seeing what they perceive to be crime trends. They like to think they can stamp it out by taking a tough line and they do not appreciate being lied to. There's an old maxim in law; that he who would seek justice should come to court with clean hands. If they can prove you a liar, you may forfeit not only your right to justice, but your life. Wife murder is front page stuff these days - take the Crippen case for instance. There are perhaps more *dis*similarities between your case and the Crippen case than there are similarities, as far as I can see. For one thing, he is a doctor, albeit a self styled one, which could either go in his favour or, conversely, might work against him, but then again, *he* has no previous convictions. However, he will still hang when they catch him. I'm convinced of it. Now, is there anything else I need to know before we go to trial?"

William Henry again shook his head. Mr Graham packed his papers away in his leather briefcase.

"One last question then, Mr Henry," his advocate turned at the cell door to look back at him, "*did* you kill your wife?"

William Henry looked up at him, "Mr. Graham ... I still don't have full recollection of that night, though wee threads of memory keeps comin' back to me. I think ... there's a chance ... I just *might* have done so."

Part Three – **THE TRIAL**

Three months later, the day of William Henry's trial finally came around. Breakfast was served to him that morning, as always, but of course, was not eaten, leaving him an hour or so to kill in his cell and feel his stomach churn. Soon, however, he was escorted down some very dark steps and along a dark and damp smelling tunnel, which took him beneath the Crumlin Road and came up in the cells of the courthouse across the road, where he was to await the call to appear. One of the warders advised him it was a beautiful July day outside, but that he would not be seeing any of it, unless, of course, he were acquitted. Billy, had called in the day before with a set of clean clothing for him and to wish him luck. Thus, William Henry was wearing his black Sunday jacket, grey Sunday trousers and a clean white shirt and black tie. His clothes were old but fairly respectable. They sat limply on him however in view of his weight loss. He wondered if that might evince a little sympathy from the jury.

He was soon called into court and climbed the steep steps to take his place in the dock. Courtroom One was the largest room he had ever been in. It was cavernous and brightly lit, with many windows placed high up near the ceiling. Various bespectacled men in black gowns and wigs bustled about, laying out files, papers and jugs of water, and whispering to each other. There was a low and steady background murmur as more people shuffled in. Up in the public gallery, people in more every day dress were now being admitted and more shuffling ensued. The odd noise of a dropped file, or a spectacle case snapping shut, echoed starkly around the courtroom and sounded much nearer to him than it actually was. William Henry noticed a couple of men up in the public gallery, with pencils tucked behind their ears, clutching reporter's notebooks. This increased his anxiety somewhat, but then he saw a woman give him an encouraging wave. It was his sister Lena. Helena Patterson, formerly Kelly, and known as Lena to her family, was a lovely woman. She had been living in Scotland for some years until her Scottish husband, Robert Patterson, had died suddenly, and now, to William Henry's delight, she was back living in Belfast.

William Henry now spotted a number of his fellow shipbuilders who nodded and gave him the thumbs up. They must all have taken the day off to attend. Was it morbid curiosity or were they here to truly wish him well? He immediately banished the uncharitable thought that they would forfeit a day's pay, or risk their jobs by leaving their bourds with workmates, for any base motive. Hughie Hewitt was there, but, disappointingly, there was no sign of Johnnie Beasant. He wondered where his other sister Charlotte was. He had felt sure she would be there, for Lottie was the most solicitous of his siblings. She was usually the first of the family to respond when someone needed support. Lottie it was who arranged funerals, consoled the bereaved and looked after folks' weans. Then he realised that she and other members of his family might be giving evidence and so would not be allowed into in the courtroom until called. He could see his daughters Jane and Alice sitting alongside Lena and he wondered if Billy and wee Belle would be there. Mr Graham had hoped to arrange for them to be witnesses, but of course there was no guarantee they would wish to do so, especially as he was charged with killing their mother.

He looked across at the sober and sombre men of the jury, hoping there might be someone who knew him and who would therefore be sympathetic, but he did not recognise a soul. They looked like shopkeepers, minor officials or managers, so they were probably all fellow Protestants, which likelihood comforted him. Soon, the judge, the Right Honourable Mr Justice Wright, was announced and everyone rose as the tall, bewigged man entered. When he sat, so did everyone else. Messrs John Gordon and Henry Hill Smith now announced themselves as appearing for the prosecution and Messrs Henry Hanna and Thomas Campbell for the defence. William Henry had not met his counsel but knew he would have been briefed by Mr Graham. As soon as all were seated, the charge was read out:

"That the defendant, William Henry Kelly, on the twenty third day of April in the year of our Lord One thousand nine hundred and ten, wilfully, feloniously and of his malice aforethought, did kill and murder one Isabella Kelly against the peace of our late Sovereign Lord the King, his crown and dignity".

William Henry wondered why the clerk of the court referred to the sovereign as being 'late', since his understanding was that, the second a monarch died, the heir automatically became the sovereign. His thoughts were suddenly interrupted when he realised the Clerk was addressing him. He was asked how he would plead, to which he spoke the only words he would speak in open court: "Not Guilty". Then the medical evidence was read out. Doctor McLorinan, who was William Henry's local GP, read from his notebook an account of being called to the Kelly household in the early hours and of what he had found there. He also continued to describe the findings of the post-mortem examination which he had conducted in tandem with the Coroner, Mr Symmers.

"I received an urgent call to Mr Kelly's house off the New Lodge Road, at four am on Saturday 23 April. I went at once and there saw the body of Isabella Kelly, lying on her back with a pillow under her head, on a sofa in the kitchen. She was fully dressed except for her boots. On examining her, I found she was dead. She had evidently been dead for some hours, as the exposed parts of her body were stone cold, although the covered parts were still warm and rigor had not set in. She had four gaping wounds on the top of her head extending to the bone and the hair was matted with coagulated blood. She had also a gaping wound on the left side of her chin, extending to the bone. Her hands and part of her forearms were covered with dried blood. Grasped in her hands were a number of long hairs which resembled her own. There were two large splashes of blood on the kitchen floor - one beside the sofa on which the body lay and one near the door leading out to the scullery. Near the latter was a large mangle with iron legs and on the leg nearest to the scullery door were splashes of blood. A strong kitchen chair from which the legs appeared to have been recently broken lay inside the parlour door and two of these legs were lying on the kitchen floor."

As Doctor Lorinan finished reading his initial statement, William Henry's face was white and drained. There was absolute silence in the court and he saw his family leaning forward in the public gallery, the better to hear the cause of death of their mother and sister-in-law. The doctor continued reading with his account of the post mortem examination:-

"Body of a well-nourished woman, aged around fifty, rigor mortis firm, both hands and forearms covered with caked blood. The whole back of the left hand was swollen and discoloured, owing to a copious effusion of blood under the skin and among the muscles, the outer edge of the right hand was badly bruised also and there was copious bruising to the backs of the hands extending up the forearms to the elbows. There were numerous individual bruises on both upper arms, each around the size of a shilling. Immediately above the right nipple, there was a bruise about the size of a half crown, and extensive bruising over the area of the left breast, continuing over the ribs of the left side. Over the shins of both legs there was discolouration extending for six inches in length and around two inches wide, with freshly effused blood found under the skin in these areas. There was a large bruise on the left cheek, the size of a crown, with effused blood flow under the skin, which had drenched all the subcutaneous tissues in the left side of the face. Immediately under the chin on the left side of the jaw, the skin was torn away down to the bone, forming an open wound with the bone laid bare. This was such as might have been caused by falling against some sharp edged object with great violence."

William Henry's daughters Jane and Alice, and his sister Lena clasped their handkerchiefs to their faces and huddled closer together.

The doctor continued: "On the left forehead, over the eye, was a bruise the size of a shilling, and the edge of the eye was torn. The hair over the front part of the scalp was matted with blood and the scalp was torn through in four separate wounds which had bled effusively. Each of these tears extended down to the bone, exposing the bone of the skull. These wounds appeared to have been caused by a blunt rather than sharp instrument. Blood was found also within the skull, beneath the pia mater membrane of the brain. There was extensive bruising to the windpipe below the adam's apple. On the right side of the body, seven ribs were fractured, the third to the ninth inclusive. The heart was normal, except for a little chronic myocarditis in the papillary muscle of the right ventricle. A large quantity of blood was found in the abdomen, having pooled in the pelvis. The right lobe of the liver, immediately under the diaphragm, was lacerated, and a hole the size of a man's clenched fist was torn in the organ in an irregular manner through the top of the lobe. The stomach contained a little undigested food but there did not appear to be any alcohol present. The kidneys appeared slightly cirrhotic. The other organs appeared normal. My conclusion regarding the cause of death was that this was due to shock and haemorrhage following multiple injuries of the body including rupture of the liver."

William Henry began to sob softly in the dock. Mr Hanna was now on his feet.

"Doctor Lorinan," he said, "did the victim die from the sum total of her injuries, or was one injury alone responsible for her death?"

"Well," said the doctor "exsanguination - loss of blood - was the *principle* cause of death, and the major blood loss was from the rupture of the liver, so it would be fair to say that the ruptured liver was the main injury which caused her death."

Mr Hanna pressed the point, "had the liver *not* been ruptured, would the deceased woman have died from the bleeding and effects of the remaining injuries or might she have survived?"

The doctor considered this carefully before replying "no, *those* injuries would probably not have killed her, although she may have suffered further life-threatening complications, were no prompt medical attention forthcoming."

"So, in essence," said Mr Hanna "it was the injury to the liver, and this alone, which was the cause of her death?"

"Yes" said the doctor.

Next Doctor William St Clair Symmers, introduced himself as professor of pathology at the Queen's University and he confirmed he had been present at the post mortem of the late Mrs Isabella Kelly. He consulted his notes and added that Mrs Kelly had appeared to be a fairly well nourished woman, aged between forty five and fifty years, who had been subjected to very great and sustained violence. He added that the vast majority of the injuries could not have been self inflicted or accidental. In response to a question from Mr Hanna, Dr Symmers agreed the deep cuts in the dead woman's scalp would not have caused her death, but that the injury to the liver was the principle cause of her bleeding to death internally. Mr Hanna asked if the deceased's bones were of normal composition or might have been unusually thin for a woman of her age, Doctor Symmers said the deceased's bone density was entirely normal. Mr Hanna next asked the doctor if he had in fact made an earlier statement to the contrary when giving his initial findings to the police. Doctor Symmers confirmed he had indeed said in an earlier statement that Mrs Kelly's bones had been thinner than normal, but he now said he had been mistaken in the first instance. There had been silence in the court as everyone took in the gory details. Now, everyone in the court, William Henry included, looked across at the defence counsel, as they expected him to pursue this inconsistency and demand an explanation, but, disappointingly, he did not.

Next, Constable of Constabulary, Thomas Murphy, gave evidence that, on the night of Friday 22 April, he had been walking his beat up the New Lodge Road when he had been approached by a Mrs Wheeler, a next door neighbour of the deceased, who said she had heard sounds of violence coming from the defendant's house and believed a woman was being assaulted. He added that this had been at around 11.30 pm and he had proceeded to the house and had listened at the door for around five minutes but had heard nothing. He had remained in the vicinity for around a quarter of an hour then continued on his beat, returning to the address again just after midnight and again at around 1.30 am but had found everything quiet. Mr Hanna waived his right to cross examination.

The next witness, Constable John O'Sullivan, gave evidence that he had been approached at the corner of Singleton Street and the New Lodge Road by the defendant's daughter, who had asked him to accompany her and her father back to his home to confirm their fears that her mother was dead. Constable O'Sullivan said the defendant was quite drunk and was crying and shouting incoherently. At one stage, he said, referring to his notebook, the defendant had said: "She has taken a

54

weak turn. Dr Lorinan attends her for a weak heart. She must have had a heart attack. She is dead from that." In the dock, William Henry shook his head to himself. He still had no recollection of having said that.

Constable O'Sullivan continued to describe the scene he had found at the house and the events leading up to the arrest of the defendant and his being conveyed to the Police office. Mr Hanna asked the constable to confirm that, in his opinion, the defendant had been drunk and incoherent when he and a fellow officer had walked him to the Police Office. The Constable confirmed this.

"What period of time had elapsed then" Mr Hanna asked, "between his being incoherent and his making the apparently perfectly *coherent* statement regarding Doctor Lorinan attending his wife for a heart condition?"

How far, for example, Mr Hanna wanted to know, was the Police Office from the junction of Singleton Street and the New Lodge Road and how long did that walk take? The Constable hesitated and then said it was perhaps ten or fifteen minutes' walk. William Henry looked expectantly at Mr Hanna, in the hope that he would pursue this line and establish whether the constable had either exaggerated his drunkenness or had attributed to him a statement he did not make, but, disappointingly again, Mr Hanna did not press the issue.

Another police officer now took the stand. Head Constable Daniel Hughes recounted how, acting on information received, he had gone to the defendant's house at 5.30 am on the morning of Saturday 23 April and had observed the dead body of Mrs Isabella Kelly. He described the position and condition of the body and the state of the room. He said he had found a damp and bloodstained pillowcase which appeared to have been used to clean the dead woman's face and hands, and a clean pillow which had been placed beneath the deceased's head. He described how he had found the solid, wooden kitchen chair splintered and blood-stained, lying in pieces around the kitchen.

He said the defendant was sitting at the kitchen table and appeared to be drunk. He further stated he had arrested the defendant and had taken him to Glenravel Barracks. He had charged the prisoner with the murder of his wife, whereupon the defendant had said: "You need not charge me with murder, for I would rather have her alive." Head Constable Hughes added he had searched the prisoner and had taken possession of a caulking knife, a pipe and a pair of spectacles. He further stated he had escorted the defendant to the Police Office and, en route the defendant had said "You may hang me. She was a good wife. I loved her. I will not live without her. I will do away with myself if you let me go."

Head Constable Hughes said that, at the police office, he had taken possession of the defendant's bloodstained clothes and had noted an abrasion on his cheek. In cross examination, Mr Hanna asked if there had been any other injuries on the person of the defendant and whether there had been any blood on the defendant's caulking knife, and Head Constable Hughes answered in the negative to both questions. Mr Hanna then asked the officer whether the defendant had still been in a drunken condition when he had made the afore-going comments at the Police office. The officer replied "he was drunk but becoming sober."

The next prosecution witness was William Henry's neighbour on the other side, William Hannan, who said the defendant and his late wife had only come to live in the street at Easter and he had not spoken to them very much but that they had often been heard arguing. On the night of Friday 22 April, at about half past eleven, he had heard a row going on in the defendant's house. He recounted how he had heard a woman screaming "stop it, Wim Henery, you're chokin' me!" William Henry now sat bolt upright on the hard bench which he shared with the two warders. Not just the words of his deceased wife, but even the way they were spoken by Hannan, sounded exactly as they had in his recurring dreams. William Henry half hoped Mr Hanna might ask Hannan how many William Henrys lived in their street, for there were two in Hannan's household alone – Hannan himself and his brother in law – and maybe a quarter of a million men named William Henry throughout Belfast. There was little point in sowing any further seeds of doubt however, as, by now, it was no longer a case of establishing *who* had committed the crime. William Henry now knew in his heart that he himself had done it. It was now a case of arguing for his life. Would they hang him?

Another William – William Robinson – was the final prosecution witness, and he appeared in the witness box in smart waiter's uniform. William Henry wondered if the uniform would create an undeservedly favourable impression with the jury. Robinson recounted how, at around ten past six on the evening of Friday 22 April, he had been walking up the New Lodge Road to the junction of the Antrim Road, when he had met the defendant, whom he had known for the past two years. The defendant had asked him to go for a drink with him but Robinson said he had declined, as he was on his way to work. William Henry couldn't imagine how drunk he would have to be to invite a child molester to drink with him. Robinson continued to say that the defendant had then remarked that he had a wife who drank very heavily, and had asked him what he would do with such a wife. Robinson said he had replied 'send her away to the country' to which the defendant had said he would 'send her out of the country by a switcher'.

Mr Hanna rose to cross examine and asked what Robinson understood this to mean. William Henry winced at this, as he had neither heard nor used the word 'switcher', though he could guess at its meaning, and he didn't think it helpful that his own solicitor was giving Robinson an opportunity to expand on his answer, especially when this expanded answer would certainly reflect badly on William Henry. He glanced at the upright and sober men of the jury. It was just possible that some of them were unfamiliar with the word 'Switcher'. Why not let that be? Obligingly however, Robinson explained that 'Switcher' was local popular parlance for a switchblade, or knife, such as one might use in a street fight for example. Mr Hanna asked what state the defendant had been in when Robinson had met him, and Robinson said that obviously he 'had much drink taken'. Anticipating Mr Hanna's next question however, Robinson added "... but yet he seemed sensible enough. We then shook hands and he told me he was going home." William Henry knew he would be able to prove he had been in the pub with his workmates at the time the meeting with Robinson was alleged to have taken place. If need be, Johnnie Beasant might be asked about this. As it turned out however, this would not be necessary.

Mr Hanna continued his cross examination by asking Robinson how he knew the defendant and whether they were on good terms. Robinson said they had worked together in the shipyard until Robinson had left to work as a waiter, and that they had got on well enough. William Henry hoped his lawyer would ask Robinson why he had left the yards. However, Mr Hanna's next question was whether Robinson considered the defendant to be a good humoured man and Robinson replied that he did. Mr Hanna then asked if he had taken the defendant's words seriously or had considered the possibility he might have been joking. Robinson conceded he had thought it was just the idle talk of someone who had got some drink in him. 'Ach, for god's sake,' William Henry thought to himself, 'sure I wasn't even there.'

Mr Hanna asked Robinson if the words the defendant had used – 'send her out of the country by a switcher' had been *exactly* the defendant's words. For example, he suggested, he might have said 'send her out of the country on a switchback' or similar, meaning the local slow train. Robinson explained he had written the defendant's words down in his notebook. He produced from his pocket a new notebook, which was immediately entered into evidence and of which Mr Hanna made the observation that it was unused, except for an undated annotation of the conversation he had allegedly had with the defendant. Asked *when* he had written this in his notebook, Robinson said he had done so at around ten o'clock that same evening when back in his lodgings. Mr Hanna pointed out that the words 'send her out of the country by a switcher' did not in fact appear in his notebook. Robinson explained "I suppose the reason for that is that I didn't write down *every* word he said. However, I do recall exactly what was said, even if I haven't it all recorded".

Mr Hanna leapt on the point. "Are you saying your recollection of the defendant's words is clearer now, *three months* after the short, alleged conversation than it was only *four hours* after?" Robinson agreed that could not be so.

"Why did you write down *any* of your conversation? Why did you think it relevant to do so?" the lawyer asked. Robinson explained that, the following Monday, he had met a local policeman on the Crumlin Road and had learned from him about the defendant's arrest for the murder of his wife, and so the relevance of their earlier conversation had become clear.

"So, are you now saying that it was *after* hearing of the death of the defendant's wife, and not immediately after you had met the defendant, that you decided to write down what you could recall of your conversation?" Mr Hanna asked.

Robinson saw which way the wind was blowing. "I made a mistake when I said it was four hours after the meeting that I wrote down what the defendant had said," he expanded, "it was after speaking to the constable."

"Why *did* you speak to the constable?" the lawyer asked, "did you approach him or did he approach you?"

"I approached the constable," said Robinson.

"Why?" the lawyer asked.

"Because I had just read about the defendant's arrest in the Monday's evening paper and I wrote down in my notebook what I remembered and was taking it out with me to the Police Office, but I met the constable on the way."

"So it was not four hours after the meeting that you wrote this account of the conversation, but *three days* afterwards. And it was not your meeting with the constable which prompted you to write the note, as you have just said, but rather your reading of the rather luridly expressed facts of the case in the press. And, furthermore, the most relevant part of your alleged conversation with the defendant, the part where he threatened to stab his wife, you omitted from your notes. Surely, it would have been the defendant's alleged threat of violence to the deceased which ought to have prompted you to make the note and to approach the police, and yet you omitted to record this seemingly relevant alleged comment. In fact, it is only now, a full *four months later* that you first mention this?   I put it to you that the conversation never took place at all but that you fabricated it, for sensationalist attention."

"No, I mean, yes, it did happen" insisted Robinson.

"Did you mention the conversation to anyone else, your wife, your family or friends, or to anyone at the hotel where you work?" Hanna pressed him, "and is there anyone else who might be called as a witness to confirm this conversation ever took place?"

"No," Robinson conceded, not wanting to qualify this by admitting he *had* no family or friends and was not even on gossiping terms with his fellow waiters. Humiliated, Robinson was dismissed from the witness box and, as he turned hurriedly to leave, he glanced up at the public gallery, where a number of the shipyard workers were all looking at him intently and one of them drew a finger silently across his throat. Robinson, now red-faced, lowered his head, hurried down the steps from the witness box and fled from court.

Now, it was the turn of the witnesses for the defence, and first to take the stand was William Henry's daughter, wee Belle. She testified that she had lived at home with the defendant and her late mother until recently when she had moved in with her married sister, who had been unwell. She lived in her sister's house in Upper Canning Street, where, when home from her work at the mill, she helped keep house and look after her sister's baby. She recounted how her father had called at the house at around a quarter past nine on the evening of 22 April, looking for her mother and said there was no food in the house and no fire lit. In reply to questions from the prosecution counsel, she said her father seemed to have had a bit of drink taken when he called at Upper Canning Street, but he was not drunk. She now stated that the defendant was a most loving and kind father and husband, though, when he and her late mother had some drink taken, they would often argue. She mentioned that her father had left all the change from his pockets for her sister's child and had said he would next call at the lodgings of her brother, William Henry Kelly junior.

She did not see her father again until around three o'clock the following morning, at which time he was crying and shouting that her mother was dead. She and Jane had accompanied their father to his house, where they saw their mother was indeed dead. She said she and her sister went to fetch their aunt, Mrs Lena Patterson, the defendant's sister, and on the way, she had decided to summon police help from the nearby barracks. On the way, she had met a policeman whome she asked to accompany her. The policeman had then summoned Doctor Lorinan. Mr Gordon, Counsel for the prosecution asked Belle if the reason she had left her parents' home to live with her sister had been because of their drinking and quarrelling. Reluctantly, but mindful of being under oath, Belle said this had been one of the reasons, the other being that her sister was unwell.

Mr Gordon asked Belle junior if her mother had been a Catholic. "No, she wasn't" Belle replied, surprised. Mr Hanna sought to re-examine and asked Belle if she believed her father had loved her mother. Belle confirmed this was indeed so and that he was a most kind and loving father, but that drink would set them both quarrelling. When they were not drinking, they lived most harmoniously. Mr Hanna asked which of her parents had been the worse when in drink, her father or her mother. Belle replied that her father drank only occasionally, whereas her mother drank almost daily and often failed to have her father's supper ready when he came home from his work, and this was the chief cause of their occasional disharmony. William Henry hung his head, as this was something of an exaggeration.

The next witness for the defence was William Henry's son, Billy. Under Mr Hanna's examination, He explained he was a hairdresser, and he had moved out of his parent's home and into lodgings a short time before his mother's death. Counsel for the prosecution asked why he had moved and he confirmed this was because of his parents' drinking and arguments. He said his parents had begun drinking particularly heavily before their move to their new house. Billy explained that, a few days before he had moved out, he had returned one lunch time and had found his mother in the kitchen with a friend, a Mrs Spence, and both were already quite drunk. He found that, on hearing him enter, they had hidden some cups of porter under the kitchen table, and he had taken the porter and thrown it down the jawbox. The clerk of the court, noticing the judge's puzzled glance, explained that the term 'jawbox' meant the kitchen sink. Finding nothing in the house to eat, Billy said, he had left and returned at two thirty and again at four thirty, to find no-one home on each occasion.

Mr Hanna asked Billy why, since he no longer lived at home, he had returned to his parents' home no fewer than three times that day. Billy explained that he was concerned about his mother, as she would then be alone for most of the day whilst his father was at work and she might be upset that all the children were gone. He added, pointedly, that he feared she might resume drinking, fail to eat and possibly fall and hurt herself. Mr Hanna asked him whether his mother had fallen over previously when in drink and he confirmed that she had often done so and had often sustained injuries, such as bruising and bleeding. Mr Hanna asked him to describe the defendant's relationship with his family and Billy said that his father had been a very kind father to all the children and had been very fond of his mother when sober. He added that his father had worked continuously over the past thirty six years at Harland and Wolff's shipyard on the Queen's Island and had always supported his wife and children. He added that his parents had always lived together most agreeably, when not drinking. Asked whether it was his father or his mother who had been the most troublesome when in drink, Billy had no hesitation in confirming that his mother was the heavier drinker.

He nodded across supportively at his father in the dock, but William Henry senior shifted about uncomfortably in his seat. He was feeling very uneasy. It didn't seem right to be blackening the character of his Belle like that when the poor wee woman, his beloved, was dead, and when he, her own husband, whom she trusted and to whom she looked for support, was clearly the cause of it. In cross examination, Mr Gordon asked Billy whether his late mother had been a Catholic. William Henry replied that she had not. Seemingly not satisfied at the dismissal of an additional possible motive for the defendant having killed his wife, Mr Gordon asked him what his mother's maiden name had been. "It was Gordon" William Henry replied, "same as yours." This brought a rare smile or two from the jury.

Next, William Henry's sister Lottie - Mrs Charlotte Condit - was called. Mr Hanna invited her to give evidence of a specific incident which had occurred a while back, before William Henry and Belle had moved to the present house. She explained she had heard from a neighbour that there was a problem with her sister in law and so she and her son had walked the few hundred yards from her own home to the defendant's house in Collyer Street, where the defendant's wife was then running a little grocer's shop, with their living quarters above. Lottie said that, to her surprise, she had then observed Belle emerging from an upstairs side window. Lottie added that her son, William John Condit, had run ahead of her and caught Belle as she emerged, worse the wear for drink and most unsteady. Lottie said she had run around the front of the shop where her brother, the defendant, was admitting the baker to the shop. The baker had been trying to deliver bread to the shop but had found the door locked. Lottie had asked the defendant what was the matter with Belle, as she was apparently climbing out of an upstairs window.

Mr Hanna asked what the defendant's reaction had been and Lottie said he had clapped his hand to his head in despair and he had exclaimed to the baker, 'You see what I have to put up with?' Lottie said the defendant had immediately run upstairs to see whether it was true that his wife had climbed out of a window and then he had accompanied Lottie to her house, where her son had taken Belle.

She added that the defendant had just returned from his work, had not been drinking and seemed greatly embarrassed by his wife's actions. Mr Hanna asked Lottie how the defendant and his wife had been living at that time and what relations were like between them. Lottie explained that her brother had taken the lease on the shop and dwelling to give his wife something to occupy her, as he loved her very deeply and was very worried about her being alone at home all day, with her son Billy coming home at lunchtime only.

Lottie said her late sister-in-law fell into drinking when she had nothing to do but dwell on past unhappiness and so forth. Mr Hanna asked Lottie what she meant about past unhappiness, and Lottie explained that Belle had never really recovered from the trauma of one of her children, a particularly sweet child, dying at the age of only three years. Lottie said that, in her opinion, this had marked the start of her drinking, and that the defendant had felt unable to console Belle. He loved her, of that there was no doubt, but he had told Lottie he did not know what else he could do to help Belle.

In the dock, silent tears ran down William Henry's cheeks – a fact not lost on the jury members. Mr Gordon rose to his feet and asked Lottie if the deceased had been a Catholic, at which Mr Justice Wright, irritated now as he felt this point had clearly been established, put down his pen and sighed audibly. Seeing another opportunity to assist her brother, Lottie quickly responded: "no, but I am a Catholic, for I married a Catholic." Although, in the back of his well trained legal mind, Mr Gordon knew he should never ask a question to which he did not already know the answer, nevertheless he tried to regain the advantage by asking: "and do you and *your* husband live harmoniously?" to which Lottie replied: "Well we do since we separated." There was laughter from the public gallery. It seemed to William Henry though that maybe neither counsel had won that round.

William Henry was very surprised to see his nephew, Samuel Condit, Lottie's younger son, appear in the witness box. William Henry was confused, as he could not remember what it was the solicitor had said young Sammy would add to the story. Sammy identified himself and advised that he was fourteen years old, going on fifteen, and was a millworker. He was asked to explain what he knew of the events of the evening on which Isabella Kelly had died, and he began his account. He said how he was out and about on the town with his cousin, Thomas Patterson, and they had found themselves in Mackey Street at around half past ten at night. They had noticed their aunt, leaning against a wall in Mackey Street, obviously under the influence of drink. They had watched her try to walk on down the street and they had followed her, taking hold of an elbow each to steady her. Despite their assistance, she had fallen on her knees at the end of the street. She had fallen over again - headlong and face first - in Edlingham Street. He and Thomas had helped her to her feet and escorted her along in the direction of her home, but she had fallen yet a third time, very heavily this time, on her side, against the step at Rea's shop. At this point, the boys had linked her more firmly and had half carried her to her home.

They had reached her house a few minutes before eleven o'clock and had found the door locked. Sammy said he had supported his aunt in the doorway, whilst Tommy called at the neighbours to borrow a key to her door and they had let her into the darkened and cold house. Sammy said his aunt had sat down heavily on one of the wooden kitchen chairs and was rubbing her side, which she complained was painful, and she had asked the boys to go to the kitchen and find her a glass of something strong to drink, to take away her pain.

Not wishing to be disrespectful to their aunt, Tommy had done as bid and had gone to the kitchen where he found a half empty bottle of rum and poured out a small amount in a teacup, putting the bottle on top of the kitchen press where she might not immediately notice it. He had given the cup to his aunt and she had drained it and then asked for some bread. Sammy had gone into the kitchen, where he had been unable to find bread but had found a few slices of beef which he brought in for his aunt and which she had eaten. She had then lain down on the small sofa in the kitchen, fully dressed and still with her boots on, and had gone straight off to sleep. Sammy said he and Tommy had waited for a while, expecting their Uncle, the defendant, to return but, when he did not, they had left, believing their sleeping aunt to be safe. It was now just about eleven o'clock, Sammy said, in reply to counsel's question.

Mr Hanna asked whether they had closed the front door behind them and Sammy said they had. Mr Hanna then asked whether Sammy had visited the defendant and his late wife often, and if he had observed how the couple appeared to relate to each other. Sammy said he visited often and his aunt and uncle had lived most agreeably together and had always treated him like a son. He said he was devastated at what had happened to his aunt and he could not believe his uncle would have done this to her, as he was a loving father and husband. Mr Hanna asked Sammy if he knew how the neighbours came to have a key to his uncle and aunt's house. Sammy explained that the key was not specifically for his Uncle and Aunt's house, but it was the case that all the houses in the row had the same front door lock, and so one neighbour's key would fit another's lock, which was very convenient if anyone got locked out.

Mr Hanna then asked about the deceased woman's fall against Rea's step and on which side she had fallen. Sammy said she had fallen very heavily on her right side. Mr Hanna asked whether she had fallen heavily enough perhaps to have broken several ribs, but Mr Gordon objected to this question as it called for speculation and the witness was not sufficiently qualified to give a *qualified* opinion. The judge allowed the objection. Mr Hanna returned to the point about the door key. "So any number of your aunt and uncle's neighbours, or their friends or associates, whether with good intentions or bad, might gain entry to your aunt and uncle's house, since their own keys would open your uncle's front door?"

"Yes" replied Sammy.

Mr Gordon, in cross examination, simply asked: "Did your deceased aunt and the defendant have anything of value in the house which might tempt their neighbours to let themselves in and attack your aunt?"

"Sure, that would depend how poor and hungry the neighbour was, for there's a lot of Belfast folks up here for stealin' food and clothes these days" Sammy replied. Mr Justice Wright glanced over the top of his spectacles at Mr Gordon, an almost imperceptible arching of his left eyebrow signifying that the youth had got away with expressing an opinion after all.

There being no further questions Sammy was dismissed and he glanced at his uncle as he left the witness box. William Henry smiled weakly back at him. Sammy was a fine and smart boy who had come close to perjuring himself, and one whose kind guile William Henry felt he did not deserve.

The next witness for the defence was Thomas Patterson, who confirmed he was aged fifteen and worked as a rivet catch boy at the Harland and Wolff shipyard on the Queen's Island, as indeed the scars on his young hands also bore witness. He echoed his cousin's account of the events of the evening of 22 April and confirmed that it was upon her right side that his aunt fell at Reas's step. He added that he and Sammy had left his aunt's house at around eleven o'clock that evening and there had been no sign of his uncle returning. Mr Gordon waived his right to cross examination.

Next, a friend of the deceased, a Mrs Norah McLean of Mackey Street, testified that, at around half past seven on the evening of 22 April, the now deceased woman had called at Mrs McLean's house, in a 'very drunk state' and asked if she might have a cup of tea. Mrs McLean had obliged her friend, but, before the tea was ready, Belle had fallen asleep and had to be roused, at which she left the house. It was by then around eight o'clock yet Belle was still quite intoxicated, in Mrs McLean's opinion. Mrs McLean added that the deceased had been most unsteady on her feet when she had set off up the road and the witness had feared for her wellbeing, but, having her own grandchildren to care for, she had been unable to accompany the deceased home.

The final witness listed for the defence was Johnnie Beasant. William Henry was pleased to see his old friend in the court after all. Beasant explained he was William Henry's under foreman, had known him for some sixteen years and could testify to the prisoner's long and constant service with Harland and Wolff in their Queen's Island shipyard. He also referred to William Henry's unswerving application to his work, his valuable skills and the fact that he attended regularly and punctually. He added that the prisoner was an honest man and 'on the square'. Johnny scrutinised the Judge's face to see if he had picked up this reference to Freemasonry. Johnny had done a little background digging on Justice George Wright and, having established that he was a Protestant and very well connected in legal circles, he thought it a safe bet that the Judge would be a Freemason. Justice Wright's face gave little away however. Beasant did not mention, since he was not asked, the occasions when William Henry had missed work, owing to his earlier periods of detention in *The Crum*. He gave a nod of support to a grateful William Henry as he left the witness box.

Mr Hanna said the prisoner himself did not wish to give evidence as he had nothing to add in his own defence, but Mr Hanna asked to call a final witness who had not been listed and the judge had both counsels approach the bench to agree this. To William Henry's great surprise and joy, his other son Jimmy appeared in the witness box, resplendent in freshly pressed sailor's uniform and with good conduct stripes upon his arm. He identified himself as James Hodges Kelly, Stoker First Class, RN, and explained he had made his way, at his own expense, from where his ship lay berthed at the opposite corner of the Kingdom, in Devonport, in order to give evidence on his father's behalf. William Henry proudly noticed a few of the women in the public gallery leaning forward for a closer look at the exceptionally handsome sailor.

Jimmy then gave evidence that he had often seen signs of drink on his mother; that his father was a kind and good father, albeit with a bit of a quick temper, and that his parents lived together most agreeably and affectionately when not drinking. Asked by Mr Hanna if he had ever witnessed his parents strike each other, he said he had seen his mother strike at his father when she was drunk, but had never seen his father retaliate. In reply to Mr Hanna's questions, Jimmy confirmed that his mother's behaviour was, in his opinion, ten times worse than his father's when they had been drinking and he said his father drank only occasionally. Mr Gordon waived his right to cross examine and, on leaving the witness box, Jimmy smiled encouragingly at this father and gave him a salute. It was only a small gesture, but clearly it had a significant effect upon the jury members. William Henry sat upright now, immensely proud of his son. He realised what treasures he had in his children - all five of them. He felt however that he was about to lose those treasures. Jimmy had been away at sea for six years now, and it had been over a year since he had been home. He had been a stoker second class then. William Henry had not heard of his latest promotion. He wished his Belle could have been here to see this fine young man they had raised. Next, the prosecution asked to recall an earlier witness, Head Constable Daniel Hughes. 'My God,' thought William Henry, 'isn't there more constables in this court than you'd normally see in the whole of Belfast of a Saturday night?'

Head Constable Hughes flipped open his notebook and began his testimony. "With regard to the earlier deposition of Mrs Charlotte Condit, on the instructions of prosecuting counsel, I went today to the house and shop in Collyer Street, formerly occupied by the defendant and his wife, and I measured the distance from the said rear side window. I found the drop to be ten feet. With regard to the depositions by Master Samuel Condit and Master Thomas Patterson, I then examined the step at Mr Rea's shop, and found it to be only five and a half inches high at the highest end and level with the pavement at the other end."

William Henry now sat cradling his head in his hands. He thought he should comfort his old head whilst he still could - before the hangman's rope parted it from his body. Mr Hanna requested a recess to confer with the defendant prior to submissions and Mr Justice Wright agreed the court would now adjourn for lunch.

William Henry was taken to the cells beneath the courthouse where he was joined by his solicitor Mr Graham, his counsel, Mr Hanna, and counsel's junior, Mr Campbell.

"Mr Kelly," Mr Hanna began, "the jury appear to be impressed with the evidence given by your children and other relatives. Mr Graham went to much trouble to track down Mrs McLean, who, most usefully, was able to confirm the fact that your late wife was very drunk in the hours prior to her death." William Henry nodded his gratitude to Mr Graham. "The doctor says he found no alcohol in your wife's stomach, but the medical evidence is already somewhat shaky, as the good Professor Symmers has seriously contradicted his own testimony on another very crucial point, regarding the soundness of your late wife's bones. The prosecution's witness, the waiter Robinson, has *totally* discredited himself – that was a rather ill-prepared attempt by prosecution counsel to blacken your character."

"Mr Hanna" William Henry began, "I wish to speak in my own defence, as I'd like to set the record straight about my wife. She was often drunk, but she was not a bad woman. I'm as much to blame for our rows as she was, more so, if I am honest, and I was never able to give her a good life, such as she deserved. I'm not right comfortable with the way her character has been made out and I want to express my sorrow and regret to the court".

"Mr Kelly," his counsel said solemnly, "there is no doubt of your guilt in this matter. Furthermore, if you put yourself on the stand, you will be liable to be questioned about your past criminal record, which I understand comprises a number of separate offences, mostly for being drunk and disorderly, but also includes one three month sentence served for assaulting your wife. Now, whilst your past record cannot be raised in court, if you are so foolish as to enter the witness box, Mr Gordon will have the opportunity to ask you outright if you have ever been found guilty of assaulting your wife and, should you choose to perjure yourself and say no, Head Constable Hughes, who is at this moment quivering with eager anticipation, will be recalled to read from his notebook the precise details of your many offences. You will then certainly be found guilty of murder and you will hang. Do I make myself clear?"

William Henry was shocked at his counsel's frankness and his throat was bone dry. He licked his lips whilst considering his counsel's words.

"But, Mr Hanna, it was many years ago that I hit my wife. Wee Billy was a toddler then and I came home and found him roaming outside in the road and Belle inside, incapable, with drink taken" he protested.

"That may be interpreted by the jury as a long standing grudge, and perhaps the only assault for which you were *caught* though necessarily not the only one you committed," Mr Hanna suggested. He continued, "It may be that the three months you were in gaol, for which your wife presumably received no income, made her reluctant to report subsequent beatings to the police. No, now you really should have been completely honest with us about your antecedents, Mr Kelly, and now you really must take my advice and decline to speak on your own behalf. Simply look remorseful and say nothing to anybody. All the men on the jury may in fact be fairly sympathetic to you but they will have no option but to find you guilty of murder if they hear of your past record. Despite the best efforts of your nephew to hint at other possible killers in your street, the police are not looking for any other suspects and therefore you have no chance of being acquitted of the present charge of murder. However, I strongly recommend that you agree to accept a finding of guilty to manslaughter. Manslaughter is not a capital offence and therefore carries only a custodial sentence."

Seeing William Henry's puzzled look, he explained; "that means, providing the judge and the prosecution counsel are willing to accept the change of plea, from not guilty of murder to guilty of manslaughter, then you might not hang, but you would instead face a lengthy prison sentence, perhaps twelve to fifteen years. The choice now is not a choice between being found either guilty or not guilty of murder, but whether, if it please the judge, you hang or go to prison. That is the situation as it stands." William Henry nodded his agreement. The warder opened the cell door and the barristers took their leave of William Henry.

Mr Graham patted William Henry on the shoulder. "Here are the day's papers for you to read. I picked them up on the way over here. They may just be the last you get to read for some time to come. And do try to eat some lunch while you have the opportunity, because the court lunches are so much better than what you get over the road. Mr Hanna and Mr Campbell have gone to see the judge and the Prosecution counsel in chambers, and you'll be summoned back after lunch to see whether the judge will accept your plea or not. Then there will be final oral submissions from both prosecution and defence counsels before the jury retires to consider its verdict."

"How long will all that take, Mr Graham?" William Henry asked.

"It could be hours or then again it could be days. That depends really on which plea is accepted. Well, I must go now. I cannot be in court this afternoon, as I have other clients to see, but I'll be thinking of you. Mr Hanna will let me know the outcome. I wish you the very best of luck Mr Kelly."

William Henry shook his solicitor's hand and thanked him warmly for all his help, and as the warder again opened the door to allow Mr Graham to leave, another warder entered and placed a lunch tray on the small wooden table. William Henry saw that Mr Graham was right. The lunch consisted of roast beef with all the usual trimmings heaped upon a sizeable tin place. There was also a tin bowl, containing a generous helping of apple pie, with a good half pint of hot yellow custard floating around it like a moat. William Henry forced himself to eat the lunch, as he knew this would undoubtedly be the last decent meal he would eat, one way or another. The irony of it being roast beef was not lost on him. That had been the last food his beloved Belle ever ate. He recalled the medical evidence that it had remained undigested in her stomach as she lay dead in the morgue. Swallowing the repast was difficult for William Henry. The strain of concentrating on the morning's proceedings had left him exhausted both physically and mentally but yet he knew he must eat. As he did so, tears flowed down his nose and cheeks and onto his plate. First his gravy, and then his custard were by turn diluted with his salty tears. He was now feeling very sorry for himself indeed, and truly very, very remorseful.

He lay back on the cell's metal cot and picked up the solicitor's newspaper, hoping it would distract him from contemplating his fate. The front and back pages were full of detail of the exciting capture of Dr Crippen and his young lover, Ethel le Neve. Remarkably, they had fled to Antwerp, following a full search of Crippen's house, during which no incriminating evidence had actually been found. Their flight was evidence enough of their guilt, as far as the British public was concerned. However, it seemed a second search of Crippen's house had turned up human remains hidden in the cellar. There were reports of interviews with the Captain of a ship, *SS Montrose*, who, shortly after the ship's departure from Antwerp for Canada, had noticed two passengers behaving oddly, one of them being clearly a young woman dressed, unconvincingly as a boy. The Captain had notified the police. One Chief Inspector Dew of Scotland Yard, had boarded a faster ship, the *SS Laurentic*, and had overtaken the *Montrose*, identified and arrested the pair and brought them back to London, to great acclaim, it was reported in thrilling terms.

"Would you look at that, Belle, sure didn't I build the Laurentic," William Henry said aloud to his empty cell as he clutched the paper. Belle was not there, of course, but there was no-one else with whom he could share his thoughts and he *would* have been discussing this with Belle if she *had* been there, so he continued regardless.

"Yes, she was called the *Alberta* then, but White Star Lines bought her even before she was out of the slips and we upgraded her with triple expansion steam engines, and triple screws and she had a speed of 11,000 horsepower. She was a prototype for the Olympic and the Titanic which we're working on at the moment. Aye, I've worked on the big ones alright. I can be proud of that, if nothing else. Sure and poor auld Doctor Crippen didn't stand a chance with a Belfast-built ship chasin' him. They'll surely hang him after all this publicity. Then again, ma wee gerl ... I don't fancy my own chances much neither."

William Henry reflected sadly on how much Belle would have enjoyed following the reporting of the case in the paper. Like most Belfast folks, she enjoyed following the gripping details of a good murder trial and would often interrupt his reading of the editorial to recount aloud the gory and exciting details of the latest criminal investigation. Little did he or she ever imagine that she would one day be a murder victim herself. William Henry wondered if *his* trial would attract much public attention. Maybe it would pale into insignificance alongside Crippen's seemingly more sensational case. He hoped so. He wondered what might have happened if *he* had jumped on a ship and sailed away. Sure, that was the main difference. Crippen *knew* he was guilty and had fled. His was, in all probability, a premeditated crime. In William Henry's case, he hadn't even been aware he had done it and so it hadn't even occurred to him that he needed to flee. He wouldn't have got far on what was in *his* pocket in any case. A fast ship to Canada, was it? Sure, William Henry's coppers wouldn't have got him as far as Carnmoney on the bus.

Shortly however, the key was grating in the iron lock of the cell door and the two warders were back to collect him. "I hope the judge has had a great lunch, too" he commented, as he was escorted back up into the brightly lit courtroom. By now, the rapid and forced consumption of William Henry's own lunch was causing him stomach cramps, or maybe it was the apprehension at what was to come? It took some time for all in court to resume their places, and William Henry now saw that all his family, those who had given evidence included, were seated up in the public gallery and were giving him signs of hope and encouragement. He saw too his shipyard mates and he nodded at them in thanks for their support. They gave him the thumbs up sign in return.

He now remembered he was supposed to make an effort to look remorseful. It was really no effort at all however. He was indeed filled with remorse. He felt the deepest regret for his actions. He felt hatred of himself and his own short temper, and was fearful for his future, if indeed he had one. Without his Belle though, there would be no future anyway. So, if he were to hang, it would be right and just. He now saw a look of concern on the face of his elder son, now up in the gallery with the rest of the family, and he assumed Jimmy must be expecting the worst. If William Henry did hang, he would bring even greater disgrace upon them, if that were at all possible. However, the cause of Jimmy's dismay was shock at his father's aged and shrivelled appearance. When Jimmy had last left home to return to sea, it was a bigger and stronger father who had embraced him.

The banging of the judge's gavel banished William Henry's self pity for the moment and restored his concentration. Mr Justice Wright asked if both counsels were ready to proceed to submissions and Mr Hanna replied that, since the evidence given in court had awakened numerous facts and circumstances which the defendant had been unable to remember following the incident, the defendant now craved the court's indulgence to allow him enter a plea of 'guilty to manslaughter', on the understanding that he would accept such a verdict without appeal. The judge asked prosecution counsel if he opposed this motion and Mr Gordon confirmed this was acceptable to him, so the judge invited the prosecution to address the jury. Mr Gordon began his submission:

"You have heard the evidence of the Pathologist and the police as to the injuries sustained by the Prisoner's wife and of the condition of the crime scene. You will therefore have no doubt that Mrs Isabella Kelly, a woman of 48 years of age and of small stature, a wife and mother to five living children, was brutally beaten to death in her own home. There were a huge number of injuries upon her body, caused no doubt by a long and sustained beating, and the bloodstained instruments of these injuries have been identified. These were a solid wooden chair and the prisoner's own bare hands. No other instrument appears to have brought in from outside to injure her. It has been suggested she might have sustained her injuries in falling over drunk, in particular during a fall against the step outside Rea's shop, yet it is the evidence of Head Constable Hughes that at its highest point this step is only five and a half inches high. To sustain seven broken ribs in this fashion seems highly unlikely."

The men of the jury all seemed to be looking at William Henry. He could not return their glances. Mr Gordon continued:

Other witnesses have testified that the deceased woman was in a very inebriated state up until around eleven o'clock that night. This would suggest she would not have been in any position to defend herself from such a brutal attack, which makes the actions of the killer all the more brutish and inhuman. However, the pathologist has testified that he found no alcohol in her stomach the following day, so this may suggest alternatively that her family and her friend have exaggerated the degree of her inebriation on that night, and thus they may also have exaggerated the degree of her habitual drinking. The deceased woman's nephews have testified that they left the deceased woman's front door locked behind them when they left and that there was no one but the soon-to-be-deceased woman present in the house at that time. If you accept their evidence that their aunt was asleep and therefore not likely to have opened the front door to callers, it is most likely that the last person to have seen her alive - the person who killed her - was known to her and was able to admit himself to the house. No other suspect has been identified and no evidence points to any other suspect, other than the defendant."

William Henry hung his head once again. He really did not wish the counsel to reiterate the awful events, but Mr Gordon went on:

"You will recall the police described the state of the defendant, who was himself greatly inebriated and bloodstained, with an abrasion to his cheek. You have also heard evidence from a neighbour who heard the dying woman call out 'William Henry, you are choking me!' These may have been her dying words. It is true to say that William Henry is a common enough name in this community and throughout Belfast, and yet with whom would the deceased be sufficiently acquainted to call him William Henry? There has been no suggestion or evidence that her own son, also named William Henry, might have perpetrated the murder. Moreover, the neighbour has identified the other voice he heard arguing with the deceased at that time as being that of the defendant. The prisoner has made no statement in his own defence. You may consider remarks he gave to the police at the time of his arrest - to the effect that he would hang himself - to be an expression of sorrow at the loss of his wife, or you may interpret these to be an admission of remorse for the awful crime he himself had committed. I would ask you to consider there is little doubt as to how the deceased met her death nor who her killer was, and I would ask you gentlemen to return a verdict of guilty against the prisoner."

Mr Hanna was now on his feet:

"Let me first address the medical evidence. The pathologist has indeed said he found no alcohol in the deceased woman's stomach and moreover no evidence of any alcohol-related condition or disease. This does not accord with evidence, given by no fewer than seven witnesses, of the deceased woman's habitual drinking. He has also observed the deceased's kidneys were cirrhotic, which in itself indicates she was an habitual drinker. You are also aware that the pathologist initially made a statement to the police to the effect that the deceased woman's bones were thinner than might be considered normal for a woman of her age, suggesting they would be

68

more easily broken and indeed may have broken during one of the three occasions that evening on which she fell over."

"Later however, he contradicted his own evidence, saying her bones were of a normal strength, but has not explained this inconsistency and this must surely throw other parts of his evidence and his opinions into equal doubt. Why indeed could not the deceased have broken a number of ribs in the fall against the step? Surely that would depend upon the angle at which she fell and how fast she was going when she fell, whether she put out a hand to save herself etcetera? And why might not those broken ribs have been responsible for the rupture of her liver – the injury which alone killed her? The pathologist has stated his opinion that the hole in the deceased's liver was the size of a man's fist. Are all men's fists of the same standard size? I think not. And has anyone given evidence that they measured the size of the defendant's fist and compared it with the size of the hole in the deceased woman's liver? No, they have not. And, as for the many bruises described on the victim's body, no account has been given of how many of these were fresh bruises and how many were old bruises, such as one would expect to be regularly sustained in falls by an habitually drunken woman."

"Let us now consider the defendant. He has been described by six witnesses as a loving husband and father. Married for over thirty years and in full time, steady employment with the same employer for thirty six years, he is a hard-working man, who has had few advantages in life but who has never shirked his responsibilities to his family. He has no recollection of the death of his beloved wife, though witnesses have confirmed that this was not the first, but one of many occasions over recent years, when he had returned home from his long and hard day's work, standing all day out in the open in the shipyards in the worst of weathers, to find no warm welcome at home from his dear ones, no fire and warmth and no supper prepared for him. This continuous lack of warmth and welcome in the home of a man who works hard to maintain his home and family, added to the effects of the drink which he himself may well have taken to some degree of excess, plus the long and fruitless search he conducted that evening for his wife, may well have pushed a sane man over the edge."

William Henry glanced now at the faces of the jurors, to see if there were a hint of agreement with this argument or a glimmer of empathy for him, but their faces gave away nothing.

"You have heard evidence" Mr Hanna continued, "to the effect that his wife's drinking was a continuous source of unhappiness and disagreement between them. You may well consider the outcome of this intolerable situation to be almost inevitable. You may ask yourselves, gentlemen, whether you yourselves would have tolerated such an *in*tolerable situation and whether you might not have snapped and lost control with the wife whom you adored but who regularly failed to repay your adoration with devotion to the needs of yourself and your children. I would ask you, gentlemen, to consider, above all things, that this was clearly not a pre-meditated or planned act. And it is an act, the consequences of which will remain with the defendant for the rest of his life, should the court decide, in its mercy, to spare him his life."

The judge now directed the jury to retire to consider their verdict and, once again, William Henry was taken down to the cells. He availed himself of the toilet facilities and washed his face in cold water, as he was not feeling any less strained by the near termination of the proceedings, despite the judge and counsel's acceptance of his willingness to plead to manslaughter. He wondered briefly if he still had a chance of a 'not guilty' verdict and of gaining his freedom but immediately dismissed the thought. He told himself he was facing an inevitable 'guilty' verdict and a prison sentence, and could only hope this would not be a life sentence. He consoled himself with the fact that at least he would not hang.

He supposed he ought to feel relieved about this at least, but yet he did not. He had an awful feeling of not being in control, and he knew he would not be in control of his life for some years to come, perhaps never. It was his own fault for allowing himself to be out of control through drink. Well, there would be no more drink where he was going, though that was the least of his worries. All too soon, he was summoned back to the court room. That had not taken long. He glanced at the huge courtroom clock and realised the jury had been out for only twenty minutes. William Henry now stood to be judged by a jury of his fellow citizens for his horrendous crime.

"Gentlemen of the jury, have you reached a verdict?" the Right Honourable Mr Justice Wright asked.

The foreman of the jury replied "We have, your honour".

"And is that the verdict of you all?" asked the judge.

"It is, your honour" replied the foreman.

"And how say you? How do you find the prisoner at the bar to the charge of manslaughter, guilty or not guilty?" the judge built up the drama of the moment.

"Guilty" was the inevitable and expected verdict.

William Henry thought that at least the judge had been spared the act of having to don the little black head covering which must have been reposing somewhere on his bench. It could not be very pleasant to have to condemn another man to death. Perhaps, like William Henry, the judge too suffered from nightmares. William Henry thought it was a good sign that he himself was now worrying about other people instead of dwelling on his own lamentable situation.

The judge then retired briefly to consider sentencing, during which time William Henry remained in the dock and had another opportunity to exchange looks with his children and his sisters. He wondered how soon, and how often, they would be allowed to visit him in the prison across the road. All too soon the judge was back however and delivered a short address before he delivered the sentence:

"Undoubtedly, the deceased died as a result of the defendant's violence. The Crown has put him on trial for murder but, during the course of the trial, the prisoner has elected to plead guilty – very properly, in my opinion – to manslaughter, and the Crown has - again rightly in my opinion – decided to accept that plea. The foreman of the jury has intimated to me, by virtue of a note to me in chambers, that this would have been the verdict of the jury in any case, and so now the prisoner is accountable for the death of his wife."

The judge continued, his English public school accent concealing his County Cork origins: "various accounts have been given by the members of the family as to the relations which existed between the defendant and his wife. It has been stated, probably truly, that, when there was no disturbing influence of drink, the prisoner was an affectionate parent. It also appeared that his wife was occasionally a victim to intemperance, but I cannot say it is clear which was the greater offender in that respect. I find that, in most cases where life has been lost, the tendency is to put all the blame on the deceased, and I do not, as a rule, give credit to that. It is clear that members of the defendant's own family would not live with him. The crime closely resembles murder. It has been proved by neighbours and others that sounds were heard coming from the house of a woman moaning and screaming for mercy and sounds of blows and of a man beating a woman."

The Judge turned in his chair to face William Henry, who straightened up and looked at him intently. The judge addressed him directly:

"It has been proved beyond all doubt that you attacked the woman and beat her ribs with a chair or your fist or something. What appears to be the worst feature of the case is that you did not summon medical aid but allowed her to die. This too may be due to drink. You left the house, leaving her there behind you. Seven ribs were broken. Her liver was burst and there were other marks upon her. She is now dead as a result of your violence. The women of this city must be protected. Men must be taught that, if their passions run away with them and they become savages, they will have to face the consequences. I therefore sentence you to be kept in penal servitude for twelve years."

William Henry was numb. He did not know if this were shock or relief. It was over. He cast a last look at his family and friends in the gallery. He saw his daughters and his sisters were sobbing and reaching out their hands in his direction, and his sons looked grave. As he was led down, he did not know whether he would be allowed to see them again to say goodbye and to say how very sorry he was, before he started his sentence. In the event, he was not.

William Henry was marched back across the road, via the dark and malodourous underground passage, to his bleak cell at *The Crum,* there to ponder his sentence. Back at the courthouse, Justice George Wright packed up his robes and made his way to the waiting car, whose police driver would convey him to Dublin, to the fifteen-room mansion at number one Fitzwilliam Square, where his family and six servants awaited his return.

As William Henry's cell door clanked open, for the usual miserable supper to be doled out, William Henry saw the warder was O'Hagan. Oh joy, now his day was truly complete.

"Well, you don't look any taller, so I suppose they didn't hang you, then" the warder said with expected sarcasm.

"No, Mr O'Hagan," said William Henry, his numbness having subsided, now that he was back in the brisk and noisy routine of the gaol, "the judge got your note saying how much you'd miss me."

O'Hagan wore his customary scowl as he slammed the door. "No doubt you had a Protestant judge. Oh and you're being transferred tomorrow" was the parting comment as his voice tailed off up the landing.

Transferred? William Henry wondered if he had heard O'Hagan correctly. Why would he be transferred? His previous short sentences had all been served in

71

The Crum. Where would they send him? He did not know of any other prisons in Ulster but supposed there might be one up in Londonderry.

That night, for the first time since his arrest, William Henry slept right through the night. He guessed it was the relief. He had felt like an over-wound clock whose spring had now been released a few turns. As usual, he was awake before the warder came around banging and shouting, but this time he was alert and well rested. He was taken to have a full bath then, once dressed, he tidied his cell, stripped his bed and left the bedding folded up. The gruel tasted no better, but at least today he was able to eat some of it. O'Hagan had been right about the transfer. William Henry and two other prisoners were summoned to the reception office where they were searched and weighed, as they had been on arrival. Their few small belongings were put in envelopes and signed over to the waiting escort which comprised three warders. The prisoners were now advised they were being transferred to Maryborough Prison.

"Where's that?" asked one of the prisoners, and William Henry was glad the other man had asked, for he had never heard of it either.

"Down in Queen's County, in the Irish midlands" the warder replied, and William Henry recognised a southern Irish accent. This warder seemed jovial, a different character from O'Hagan.

"But my family won't be able to visit me down there," the other prisoner complained, "for they won't have the fare."

"Well, mebbe so," said the warder, "but even so, you're the lucky ones, for there's another contingent going from here to English prisons."

The first stage in the transfer process was the official prison transport vehicle – the horse-drawn *Black Maria* - to take them to the station for the train to Dublin. William Henry's hands were cuffed together in front of him. The other two prisoners, who were a little younger than William Henry, were handcuffed together. William Henry was glad to be handcuffed separately, since he learned during the journey that these men were both sex offenders.

"There's a whole wing of sex offenders in *The Bog,* so these won't be the last one's you'll meet, not be a long way" said the jovial warder.

William Henry took it that *The Bog* was the popular name for Maryborough Prison. He now remembered from his school geography that the town of Maryborough had been known as Portlaoighise up until the sixteenth century, when the name had been changed in honour of Queen Mary. Indeed, the county in which Maryborough was situated had also been renamed from Laoighise to Queen's county. This gave him the germ of an idea. Perhaps, if he lived to see his release, he might change his *own* name. 'William Henry King,' he thought to himself, 'in memory of King Billy. Then again, since I'm a subject of the Queen, have worked all my life on the Queen's Island, and will now be living at the Queen's pleasure down in the Queen's county, perhaps William Henry McQueen would be appropriate.' Somehow, the thought did not amuse him as he had hoped it might. Perhaps this was because he knew he would have twelve years in which to consider this.

The two middle-aged warders sat up front with the driver and the third, a younger and bigger built man, sat in the back with the prisoners. There was only one small window in the back of the wagon and naturally this was located too high for the prisoners to see much or to be seen, but they could just about see the tops of some familiar landmarks as they passed them and by this they recognised the route. As they went around Carlisle Circus, William Henry espied the statue in the middle of the roundabout and was certain that the dour, stone face of fundamentalist preacher 'Roaring' Hanna was giving him a highly reproving look. Beyond, in Clifton Street, he glimpsed the seven ton statue of King Billy, seated defiantly on horseback, atop the Orange Order building. These were the symbols of William Henry's Protestant faith, a faith whose tenets he felt he had betrayed. It also occurred to William Henry though that he wasn't too far away from the streets where his children lived. Indeed, shortly, he might be passing his son Billy's place of work. If only he could stop and say goodbye and let them know where he was being taken. This was out of the question of course. His punishment entailed the loss of all aspects of his freedom.

At the railway station, another ordeal began. The prisoners were marched out of the wagon, into the station and up to the ticket office. The station was still quite busy from the morning rush and the crowds parted to stare at the handcuffed men. The travel passes having been exchanged for tickets by one of the warders, the group next moved to the platform where they stood in an awkward looking line against the station wall, there being no convenient corner in which to hide their shame. William Henry saw a couple of people he knew, but they looked by turns shocked and embarrassed and turned away to avoid his glance. However, the station newsvendor, Mickey McAdorey, an elderly ex-soldier with one arm, had been a friend of William Henry's father. He recognised William Henry and came over with a couple of newspapers and a chocolate bar and asked if he could give them to William Henry. William Henry fully expected a brusque refusal, but the jovial warder, a kindly middle-aged man, agreed and took the gift on William Henry's behalf, checking it over first.

"All the best, William Henry" said the news seller earnestly, patting William Henry on the arm with heartfelt emotion, "all the best, son!" William Henry was deeply touched.

Soon the train pulled in and the kindly warder walked the length and breadth of the train, searching in vain for the compartment which the booking clerk had assured them would be reserved for them. "Never mind," said the other middle-aged warder, "let's just choose the least full compartment, it'll empty soon enough when we get in!"

The prisoners had the indignity of being herded along the train's corridor and having to push past other travellers. Eventually, they found a compartment containing only one businessman passenger. The warders wore plain jackets over their uniforms and so the man noticed nothing at first. However, as the group took their seats and the train pulled out of the station, the businessman spotted the fact that some of his fellow passengers were handcuffed. His gaze wandered slowly from the warders to the prisoners and back again several times until the penny began to drop. His face a picture of horror, he scrunched up his newspaper, gathered up his briefcase and overcoat and left the compartment hurriedly, glaring back at the group as he slammed the compartment door shut.

The younger warder guffawed and rubbed his hands together. "Right, giz the chocolate, then" he demanded of his colleague.

"No, son, this is fer yer man" said the kindly warder and handed it to William Henry. William Henry nodded his thanks and, with some difficulty, owing to his handcuffs, he peeled off the wrapper, broke the bar into its six squares and offered them to the warders. The younger man leaned forward but the older man stopped him.

"Now, don't be an arse, son," he said to his young colleague, "this'll be the last chocolate he has for twelve years. Ye could have got yerself some at the machine on the platform. Yer on expenses, aren't ye? Ye don't want to be takin' the poor fella's chocolate."

William Henry was touched by this display of humanity, which, like Mickey MacAdorey's chocolate, might be the last such kindness he would see for twelve years. He had not a minute's hesitation in offering some to his fellow prisoners however, and they looked very grateful and humbled by the gesture. They would only take one square each however and declined William Henry's offer of more.

"We'll have a read of yer papers when ye've done with them though, if we may" said the kindly warder, "I'm John O'Farrell, be the way. This here's Daniel Dinan and the young fellah's moniker is Murray, but don't mind him."

'A different kettle of fish from O'Hagan' thought William Henry.

After ten minutes or so, a small clutch of passengers, mostly youths and children, came along the corridor to stare in at the prisoners. O'Farrell shooed them away. He suggested to the sex offenders that they should keep their jointly handcuffed hands on the seat between them and he gave William Henry his own jacket to spread over his lap so that, if anyone came looking in, William Henry could slip his handcuffed hands beneath the jacket. William Henry was heartened by this further small kindness also.

O'Farrell took the opportunity offered by the long train journey to explain how things would go at *The Bog*. He explained why they were being transferred. Apparently, a sentence of two years or less was normally served in a local prison, but greater sentences meant the convicted men must be transferred to a prison away from their home. *Penal servitude*, which William Henry was to serve, could only be given for an *indictable offence* – that is, one tried by a judge and jury. Three years was the minimum sentence which might attract *penal servitude* or *hard labour*. Men who received shorter, local sentences would be still be termed *prisoners* but those sent to do longer sentences, were known as *convicts*. William Henry had graduated, it seemed.

O'Farrell advised them that, although discipline was much stricter at *The Bog* than in *The Crum*, they would find conditions better, especially the food. There would still be no free association though. There would also be very few visits and very few letters or other privileges allowed. O'Farrell explained they would be allowed one visit every four months, but they could send a letter in lieu of a visit and were entitled to receive one reply to that letter without it counting against a visit. William Henry listened carefully and tried to take in all the rules and procedures.

"It's no holiday camp, but then ye weren't expecting one, were ye? So ye'll need to knuckle down and use the time to improve yerselves," O'Farrell said. He explained there was a thirty acre farm at *The Bog* which produced first rate food for the inmates, who could earn a little money from their work, if they kept their noses clean and did not lose marks.

"What about the Guv'nor?" his colleague, Daniel Dinan, chimed in: "tell them about the Guv'nor!"

"You do it," said O'Farrell, "sure, you're the best at doing him, indeed so."

Thus encouraged, Dinan gave an impression of the Maryborough Governor. William Barrows, an Englishman, had an earnest manner, somewhat adenoidal intonation and a restrained English accent, it seemed. Dinan read the Governor's traditional welcoming lecture and all the usual warnings about keeping one's head down, one's nose clean and one's feet in step whilst towing the line. The warder's up-tilted jaw, and the almost priestly way he delivered his mixed metaphors, made William Henry laugh. He had not laughed in a very long time. He suddenly felt a little bit like a human being again. He beamed at O'Farrell. O'Farrell smiled and nodded back at him.

Part Four - **THE BOG**

The following morning, William Henry awoke to the usual sound of heavy footfalls along concreted corridors and the clanking and slamming of doors. Nothing unusual there, of course, and yet today it was somehow different. He was in a different cell. The window was in a different place in relation to his bed. The smell of the cell was different. Generally, the bedrooms of the little, rented houses he had shared with his wife had smelled of the wintergreen ointment which Belle would rub on his shoulders and back each night. His cell at *The Crum*, indeed all the cells and the landings too, had smelled strongly of urine. Here in his new cell at *The Bog* however, whilst he could indeed smell the unmistakeable odour of urine, not all of it his own, there was a more dominant smell of carbolic.

He had been exhausted by the journey. He had little recollection of the latter part of it, after they had changed trains in Dublin, arriving late at night under escort at Maryborough Gaol. The quarter mile or so from the station to the prison had been a march at the double. If William Henry had found it difficult to sustain a marching rhythm whilst handcuffed, it had been nigh on impossible for the two men who were handcuffed to each other. On arrival, the Belfast prisoners and their warders had been starving as, apart from the tiny squares of chocolate and some sandwiches which the two older warders had bought for everyone - at their own expense too, William Henry had noted - they had not eaten a great deal that day. A very reasonable soup and bread supper had been served to them in their cells and, once he had made up his bed, William Henry had slept like the dead.

He now had a good feeling on awaking. Exhaustion apart, he thought the reason he had slept well was perhaps the lack of uncertainty about his future. The trial was over and he now knew pretty much what the next twelve years had in store for him. Being a prisoner on remand had been stressful, more stressful than being convicted and sentenced. Oddly enough, in that misty transition between sleeping and waking, he had fancied himself back in the wee Belfast house, awaiting Belle's return. Now that he was fully awake however, the good feeling started to dissipate. Now, disappointing reality flowed over him, like a chill Mourne mist. The slow realisation that his Belle was not lying by his side - and never would again - made him miserable again. The bed was still a prison cot - a single cot. He rose and had a look around his new cell however.

He had ascertained the previous night that he was in B Block, which was one of the older blocks and consequently had cold stone floors. The single window was set very high in the cell's external wall. He guessed he would have to stand on the wooden table if he wished to look out. The window frame was around three feet wide and some fifteen inches high in the middle but, owing to its curved top, it tapered away at each side. He counted fourteen small, thick panes of glass, though

76

two of these were missing. He wondered if these had been broken in some fit of rage - surely not in an escape attempt - or whether they had been removed for ventilation. He also noted three, stout, iron bars running horizontally across the window on the outside. Both the window and the standard heavy, iron door seemed fairly escape proof, not that he harboured any thoughts of escape.

To the left of the window, in the corner of the cell, were two quarter-circle shelves, set into the wall about twelve inches apart. The top shelf was empty but the one below held two enamelled tin mugs, each of around one pint's capacity; a spoon and knife, but no fork; a small salt cellar containing some salt; a toothbrush and comb and a writing slate and slate pencil. Beneath the shelves was a small table and a small, three-legged stool, both made of deal, and both scrubbed to an unnatural whiteness. On the floor, there was a white enamel basin and next to it a chamber pot, also of white enamel. Also on the floor was a tin, in which stood a small floor scrubbing brush, a coarse cleaning cloth and two pieces of brickbat, which he supposed were for him to use to clean his eating utensils and indeed his cell also. Looking around him, he noticed that the cell was surprisingly clean, unlike those back in *The Crum*.

The previous night, he had been obliged to remove his boots and leave them outside his cell. He now noticed a pair of felt slippers just inside the door. He put them on and immediately his feet began to feel felt warmer, despite the cold stone floor beneath them. He had never owned a pair of slippers himself, but had usually gone about in stockinged feet when at home. There was something civilised about slippers. He began to feel a little civilised himself. Soon, the bustle in the corridor reached his cell door, which was unlocked and clanked open and a warder and a prisoner orderly entered. The orderly dispensed hot water and the ubiquitous ration of gruel and bread. He advised William Henry to drink a little of the cooled hot water first - 'to cleanse the system' - and to use the rest for washing and shaving, after which he should use it to clean his utensils and then his cell.

The warder now placed a pile of clothing upon William Henry's cot. There was a suit of thick, woollen frieze, with broad black stripes down both front and back of jacket and trousers; a white cotton shirt and three sets of woollen socks, vests and underpants. The warder also produced a white cotton muffler which was to be worn like a necktie. He gave William Henry a brief demonstration of how this was to be tied. It was not unlike William Henry's usual neckwear, but it was to be worn with a collar, and not tied directly around the neck. The warder explained that, although the underwear was of rough woollen interlock fabric, he should wear it, as the suit was rougher still and would chafe even the toughest convict's hide. He now asked if William Henry wanted his own clothes to be sent home to his family. William Henry was about to say that this would not be necessary, when he caught sight of the orderly, now standing behind the warder, nodding his head vigorously, so he agreed he would like this. Before departing, the warder advised that William Henry was to have an audience with the Governor after breakfast, and he reminded him not to speak to the Governor until invited to and to call the Governor 'sir' whenever he did so.

Once he was washed, dressed and fed - and to his surprise the Maryborough gruel was far superior in taste and quality to that of *The Crum* - he washed his mug and eating utensils, using the remaining water and the brickbat. He scrubbed down his table and the floor, and endeavoured to replace the cleaned hardware on the shelves, all pieces in their former order, before folding up his bed linen and laying it out on his bed for possible inspection. He recalled the warder Dinan's advice on the journey down, that the Governor was an ex-military man and was a stickler for cleanliness and kit inspections. A short while later, the warder returned and escorted William Henry, along with five other convicts, along the landing to a communal sink, where the convicts emptied and rinsed their chamber pots and mugs, before replenishing the latter with clean, cold water to take back to their cells.

William Henry stood in the centre of his cell and ran over the routine in his head. He would need to remember all of this until such time as it would become automatic. He was still on his feet when the warder returned to escort him to the Governor's office. William Henry left his slippers in his cell, at the same right angle to the wall as that in which he had found them, and bent down outside the door to retrieve his boots, only to find a different pair had been left for him. These must be standard issue in *The Bog*, he supposed. He slipped on the new boots and quickly laced them up. They appeared better quality than those issued to the convicted prisoners at *The Crum,* for he had heard many complaints about the mismatched and ill-fitting footwear available to the short-sentence Belfast convicts. So, a cleaner cell, better breakfast and more comfortable footwear than he would have had if he had remained at *The Crum,* this all represented a promising start, he thought.

"Take a seat, Kelly" the Governor said, without looking up, as William Henry entered his office and the warder took up a position by the door.

"Thank you, sir," William Henry responded, hoping to make a good first impression on the man who would determine the course of his life for the next twelve years.

The Governor was perusing papers in a file, which William Henry presumed was his own that had travelled from Belfast with his escort. This gave William Henry a moment or two to observe the other man. William Barrows was a tall man. William Henry could tell this even though the man were seated, and he was also thin, with neat hair, and a tidily trimmed moustache and the upright bearing of a military man, though he wore civilian clothes rather than uniform. William Henry had met many prison warders previously but this was the first time he had spoken with a governor. Barrows spoke again:

"Now then, upon conviction, you were immediately assigned a unique number in the penal system. Yours is D995 and henceforth it is by this number that you shall be addressed by the warders. It will be chalked up outside your cell door and you must use it in all correspondence, both within the prison and to the outside. Now, you were charged with the murder of your wife, I see, and were sentenced to twelve years on the lesser charge of manslaughter. Well, no doubt you consider yourself lucky not to be facing the hangman's noose."

William Henry did not know if this were a question or a statement, but he felt he ought to respond.

"For each man kills the thing he loves, yet each man does not die... sir" he intoned,

The Governor looked up quizzically. "That's ....?" he began.

78

"Oscar Wilde, sir, from *The Ballad of Reading Gaol*" William Henry explained.

"Yes of course," the Governor's serious and official manner dissolved, and he smiled and sat back in his chair, crossing his long legs, "you like Oscar Wilde, do you? Enjoy reading? Well you'll have access to our fine library here, you know. We have thousands of books in our library. You'll be allowed to borrow two at time, though you must treat them with respect."

"Oh yes, indeed I will, sir" William Henry responded, surprised at the thought that, notwithstanding the fact that he was here to be punished, he would be able to continue to enjoy reading.

"Who else do you like to read?" the Governor was now smiling at him.

"Oh well, Mark Twain, sir, and HG Wells, and of course Rudyard Kipling ..." he could have continued, but did not want to be presumptuous, for it now occurred to him that the prison library might be full of religious tomes, designed to improve the soul.

"Ah yes, Kipling," the Governor beamed, "and his wonderful stories of India. I served in India with the army, you know. So did the Assistant Governor, Mr Shewell. You ever been to India, Kelly?"

"No, sir, but I might have built the ship you sailed to India on," William Henry replied, thinking that he and the Governor were about the same age. He noted the Governor had the better set of teeth, however.

The Governor leaned forward and took another look at the file notes.

"Ah yes, you were a shipwright at Harland and Wolff in Belfast, weren't you? So, you have lost your wife, your liberty *and* your job. That's what happens when you commit a crime, Kelly. Would all this have come about through drink, perhaps?" he asked.

William Henry indicated that it had. The Governor then launched into his speech of welcome, emphasising the advisability of keeping one's head down, one's nose clean, one's feet in step, whilst towing the line and maintaining standards of good behaviour, etcetera, etcetera. William Henry tried not to smile, though he had heard the speech before, from Warder Dinan's lips on the journey to Maryborough. Dinan was clearly a good mimic. William Henry confirmed he understood what was required of him.

"Well, Kelly," the Governor rose to his feet to signal the end of the interview, and William Henry did likewise.

"You must now see the Medical Officer, Dr Kinsella" the Governor said, "but you and I will speak again. In the meantime, I have assigned you to work in the tailoring shop."

William Henry felt the interview had gone well. Not for the first time that day, he felt he was being treated in a humane and civilised way. This was indeed different from *The Crum*. Next, he and his file were marched – there was no walking in *The Bog* for prisoners were marched everywhere at the double - to the Medical Officer's room, where he was weighed and measured by an orderly and his details were recorded on the file. The MO, Doctor John Kinsella was a local man, a practising GP who also attended the prison on a daily basis. Here too, William Henry was treated civilly, although the MO did not call him 'Kelly', but 'D995'.

William Henry began to think that, after all, he might in fact survive his twelve years in this institution.

Over the course of the next week, there was much routine for William Henry to assimilate. There was an hour's daily exercise, which took place on one of two exercise areas which flanked the cell blocks. Each area comprised three flagstoned rings. Twenty-five prisoners were allocated to each ring, where they were to walk briskly around in total silence, until prompted by the warder's cry of "about turn!" when they must immediately spin around and change direction. Each ring walked in a different direction, the outer rings starting off clockwise and the inner one anti-clockwise, which gave William Henry an opportunity to observe the men's faces in the next ring. Naturally, he recognised no-one. During their drilling, warders counted them continually. William thought this completely unnecessary, since it would have been impossible to break out of the ring and scale the high wall unnoticed by the guards. Still, he supposed it was a useful exercise for the brains of a seemingly overstaffed and under challenged team of warders.

The tailoring job was similar to that he had held at *The Crum* and not difficult, though his stiff fingers were not as nimble as the task required. Over the next few days, he managed to get up to speed and produced his required quota of stitched and bound floor mats or to stitch the long seams of frieze trousers, as demand required. A new batch of younger prisoners arrived in the tailoring shop towards the end of the week and so William Henry was reassigned to the much easier task of pressing the finished sections of garment. One of the older lifers, who virtually ran the tailoring shop under the disinterested supervision of the warders, instructed him in use of the Hoffman press. This was an ingenious device which acted like a large scale iron, and could press long seams quickly and effectively. It was mainly foot operated, which demanded less of William Henry's tired fingers.

The lifer declared himself lucky that the Governor had ordered the press, as Maryborough was the only prison laundry in the British penal system to boast such a sophisticated and efficient machine. William Henry must not have seemed sufficiently impressed at this fact, for the lifer expanded on its fame. He explained that it had been invented by a New York tailor, who had feared losing his business, following a shoulder injury which left him unable to lift a heavy iron. A businessman had come into Hoffman's tailor's shop to escape a rainstorm and to have his suit dried, had spotted the prototype pressing machine and had offered to fund its development. Both men were now millionaires, the old lag added. William Henry realised how much this machine, which nowadays was to be found in many a high street laundry, had improved the convict's life.

The warder interrupted their conversation and said that William Henry had had sufficient instruction and so silence must now resume. The separate and silent system of convict control was enforced most strictly at Maryborough. Prisoners were forbidden to speak to each other or to warders, unless given permission to do so. The rules said that prisoners only spoke when spoken to by a member of the prison staff, on pain of loss of points. A certain number of points might be earned by the prisoners and their weekly totals were recorded in their prison files. Points earned the prisoners a small amount of monetary credit, which remained in each man's 'account' for him to spend on newspapers or soap in the prison shop. A convict did

80

not receive any actual cash in hand until his release, if he had any credit left. Points also added up to remission of sentence. Equally however, points might be lost for the merest of transgressions, and loss of points meant loss of remission.

Many of the convicts seemed to get around the rule of silence. William Henry had noticed them twisting their lips to one side and speaking in a low snarl out of the corner of the mouth. The fact that they were speaking was thus less obvious to the prison guards. William Henry noticed this infringement was widespread during the monotonous circular marching at the daily exercise. This odd pose now rang a faint bell with him. He had seen some odd types in pubs around Belfast who also spoke like this and who continually glanced over their shoulders, even when sitting with their backs to the wall. He now guessed that they were ex-convicts and had kept up these habits acquired during long term incarceration.

Maintaining silence did not sit easily with William Henry, who was by nature a garrulous fellow, even in a city of great talkers. It was punishment enough that he spent hours alone in his cell but to be denied the basic need of communicating with other human beings was increasingly unbearable for him. He found himself thinking aloud at the end of each day, before lights out. He was talking to himself of necessity, but there was little pleasure in that when there was no reply, and no-one with whom he might argue. He could hear others murmuring in their cells also. Perhaps they were praying? More than likely though, they too were simply engaging in voicing their thoughts. The deprivation of human discourse was William Henry's second greatest loss.

Sunday came around and there was a significant change to the prison routine. The convicts were roused half an hour later than usual, allowing them a little more sleep, and were paraded down to the prison chapel some half an hour prior to the commencement of the Sunday service. Rather than rows of pews, the main body of the chapel was taken up with rows of three-sided wooden cubicles, so that each man must sit in isolation to pray. Each would face the altar and could concentrate on his private prayers and the service and sermon, without being tempted to communicate with his neighbours. Immediately after the service, the men were locked in their cells, where they were fed but otherwise remained in solitude until the following day. William Henry contemplated the expense and the ingenuity of design which had gone into depriving the men of all human contact. The miserable confinement in cells on Sundays in Maryborough was very slightly compensated for by the Sunday lunch however. This was the one day of the week on which soup was not served, but the four ounces of corned beef and the boiled cabbage and full pound of delicious, prison grown potatoes served with it, was a delight to be savoured. Of course, the prisoners would have enjoyed this all the more had good Irish butter been drizzled over the cabbage and potatoes, but this was a prison, after all. The ubiquitous four ounce hunk of bread also graced their Sunday ration.

Fortunately, William Henry had taken the opportunity to select a couple of books from the library trolley the previous Friday so at least he had something to occupy him during the long hours locked in his cell. The library orderlies came around three times a week, on Mondays, Wednesdays and Fridays. The trolley they brought did not hold many books, and the books which remained by the time it reached William Henry's cell were those which had been returned or rejected by the prisoners on the lower floors of B Block. William Henry learned that there were some twenty four thousand books in the prison library, and yet it was an unappealing selection which was open to him for his first weekend. He had selected an ancient and well-thumbed bound volume of copies of the *London Illustrated News* and a Wilkie Collins' classic, which he had often read before.

The warder accompanying the library orderlies that Friday had been the kindly John O'Farrell, one of his escorts on the way down from The Crum, and O'Farrell had asked after his health. William Henry had jumped at the chance of engaging O'Farrell in small talk. O'Farrell had noticed his former charge's disappointment at the choice of books and advised him he should chalk up on the slate outside his cell a request for a particular book or two, or a favourite author, and the orderly would bring them next time, if they were available. It was such a small and incidental piece of information, yet the joy it brought to William Henry's heart was immeasurable. The orderly had then stepped into the cell to hand over the books and immediately flashed his eyes towards the uneaten hunk of bread reposing on the deal table. The message was not lost on William Henry, who covertly passed the bread to the orderly as he accepted the books. So the currency in *The Bog* was bread? In *The Crum* it had been tobacco. However, although smoking was permitted, indeed encouraged, in Belfast's main prison, it was prohibited here in Maryborough. If the regular cell searches turned up so much as a tiny flake of tobacco, the cell's occupant would be punished.

William Henry desperately missed puffing on his pipe as he read, as was his habit. He lay on his bed and read until the light was fading. Outside, it had begun to rain. He was to learn that it often rained here in the Midlands, even in summer. He heard the large drops bouncing off his window panes. Where two of the panes were missing, the rain came in. He heard it splat on the stone floor. It seemed odd reading such old news in the *London Illustrated*. In those pages, journalists had called for Queen Victoria to curb her son's scandalous behaviour, and to consider abdicating in favour of her heir, in order that his he might have less leisure time and more responsibility. This was old news indeed, for both the old queen and her son Edward were in their graves now. William Henry felt that Edward had not been a bad monarch at all, despite the dissolute lifestyle he had enjoyed whilst being a king in waiting. Then again, it was probably the excessive wining, dining and wenching which had shortened his life and his reign. It would be interesting to see what sort of King the monarch's heir, Prince George, would prove to be. His wife, Princess Mary of Teck, now Queen Mary, was a bit of a sour-faced woman, William Henry thought. He wouldn't have liked to be married to that woman at all, he mused, as his eyelids began to grow heavy.

"That's no way to speak about the Queen, Wim Henery!" Belle reproached him, "you should show a bit more respect for your betters, so you should."

"Ach well, she's a face that would drive rats from a barn," he chuckled, "not like my missus though. For you're a true beauty, Belle. Mebbe I should have tellt ye that more often. I wouldn't swap ye for another, not even for a Queen, so I wouldn't."

He slowly raised himself up the bed in the darkness and looked fondly across at Belle, as she sat on the hard wooden stool just a step or two away from him, the moonlight gilding her petite form. It seemed natural that she should be here and that he should be talking to her. He knew he was only dreaming of course, but the dream was so real, and Belle was so real, that he would not risk her disappearance by questioning the reality.

"Can you forgive me, Belle?" he asked gently, "for I wouldn't have hurt ma wee gerl for the world - not if I hadda been in my right mind."

"Ach, it's done now, Wim Henery," she smiled ruefully, "and there's no turnin' back the clock, sure there isn't. I think the time is going to pass very slow for ye in this place though."

He hardly dared blink, lest she pass from his gaze. "Could ye come nearer, and lie here with me a while?" he asked.

Noiselessly and instantly, she was by his side. He moved onto his side to make room for her alongside him on the narrow cot. He gazed at the familiar, sweetly lined face. He did not know if he would be able to touch her, if she would be as tangible as she was visible, but he inclined his head to kiss her pale face, closing his eyes in earnest expectation. His lips tasted something cold, damp and clammy. He drew back and now saw her face was bloodstained, her eyes watery and fixed, her body cold and stiffening, as it had been that night. He cried out, his voice rising in a desperate crescendo. The cruel deception of his conscience now let him alone. Belle was gone. He awoke to the sound of his own voice, albeit screaming into his pillow. The pillow, which his lips had touched, and indeed most of his mattress also, were soaked through from the intruding rain. He arose, shivering, and pushed his bed further along the wall, away from the broken window. He hoped no-one had heard him. Nobody came however. He sat on the stool, his elbows on the table and, head in hands, he awaited the forgiving light of morning.

That Monday morning he was back at work in the tailoring shop. He threw himself into the work, in order to avoid thinking about his dream of the night before. There was no heating in the prison, this being officially spring and the prison's heating was switched off between April and October, regardless of the weather. He supposed he ought to have moved his pillow and mattress to that corner of the cell which caught a few of the sun's fleeting rays, in order that they might dry out. Then again, he secretly hoped he might catch pneumonia and die. That way he might be with his Belle again. The thought that death might not reunite them however, and that some far more horrific punishment awaited him in 'Roaring' Hanna's promised inferno, kept slipping into his tired brain. He had slept little following his dream. He did not deserve the bounty of sleep. He did not deserve to be alive, not when his Belle was dead.

It now struck him that he did not know where she was buried. Had there even been a funeral? Would they have buried her in the family plot which he had purchased at the time they had lost their first little daughter, wee Belle. Like the first little Isabella, William Henry's little nephew Hugh, his brother Patrick's only son, had also died of *marasmus*, and the little fellow had been buried in the plot alongside his wee, curly-haired cousin. William Henry expected to be buried there too, that is, if his children thought it appropriate for him to lie next to Belle for eternity. Did convicted murderers have to be buried in the prison yard, he wondered, or was that just for those who were executed for their crimes? He supposed he might be buried there if he died in prison, otherwise... otherwise what?

His gruesome train of thought was suddenly interrupted by sounds of a scuffle immediately behind him, by the tailoring shop's cutting table. An ongoing disagreement between two of the other convicts in the tailoring shop had suddenly escalated into an all out fight. The warder blew three sharp blasts on his whistle and other warders came running, but not before one of the protagonists had seized a pair of tailor's scissors and plunged it into the neck of the other. A sudden arc of warm blood slapped against William Henry's face and down the front of his body. He saw the raised arm of the attacker before him, still wielding the bloody scissors, about to descend once more into the already fatally wounded victim. Instinctively, William Henry grabbed the arm, pulling it backwards away from the wounded man, who now slumped to the floor, and continued to wrestle with the assailant until Warders took over and subdued the man. William Henry now turned his attentions to the fallen man. He took a fistful of off cuts from the floor and held these firmly against the casualty's neck to stem the flow of blood. Helpless, he watched the man's shocked eyes lose their focus as his life quickly ebbed away. The sight disturbed him deeply.

William Henry had little recollection of what happened immediately after this, but was vaguely aware of urgent voices and equally urgent footsteps, then John O'Farrell guiding him to the large sink where the night soil was normally sluiced away and helping him rinse the blood from his hands under the cold tap. O'Farrell seemed relieved to find that the blood was not William Henry's but that of the victim. He escorted William Henry back to his cell and left him alone whilst the mayhem in the tailoring shop was sorted out and order restored. The incident had shocked William Henry, who had hitherto felt safe under the prison's heavy discipline and constant vigilance. He glanced down at the blood which was now drying on his clothing. He was shaken by the memory of the man's dying face and by the violence of the attack. He wondered if Belle had looked like that, helpless and distressed. He could only wonder, for he still had no clear recollection of his misdeed. Was he himself every bit as vicious and murderous as the convict in the tailoring shop? Had Belle suffered as the victim had? Had she been terrified as she realised her life blood was draining from her? It began to dawn on him that perhaps incarceration was not the *real* punishment. No court-imposed penalty could be so effective or so fearsome as the torture of his own mind.

Soon the lunch orderly was thrusting at him the tin of hot Irish stew and the hunk of bread. William Henry lifted a spoonful to his mouth, but could not swallow. He watched the stew grow cold and congeal in the tin. He now felt partly a victim and part vicious killer. Even the arrival of the library orderly with his chosen books did not move him. The orderly placed the books on the table beside him and simultaneously relieved him of his unwanted bread. He briefly placed a reassuring hand on William Henry's shoulder. Everyone in the block, indeed possibly the whole prison, had heard what had happened. The sudden touch of the orderly's hand surprised William Henry. It was an unexpected gesture, if a fleeting one, but it comforted him. He shook off his torpor and was ready to return to his work when the warder returned to collect him. He worked frenetically now to press the sizeable

84

pile of garments which had grown in his absence, as he needed to meet his daily quota.

The next few weeks passed relatively monotonously. He had now fallen effortlessly into the prison routine. Mondays, Wednesdays and Fridays saw the arrival of the library orderly. On Tuesdays, Thursdays and Saturdays, the highlight of the day was the pint of good vegetable soup served at midday, along with the hunk of bread and the tin of meat and vegetables, with potatoes in a separate tin. On Mondays and Wednesdays, there was no soup, but a tin of Irish stew and the four ounces of bread. On Fridays, in deference to the Catholic majority, no meat or fish was served, but a sustaining lentil soup was accompanied by wholemeal bread this time. The food was good, far better than prison fare he had experienced in *The Crum*. However, he sometimes dreamed he was eating fried fish and chips from McGurdy's chip shop. He could not understand however why the convicts were not allowed forks. Surely knives were the more dangerous implements, so why deprive the men of forks? Although he had not been raised to use silverware, side plates and the like, he had always used a knife and fork. He now learned to manipulate his meat and vegetables with a knife and spoon however.

The last meal of the day was always served at four thirty in the afternoon, which was not sufficiently long after the substantial midday dinner for the prisoners to be hungry enough to do it justice. He presumed this was to ensure all the convicts, including those who worked in the kitchens, were settled down in their cells before lights out at eight thirty, when the night watch arrived. The supper comprised half a pint of very good, thick oatmeal porridge, with the inevitable eight ounces of bread, precisely nine-sixteenths of an ounce of butter and a half pint of milk. William Henry had learned to keep some bread aside to eat later on, before bedtime, for it was a long time from the serving of the afternoon supper until the serving of breakfast the following morning. The bread was soda bread, baked by convicts in the kitchens and although it was not as good as the soda bread Belle used to make him, it was pretty good nevertheless.

He had never been able to sleep on an empty stomach – unless of course he had consumed a bellyful of drink, and he now vowed he would not drink to excess, if at all, ever again. Many years earlier, in his childhood, there had been a zoo on the Queen's Island where the shipyard now stood, and he had once paid his penny to visit the zoo where he had observed, at a certain time of the day, the various animals, standing in little huddles, gazing anxiously and expectantly at the door through which they expected the keeper to emerge with their food. He now appreciated how those animals had felt. To be so institutionalised, wholly dependent upon other people for one's food, and disciplined to set times, served to remove all personal choice and control.

All convicts were allowed, upon their arrival at the prison, to write a letter to their families. William Henry had not been able to do so thus far, as he could not imagine what he would say to his children. He realised now however that he must avail himself of this opportunity though, as otherwise he would not be eligible to communicate with them for another four months, just as O'Farrell had explained. Convicts were allowed one visit every four months or, if there were no visit, they might send or receive a letter in lieu of that visit. That meant just three visits a year, a maximum thirty six visits in all during the course of his twelve year sentence. It did not sound much. Replies to his letters would not count against the four monthly entitlement, though he knew his family were not great letter writers. Although he usually felt comfortable with the written word and, had the circumstances of his birth been otherwise and his education better, he often thought would have enjoyed being a writer by profession, yet he now sat in the prison classroom, under the cynical eye of the prison school master, struggling to find words to adequately express his contrition. He realised, of course, that all letters in and out of the prison were scrutinised and censored by the school master. After much thought, he wrote just a couple of lines, saying he was deeply sorry for all the pain and shame he had inflicted upon them, and for depriving them of a wonderful mother. He had added a bit initially about his having lost a wonderful wife also, but immediately deleted this as he did not feel deserving of anyone's pity. He ended by expressing the hope that they might find it in their hearts to come and visit him one day.

Outside the prison walls, the summer continued to bestow its early light and cheerful birdsong upon the Irish Midlands. William Henry did not really enjoy the daily exercise around the flagstone circles, but he did enjoy the exposure to fresh air and sunlight. He tried to lessen the tedium by reciting, in silence and in his head, and to the rhythm of his walking, one of the many poems he had learned by heart. A particular favourite was an old sea story, *The Yarn of the 'Nancy Belle'* which he had taught to all his children. It was an odd poem, about a shipwrecked mariner who turns cannibal and eats his shipmates, but, perhaps exactly *because* of its gruesome subject, his children had loved it. Another rhyme which came into his head was a snippet from Wilde's *The Ballad of Reading Gaol*:

'I walked with other souls in pain
Within another ring,
And was wondering if the man had done
A great or little thing.'

Keeping one eye upon the progress of the convict in front of him, to avoid a collision and probable retaliation, for after the incident in the tailoring shop, he realised he did not know which among the men in his ring might be a savage murderer, he nevertheless managed to steal glimpses of the changing scenery around him. Beyond the cheerless prison blocks, he caught sight of what appeared to be a garden. There was verdant shrubbery and a profusion of colourful flowers, half hidden midst the dismal, grey, granite correctional buildings, over towards the front gates. He must have passed by this garden on his arrival, but it had been so late at night and he had been very tired. He knew there was also a thirty acre farm somewhere, which produced the potatoes and other vegetables the prisoners ate, but he was unclear as to whether this were within or without the high walls. He enjoyed being out of doors for, despite the two absent window panes, his cell was stuffy and airless. The missing panes did allow him to access the outside of the window in order to clean it and thereby let in the maximum amount of light possible, but he had begun to miss his days working out in the windy shipyards, especially now that the weather had turned so pleasant.

One morning, the warder announced that he was to see the Governor immediately after breakfast. Waiting outside the Governor's office, he could not think what the reason for the summons might be. He hoped he had not committed some unwitting infringement of the rules. He ought not to have, especially as the only adornment to his cell walls was a printed copy of those rules and thus he now knew them by heart. He feared that perhaps he was to be moved back to *The Crum*. The pessimistic twists of his imagination had just reached the point where he was anticipating receiving news of the death of a family member, when the door opened and the escorting warder brusquely ushered him inside. His foreboding increased somewhat when the Governor bade him be seated, for, in William Henry's experience, persons in authority usually delivered bad news to *seated* recipients. Thankfully however, the Governor put him at his ease immediately by saying he wished to thank him personally for the prompt assistance he had given to the warders in tackling the convict who had perpetrated the attack in the Tailoring shop. It was unfortunate that the victim's life could not be saved of course, but William Henry's quick thinking and positive action, without regard for his own safety, had doubtless saved further persons from injury.

The Governor now recognised him as the man who had quoted Oscar Wilde on his arrival. He remembered William Henry as the new convict who enjoyed reading. Mr Barrows now remarked how surprising it was that so many men who could read did not bother to.

"A person who *won't* read has no advantage over one who *can't* read, sir" William Henry said.

The Governor wagged a knowing finger at him. "Mark Twain?" he suggested.

"Yes indeed, sir" William Henry smiled, "he is one of my favourites, along with Kipling, sir"

He had remembered the Governor's expressed preference for Kipling and his love of all things Indian, and thought it would do no harm to establish common ground. He racked his brains for something to quote from one of Kipling's many poems about India, but all that would come to mind was not a story of the east, but a snatch from *The Ballad Of The Red Earl*:

> *"For some be rogues in grain, Red Earl,*
> *And some be rogues in fact,*
> *And rogues direct and rogues elect:*
> *But all be rogues in pact."*

"Well, there are plenty of rogues in here," the Governor laughed, though he seemed suitably impressed at the former shipwright's erudition. "Of course, I prefer his Indian poems," he added.

A flash of inspiration now struck William Henry. "Oh East is East, and West is West, and never the twain shall meet," he intoned.

"Till earth and sky stand presently at God's great judgement seat," the Governor continued dramatically, "but there is neither East nor West, border nor breed nor birth, when two strong men stand face to face, though they come from the ends of the earth."

William Henry looked down at his feet. These lines had served to remind him that he and the Governor might well have come from the opposite ends of the earth, for all they had in common, and he had no right to try to cultivate this cultured

87

man. The Governor would surely see through his sketchy learning. However, when he looked up, he saw the Governor was beaming at him. He guessed that perhaps the Governor did not often get to discuss poetry during the course of his working day.

"You appear to have had a good education, then?" the Governor asked.

William Henry said it had been as good an education as the son of a gardener might expect, but that he was largely self-taught since the age of fourteen and read whenever he could. The Governor seemed quite interested in William Henry's father's occupation, and asked him where he had worked and whether he had taught his son any of his gardening skills. In truth, though his father had been head gardener on a grand estate, and later at the city's Botanical Gardens, James Hodges Kelly had not passed a great deal of his knowledge on to his children. William Henry recalled yesterday's tantalising glimpses of the unexpected garden however. How hard could it be to tend a garden? He could dig and hump around a barrow well enough. He sensed there might be some advantage in claiming to have green fingers. Before he could think it through properly, he realised he had talked himself into a new job. Back in his cell however, he cursed his own impetuousness, for he might soon be found out and dismissed as a fool or an opportunist.

The following morning, William Henry discovered that the colourful flora he had seen was in fact in the Governor's private garden, and that the two acres of herbaceous borders, island beds, fruit trees and neat paths, to which he was now assigned, were the Governor's great pride. In fact, this was alleged to be the best garden within any prison in the British penal system. He now began to regret his folly in exaggerating his gardening skills, but he soon learned he would be joining two other gardeners who were currently charged with tending the precious plot. In overall charge was a lifer, an elderly man who clearly was the driving force behind the garden and had been so for many years. William Henry and he were not introduced by name, only by prisoner number, and William Henry promptly forgot the other man's number, but he was pleased to be able to engage in legitimate discussion with him, albeit once again solely for the purpose of receiving instruction.

Despite being granted permission to speak with William Henry, the elderly convict divulged his name, in prison style, from the corner of his mouth. "David Deasey" he snarled. William Henry responded in like fashion.

"What's your gardening experience? Deasey asked.

William did not want to spoil things at this early stage, but equally he did not have sufficient knowledge to maintain the pretence, so he mentioned his father's antecedents and added that he himself, as a former shipwright, was happy to relieve Deasey of any of the heavier work and that, since he had a good head for heights, climbing ladders to fix trellising or to prune the fruit trees was within his capabilities. The old man considered this for a moment, and the idea seemed to appeal to him well enough. He nodded in the direction of a skinny young man who was engaged in wielding a hoe around the borders.

"That there's Diarmid. He'll not be with us long, as he's halfway through a five stretch, but he's a country boy and knows the soil well enough. I can't remember how many boys I've had here and had to teach all of them the basic gardening skills afore they were any use. How long you in for?" he asked.

88

William Henry told Deasey he had just started a twelve year sentence, which seemed to satisfy him. Doubtless it would be worth the old man's time to pass on his knowledge to someone who would be around for a reasonable length of time. William had realised that prison etiquette forbad convicts from enquiring into the nature of each other's crimes. It simply was not done. However, Deasey now felt it his duty to confide to William Henry that Diarmid was currently housed in the sex offenders' wing. William Henry glanced across at the youth, who saw him looking and bowed his head. William Henry suddenly felt embarrassed that the youth would have guessed they were talking about him. Deasey too caught the look and saw William Henry's embarrassment. He explained however that it was important for William Henry to know this, for they would both need to keep an eye out for Diarmid, particularly with regard to what gardening implements he took out of the tool store. They must ensure he put them all back again, especially the sharps, since sex offenders had a higher rate of suicide than the rest of the prison population. Deasey added that the warder held the key of the tool store and would have to authorise their release anyway, and, like all the prisoners, they would be searched by the warder at the end of each work shift.

Deasey showed William Henry around the garden, giving him an explanation of the plants. He produced a small notebook which contained pencilled diagrams and plans of all the beds and details of each species of flower and shrub and some notes regarding their care. He said William Henry might borrow the notebook for a few days, if the Governor were agreeable, to take back to his cell in order to familiarise himself with its contents. At the end of the garden were two white-painted, wooden beehives. Deasey explained that the gardeners need not service the bees, as one of the warders acted as beekeeper, though the bees obligingly serviced the rest of the garden, by pollinating all the plants and fruit trees. There was also a small greenhouse which had trays of potted flower seedlings and also some tomato and runner bean plants.

Deasey explained that the vegetables would be presented to the Governor for his table, but that the gardeners were allowed to help themselves to the undersized tomatoes, and this was a useful supplement to their diet. Clearing with the supervising warder the release of a pruning knife, Deasey then gave William Henry some light seasonal jobs to do, including removing the yellowed lower leaves from the tomatoes, cutting back the flowering chives to ground level, so that they would miraculously re-grow, and thinning out a rampant climbing clematis, which had flowered back in May. Deasey explained that many of the plants had been pruned back in the autumn, but not the spring flowering ones.

"If it blooms before June, do not prune" he chanted.

This was the first of many pearls of old gardeners' wisdom Deasey was to impart to his new assistant. It was a whole new world to William Henry but he was eager to learn some new skills. Even at his age, he might be able to embark upon a new career when released as, he reflected with sadness, his career in shipbuilding was likely over. His new role in the garden however felt like the opportunity to make a fresh start. The morning went quickly and soon it was time to wash up and return to his cell for lunch. William Henry realised he no longer had to engage in the daily exercise yard routine, since it was expected the physical exertions in the garden would suffice to keep him fit and healthy. He decided he would not miss the endless mechanical perambulations. The afternoon passed pleasantly enough, and it was clear that Deasey did not, after all, mind having to share his knowledge with another 'new boy'. After supper, William Henry avidly leafed through Deasey's notebook, determined to memorise the plant names, both the familiar names and the Latin Ones. All too soon, the lights went out however, and he settled down on his cot, feeling physically exhausted but curiously optimistic.

Belle came to him again that night, as indeed she would now most nights. He no longer tried to embrace or kiss her, however much he might ache to do so, as he realised that the rules of retribution did not permit this.

"So, Wim Henery, ye fancy yerself a gardener now?" she smiled.

Her smile however was never anything other than rueful. He wished he could make her laugh as he had done formerly. He reminded himself however that she was simply the manifestation of his conscience and as such was unlikely to do anything to please him. He told her about his experiences in the Governor's garden and how Deasey had seemed pleased with his endeavours. He reeled off for her some of the plant names he had memorised;

"*Nigella Damascena*, that's what we call love-in-a-mist; then there's *Santolina*, which is cotton lavender; *Lavandula Angustifolia*, that's blue lavender, and *Papaver Orientalis* is them great big, fancy poppies, not the wee red ones you get along the fields. Then there's the roses, which are mostly French ..."

Belle raised her hand and held out a small bunch of withered flowers. They looked like limp, blacked little bottle brushes. He could see they had been blue grape hyacinths, the ones he had picked for her the night they had spent at their daughter Jane's, surrounded by family. That was the last time he had seen Belle truly happy.

"If you and me wuz back in our wee house, it'd be red roses I'd be bringin' ye, Belle" he said wistfully.

"Sure, when did ye ever bring me roses, Wim Henery?" her expression was rueful again.

"Aye, I never brought ye nothin' but trouble. I can see that now. Them things they said about you in court ... I'm so sorry about that. That wasn't my idea. Ye wouldn't have been out drinking if I'd been a better husband, sure ye wouldn't?" he said, hanging his head.

"Mebbe not," Belle whispered, as she arose from the stool, "but I suppose it was necessary to put tha blame on me, for sure ye wouldn't have let tha weans see you hang, now would ye? It's shame enough for them that yer in prison. How d'ye suppose our Wee Belle will find a husband, with everyone knowin' her father's in gaol?"

He had not considered this. The thought made him sad. Belle turned her back on him, climbed effortlessly onto the stool and from there onto the table. She gazed out of the window, into the darkness.

"So this is Laoighise?" she said, "well, I was never out of Belfast when I was alive. You've taken me somewhere at last, Wim Henery. It's awful quiet here, though. Do you not miss the noise of the yards?"

"Yes, Belle, I do. I miss tha men, and tha chat and tha work. Most of all though, Belle, I miss you. Will ye come and see me every night, Belle? I'd love that, though I don't deserve it at all, so I don't."

The sad smile was her response, and she began to fade into the gloom of the cell.

"Ah, don't go, Belle" he pleaded, to an empty cell.

The next four months passed almost imperceptibly, in the dull routine of prison life. William Henry enjoyed the weekly bath however. Unlike the basic daily ablutions, the bathing ritual did not seem to run to any particular schedule and nor was any of the process in the control of the convicts. They would be summoned to the bathrooms, which in fact consisted of one huge room, partitioned into cubicles, each containing a bath without taps and a hook for hanging clothes upon, but no curtain or door for privacy. Ordered to undress in the cubicles, the men were at all times observed by warders who controlled the filling of the baths via external taps. How pleasant the temperature of the water was, and how long they were permitted to enjoy their soak, was down to the warders. Then, clean underwear and a freshly laundered shirt each would be brought around by a laundry orderly and thrust into each cubicle, as the water was suddenly drained away. William Henry now started to notice how thin his legs had become, and his arms too. He still had some muscle, from the gardening, but it was noticeably less than before.

All too soon, summer was at an end. However, the autumn proved to be a good time for William Henry, as the fruits ripened and Deasey encouraged him to sneak the odd fruit or small tomato into his mouth, as they were picking them for the Governor's table. Their prison jackets and trousers had no pockets, and they were searched at the end of their working day, so there was no possibility of taking the fruits of their labours back to the cell to be consumed later. Therefore, William Henry made sure he ate his fill surreptitiously as he worked. Soon, Deasey was admitted to the hospital wing, suffering from pleurisy, and the care of the garden was left to his two assistants. October was a mild month and, one warm afternoon, the supervising warder having fallen asleep in the sun, William Henry quickly picked two nice, red apples and offered one to Diarmid. The two men took advantage of the warder's lack of vigilance and they sat on one of the Governor's ornate, cast-iron benches to eat them.

"Howayiz, son?" William Henry asked the youth, "how's yer time going, all right?"

"It's goin' foin" Diarmid replied, "though, be the grace o' God, I'll be glad to be outa here in just over tew yeeyers."

The two men chewed their apples contentedly, each keeping an eye on the warder however. William Henry knew it was not the done thing to acknowledge another's crime, but he had never had an opportunity of exchanging words with a sex offender, not even with those with whom he had shared his chocolate on the train down from Belfast, and his lurid curiosity was aroused. 'Sex offender' was the blanket term given to men whose homosexual tendencies had got the better of them and who had been somehow caught in the act. They were housed together on the ground floor in each block. Men who had committed sexual offences against women or children were, however, mixed in with the general prison population, to whom they were not considered a threat. That the sex offenders had such perverse predilections was a baffling concept to William Henry, and he just could not pass up the opportunity to discuss this. He asked Diarmid, with the greatest respect, how and why he had fallen into committing such unnatural acts. Diarmid, taken aback at first, thought for a while, then made reply.

"Well, how shall I explain meself?" he started, "let me ask first, are yew a married man, yerself?"

William Henry confirmed he was. He immediately corrected himself however and said he was in fact a widower, adding that he had fathered six children, of whom five were still living and thriving.

"Well then," Diarmid continued, "imagine how yew'd react if the priest, and mebbe the poliss too, came to yew and said yew must stop having relations wit yer wife, for such a thing is forbidden now, and that, instead, yew should seek your gratification only with men, on pain of excommunication or imprisonment?"

William Henry sat back on his side of the bench and regarded the younger man with some surprise.

"Why I'd massacre the lot of 'em, so I would, for how would a man go against his natural instincts?" he declared.

"Well, exactly so," agreed Diarmid, "and in moi case, God forgive me, moi instincts are to be attracted to men. It isn't something Oi can help and nor is it something Oi dew to be controvairshal, and Oi certainly have not been prompted to do this be the devil. But, see, Oi feel as much revulsion at the thought o' sleepin' wit a woman as yew would at sleepin' wid a man. The church says what I feel is wrong, but yet there's mention of it in the boible, so it musta been a man's instinct since way back in those toimes. That's why, accordin' to the boible, God destroyed Sodom, for that's the sort of relations as prevailed there. D'ye know that the church calls us 'sodomoites'? Now, Oi'm not sayin' that we're roight, and the rest of the world's wrong, but sure, we can't go against our nature, any more than yew can, no, nor any more than a loin could change his nature and just eat vegetables."

William Henry struggled a bit with Diarmid's Dublin accent, but now guessed that by 'loin' he meant 'lion'. Whilst he was contemplating that his own pronunciation of the word might be mistaken for 'layin', Diarmid drew him back to the subject in hand.

"What Oi done wasn't done to anyone against his will, but 'twas done in total proivacy with the consent of the other party. Oi would never hert a livin' soul, as God is moi witness, but the Catlick church dictates than any act of luv, which doesn't have the possibility of leading to procreation, is a sin. Are you a Catlick, be the way?" he asked.

William Henry confirmed that he was not a Catholic. That did not, of course, mean that he condoned Diarmid and other men of his persuasion, but he certainly was surprised to hear Diarmid's point of view. It occurred to him that perhaps, just perhaps, a person like Diarmid had as much right not to be persecuted as did, say, a Catholic, a Protestant or a Jew, and more so in fact, since a man had a choice in his religion, but not necessarily, it now seemed, in his sexual persuasion. It had not occurred to him that not everyone's sexual natures were the same, and yet a religious man might say one's nature was God given. It certainly was food for thought, he realised, as he chewed on his own forbidden fruit. However, before he could give this revelation further consideration, a sudden loud snort from the warder signalled the man's awakening. Automatically, William Henry and Diarmid both plunged their apple cores into the soil, took up their tools again and laughed, as two schoolboys might who were sharing a secret joke or a confidence.

That night, William Henry thought over his day and he recalled what he and Belle had read of the trial and imprisonment, some fifteen years back, of one of his writer-heroes, Oscar Wilde. Wilde had been a sex offender. His crime had been to love the young Lord Alfred Douglas. Like Diarmud, he had been sentenced to penal servitude, albeit for only two years. Whilst William Henry himself could not see the physical attractions of another man, he began to wonder if it mightn't be wrong to persecute those who did. '*Forgive them that trespass against us*' the Lord's prayer urged, and indeed William Henry had now taken to intoning it in the dark of night, whilst awaiting Belle's appearance. Did giving in to the temptation of the flesh with another consenting human being, albeit of the same gender, in any way constitute *trespass*, he wondered? He thought not.

He had enjoyed his past reading of *The Ballad Of Reading Gaol*, though it did not deal with Wilde's own crime, but with the execution of another prisoner for the murder of his wife.

> '*And blood and wine were on his hands*
> *When they found him with the dead,*
> *The poor dead woman whom he loved*
> *And murdered in her bed.*'

The twenty fifth of October was a Friday, and Friday was the one day in the week when William Henry was permitted a newspaper. After a long day spent 'wintering-down' the Governor's garden, William Henry was relieved to be lying on his cot again, reading his paper. It seemed the entire journal was taken up with the account of the verdict and sentencing, earlier that week, of Doctor Hawley Harvey Crippen. To William Henry's surprise, the American doctor had been sentenced to hang. With every tiny detail of the case rattling around in his head, William Henry could not wait for Belle to put in an appearance.

"Belle, did ye see tha news?" he blurted out, "thon Crippen's goin' ta hang for killin' his wife. What a turn up. That cudda been my fate too, I suppose."

"Aye, ye had a lucky escape, right 'nuff, Wim Henery," Belle remarked.

"Fancy gettin' rid of most of tha corpse and then buryin' just that bit with th'identifiable operation scar down in tha cellar of his own house. That's just plain stupit, that is," he declared.

"Yes, surprisingly stupit for an educated man," Belle agreed, "so mebbe that's not his wife in the cellar."

"Ach, who else would it be then, fer gawd's sake?" her husband asked.

"Mebbe it's just a bit of torso cut affa some auld tramp in the morgue and left there by the police to make a case against Crippen. For they didn't find it when first they searched the house, did they? You and I know fine well the police is always doing that sort of thing, and sure who'd miss a bit aff a dead tramp? That there Inspector Dew has Crippen stitched up like a kipper, I'll bet," she nodded knowingly.

William Henry was surprised at this suggestion, but the more he thought about it the more he suspected his wife might be right. He began to wonder if the dead might be able to see the most intimate acts of the living, and whether Belle therefore had some inside information. Then again, he reasoned, this conversation was purely in his own imagination, wasn't it?

"So yer sayin' he didn't kill his wife after all?" he asked.

"Ach, I'm sure he did," Belle corrected him, "for doctors is always seein' aff their wives, an' he's a smart fellah so he would have done a good job of disposin' of her body, too. Tha police knows he done it but they might not have convicted him if they hadn't planted someone else's remains in the cellar. I'll bet that auld tramp never thought he'd be assistin' tha police in a murder case by givin' evidence in court!"

"Well, he *was* the evidence, it seems," William Henry now acknowledged his wife might well be right, "and that's a persuasive theory you have there me gerl. But you know, I think that jury would have convicted him anyways, for his immorality in carrying on with tha typist."

It occurred to him that young Diarmid had also been convicted for what was perceived as *his* immorality. Well, wasn't it Shakespeare who had declared the law to be an ass? Or maybe it had been William Henry himself, on the many occasions he had fallen foul of it. That would not happen again, he reminded himself - if he ever got out of prison alive, that was. The more he thought about it, the more convinced he was that Belle must have some other worldly ability to know what was going on elsewhere and maybe she could forsee the future. He wondered if he dared ask her about this, whether, if she knew she would tell him and even whether he wanted to know what she knew.

"So, what else is happenin' in the world, Belle, for you seem to know more about it than me?" he asked, lying back on his cot.

"Well, that Robinson fellah who gave false evidence against ye at yer trial, he's took a bit of a batin', so he has," she confided, "for some of the men from tha yards gave him a goin' over. When he's walking again he'll be leaving Belfast for good".

William Henry was surprised to hear this, but also pleased - not so much for the sake of revenge, but at the thought that his pals still thought enough of him to do it. He decided he did not want to know about the future, for, if there was the slightest chance he would not live to enjoy his freedom, the knowledge might destroy him right here and now.

Later that month, to his delight, he was advised he was to be granted a visit. However, he did not know until the day of the visit exactly who would turn up and so it was with great excitement that he was led to the visitor meeting area. On this occasion, it was his sister Lottie and his daughter Jane. He realised they had undergone a long and tedious journey to see him and he felt enormously grateful. The arrangements for visits were not as intimate as he would have liked however. The prisoners receiving visitors were all herded together into a large shed, separate from the main prison wings. This annexe comprised a large room, divided into two

94

long, narrow and barred, cell-like compartments, separated down the middle by a three foot wide corridor. The prisoners entered their half via one door and the visitors entered the opposite side via a separate door. A warder sat on a seat in the corridor. The iron bars, the distance of separation and the warder all served to keep the prisoners apart from their visitors and prevented the visitors from passing over anything which might be termed contraband.

William Henry longed to hug his sister and daughter, but of course any physical contact was impossible. He found himself squinting at them now, for his eyesight was not what it was. For their part, Lottie and Jane were greatly taken aback at his physical deterioration since they had last seen him at his trial. They imparted the highlights of the family news, including his daughter wee Belle's engagement to John Stewart. They were to be married next month. William Henry was glad that Belle's fears over wee Belle's marriage prospects had proved unfounded, but he was also sad he would not be at his youngest child's wedding. He would not even be able to buy them a gift. He thanked Lottie and Jane for travelling for what he knew must be more than a hundred and fifty miles to see him. They had only twenty minutes in which to exchange the more important family news however. They had brought some recent family photographs, which the warder took. William Henry would be allowed to keep just four of them in his cell whilst the rest would remain in his prison file. Later on, he might exchange the four photographs for a different four, but no more than four at a time were permitted in his cell. He so longed to reach out and touch his loved ones, but all too soon their time was up. Jane had started to cry as the warder summoned William Henry to leave, and Lottie had put an arm around her.

Later in his cell, he had spent a long time gazing at the four photographs, chosen at random by the warder, and had admired those of the assembled grandchildren, nieces and nephews, including the latest baby, his brother John's fair-haired son James, now six months old already. William Henry began to realise just how much he was missing of his family life. By the time he was released, that particular wee James Hodges Kelly would be going on for thirteen and getting ready to leave school. He also realised, to his great sadness, that he had no photographs of his beloved Belle. He would have exchanged all these family photographs for just for one image of her. There had been a lovely portrait of her over their mantel in the house. He wondered who had this now? It would have been too large for him to have kept in prison, but all the same, it was an image of her which he would remember always.

The year began to draw to a close, and William Henry thought he would not be sorry to see it go. Naturally enough, he considered nineteen ten to have been the worst year of his life. All that year's misfortunes had been entirely of his own making however. The prospect of Christmas did not dispel his gloom, since he would be spending it without his family. Around the middle of the month, he went to the schoolroom with the intention of writing a Christmas letter to his family, but the room was full of men writing their petitions for early release, to be sent via the General Prisons Board to the Governor General of Ireland. It was rumoured that clemency was more likely to be exercised by the Lord Lieutenant during the emotive season of Christmas, so William Henry might have foreseen he would have difficulty finding a place in the schoolroom. Indeed he presented himself there unsuccessfully several days running before he was able to enter and access a desk, pen and prison stationery. He wondered how long it would be before *he* would be eligible to apply for early release.

He had learned that, on Christmas Eve, Christmas Day, St Stephen's Day, New Year's Day and Twelfth Night, the prisoners would spend most of the day locked in their cells, as they did every Sunday and bank holiday. He guessed the reason behind this would be that most of the prison staff would be granted the holiday, in order to save the prison authorities money. On the Wednesday morning before Christmas, William Henry and Diarmid found themselves, not in the Governor's garden, but in the library, with a host of other prisoners who normally tended the farm. They were now given brooms, scrubbing brushes and buckets of water and ordered to clean the floor until it was hygienic enough that someone might eat his dinner off it. William Henry could not imagine that anyone might actually be intending to do such a thing, but he felt nonetheless that something out of the ordinary prison routine was about to happen. They were then set to arranging chairs in rows along the length of the library.

About an hour after their early supper that evening, the entire cadre of prisoners was marched in double time down to the now sparkling library, where they were seated in the rows. The customary order of silence appeared to have been relaxed a little, for the warders paid little heed to the whispering and corner-of-mouth murmuring. Shortly however, a voluntary silence descended, as, to the surprise of all the prisoners, a band of beautiful children entered the library, filing in and arranging themselves in four curved rows, followed firstly by a middle-aged lady who seated herself at a piano, and then by a priest, who took up his position as conductor. William Henry was put in mind of a poem he had once read - *The Jackdaw of Rheims* - in which a procession of 'nice little singing boys, dear little souls, with nice clean faces and nice white stoles' had floated into the cathedral, to the admiration of the congregation. He hoped there would be no squawking auld jackdaw to spoil the magic of the proceedings on this occasion. The piano introduction broke the awed silence in the room and then the children began their little carol concert. They commenced with *Silent Night,* sung partly in English and partly in German – William Henry had not realised the Germans sang the same hymns as the Irish - and then proceeded to sing all the old, familiar favourites. There was total silence as the children sang, since it truly was like the singing of angels.

William Henry scarcely dared stir, lest he disturb the magic of the moment, but he stole occasional glances at the faces of the men around him and saw that many of them were crying. He then realised that his own face was also wet with tears. The end of each carol was met with thunderous applause from the convicts, who had been deprived of music of any kind for so long, let alone the sight of small children. William Henry couldn't help thinking that there was a cruel irony in the well-meant performance, in that it served to remind every family man of his much-missed innocents at home. Clearly, each man felt within him a spark of hurt and regret. However, as the little concert came to an end with the opening notes of *Hark, The Herald Angels Sing!*, the priest indicated that the men should all rise to their feet and join in. They did so with great enthusiasm, each prisoner giving it his all. The applause at the end was accompanied by rousing cheers, as the little angels and their conductor took several bows, before filing out of the library again, with the same sweet discipline as their arrival.

The twin emotions of joy and sadness which the little concert had inspired, seemed to last for several days, until eventually Christmas Day came around and the prisoners were marched down to the chapel for the service. William Henry did not concentrate on the Christmas sermon and blessings, but instead sat wondering what his own family would be doing at that very hour back in Belfast. Would anyone be thinking about him, he wondered? Normally, Belle and his daughters would be preparing food for a bit of a family get-together, most often held at his and Belle's house. Whose house would be hosting the celebration today, he wondered, and would they know that he would be passing the rest of the day locked in his cell? Would they care? He tried to picture them all assembled and happy, but he realised there would be some children present whom he had never met and whose faces he could not imagine. Would wee Belle's new husband be there? William Henry had no idea what he looked like. It now occurred to him that his family was growing in his absence, and he wondered if they would also grow away from him. The thought made him feel indescribably sad.

He perked up considerably however when the Christmas meal was brought around to the cells at midday, for a pig or two had been killed on the farm and had been roasted on the big old range over in the binding shop. Normally, their meals were steam cooked in the large kitchens, but a meal of Christmas quality required roasting in real ovens, with oven-roast potatoes. Carrots, sprouts and parsnips had been boiled on the gas and real gravy prepared in the roasting tins, for extra flavour. There was even a dollop of apple sauce and a small strip of crackling for each prisoner. The meal was truly outstanding. Furthermore, Christmas Day was the only day in the year when the prisoners were allowed a dessert of any kind, and this year it was a fine rice pudding.

There was also an apple for each prisoner, the only time fruit was included in the prison diet. William Henry saved his gift apple for the library orderly however, and he looked forward to seeing the surprise and delight on the orderly's face when next he came. William Henry savoured every mouthful of the sweet and creamy pudding however and, as he did so, he thought again of his family. They had all sent him greetings cards and he was allowed to display these around his cell until Twelfth Night, when they would be taken away from him. He wondered if they were enjoying their meal as much as he was enjoying his. He hoped they would raise a glass of Bushmills whiskey to toast his health. Of course there would be a certain irony in that, given that alcohol was the major factor in his absence from the festivities, and Belle's too. Whenever he began to feel sorry for himself and to regard himself as a victim of circumstances, he had to remind himself that Belle was the true victim. She would always be there in his conscience, directing his thoughts and ensuring that any self pity he felt was quickly dispelled and replaced by pity for her shortened life.

He sometimes pictured alcohol as a demon. Well, wasn't that how the preachers regarded it, as the *Demon Drink*? He did not understand however why drink affected people differently. Why did some drinkers become amusing and affable or simply fall asleep, whilst others, like himself, became argumentative and violent? Some decent men fell into bad company and got led astray. In William Henry's case, he decided, drink was the bad companion, and one which he would have to avoid for the rest of his life. He spent the afternoon of Christmas Day in his cell, waiting for Belle to come to him. She did not come. He realised this was the first Christmas Day in thirty years that he had spent without her. It would not be his last Christmas spent alone. His cell was very small. However, he felt much, much smaller even than his surroundings. He sat on his cot, alone and reflecting, as the lonely hours passed. Somewhere down the corridor, the appropriately cheerless voice of a lone convict sang croakily, hastening the day to its close.

"In the bleak midwinter,
Frosty wind made moan,
Earth stood hard as iron,
Water like a stone ..."

Part Five – **THE TITANIC**

Nineteen eleven was an unusually mild year in the western hemisphere. The press quoted scientists' fears of worldwide warming, but William Henry did not need weather reports to tell him of the unnatural heat. When the heating boilers were switched off again in Maryborough prison in late April, it made little difference to the temperature in the prisoners' stuffy cells. May brought record temperatures. William Henry realised how much he missed the fresh coastal breezes of the Antrim spring and summer and the cries of the herring gulls, announcing the arrival of the fishing boats. He did not like being so far inland. He dreamed he was back in the shipyards, surrounded by familiar accents, cloth caps and clanging steel. Gazing out of his cell window, at his own tiny allocation of the cloudless, periwinkle blue sky he was reminded of Wilde's description of the condemned wretch at Reading Gaol:

'*I never saw a man who looked*
With such a wistful eye
Upon that little tent of blue
Which prisoners call the sky.'

Back in Belfast, according to his weekly paper, the thirty first of May had brought some of the biggest crowds ever seen for the launch of *Titanic*. Her completed sister ship *Olympic* sailed out of Belfast the same day to begin her transatlantic service, but *Titanic* would proceed only as far as the fitting out wharf to have all the fine finishing and fripperies added. When William Henry had last worked on her, electric lifts were being fitted. Now, he imagined, the hand crafted crystal chandeliers must be hung in place, and also the best porcelain toilets and washbasins, marble fireplaces and wooden panelling installed. The sumptuously appointed first class cabins, saloons and dining rooms were to die for, according to the reports in his weekly journal.

William Henry would have given anything to have been there to witness the excitement and the glory of the launch at first hand, but he had to be content with reading about it in his newspaper, some days after the event. He was delighted to spot a few faces he recognised in the press photographs, however. Lord and Lady Pirrie were in the specially constructed VIP stand, along with their nephew and *Titanic* designer, the much loved Thomas Andrews and his wife; Lord Pirrie's brother-in-law and Head Designer Alexander Carlisle, and also Bruce Ismay, wealthy chairman of the White Star Line. The distinguished party of guests was completed by J. Pierpoint Morgan, American owner of the International Mercantile Marine Company, of which the White Star Line was a subsidiary, and, of course, the Lord Mayor and Lady Mayoress of Belfast. 'No show without *Punch* and *Judy*' William Henry thought to himself. He started slightly at the name of the American, as he was familiar with the name Pierpoint as being that of the British official hangman. That name made him shiver. In fact, had William Henry been found guilty of murder, instead of manslaughter, it would have been Henry Albert Pierpoint who would have carried out his execution. He could not imagine there would be any family connection between the British executioner and the American millionaire, though doubtless Belle would have something to say about that if she were reading over his shoulder.

William Henry's eye was drawn to a quote in the press from Johnnie Beasant, given in his capacity as the shipwright's union representative. Johnnie had ensured the glory of the moment was linked with the virtues of the hard working and dedicated, if modestly paid, Belfast shipyard workers.

"Ah, Johnnie Boy, trust you to bring tha working men into the picture!" he chuckled, "ye always put yer own kind first, so ye do."

There would have been no shipwrights in the VIP box of course, although those who had not minded being docked an hour or two's pay in order to attend the launch, would have lined up along the slips, dunchers doffed and bowlers respectfully in hand, to watch the great lady enter the water. Whilst the party of distinguished guests had then been given a magnificent lunch on the Queen's island, and other *bigwigs* and their ladies had repaired to the high class dining room of the Grand Central Hotel on Royal Avenue for a special *Titanic* dinner menu, the ship builders would, of course, have returned to their labours. William Henry's heart swelled with joy to read of the event. Even the Governor was moved to mention the *Titanic* to him when he came around on his regular inspection visit the following day.

"You must be immensely proud, Kelly, to have been instrumental in such a great achievement," Mr Barrows had said, and William Henry had realised that, aside from his children and grandchildren, the small part he had played in building *Titanic* might be the only trace he would leave of himself on earth .

Every four months, without fail thus far, William Henry had received a letter from one of his sisters or his children and he had replied promptly. He was greatly relieved to see that they had not cut him off, even if they could not manage to visit, and he appreciated their letters all the more letters for knowing they did not normally engage in written correspondence. Their letters did not mention their mother or his crime - he now acknowledged it as his crime. Somehow, the fact that he now fully accepted the blame, and no longer tried to persuade himself that Belle had been at fault, made him feel slightly more at ease with both his conscience and his situation. To his relief, despite her Christmas absence, Belle still came to him most nights and they talked the night away. He was grateful for her visits and grateful that she never raised the subject of his ending her life prematurely, though her customary doleful look was sufficient expression of her disappointment and regret. He would avoid mentioning *that* night naturally enough, but would discuss instead their children's news and those developments in Belfast and the wider world which he could now only experience vicariously through his weekly newspaper.

He still missed the lively and intense discussions he used to have in the pub with his workmates, when the one with the loudest voice and most passion – often himself - would win the argument. However, he tried to ensure that, in his nightly discourse with Belle, they never argued. Oddly enough, he felt their conversation was more harmonious now than ever it had been. With the clarity which distance and time inevitably gave to his past life, he now saw her virtues, and his own vices, in sharp contrast. Belle always had a way of seeing things from a practical point of view. Despite her superstitious forebodings, she was the pragmatist. William Henry however was the one tilting at windmills and other imaginary foes. It was he who saw conspiracies where perhaps there had been none and who wanted to change the world. He still felt passionate about a lot of things, and he did not think he could ever change this side of his nature, for after all he was an Ulsterman through and through. Surrender was not a word in his vocabulary. Yet he accepted that he could be extremely argumentative, and indeed violent, when he had drink in him, and this must change. He must never again surrender to that viler part of his contradictory nature. He felt that, at heart, he must have been a kindly man on his good days, for Belle had loved him and clearly his children still cared for him too. He wondered however whether his shipyard comrades had forgotten him.

He was comforted by Belle's nocturnal presence, even though he realised it was no more than the illusory embodiment of his remorse. He did not question her appearance of course, for he feared that, if he did, reason would banish her from his little cell and perhaps from his life, forever. If that should happen, he knew he would have nothing left to live for.

Sometimes, the letters he received from home would include enclosures, little notes from other family members or perhaps a photo of his son Billy's wedding to Edith, or of another newborn grandchild, nephew or niece. He was allowed to see the photos but not to keep them all in his cell. He understood his punishment was multi-faceted, as befitted his crime. He had denied his children their mother and, through his actions, some of his grandchildren would never know their grandmother. Although the news from home was delivered mostly in a cheerful vein, it sometimes left him saddened. Every birth, marriage or death in the family served to remind him of time passing and of how much of life he was missing.

He now realised he was having increasing difficulty reading the letters. Lottie's handwriting seemed to be degenerating to the size and clarity of a sparrow's scratchings, whilst Lena's enclosed notes were positively microscopic. He began to wonder however if the gloom of his cell had caused the further deterioration of his already less than perfect eyesight. He asked to see Doctor Kinsella, who conducted some basic eye tests and confirmed that William Henry was indeed losing his vision. A box of assorted prison spectacles was produced and William Henry tried out a few, focusing through them upon samples of newsprint of various sizes. When he found a pair with lenses that offered a significant degree of improvement, and he saw the print suddenly spring forth into easy legibility, he now realised the extent of his visual impairment. He was suddenly overwhelmed with emotion. He became tearful when Dr Kinsella advised that his precious sight would continue to deteriorate, for reading was his greatest pleasure. His tears turned to tears of gratitude however when the MO said he might borrow the spectacles for the duration of his prison term, though he must hand them back prior to his release.

With the almost unbearable heat of early summer, and his discomfort increased by the heavy woollen frieze suit, for there was no alternative summer uniform, William Henry was gladder than ever of his job in the Governor's garden.

Mr Barrows himself would stop by every now and again and would engage him in conversation, either about the progress of the garden or about the books he was reading currently. The Governor would also speak longingly about his days in India and, one hot June day, he advised William Henry that, not only would the coronation of King George and Queen Mary take place on 22nd June, but the Royal couple would be ceremonially received as Emperor and Empress of India during a grand *durbar* in Delhi later in the year. William Henry had no idea what a *durbar* was, but avoided revealing his ignorance, lest the Governor tire of his company. William Henry supposed a *durbar* must be some sort of party. He wondered if being an empress and having a bit of a knees-up might bring a smile to the face of the dour queen.

Whilst William Henry was picturing this unlikely scene, Mr Barrows had then remarked that William Henry had almost reached the end of his first year in prison and he asked whether he would be submitting a memorial to the General Prisons Board, requesting a reduction in his sentence. William Henry was taken aback by this, as he had not realised such a thing were possible. It had given him a glimmer of hope however. Mr Barrows explained that, should he decide to forward such an appeal, he should request an appointment with the schoolmaster who would oversee his application and advise him. The request to attend the school room was to be made in the usual way, by chalking it on the board outside his cell. The Governor further explained that a prisoner might apply for his sentence to be remitted at any time after he had served one year of his sentence, although the first few applications were almost invariably rejected. He added that these applications might take a month or more to be decided, as they went to Dublin Castle, so he should not expect an early reply, and nor should he pin his hopes on being released until at least half his sentence had been served.

The following week, William Henry duly presented himself at the classroom, where other prisoners were writing their lessons or composing letters. Armed with his prison issue spectacles, he was now furnished with the appropriate form, some ruled continuation sheets, a bottle of black ink and an old, scratchy pen. The prison schoolmaster advised him on the appropriate form of address to use, as the appeal would be directed to the Lord Lieutenant, Governor General of Ireland, the Earl of Aberdeen. The large windows of the classroom let in a great deal of light. This and the overall air of literary endeavour in the room inspired William Henry as he wrote his contribution after the pre-printed preamble:

"To His Excellency the Lord Lieutenant of Ireland: The petition of: *William Henry Kelly D995* humbly sheweth Your Excellency: *that the petitioner was convicted at the Belfast Summer assizes on the 22nd day of July 1910 for the manslaughter of his wife, and sentenced to twelve years' imprisonment. I now earnestly appeal to Your Excellency to reconsider my case and I humbly beseech you to take a lenient view of my case, and remit a portion off my sentence.*

I am almost fifty-seven years of age and I lived with my wife for upwards of thirty-one years, and I was never charged with assaulting her. I reared three daughters and two sons by honest work. I worked upwards of thirty two and a half years on Messrs Harland and Wolff's shipyard and I never had a quarrel with any person in the firm, which the Right Honourable A.M. Carlisle can testify, as he was manager during my engagement.

My wife became addicted to drink about twenty seven years ago, which I am sorry to state was the downfall of our home. Upon several occasions I started her in business, but the love for drink was the cause of failure every time. I started to take drink myself, which I am sorry to confess did not improve matters. For when my wife got me to take drink she got regardless, so the children had to suffer, as I got regardless myself when I had too much drunk. I state this to let Your Excellency know what I had to contend with for upwards of twenty seven years, and yet I never abused my wife through all those years, all because my Father, on his death bed, made me promise never to abuse my wife, so I kept my promise, up to the time of the sad occurance.

I now give Your Excellency a full account of the case, as far as I can remember. I was working up till the night of the twenty first of April 1910, which was my pay day. I arrived home about six fifteen. When I knocked at the door I could not get in. I then opened the door with my own key. When I entered, I found the fire out and the house in confusion. I then went to my son's shop in North Queen Street, where he carries on business as a hair dresser, to ascertain what was the matter with his mother. He told me she had started to drink again, but he could not tell me where she was.

I went to several houses to enquire for her but I could get no information about her. So the consequence was that I got tired looking for her, as the people seemed to think that I was foolish to trouble myself about her. After that, I began to take drink. That was about 8 o'clock pm and before 11 o'clock, I was completely helpless. I don't remember how I got home, but as far as I can recollect, my wife wanted to take some rum out of my pocket, which I had in a bottle, and I would not let her take it. So there was a scuffle between us, and we both fell and before I got up again she went out of my sight somewhere.

I then went out again to look for her but I can scarsely remember where I went. However, I returned and found her in the house. She began to abuse me for not giving her some drink. Then there was another scuffle and I remember her falling several times in the kitchen against the mangle and chairs. After I got separated from her, I went out to the street, but I don't remember where I went because I was that drunk after taking the rest of the rum that was in the bottle.

Sometime afterwards, I returned and found her on the kitchen floor moaning. I tried to make her get up but all she said was "Ah, Wim Henery". Then I lifted her up onto the sofa and got some water to bathe her face. I clapped her hands and beat them with my hands but she would not answer me. It was then that I went to my married daughter's and told that their mother was dead. I was distracted and, only the drink was not clear in me in time, I believe I could have got some medical aid in time to save her life.

This is the truth of the case and I sware that I never used any instrument to my wife. There was no malice or forethought in the case. It was a drunken brawl that ended fately. I never done a complete term of imprisonment but once, eighteen years ago, when I myself got drunk and got the police to take me and they charged

103

me for assaulting them, which was not true. There were several convictions against me for simple drunkeness, but the fines were always paid.

Judge Wright said, at the time of my trial, when my five children swore that I was a good father to them and a kind husband to my wife, and that my wife was addicted to drink, he discredited all they said.

I now trust that Your Excellency will look with a single eye at my case and be as merciful as you possibly can, for the Almighty Judge knows that you have the whole truth and nothing but the truth. I remain Your Excellency's most humble servant,

No D995 William Henry Kelly.

Ps I am a little deaf and I did not know what Judge Wright said when he sentenced me. I was in prison three months and was in a few days waiting for my fines to be paid on two occasions. WHK."

William Henry read over his memorial and was a little unsure about the date of the incident and also about the spelling of a couple of the words, but he did not want to compound any errors by making crossings out, so he handed his paper to the schoolmaster and went back to his work.

That night, he was not surprised to be reproached by Belle for the content of his letter.

"So yer still blamin' me for yer misfortune, Wim Henery?" she said, her face a picture of hurt and disappointment.

He tried to explain his motives, in that the truth would not earn him a reprieve, and he said, in mitigation, that so long as he remained in prison, he was giving their children continued cause to be ashamed of him. Belle simply shook her head. He had not exactly expected her approval, but he was now stricken with guilt. He felt angry that she had not understood his situation and moreover she made him feel he had been cowardly. In his anger, he turned his face to the wall and ignored her. Almost immediately, he regretted this, for when he looked back, Belle had disappeared. He did not sleep at all that night and spent the next day worrying that he had offended her so deeply that she might not visit him again. However, she came again the next night, and indeed every night, to help him ease his conscience and to keep him company in his loneliness.

From July to September, the record-breaking heat wave continued. Despite the fact that Deasey was a Cork man, and therefore used to the milder temperatures afforded that county by its proximity to the Gulf Stream, he now suffered terribly in the heat. Thankfully, the warders allowed him, William Henry and the youth to relieve their thirst at the garden tap as they needed. They would not however permit the men to remove their shirts and work in just their woollen vests. William Henry assumed this to be in case the Governor's wife and daughters came into the garden unexpectedly. This was not necessary however for, normally, their impending arrival would be communicated to the warders in advance and the 3 gardeners would be marched indoors and found other tasks to occupy them, and thus these genteel ladies would be spared the site of the rough convicts, properly dressed or otherwise.

William Henry could not remember ever having experienced such heat. According to his newspaper, scientists were concerned that the Greenland ice shelf was melting at a much greater rate than was normal.

"We could use a bit of that ice here, right enough," Deasey had joked.

The octogenarian was getting forgetful these days and would repeatedly tell William Henry that his first indulgence upon release would be a cool glass of porter, to be followed swiftly by another. Asked what his own longed-for treat would be, William Henry would answer, honestly enough, that it would be Belfast tap water, cold and pure, fed by the soft rain from off the Mourne mountains.

October proved to be the most pleasant month of the year so far, however, and the men who laboured in the Governor's garden could again help themselves - whenever able to do so covertly - to the ripening fruits. William Henry had become adept at slipping a strawberry, blackcurrant or raspberry into his mouth and squashing it between his tongue and palate, before swallowing it, without any telltale chewing motion which might alert the warder to his theft. He had learned that any produce not required for the Governor's family was sold off cheaply to the warders, so he derived a small satisfaction from the knowledge that he was getting one over on the warders, not all of whom were as sympathetic towards the prisoners as was his friend Mr O'Farrell.

When Warder O'Farrell supervised the gardens, William Henry would wash any windfalls or fallen berries under the tap and would suggest O'Farrell tasted them - purely of course to ensure they were ripe and sweet enough for the Governor's table. One highly memorable day, O'Farrell came down to the gardens for the start of his duty, bringing with him four tin bowls and spoons and some extras he had brought from the prison kitchens. In the privacy of the glass house, sitting on upturned clay pots, the warder and the three prisoners together savoured a rare repast of autumn – some of the Governor's raspberries with sugar and cream. Deasey remarked that it was a grand treat altogether and that it felt like his birthday. O'Farrell said that, in fact, it was his own birthday that very day, hence his generosity. William Henry felt that no rich and privileged man, who might enjoy raspberries whenever he wished, could possibly have enjoyed the treat or indeed the company as much as William Henry had that day. It was a rare sort of a day and one he would never forget.

William Henry now observed the Virginia creeper taking on its deep red autumn hue. Likewise the prolific *Rhus Typhinus* trees were turning to crimson, and he marvelled at the russet, lime green and scarlet shades of the fallen leaves which he now had to sweep from the paths each day. It struck him that nature bestowed a rare and magical kind of beauty on the leaves just before she killed them off. Butterflies too displayed their finest colours just as the weakening sun hastened their demise. It was a sort of final kindness, a gift of glory at the end of a short and frenetic life. He reminded himself of his own good fortune in being allowed to tend this magnificent garden. He felt that, in the autumn of his own life, he was perhaps glowing and ripening himself, in that he was developing new skills and experiencing new wonders of nature each day. The garden afforded him more pleasure than he had any right to expect. He wondered if his own gardener father had felt the same wonder.

He now marvelled that, even here, within these grey, stone perimeters, the most miserable wretch might find a little magic.

November brought a reply to his *memorial* and he was summoned to the Governor's office to read the papers. The Chairman of the General Prisons Board, had written a brief summary of William Henry's appeal in the broad left-hand margin of his petition, and had then submitted it to the Under Secretary to make a decision on behalf of the Lord Lieutenant. William Henry was mildly disappointed that his missive had not been read by the Earl of Aberdeen in person. The Governor showed him also a letter written by the Judge in his case, George Wright:

"This prisoner was tried at last July Assizes in Belfast for the murder of his wife. The trial lasted the greater part of a day. The case for the Crown was completed and several witnesses were examined for the defence, when Counsel for the prisoner offered to plead guilty to manslaughter. This plea was accepted by the Crown and I passed a sentence of twelve years' penal servitude.

I beg to refer to the copy of an extract from a newspaper report of the trial (annexed to petition and papers) which accurately sets out my view of the case. The crime was very close to murder, the story of the woman's intemperance was in my opinion grossly exaggerated, and the violence used towards her must have been very great – seven ribs were broken and her liver was ruptured, in addition to other injuries, and what impressed me as a very grave fact in the case was that, during that night, the prisoner attacked his wife twice, the second and fatal attack being some hours after the first, when the prisoner may be supposed to have recovered from any effects of drink recently taken. This seemed to me to show a very deliberate and determined intention to beat this wretched woman in a savage way.

The weapon used was a chair, which was broken and on which blood was found. The Crown Counsel were somewhat doubtful as to accepting the plea of guilty of manslaughter, but I think they were right in accepting it and the jury, with all the facts before them, stated that they would have found such a verdict. I see no ground for reconsidering any reduction of the sentence."

William Henry declined the Governor's offer to read the attached newspaper clipping, for he was already familiar with all the pre- and post-trial press reports. He had not realised the trial Judge would be invited to comment on the evidence or that he would continue to have a say in his continued detention. He now thought perhaps he had approached his appeal in the wrong way. He did not know how long it would be before he might appeal again, but he decided he would give more careful consideration to his next *memorial*, and he would perhaps take a more contrite stance. The Governor now showed him a final comment, written in a dark and sombre lettering and given at Dublin Castle. It read: *'let the law take its course'*.

William Henry was disappointed, naturally enough, yet at the same time, he had not really expected to be considered for release so soon. Justice was not done with him yet and nor was his conscience. The Governor sought to cheer him up however by telling him he was to have another visit the next day. He was not told who the visitor or visitors might be, but, on a sudden impulse, he asked if the visit might be extended from thirty minutes to forty minutes, given that his visitors had to travel more than a hundred and fifty miles from Belfast. To his surprise, the Governor granted his request without demur. A greater surprise met him the following day when he entered the visiting area and saw Johnnie Beasant and Hughie Hewitt waiting for him. He could not greet them with a friendly handshake or a warm shoulder slap, as once he would have done, for the narrow passageway and two barred partitions separated them, but he sat, and then rose, and then sat again, clutching at the bars and fighting back tears. He was beside himself at the very welcome sight of his old friends.

Not having seen him since the trial, Johnnie and Hughie were as shocked at his appearance as his family had been, but they did not let him see this. They smiled warmly at him and asked after his health. He had to strain to hear them however, for his already defective hearing seemed to have declined further in the comparatively silent world of the prison. He thanked them for giving up a day's pay to visit him, but they told him they were in fact on strike at the moment. He begged them for news of the yards. They told him as much as they could think of, for example that Alexander Carlisle, the popular Chief Designer and manager of the *Titanic* project, had retired, which William Henry was sad to hear. Johnnie said that Harland and Wolff were employing more unskilled men than ever before, thanks to the new technology which required little skill to operate. He added that the tradesmen's unions were worried about the increasing unionisation of the unskilled men. Firstly, the National Amalgamated Union of Labour had been allowed to join the Federation of Engineering and Shipbuilding Trades, and then the National Union of Gasworkers and General Labourers had also been accepted into that elite body, and together, the unskilled men's unions were forming a pressure group within the Federation which might work against the hard-won position of the skilled tradesmen.

William Henry asked whether the pay gap between skilled and unskilled men had narrowed, for this would be a major issue to divide the men and could only work to the advantage of the management. Johnnie said the pay differentials had not vanished as yet, but that he could not rule it out in future, since the unions were now set against each other, with the shipyard management taking a comfortable back seat in the negotiations. Seeing William Henrys' worried expression however, Johnnie remembered that this was not the main news which he and Hughie had come to impart. He now advised him that he had secured the management's agreement in principle to William Henry's re-employment on his ultimate release, whenever that might be. William Henry was overjoyed. He had not dared to imagine he would ever be allowed back in the yards. The tears he had been holding back now defied him and he quickly wiped them away with the sleeve of his coarse jacket, for Ulstermen did not cry. He told Hughie and Johnnie about his recent unsuccessful petitioning of the Lord Lieutenant of Ireland and said he would not give up seeking early release. Johnnie promised him that, if there was anything else he and Hughie could do back in Belfast to assist him in this, they would surely do it. When they took their leave of him, they left him a more optimistic man.

William Henry learned he had to wait another year before he could re-apply for early release, and indeed Deasey now told him he himself had applied every year for the past five years. Though the long, hot summer had now given way to a very chill winter, William Henry's optimism stayed with him through Christmas and over into the New Year. January brought with it a minor influenza epidemic which affected both prisoners and warders. The prison infirmary was full of sick inmates and the number of warders reporting unfit for duty led to the rest of convicts spending more days of inactivity locked in their cells. William Henry believed that the fruit he had surreptitiously consumed through the summer and autumn had given him some immunity. The same could not be said for David Deasey however, and when he failed to appear for work one day, the warder advised William Henry that Deasey too was in the infirmary. Two weeks later, he learned that Deasey had succumbed to the combined effects of bronchitis and pneumonia and had passed away. William Henry was deeply saddened to hear this, as he had become quite fond of his old mentor, and felt he owed the man a great deal for his patient instruction and friendship.

William Henry was not allowed to attend Deasey's funeral. In fact, he did not even know if there had been a funeral service for the old prisoner. Deasey had never mentioned having any family living, so William Henry wondered where they had buried him. He did not like to ask for, in the back of his mind, he harboured a fear that he himself might die in prison also, and he could not imagine his family having the money or inclination to have his body brought back to Belfast for burial. If Deasey had, of necessity, been interred within the prison walls, William Henry did not wish to know about it. William Henry and Diarmid carried on their labours in the garden alone for the time being, and of course there was comparatively little to do in depths of winter anyway. When the spring blossom was on the trees however, Deasey's replacement was introduced. Michael Morley was a quiet Mayo man in his early forties and was an experienced gardener. He only needed to be shown the layout of the gardens and have the prison garden routine explained to him before he was functioning with full efficiency. William Henry believed that calm men were chosen for the gardening duties, and he reassured himself that he and Morley would get along fine.

Throughout the spring of nineteen twelve, William Henry read with growing concern the press reports on the progress of what was generally known as the third *Home Rule Bill*. The bill appeared to pose the most serious threat yet to the future of the Protestants in Ulster, and violent opposition was growing daily to the proposal to bestow or enforce – depending upon one's point of view – a degree of self government upon Ireland. Naturally, the Unionists were opposed to this, but the Nationalists also rejected the bill in its current form in favour of a *wholly* independent Irish state. William Henry had been shocked to hear that, back in February, hostile crowds had turned out onto the Belfast streets during the visit of Winston Churchill who was to address the Ulster Liberal Association, and that, not content with vocal expression of their discontent, a large gang of loyalist shipyard workers had attempted to overturn the car in which Winston and his wife were travelling. Lord Pirrie, another supporter of Home Rule, had also been subjected to the anger of the crowds and had been pelted with rotten eggs, herrings and flour. The King's speech upon the opening of Parliament now announced the imminent introduction of the *Government of Ireland Bill*, as it was to be known. The predictable outcome of this was a series of both rallies and riots over the Easter period, and press reports were that sixty casualties were treated at Belfast hospitals.

A week or so following the Easter rioting, Governor Barrows stopped off at William Henry's cell during his routine inspection. William Henry expected he wished to discuss the Ulster situation with him, as he often did. To his surprise however, he saw Warder O'Farrell, who was not scheduled to be duty warder on B wing that week, also step inside and pull the cell door to behind him. William Henry leaped to attention but the Governor bade him be seated on his bed, whilst he himself perched his lanky frame awkwardly upon the small stool. William Henry feared their raspberries and cream feast had been discovered, and that he might lose his remission over the theft of fruit from the Governor's garden. However, the Governor appeared quietly grave, rather than angry. William Henry glanced across at O'Farrell, but the warder lowered his eyes to the floor.

"I am afraid I have some rather sad news for you, Kelly, since you will not have seen the day's news as yet," Mr Barrows began, "there is no easy way to say this, and I hate to be the bearer of such bad tidings, but the fact is that the *Titanic* has had a serious mishap on her maiden voyage. I am afraid she is believed to have hit an iceberg the day before yesterday and she then sank, with, it is feared, significant loss of life. I thought I would prepare you for some of the disturbing detail which you are likely to read in the press reports. I know you will be disappointed to hear this, in view of your close links with the vessel, and I am so very sorry to have to tell you this."

William Henry found himself mumbling his stunned thanks and, before he could rise to his feet, the Governor had departed. O'Farrell came and patted his shoulder and asked if he would be all right. William Henry said that the news surely could not be true, for *Titanic* was unsinkable. O'Farrell said it was indeed true, and he expressed his own sorrow at the disaster. Left alone for a few brief moments before breakfast arrived, William Henry was stunned. Surely there must have been a mistake? Perhaps they had found the wreck of another ship and had concluded, wrongly, that it was *Titanic*. But he now remembered that the new liners had Marconi wireless facilities on board, so surely *Titanic*'s crew would have been able to report the fact if they were in any difficulty.

The day passed in a haze for William Henry, who did not discuss the incident with Morley or Diarmid, since neither of them would understand about shipbuilding and such. Moreover, the warder who was overseeing them that day was one with exceptional hearing and one who strictly enforced the rule of silence. What useful opinion might a gardener and a florist add to the tragedy anyway? That evening, he imagined Johnnie and Hughie, and a great many other shipwrights, would be huddled together in the pub discussing it right now. Johnnie and Hughie would have a theory or two to put forward as to the cause of the disaster. How he wished he could be there with them, instead of here alone in his cell. He clung onto a raft of hope until he might read for himself the extent of the disaster, and so he was able to eat his breakfast and lunch with ease that day. When evening came and he was given his copy of the *Evening News* to read however, he could not believe the headlines which met his anxious eyes.

'MORE THAN 1,500 PERISH AS THE GREAT TITANIC SINKS'

The number of dead was so great that he could not take it in at first. Surely, that figure must represent most of the passengers and crew? He read further. Only six hundred and seventy-five of her passengers, mostly women and children, had been saved. How could that be? What about the lifeboats? He realised there might not have been lifeboats enough for all the passengers and crew, but wasn't *Titanic* designed to remain afloat and so act as her own lifeboat? So why had not more souls been rescued? He scanned the pages for the answers to his questions, but all he could glean was that she had sunk in the early hours of the previous morning, at around two-thirty, according to reports from other ships, and that the disaster had occurred about five hundred miles from the Canadian port of Halifax, south of the Grand Banks. The ship had quickly disappeared into two miles of ocean, taking most of her passengers and crew with her. It appeared she had stuck an iceberg of a particularly dangerous nature, one known as a 'growler'.

What appeared at first to be a photograph of passengers, their faces showing only mild concern, deserting the stricken ship, in darkness, for the lifeboats, turned out, on closer inspection, to be merely an artist's impression. He noticed that the perspective was all wrong and furthermore the ship appeared to be fairly small. In fact the scale suggested it was less than a quarter of *Titanic*'s actual size. The fanciful picture annoyed him, for he guessed that the hurried evacuation of so large a ship would not be so restrained or orderly an affair. The newspaper recounted the fact that distraught families of the passengers and crew had begun to gather outside the White Star Line offices in London and Liverpool and even on New York's Broadway, but that no names of survivors were available as yet. He scoured every page of the paper for detail and noticed, with surprise, that this edition still carried an advertisement, inviting bookings for White Star Line departures to New York.

In the weeks following the tragedy, more and more detail of the sinking was released to the world's press, though William Henry could only receive these in weekly instalments. It was now confirmed that the ship had sunk in a matter of a couple of hours. He could not understand how this had happened. Principal amongst the safeguards on *Titanic* had been the automatic, self-closing bulkhead doors and the series of buoyant air chambers within the bulkhead. The caulking squads, William Henry's squad amongst them, had been assiduous in waterproofing the hull and also every inch of those bulkheads, yes, and the decking too. How could sea water have penetrated the vessel to such a degree, and so quickly, as to sink her before help could reach her? He noted that the Canadian Pacific Steamship Company's vessel, Empress of Britain, had arrived in New York the day following the sinking and her captain had reported encountering an ice field some one hundred miles wide just three miles off Halifax. In fact it was now reported that icebergs had been encountered of late in waters much further south that they had ever been seen previously.

The names of some of the dead were now released. The details of the many wealthy individuals, who, between them, had been worth five billion dollars, did not interest William Henry, and nor did the one million dollars' worth of cargo she had on board, nor the ten million dollar loss to Lloyds' underwriters. He sought out the

110

names of the deceased men of the Harland and Wolff guarantee group, a small band of tradesmen who had accompanied the ship on her maiden voyage to deal with any teething troubles which might occur at sea. He recognised none of them. They were mostly electricians, fitters and plumbers, since it was expected that any small faults would most likely involve electrics, plumbing or the interior structures. On a maiden voyage, one would not usually expect problems with the integrity of the hull, so no riveters or caulkers would have been aboard. He also examined the list of missing crew members, a significant number of whom were Ulstermen.

He next scanned the lists of the wealthy and prominent first class passengers who had perished on *Titanic* and was deeply saddened to see that of her designer Thomas Andrews. Andrews was a much respected young gentleman, a gifted design engineer and a man who often took the time to come down and speak with the shipwrights. He had been unafraid to share his ideas and his dreams with the men whose brawn made them a reality. The press said he had had a bright future in the shipbuilding industry and it is likely he would one day have been a director of Harland and Wolff. William Henry thought it a tragic waste. He wondered about the designer's poor, grieving widow, and the little girl who would too young to remember her Daddy. Which was the sadder loss, he wondered, a little girl losing her daddy, or a daddy losing his little girl, as William Henry himself had?

Weather experts now attributed the presence in the Atlantic of so much dangerous ice to the unseasonably hot weather of the previous summer, which was when the iceberg which had struck *Titanic* would have commenced its long journey south from the Arctic to the busy shipping lanes of the transatlantic routes.

"Just imagine that," he told Belle, when regaling her with the latest accounts of the sinking , "when I wuz sweatin' meself away to nothin' here in this wee cell all last Summer, there wuz thousands of tons of ice floating down from Greenland and gettin' ready for its encounter with *Titanic*."

"Sure an' it was a terrible loss of life altogether," Belle agreed, "and heaven's fillin' up with all the poor drowned men, women and children, aye an' with millionaires too, so it is."

"Is that where *you* are Belle?" he asked tenderly, "are you in heaven too?"

"Well, I'm not in *The New Lodge*, that's for sure!" she exclaimed impatiently, "but why are ye concernin' yerself with tha *Titanic* dead, Wim Henery? What about yer own kin? What about sheddin' some tears for our own wee gerl?"

William Henry started. He looked across at the apparition of his wife and now saw she held a small infant in her arms. He saw the tiny white face of their curly-haired little daughter, the first little Isabella, the little girl he never would see again on this side of life. He felt guilty that, though she had been his favourite, he had not exactly thought about her every minute of every day of his life since her passing. He knew however that Belle had. Belle had thought of her little lost girl at every moment of her waking life, every sober moment, that is.

"Could we have saved our wee Belle, d'ye think?" he asked, gazing in awe at the child.

"Mebbe, if we'd had tha money for a good doctor," Belle sighed resignedly as she stood, and taking the toddler by the hand, turned to depart, "but we drank woor spare cash away, didn't we Wim Henery?"

William Henry slipped slowly to his knees by his bed in the now empty cell, his elbows on the mattress and his face in his hands, and he sobbed. He shed tears for wee Belle who had not made her mark upon the world but had slipped anonymously away. He wept also for the fifteen hundred souls who had sailed to their deaths on the ship that he had built. He mourned Thomas Andrews, that estimable gentleman, who had also gone down with *Titanic*, and he pitied the others of the Harland and Wolff guarantee group who had perished. He felt bereaved. He *was* bereaved. When he had cried himself out and his sorrow had subsided, he became angry. His anger was not directed at the ship owners and designers however, nor at God, nor at capricious fate. No, it was focused upon himself. He was angry that his daughter was dead, and angry that Thomas Andrews, and the other Harland and Wolff men, and the crew and passengers had died, whilst he, who had caused so much heartbreak to so many people, lived still.

Only the next day, he received letter from his daughter Jane, advising of the sad deaths of yet another Isabella, Billy and Edith's six week old baby, and of Edith herself, whose heart had not been strong enough to carry the frail twenty year old through the rigours of childbirth. This was too cruel indeed. William Henry now had no tears left to shed and moreover felt numb, both inside and out. Over the next few days, he could eat nothing and the warders began to notice him having to hold onto his coarse trousers to prevent them sagging about his increasingly bony frame. In due course, he was sent to the Medical Officer who was immediately surprised at his condition.

"How long have you had these boils on your back?" Dr Kinsella asked him.

He had to repeat his question, since William Henry's hearing seemed to have worsened, either from shock or neglect. William Henry could not tell him, for he was barely aware of, and little interested in, his own condition these days. The doctor prescribed a tonic for him and signed him off work for a few days. However, this gave him even more time to sit and reflect on life's bitter irony and to dwell further on both the greatest loss of life in a maritime disaster and on the loss of his daughter in law and his latest little granddaughter. As he sat in his cell, he reflected upon the care he had taken in checking over each of *Titanic*'s watertight compartment which had been caulked by his own squad and which had fallen within his remit to scrutinise. He reassured himself that he had had each stage of the work checked and re-checked by Johnnie or Hughie. He remembered his last day in the yards, that balmy, breezy day when he had sat enjoying his pipe, his tea and the view, high up on the staging above the ship, as the water drained back into the Lagan. Of course that was a day which had ended terribly badly. He had not returned to his work since that fateful day, the day of his arrest. Someone else would have had to tell the riveters to repair the drain hole the following morning.

The thought suddenly hit him like a hawsing mallet. Supposing nobody had repaired the hole? It had been *his* responsibility to ensure this was done. Would Johnnie or Hughie have realised that, in his absence, no-one might have arranged for it to be done? It was possible that nobody else would have done so, for the section had already been fully checked for leaks and signed off. He started to feel sick to his stomach. Surely to God, one wee drain hole wouldn't sink a whole ship, would it? He tried to think what he had been told about the watertight compartments. Hadn't

112

Thomas Andrews himself said that a number of them could flood and the ship would stay afloat? Yes, that was true, of course it was, but then, supposing his was not the only drain hole to have been left unsealed? What then? No, even if five or six such drain holes had been left unsealed ... well, how long would those compartments have taken to fill up? No, that could not have been the cause. Surely, a ship with half a dozen holes in her would have sunk long before she made it to the ice fields and met that iceberg.

He began to think over his last day in the shipyard and he now recalled the incident with the rivet which had sprung out of the *Titanic*'s hull that day. Could that rivet have had any significance, he wondered? The press reports on the forty-six thousand ton leviathan had said she was held together with three million rivets. Surely *one* deficient rivet could not have sunk her, could it? But then he remembered the discussion in the pub, before the drink had got him up on his metaphorical soapbox yet again. Someone had asked whether there might have been more than one dud rivet. Supposing *all* of them had been made of inferior iron instead of steel? It was well known that Harland and Wolff were desperate to save costs, and that was why men were being replaced by machines. Machines cost money to buy too, so did materials. William Henry had read in the papers that Lord Pirrie had been trying for some time to buy a steel manufacturing plant in Scotland in order to produce his own raw materials, because importing them was expensive. Was it possible he had been saving money by using inferior materials?

The thoughts rattled back and forth in his head. Could iron rivets have held together all those steel plates in the heaving of those sub-zero Atlantic waves? Perhaps they would have done so, but not for the collision. Should he have said something about the popped rivet head? But Hughie and Johnnie had seen it too, and so had Jim Thompson and the others in the pub, and then there was the foreman caulker who had hit it with the hammer. Wouldn't they have said something about it to the management? It now occurred to him that they might not have wanted to jeopardise their jobs by highlighting the management's use of shoddy materials, but what about now, now that the ship had sunk? Surely they would speak out now? He realised though that, if this were the cause of the tragedy, then all evidence of it would be at the bottom of the Atlantic. What about the rivet head he had pocketed? Where was it now? He had no idea. He had last seen it in the pub. He could not bear the thought that he might, by some small act of either commission or omission, be responsible for the tragedy. The thought was to stay with him for a very long time, however.

One evening, after he and the spirit of Belle had said their farewells for the night, he sat at the table in his cell for a while, deep in thought. The melancholy which had come upon him since the heartbreaking events of April would not leave him. His conscience trouble him and the dark thoughts in his head turned into the accusing voices of people – drowned people. The noise in his head was too loud and the fear in his soul too great for him to bear. The light of a large harvest moon now filled his darkened cell and reminded him of the moonlight rays which had awoken him to awful discovery on the night he had killed Belle. He now removed the cotton muffler from around his neck and climbed unsteadily onto the stool, and from there he mounted the table. Almost mechanically, he fed one end of the muffler through the broken window pane and tied it firmly around one of the external iron bars. Standing on tiptoe, he wrapped the other end around his neck. It was the right thing to do, the only thing to do. He managed to wind it around and loop it over itself just beneath his chin, but there was not enough of the muffler to achieve a double knot. It was too short. He tried to hold it secure with his hand and launched himself forward heavily, his entire weight suspended forward onto the point where his neck rested against the muffler. He felt his windpipe begin to constrict and his eyes began to bulge. His peripheral vision now started to blur and he began to feel faint. However, as he came to the point of losing consciousness, his hand involuntarily relaxed on the end of the muffler and it loosened from around his neck. He toppled down from the table and landed on the floor. Exasperated at his own incompetence, he broke down once more in tears. He remained in a heap on the floor for some time, before eventually he picked himself up and slipped silently into his bed.

The next morning, it was O'Farrell who was on early duty in B Block. O'Farrell worked mostly early duties, for he liked to spend the afternoon with his young grandchildren. He now accompanied the orderly with the hot water for washing. As he entered the cell, he was surprised to find William Henry still lying in his bed. This struck him as odd, for the shipwright usually rose with the sun. He then noticed the muffler knotted up at the window, and his face fell. Briskly he took the water from the orderly and ushered him away. Pushing the cell door closed, he climbed up onto the table and untied the muffler.

"Ah, come on now, Kelly," he said, "sure this is no time to be layin' in bed, with the sun comin' up and the birds singin', is it?"

His charge slowly sat upright but was unable to respond to O'Farrell's cheeriness, partly out of despair, but also because his throat hurt and his voice had deserted him.

"What's the story with the necktie then? Is it tryin' to top yerself ye were? Sure that's no way to be goin' on, is it? Why would ye be wantin' to commit another crime, and a mortal sin into the bargain? Wouldn't you lose your remission and yer soul too? Listen now, I won't say anythin' about this, and you'd better not either. Come on and get up now, good man, for there's a fine breakfast on its way up to ye."

William Henry swung his legs over the bed and tried to stand but he felt strangely weak. O'Farrell helped him to his feet, but lost his grip when, suddenly, William Henry lost all consciousness and the floor rose up to meet him.

He came to in the infirmary. He had wondered at first if he were dead, for everything around him seemed strangely bright and clean. The bed beneath him was soft and the sheets white and starched. A small log fire crackled away at one end of the room, the walls of which were painted a shiny ointment pink, and there was a reassuring air of disinfectant in place of the usual morning odour of urine. The ache in his head told him he was indeed alive. Putting a hand to his forehead, he found it tender and covered with a gauze dressing. The medical wardsman, a short, thin and hollow-cheeked convict of about sixty-five, who looked as though he ought to be occupying one of the beds himself, approached on seeing William Henry awake.

"Howayiz now?" he asked, "for ye give yersel a rare crack of tha iron bedstead, roit on tha crust a tha head, ye did."

William Henry nodded and reclined back on the pillow, but the wardsman wasn't going to go away. He pulled up a chair and sat looking at William Henry for a few seconds, then he indicated a bunch of red grapes in a tin bowl on the side table by William Henry's bed.

"Them's what Warder O'Farrell bronged ya," he confided, and William Henry recognised them as being from the Governor's greenhouse. He had occasionally helped himself to the odd single grape, never more than one from each bunch though, as the empty stalks might be noticed, so a whole bunch of grapes sitting by his bedside caused him a momentary alarm and he wondered whether he ought to hide them somewhere.

"The Guvnor had them sent tew ya," the orderly reassured him, "on accounta yew bein' upset about the collision o' tha Toitanic and that. Didya have somebody related ta yew on there then, didya?"

William Henry managed to rasp out that he had not, but that he had worked in the shipyard where she'd been built, and of course he knew the late Mr Thomas Andrews to speak to. The medical orderly had a slightly effeminate manner about him, but seemed all the more solicitous and kindly for that. He leaned over to pull up the counterpane slightly and smoothed over the turnover of the sheet.

"Will oi give yer pillows a bit of a puck for ye?" he fussed.

William Henry confirmed he was comfortable enough. The wardsman, who introduced himself as Thomas, pronouncing the 'h', which William Henry thought unusual, advised he should not eat any of the grapes just yet, for the doctor thought he'd been in shock, so he wasn't to eat anything until supper.

"Well, oi'd better be gettin' on wid me chores," he said, smiling, "but tell me now, before I go, is there any news at all o' that poor auld oiceberg?"

William Henry looked puzzled for a second, then found himself laughing almost uncontrollably at the awful joke.

Upon his release from the medical block, William Henry found that, at the Medical Officer's suggestion, and with the assent of the Governor, he had been assigned to work in the prison library. He would be sorry to lose his fresh air job, but he was looking forward nevertheless to having free access to the prison's books, which, he had learned, now numbered the best part of a quarter of a million. The library orderly, Michael Whelan, whom he already knew by sight, as he was the one who usually brought William Henry's books around, now introduced him to the library routine. Whelan also taught him how to catalogue the new books which were received regularly from various beneficent organisations and private donors. William Henry was now glad he had been so generous in sharing his bread ration with Whelan. Few people actually ventured into the library, except at Christmas, when it was used as a secondary dining room, and so there were piles of books stacked around in corners, which Whelan advised him were awaiting either sorting or repair. Whelan was glad to have some assistance.

To William Henry's surprise, he and Whelan were not supervised directly by warders whilst in the library, unless they needed to borrow scissors from the locked cupboard in the corridor outside, but were left largely to their own devices. This meant they could also chat whenever they were alone, although each man had now fallen out of the habit of doing so. There was a flush toilet also out in the corridor and, to William Henry's delight, he did not have to ask permission to use it and nor was he timed in his use of it. Whelan looked baffled whenever his fellow librarian announced he was "away the minutes". William Henry enjoyed the silence and tranquillity of the library, particularly as his own world was gradually becoming more and more silent with the deterioration of his hearing. There was a large wall clock, the ticking of which seemed to annoy Whelan from time to time, though William Henry's deafness permitted him to hear only the striking of the half hour.

Being able to observe time passing by means of a clock seemed to him to be another small kind of freedom. Also, the limited communication that his new job required, meant he did not have to keep asking warders and orderlies to repeat those orders he had not heard. He was not as deft as Whelan with the paste brush and so it took him a while to turn his shipbuilder-gardener's hands to the delicate task of re-attaching torn endpapers to the volumes and repairing split spines. However, he greatly enjoyed accompanying Whelan as they manoeuvred the book trolley around the landings, and in this way, he got to see more of the prison itself.

More than anything, William Henry was delighted to have unfettered access to a selection of daily newspapers. He now read avidly the reports of the Board of Trade's enquiry into the Titanic disaster. In his cell each evening, he and Belle discussed in detail the evidence as it emerged in the press reports. The general findings of the enquiry were that, whilst some censure was due to the Board of Trade itself for not increasing both the lifeboat requirements and the adequacy of the subdivided watertight compartments for the new super liners, the Titanic's drowned captain must shoulder the bulk of the blame. Apparently, Captain Smith, despite being acknowledged as one of the company's longest serving and most respected captains, had been sailing at record-breaking speed through a known ice field.

William Henry said he felt it was all too easy to blame someone who was conveniently dead and therefore unable to refute any such allegations. Belle reminded him that the judge at William Henry's own trial had said something similar. Allowing Belle this barb, William Henry said he had been shocked to hear of the actions of the White Star Line's director, Bruce Ismay, who, according to highly critical press reports, had appeared incapable of making any decisions during the evacuation of the passengers but had in fact saved his own skin by calmly stepping into one of the lifeboats along with the women passengers. Harland and Wolff came out of the enquiry relatively unscathed however. There was certainly no mention of inferior materials or workmanship - to his immense relief.

As William Henry's third Christmas in Maryborough approached, he no longer harboured any suicidal urges and his former gloom and dejection were now dispelled by one piece of news in particular. He now learned that Johnnie and Hughie had organised a major petition asking for his early release and had submitted this to the General Prisons Board, for processing and forwarding to the Lord Lieutenant once more. Johnnie had written to William Henry to advise him of this and had said that, whilst it might not work, at least it would put evidence on his file, for the benefit of any future consideration, that he had numerous friends and people who respected him back in the city of Belfast.

Johnnie had arranged for a friend of his to draft the petition. John Kirkpatrick, from Barrow Street, was general clerk to a local solicitor and therefore had both legal vocabulary and decent stationery at his disposal. Kirkpatrick had persuaded some of the more noteworthy professionals who came to his Solicitor's chambers to append their names to the petition, and William Henry's son Billy had then kept it a week or two in his barber's shop, so all the shipyard workers might be asked to sign it as they came in for their haircuts. In all, seventy-eight of Belfast's citizens, including a Solicitor, two ministers of religion and some local traders, had added their names and addresses to the document.

It was late January of nineteen thirteen before William Henry got to see the petition for himself, by which time it had, of course, been rejected. He had not expected a more favourable result however. He went along to the schoolroom with eager anticipation anyway to view the papers. He was impressed to see Kirkpatrick's copperplate handwriting on the foolscap sized vellum:

'Memorial – To The Right Honourable The Earl of Aberdeen, Lord Lieutenant Governor General of Ireland:

The Memorial of your undersigned memorialists, on behalf of Wm. H. Kelly, a prisoner in His Majesty's Convict Prison at Maryborough, humbly sheweth:

1.   That the said prisoner Kelly was indicted before Mr Justice Wright at the Summer Assizes held at Belfast for the City and county at Belfast on the 14th day of July 1910, and charged that he did at number 11 Shandon Street, Belfast, on the twenty third day of April 1910, feloniously kill and slay Isabella Kelly, his wife. The capital charge having been reduced to one of manslaughter, Kelly was sentenced to twelve years' penal servitude.

2.   That the said prisoner Kelly is a man upwards of sixty years of age, and was, during the period of his married life, a model father to his family and highly esteemed by his many friends and relatives in and about the district where the alleged manslaughter took place, and truthfully be it said that that Kelly never in all his life stood charged with any offence known to the law, save the present one which he strongly resents and denies.

3.   That Kelly's family having grown up and able to do for themselves (having received a good father's attention during this period) and prisoner having given them all a sound national education and enabling the majority of said children to go to United States with full expectations, also a girl and a young man both of whom are married in this city and enjoying the utmost respect of their friends and neighbours. The son, William Henry Kelly, resides close to the vicinity of his father's alleged offence, viz. at 217 North Queen Street, where he carries on the business of a master hairdresser with the greatest respect and confidence of his numerous customers. The daughter is a married woman living also in said vicinity, and named Alice Anderson of 115 Mervue Street Belfast and either of whom would gladly keep their father during the remainder of his declining years.

117

*4.	That prisoner had worked on the Queen's Island for upwards of thirty years and on the night of the offence came home to 11 Shandon Street and on his arrival there found his wife hopelessly intoxicated and utterly unable to prepare his evening meal. The prisoner, upon seeing his wife's condition, went out of the house heartbroken and unfortunately took some drink, as, previous to this, Kelly had tried his best to try to get his wife to abstain from the liquor, but was unable to do so as she was habitually addicted to it and was seldom sober. This finally had the effect that, through that mother staggering about the locality, intoxicated, of driving the prisoner's family gradually away from the home entirely.*

*5.	That the evidence upon which Kelly was convicted was purely circumstantial as the bruise found on deceased's body might have been caused by a fall in the house over a chair or other obstacle or may have happened in the street, as she was continually stumbling about whilst under the influence of drink. The Kelly family have always to the knowledge of their neighbours been inoffensive and industrious members of the community with not a stain on any of their characters up till the time of this lamentable occurrence.*

Your memorialists therefore would respectfully press upon Your Excellency that under the circumstances of this case (and owing to the very indifferent state of the prisoner's health and mind) it is one which they can confidently recommend to Your Excellency's attention, and ask that the clemency of the Crown may be extended to the prisoner, who has already served two years and nine months of his sentence, and your memorialist will ever pray.'

William Henry's excitement at seeing the petition was tempered with some dismay at perceiving the lack of contrition expressed on his behalf and the fact that blame was again laid firmly at Belle's door. He would not have signed his own name to that petition, had he been asked. Also, he had no idea where notion had come from that some of his children were in America. His son Jimmy might have visited there with the navy perhaps, but this would not have been any of William Henry's doing. Still, he was grateful for the considerable effort which had been put into drafting the memorial and in gathering so many signatures. He scanned the names and his heart warmed to see that Johnnie Beasant and Hughie Hewitt had signed it, as had a number of his former workmates and indeed other shipyard employees who would not even have known him. He recognised the same bold hand as before in which the now familiar phrase '*let the law take its course*' was inscribed on the papers. He now saw, for the first time, the signature of the man who dictated the course of his life – 'MacDermot'.

Handing the papers back to the prison schoolmaster, he ventured to ask whether he knew who this 'MacDermot' was and why it was that the writer used no forename or initial. Charles Edward MacDermot, he learned, was '*The* MacDermot', that is chief of the MacDermot clan, and Prince of Coolavin. He was also a Justice of the Peace, Chairman of the Irish Prisons Board and a prominent Catholic, who was currently seeking to persuade Irish Bishops to change the Catholic custom of abstaining from meat on Fridays in favour of abstinence from alcohol instead. 'Well,' thought William Henry, 'that's me scuppered on all counts!' It seemed his petition and memorials went no further than the Chairman, which was a pity, as he felt he might have stood a better chance of clemency from the Protestant Earl of Aberdeen, Sir John Campbell Hamilton Gordon, to whom all petitions were routinely addressed. 'Ach well,' he sighed, 'there's always next year.'

It was with relief that, during the following year, William Henry read in the prison library's newspapers that *Titanic*'s sister ship, *Olympic*, and also *Britannic*, a third ship built on this grand scale, had been modified in line with the recommendations of the Board of Trade's enquiry and had been fitted with lifeboats sufficient to accommodate all passengers. He noted that the new ship also had motor powered davits to facilitate faster launching of those lifeboats. The designer who had taken over from the late Thomas Andrews had devised numerous additional modifications to increase passenger safety. Luxury continued to be a priority however and further passenger facilities, such as hairdressing salons and even dog kennels were planned for *Britannic*. William Henry wondered if it had occurred to his hairdresser son Billy to seek employment on board. He thought this would not have been Billy's cup of tea, however. He wondered why some Belfast hairdressers' establishments and public houses were termed *saloons*, whereas those hairdressers and tea rooms frequented by the rich were termed *salons*. Whatever the reason, Billy would not have enjoyed the same *craic* with the wealthy liner passengers in their high class *salon*, though perhaps the tips might have been better than those in his own *saloon*. William Henry pictured Billy now, back in his barber's shop, for he had recently bought his own establishment in the Ormeau Road. Billy would be enjoying the gossip with all the shipwrights who placed their heads, and their thoughts, in his hands. In fact, it was also through Billy's regular letters that he heard and savoured snippets of news about developments in the yards.

As things turned out, no sooner were all the luxury installations designed and ordered for *Britannic* than they were immediately cancelled, for the latest *White Star* liner would now have a vey different role to play. The bright and balmy summer days of nineteen fourteen were suddenly darkened by the frightening prospect of war. William Henry had been following closely accounts of the tense diplomatic exchanges which had seen the super powers of Europe squaring up to each other and siding with smaller states, according to incomprehensible treaties, and he had seen those exchanges fail. He had also been enjoying Erskine Childers' prescient thriller *The Riddle of The Sands*, in which two British men, on a yachting holiday around the coast of the Frisian islands, uncover a German plot to invade Britain.

Fictional though the story was, the British government had taken its predictions seriously, and many thought that this was why new British naval bases had been established in the northern ports of Rosyth, Invergordon and Scapa Flow. Hitherto, British naval forces had been located in south coast ports, facing the French – the traditional enemy. Now however they had been re-located to face the new threat from Germany. It was no secret that Germany had been building up both her army and her navy and there seemed only one plausible explanation for that.

William Henry had wanted to read Childers' book, ever since he had read of the arrest for spying of two British men in Germany. They had been tried in Germany in 1910, whilst he was awaiting his own trial in Belfast. He wondered whether that incident had been the inspiration for the story, and he had been delighted to find a copy of the book in the prison library. The message of the novel was a warning about Britain's unpreparedness for a possible war with the developing German empire, and, eerily enough, Childers had been right.

In view of the declaration of war, William Henry decided that an appropriate theme for his petition this year would be an appeal to the Prisons Board to allow him to do his bit for King and Country in helping to build the ships necessary to win the war. However, his timing was not good, and *The MacDermot* was not impressed by his latest plea. The law would continue, he wrote with irritating predictability, to take its course. Back at the Queen's Island, *Britannia* remained unfinished in her slips for the time being, as Harland and Wolff found their usual raw materials being channelled into urgent war production elsewhere. Johnnie Beasant wrote to William Henry of his concerns at the possibility of there being no ships for the men to build, as all commercial shipping contracts had been cancelled. Men were in fact being laid off and the yards were at standstill. William Henry now thought he had misjudged his nation's need for the services of skilled shipbuilders. Having reached a similar conclusion themselves, some six thousand of the men at Harland and Wolff had exchanged their working clothes for uniform and had enlisted in the Ulster Division. The majority of them had joined the battalions of the 107th Brigade and were undergoing scant training before being despatched to fight in the war. Muscles which had swung hammers would now be put to digging trenches. Hands which had pounded six inch rivets into steel plate would soon be pumping nine inch shells into German defences.

Of greater and more immediate concern to William Henry, was the threat that German submarines now posed to the British Grand Fleet at its base at Scapa Flow in the Orkney Islands. When he had last heard from him, his own sailor son was at Scapa Flow and, alarmingly, sightings of German U boats in the North Sea were being reported daily. He was therefore pleased and relieved to receive a letter from Jimmy. The letter was postmarked County Donegal, which puzzled William Henry at first, until he reasoned that the British fleet must now be safely positioned in the virtually impregnable Lough Swilly. The letter mentioned nothing of Jimmy's whereabouts, since that sort of talk would have been censored by the authorities. Its contents were not entirely pleasing however.

Jimmy advised of further promotion since his last letter and he announced that, the previous September, he had married Mary Rowney, a girl from Carrickfergus, whose father was a retired sea captain who now ran his own fuel business in the little seaside town. This news pleased William Henry of course, but, on reading further, he was dismayed to learn that Jimmy had told his new bride's family that his own father was dead. Jimmy said he hoped William Henry would understand this and the fact that it was therefore unlikely his father and his wife would ever meet. In his exchanges with Belle later that evening, William Henry expressed his hurt and disappointment that Jimmy's shame would lead him to deny his own father's very existence.

121

"Ach, think about it, Wim Henery," she commiserated, "sure tha gerl's family is respectable, and they wouldn't want her marrying a murderer's son, now, would they? Ye wouldn't want your mistakes to spoil yer boy's chance of happiness, would ye?"

William Henry grudgingly agreed that he understood Jimmy's reasons, but at the same time he realised he might one day have more grandchildren whom he would never meet. Would future generations of the Kelly family disown him? Would he never be spoken of to his grandchildren, not even as a warning against the perils of insobriety? It was one thing for a deceased ancestor to be forgotten with the passage of time, but for a family to actively conceal their black sheep was something else. He now realised that his punishment would extend far beyond the twelve years of his sentence.

The autumn saw a bitter campaign being fought in the Dardanelles. The *Olympic* was now pressed into service as a troopship, conveying the fighting men from Liverpool to the eastern Mediterranean. This brought some conversion work to the men who remained at Harland and Wolff, safeguarding their jobs for the time being at least. The *Britannic,* still sitting in her slips, was now being fitted out as a hospital ship to serve the huge numbers of casualties of that particularly brutal theatre of war and to convey them home. William Henry's sources had told him of the new facilities on board, with operating theatres, hospital wards and accommodation for doctors and nurses now constructed on those decks formerly earmarked for dog kennels, hair *salons* and restaurants.

According to shipyard talk, *Britannic* was better equipped than any city hospital. William Henry was therefore devastated to read reports that, on the nineteenth of November, on her third rescue mission to Gallipoli, *Britannic* had struck an enemy mine and the captain's attempts to beach her on one of the Greek islands failed. She had taken on water rapidly and sank in less than an hour. Over a thousand of the crew and medics on board were saved, some escaping in lifeboats whilst others were rescued by Greek fisherman. Thirty died however, mainly because they had abandoned ship before the order had been given and had been sucked into the ship's still struggling propellers. This was tragic, but William Henry realised that it could have been much worse. Had *Britannic* been on her return journey, laden to her full capacity with casualties, this might have proved a disaster far worse than that of her sister ship *Titanic.* It still worried him however that *Olympic* had sunk in less than half the time it had taken for *Titanic* to do so.

Belle's view of these developments reflected her continued distrust of Belfast's Titans, which had been originally nicknamed by some *The Three Graces.* Following the demise of *Titanic* and *Britannic,* Belle now dubbed them *The Disgraces.* William Henry did not like it when she spoke irreverently of Harland and Wolff's ships, but he had ceased to argue with her, for it seemed even ghosts could be offended, and he hated it when she took umbrage and disappeared before their conversation was exhausted. These days, he did not derive the same satisfaction from his chats with the Governor, mainly because he could not hear him so well, and the Governor's patience would run out with having to repeat himself. Ever kindly however, Barrows had tasked William Henry with collecting for his attention news articles about the progress of the war, which articles were pasted into a scrapbook in the library. The Governor did not come around to see him quite so often now and, when he did, it was mostly to peruse the scrapbook. The other library orderly, Whelan, was friendly enough but had little conversation himself, so William Henry depended more than ever now on his evening chats with Belle.

Strangely, he had no difficulty in hearing Belle's voice. It was as though she were inside his head, which indeed, he supposed, she were. He wondered if she had a better view of the war from the afterlife than his own confinement afforded him, and so he dared to ask her whether she knew if their Jimmy were safe. However, Belle would say only that no news was good news. There was indeed little news in the press of what the navy was up to. William Henry supposed this must be because, so far, there had been no naval engagements. This situation was about to change however, and soon, he was reading thrilling reports of a British victory at the Battle of the Falkland Islands and of how *HMS Kent* had routed and sunk the *Nurnberg* after a long and exciting chase, during which the stokers had hammered the engines beyond their expected capability. The last letter William Henry had received from Jimmy had been sent from *HMS Kent*. He could not resist adding a handwritten annotation alongside the press cuttings of the battle in the library scrapbook, to the effect that his own son, Stoker First Class James Hodges Kelly, had been a crew member on the *Kent*. The Governor noted this addition with interest, but wondered whether this were true or simply a flight of fancy on William Henry's part. After all, the prisoner had seemed to be less communicative and was becoming a little odd of late. Moreover, Warder O'Farrell had reported regularly hearing Kelly talking to himself in his cell after lights out.

The early months of nineteen fifteen saw William Henry's health beset by a succession of complaints. The cold winter nights prevented him from sleeping and Doctor Kinsella recommended he be given an extra blanket. William Henry then developed an ear infection which was alleviated by syringing and actually left him able to hear a little better than before. However the joy of this improvement was tempered by the return of the boils on his back, probably brought on by the withdrawal from his diet of the forbidden fruits from the Governor's garden. To cap it all, a bout of influenza, combined with a chest infection, had laid him low and brought him to the prison infirmary once more. Thomas - with an 'h' - was pleased to see him back and fussed over him once more, despite the fact that he had nine other influenza patients to tend.

"Ah, is it yerself, back again?" he asked, seemingly delighted, "an' what ailment is it that's brought yew back in heeyer?"

William could hardly speak through the effects of the bronchitis which now gripped him worse than ever it had in the shipyard winters. He managed a feeble smile for Thomas however.

"Is that yew wheezin' or is it tha wind houlin' outside?" Thomas asked as he poured out some of the lemon-flavoured mixture the Medical Officer had provided, "well never mind, for amen't I heeyer to look after ye?"

William Henry found the man's lyrical cadence most pleasant and reassuring. It would be three days however before he found himself able to speak to the wardsman. He had slept for much of that time, waking only for his medicine or for the few spoonfuls of gruel or soup he could manage. Little by little however, the

123

infection began to leave him and his strength gradually returned. One morning, the squeak of unlubricated wheels and the clatter of a tin trolley announced Whelan's arrival with some books for the patients and William Henry managed to raise himself to a sitting position in the bed. As Whelan handed him two Rider Haggard novels and a newspaper, William Henry felt a round, hard shape beneath them. He slipped the apple under his pillow and nodded his gratitude at Whelan. He wondered by what circuitous route the Governor's stored apple had come to him, but he was glad of it and of several others which came his way over the next week.

"I thought I was a goner there, so I did," he told Belle as she came that evening and sat down noiselessly by his hospital bed.

"It's not your time yet, Wim Henery," she said, "don't be impatient for death now, it'll come to ye some day when yer not expectin' it – like it did to me."

Ignoring his sheepish look, she ran her scarred hands over the bedding, "but will ye look at them gorgeous soft sheets. Sure them's whiter than anything I ever had roun' me?"

The two chatted until William Henry succumbed to sleep. From Thomas's point of view in his small bedroom at the end of the ward however, his charge appeared to be talking to himself. He reported his observations to Doctor Kinsella one morning during the physician's daily round of the hospital.

"I think he's mebbe disturbed," Thomas ventured his opinion, "for I see this typa thing often wid da long termers. It's the depression, so it is."

The Medical Officer was not impressed with Thomas's unqualified view, but asked him nonetheless to keep an eye on William Henry.

Now that he was feeling better and able to sit up and eat more, William Henry began to take more notice of his surroundings. He guessed the influenza had again reached epidemic proportions, for the little hospital ward was fast filling up with new sufferers and another convict had been drafted in to assist Thomas. William Henry now noticed a man, who appeared vaguely familiar, lying in the bed opposite him. The man's name, O'Byrne, chalked up on the board above his bed, meant nothing to William Henry, but, after a few moments racking his brain, he remembered him as the convict who had killed one of the others in the sewing shop incident. William Henry had heard that the man was now serving an additional life sentence for his crime but he was surprised to find him serving it here at Maryborough. William Henry now hoped that either he would be released from the hospital before O'Byrne was well enough to recognise him or that O'Byrne might have forgotten his role in the incident.

His optimism was to prove unfounded however for the next morning, without a word, O'Byrne leapt from his bed and rushed across to where William Henry lay. He threw his fist with some force into William Henry's face, smashing his spectacles and dragged him out of bed and onto the floor, where the suddenness and ferocity of the attack left William Henry barely able to defend himself. William Henry managed to throw a few kicks and punches at his assailant however, before curling up under his bed, and trying to protect his head. Moments later, the warders, summoned by Thomas, arrived to subdue O'Byrne and remove him, still in hospital pyjamas, back to his cell. William Henry also found himself back in prison uniform later that day and up before the Deputy Governor. Mr Shewell said he was aware that O'Byrne had instigated the incident, but it appeared William Henry had got in at least one or two retaliatory blows before the Warders had arrived on the scene, and so a caution for 'wrangling' would be entered on William Henry's prison file. He was advised that this incident might affect his remission. It was perhaps a measure of the extent to which William Henry was now institutionalised that this fact did not cause him anything like as much concern as did the loss of his spectacles and the consequent curtailment of his reading pleasure. A few days later however, he was given a replacement pair of prison spectacles and Doctor Kinsella assured him that O'Byrne was on his way to *The Joy*, as Dublin's Mountjoy Prison was familiarly, if inappropriately termed.

Johnnie Beasant's latest letter advised that Harland and Wolff were now fully productive again, turning out both war ships and also cargo ships to replace the huge numbers which were being lost to enemy submarines. Feeling more hopeful following this piece of good news, William Henry was also overjoyed to read that a second petition had been raised in Belfast, requesting his release. Johnnie said that, this time, no fewer than four hundred and thirty one men had signed the petition. This greatly surprised William Henry, for he knew that many of his former colleagues were away fighting the war and he had thought that those who remained might by now have forgotten him. The news gladdened his dulled heart for the time being.

Thus encouraged, he decided now might be a good time to submit his annual memorial to the Vice Chairman of the Prisons Board, adding weight to the petition from Belfast. He maintained the theme of his skills being needed now more than ever for the war effort. He really felt optimistic this time. As always however, his optimism was short-lived. When called to the school room a month later to receive the verdict, he saw *The MacDermot*'s stern handwriting once again determining that the law must take its course. Once again however he derived some comfort from perusing the names of those who had signed his petition. Naturally, Johnnie had signed it, as had Johnnie's brother Hugh Beasant, plus Hughie Hewitt and his brother David Hewitt. He saw the signature of the local Congregationalist Minister, William Davey, and he noted the occupations of the signatories, mostly shipyard workers, skilled and unskilled. He saw the hand of his own nephew, Tommy Patterson, who, he noted, was now employed as a baker. His own close family members did not sign the petitions, but he realised this was because their signatures would not count. There were many names there that he recognised, but equally, many names he had hoped to see were missing, presumably because they were away fighting. The conclusions he drew from the signatures in the petition were as informative as half a dozen letters from home might have been.

Back in the library, he now snipped and saved for the scrap book a newspaper photograph showing the seventeen thousand men of the Ulster Division parading through the streets of Belfast on the eighth of May, cheered on by many more thousands of their family and friends who had come, in tramloads and trainloads, to see them off to the battlefields of France. He squinted at the faces in the photograph, but they were too small to recognise. Also awaiting his paste brush were articles concerning a devastating incident which had occurred only the day before the parade. The Cunard liner *Lusitania* had been torpedoed by a German U-boat off the *Old Head of Kinsale*, sinking in just eighteen minutes, with the loss of almost two thousand passengers and crew. He imagined the shock waves from this incident had cast a pall over the departure of the Belfast troops but perhaps it had also made them more determined than ever to beat *The Hun*.

The *Lusitania,* built at John Brown's Clydeside yard, had not been as big as the Belfast-built White Star Liners but had successfully and safely completed over two hundred transatlantic voyages since her launch in 1907, according to press reports. William Henry was saddened to read the news of her demise, and stunned that it had taken only eighteen minutes for this disaster to occur, yet he hoped that this latest shipping disaster might push the *Titanic* disaster to the back of people's minds. Perhaps *Titanic* would, like William Henry, be forgotten in time. Press reporting on the *Lusitania* had even eclipsed the accounts of the fighting in France and Flanders. The continuing detail of casualties from the Battle of Ypres was now relegated from the front to the back pages. William Henry guessed this was because a number of wealthy and prominent American citizens had perished in this latest attack on a civilian vessel. It hurt him to think that their deaths deserved greater prominence than those of the brave sons of ordinary folk. He followed the American reaction to the sinking in great detail however. Belle's prediction that this would bring America into the war did not seem to be coming to fruition however, for President Woodrow Wilson remained reluctant to become Britain's ally. This did not sit well with the British public. Gossip from the front suggested that shells which failed to explode were now being referred to contemptuously as *Wilsons*.

All seemed quiet again on the navy front and this led William Henry to hope that Jimmy might yet make it through the war unharmed. The prospect eased his mind, as he now entered his sixth year of incarceration. Belle now reminded him that he had almost half his sentence served already, but this fact did not console him greatly, as he did not think he would make it through another six years. She admonished him for his self pity. A letter from Billy now announced his own re-marriage and the news that Jimmy's wife Mary had given birth to a baby boy over Christmas. The couple had decided to ignore Irish tradition and would not name him William Henry after his paternal grandfather but he would instead be called James, after his own father and great grandfather. It seemed the Kelly family tradition of giving each James the middle name Hodges had also been abandoned. William Henry supposed this was to further reduce the links between the infant and his gaolbird of a grandfather. William Henry now found himself becoming depressed by his nocturnal discussions with Belle, mainly because there seemed to be no truly cheerful news to discuss. The carnage that was taking place over in Europe, and the absence of any prospect of his release before 1922, seemed to be their sole topics of conversation. Warder O'Farrell, on his silent nightly patrolling of the landings - silent because the warders were now under Governor's instructions to wear felt overshoes so as not to awaken the prisoners – regularly stopped outside William Henry's cell. Disturbed to hear him talking to himself and weeping, O'Farrell made a report to the Medical officer. William Henry did not realise it, but he was now officially deemed to be 'under mental observation'.

Doctor Kinsella now visited William Henry in his cell three times a week and asked him how things were going. If William Henry noticed that the MO had softened his normally brisk and business-like manner, he overlooked it in his eagerness to have someone new to talk to. He found himself telling the doctor of his concerns for his son Jimmy, who was away facing the enemy at sea and had not written in some months. He told the doctor of the support he had received from his friends and comrades in Belfast, about the petitions and his hopes of returning to useful employment there. He added however that it had now been some six months since he had received any letters from Belfast, and he said he feared his family and friends might now have turned their backs on him. The doctor asked him why he thought that should be. He considered this question for a moment or two. Able nowadays only to look back and not forward, William Henry saw once more the concerned faces of his family, looking down at him from the gallery of the court at his trial. He remembered how he had felt upon seeing them - the mixed emotions of shame, self pity and gratitude, and the idea that he did not deserve their support. Another less appealing face from the trial now came to his mind. He recalled Robinson, lying about him in the witness box, then, having been exposed as a liar, skulking away in his own shame. William Henry wondered if Robinson had continued to repeat his lies. Supposing he had convinced others that William Henry's crime had been premeditated? He shared his thoughts with the Medical Officer, who did not seek to reassure him his fears were irrational, but simply took notes.

As nineteen sixteen dawned and news arrived of more heavy fighting on land, but still no engagements at sea, William Henry's scrapbook grew to a fourth volume. However it was the political rather than military events of the Easter of that year which now preoccupied him. He followed news reports of the events with incredulity, as Irish nationalist volunteers, led by school teacher and barrister, Padraig Pearse, joined forces with the Irish Citizen's Army, led by James Connolly to attack various locations in and around the city of Dublin. British troops had turned out to confront the volunteers and a major stand-off at the city's general post office had developed into a full-scale insurgency. Fighting next broke out in other cities around the southern counties and for a while it looked as though an Independent but Catholic state - long feared by Irish Protestants - might be about to appear. William Henry read all the press reports he could find about the developments. Nothing in this *uprising*, as the Irish press called it, or *rebellion* according to the British press, seemed clear cut.

Although the press photographs showed Dublin's Sackville Street in a state of almost total destruction, just seven days later it was reported that the siege had collapsed. Reports suggested it did not have the full support of the people. Moreover, Dublin's citizenry had taken to the streets and had prevented the volunteers from seizing Jacobs' biscuit factory in the south of the city. In this and other locations, ordinary Dubliners had been clubbed and even shot by the volunteers. The situation was a bewildering one. Indeed, once the insurgents had been arrested and marched out of the various occupied buildings, British troops had had to protect them from attacks by the locals who were angrily swarming in the streets. William Henry shook his head, as he discussed the situation with Whelan. They agreed this was nothing like the rebellion of seventeen ninety eight. During the subsequent trials, held throughout May, some ninety people were sentenced to death.

Whelan was especially dismayed to read of the subsequent court martial and execution of the ringleaders, one of whom, O'Connell, had been wounded in the fighting and could not walk, so he was tied to a chair to be shot. Despite his own vision of what the uprising might have meant for him and his kind, had it been successful, even William Henry had to admit this was shocking.

The Irish Republic, free of British involvement, whose birth the rebels had triumphantly announced, had quickly fizzled out, leaving the bitter taste of wasted human sacrifice, but also perhaps introducing the idea of physical force Republicanism. As June commenced however, William Henry's attention was fully diverted by emerging reports of a major sea battle off the coast of Denmark, involving almost every vessel in the Royal Navy's Grand Fleet. The largest navies the world had ever seen assembled together in one theatre of war had confronted each other face to face in a twenty-four hour engagement – the first such major naval engagement of the war so far. The battle had however left thousands of sailors dead. The first reports, which had in fact been reproduced from the German press releases, described the battle as an overwhelming German victory. What baffled William Henry was the fact that, although for the past decade, both nations had been building up their naval strength, in an atmosphere of tension and distrust, yet no major sea battles had taken place until now, two years into the war.

The British public, horrified at the stories of carnage in the Dardanelles and on the Western Front, had long been asking when the navy was going to play its part. The press had regularly voiced the nation's disquiet. Several isolated skirmishes at sea involving surface vessels had mostly been successful for the British but, for the past two years, German submarines had been picking off British battleships and destroying merchant vessels, virtually unchallenged. The British fleet being greatly superior in size to that of the enemy, the Germans had avoided all out confrontation, preferring instead to deploy hit and run attacks by their wolf packs of submarines. On the thirty first of May though, the Germans had ventured out to try to attack what they believed was simply a part of the British Fleet. Through interception of German signals however, the attack had been expected, and Admiral Jellicoe had manoeuvred the entire might of the British navy face to face with the enemy. It was as if all the fury and aggression had been saved up for one major battle, and now all hell had been let loose.

At last, the British Grand Fleet had confronted its counterpart, the German High Seas Fleet, in the fiercest battle ever waged at sea, but seemed to have suffered a major defeat. Confusingly, although the British Admiralty's statements appeared initially to concur with the German claims of victory, it later transpired the Admiralty had been somewhat hasty in their acceptance of defeat. Some days later, the Admiralty appeared to have a change of heart and, in an astonishing volte face, now declared the engagement a British victory. The press now reported that, although the British Grand Fleet had lost fourteen of its ships and six thousand and ninety four men, in contrast to the smaller German losses of eleven ships and two thousand five hundred and fifty one dead, and whilst, numerically, this might have appeared a defeat for the British, strategically speaking, it was a win. The German intention had been to thwart the British blockade of its North Sea ports and re-open the waters to German shipping, and in this aim they had failed. They had retreated to port and were to remain there for the time being.

Each day, his rounds of the prison with Whelan and the book trolley completed, William Henry settled down to his task of cutting out the reports of the *Battle of Jutland*, as the engagement was now being called, and he pasted them carefully into the scrapbook. Reading between the lines of thrilling reporting on the glorious manoeuvres of magnificent ships and the heroic actions of individual seamen however, William Henry could see only horror. He imagined the thunderous noise of the continuous shell bombardment, the alarm of the sailors whose ship is hit and lurches violently, sideways at first and then slowly downwards into the darkening sea. He pictured those brave men, trapped behind watertight bulkheads and beneath airtight hatches, slowly suffocating or drowning. He felt their desperate panic rising in the pitch darkness of the holds, with the knowledge that death was certain. He tried to imagine what six thousand dying seamen looked like. Six thousand - the same number as those brave men who had set off to war from Harland and Wolff. He pictured them, men and boys, lost in the deep, leaving behind them an irreplaceable void, both in the nation's workforce and in the hearts of their families.

The worst deaths, he reasoned, would have occurred in the engine rooms - men gone to their deaths with no notion of the extent of their heroic sacrifice, men choking in the bulkhead compartments - compartments which caulkers like himself had sealed to keep the sea out but which now trapped the men in. Men were dying in their riveted steel sea coffins, men like his son, Stoker First Class, his own wee Jimmy. Men were dying in the cold North Sea whilst those educated dandies up at the Admiralty were dithering in their conclusions as to whether their deaths represented victory or defeat. William Henry laid his head upon the scrapbook in an exhausted stupor. As the library clock ticked the afternoon away, and in the absence of strong liquor to drown his despair, he wept silent tears of frustration.

Back in the infirmary once more, William Henry was told by Thomas that he had had 'some sorta breakdown' but that he would be all right soon with a bit of special care from his pal Thomas. It seemed Doctor Kinsella had been in twice to see him over the previous few days, but William Henry had no recollection of his presence. Perhaps because of self-induced shock, William Henry's hearing had again deteriorated. He had no trouble falling asleep in the hospital bed, but his nightmares soon awoke him. He kept one eye on the two other convicts whose beds were side by side at the opposite end of the ward, lest one of them should attack him, as O'Byrne had. He had no cause to fear the two, who were older and feebler than himself, but still he felt uneasy. They both chatted together and he knew they were talking about him. It did not matter that they smiled in his direction from time to time, for he could see beyond their smiles. They gossiped about him, in the same way the warders did.

Even the kindly O'Farrell had turned against him. He had seen O'Farrell speaking with the Medical Officer and both of them had glanced at him. They had clearly been discussing him. Even Thomas's well-meant and humorous chat now began to irritate him, for he realised it was superficial. They were all conspiring together, plotting against him. Even Belle had not been to see him during his recent stay in the infirmary. He was alone. He felt vulnerable here in the hospital. He knew he must cultivate the appearance of being well and get back to his cell again and engage himself in his work.

Nineteen seventeen brought better news in both press reports and in correspondence from Johnnie Beasant. In February, Germany's announcement of its intention to resume unrestricted submarine warfare, with the inevitable threat to passenger ships, brought America into the war at long last. William Henry's fears for Jimmy proved unfounded. Jimmy had participated in, but survived the carnage of *Jutland*. Jimmy's latest letter included a photograph of his son, who was named just James. William Henry was pretty sure that *just James* resembled his convict grandfather, a thought which caused him some ironic amusement. Jimmy had indeed survived the terrible battle which had claimed the lives of more than six thousand of his fellow sailors and had subsequently been allowed a brief period of leave to spend with his small family in Carrickfergus. William Henry was touched that Jimmy had taken a moment or two out of that leave to write to him. His belief that people were discussing him behind his back was not entirely paranoid, albeit that his interpretation of their motives was incorrect. Doctor Kinsella now penned his report for the Governor to approve:

"I have the honour to report that William Kelly's mental obliquity is of the undemonstrable kind, and apparent only to those in close contact with him or after a long conversation. Kelly believes people speak badly of him and thinks when people are talking that it is of him, and when his friends did not write to him he thought someone corresponded with them and prejudiced them against him. He is somewhat morose and would not agree with others, but works well alone. However, today, the Convict appears much better, consequent, I believe, on getting a letter, or letters, from his friends, which has made him comparatively cheerful and hopeful. Kelly's bodily health is quite good enough, although he has lost about nine lbs since he came to penal servitude."

The Governor, Mr Barrows, appended his own note to send with the medical report to the Chief Secretary of the General Prisons Board:

"The convict urges in his memorials that he is old and in ill-health and that his daughter and son are willing to look after him if released. Health – fair, but his mental state has on occasion been under consideration. The Medical Officer fears the convict will not improve in prison, - he thinks people speak badly of him – still he is quiet. His general health, eyesight etc, causes no anxiety. Conduct in prison – good."

Back in the library once more, William Henry now gleaned from the press that the tonnage of British merchant shipping lost was greater than ever, as a result of the attacks by German U-boats. Britain's total losses to date stood at more than five hundred and fifty-six tonnes and very little commercial shipping was being built to replace the lost vessels which brought essential food supplies to Britain. Moreover, critics of the Government now claimed that food stocks were fast running out, and

130

that, if Britain lost the war, it would be through starvation, brought about by the indecision and incompetence of government. A Ministry of Shipping had been established the previous December and this body now responded to the criticism by a kicking off a scheme to create a vast fleet of merchant ships, to be built to a standard design and whose parts would therefore be interchangeable, for speed of construction and ease of repair. Johnnie's latest missive advised that Harland and Wolff had orders to build seven of these, as well as orders for replacement war ships to compensate for the losses at Jutland, and the Queen's Island slips were now being cleared to give the new ships priority. The new Ministry had directed all shipyards to increase productivity by fifty percent and had promised machinery and materials would be made available to facilitate this.

The Belfast press now announced that Lord Pirrie had finally managed to purchase shipyards on the Clyde and was also seeking to acquire the steel company which normally supplied Harland and Wolff with its steel plates. The first of the standard merchant ships, *War Shamrock*, was already under construction, as was a naval light cruiser, *HMS Glorious*. Johnnie said that one of the main stumbling blocks to the proposed increase in output was the lack of skilled shipwrights. He was also engaged in yet another round of demarcation disputes with the management who wanted to use unskilled labour to replace those shipwrights who were away fighting the war. None of the shipwrights wished to go on strike whilst the nation was at war, but Johnnie feared that the war situation had given Pirrie the excuse he had long sought to replace skilled labour with unskilled, thereby reducing his costs, increasing his profits and fending off the competition. However, the prospect of the gallant six thousand returning home from war, only to face unemployment, was unthinkable.

Negotiations had just begun however, so Johnnie was fairly optimistic that good sense might yet prevail and that the use of unskilled labour to do skilled men's jobs would be a purely temporary measure. Johnnie was also optimistic that any representations made now on William Henry's behalf might stand the best chance yet of success. He said he did not think another petition from Belfast was worth undertaking, since there were now two such petitions already on file, but he said he would approach someone higher up in the Harland and Wolff management for a written request. He urged William Henry to compose yet another memorial.

"Let's attack them with the classic pincer movement and hit them on both flanks!" he wrote.

Before William Henry could put scratchy pen to official notepaper however, he was advised by the Governor that the Chairman of the Prison Board would be visiting Maryborough in person on Saturday the twenty-sixth of May and was prepared to hold brief interviews with some of the prisoners. Clearly, the important man's time was limited and he would see only a chosen few, as recommended by the Governor. Mr Barrows offered to put William Henry's name forward to see the great man. Although William Henry's first thoughts had been of placing his caulker's iron fist in *The Macdermott*'s pasty privileged face, he immediately checked his uncharitable response and realised that this would in fact be a rare chance. The Chairman might be more inclined to accept his plea for early release if he met him face to face and could see how harmless he was. William Henry

131

gratefully accepted the Governor's gracious offer and headed back to the library to check out his illustrious visitor in the current edition of the *Catholic Who's Who.*

The fifty-five year old Charles Edward MacDermott – *the* MacDermot, Prince of Coolavin, descendant of the Kings of Moylurg and His Majesty's Inspector of Prisons - appeared to William Henry to be every inch the gentleman one would expect of such a prominent Connaught family. Taking in the well groomed appearance and the soft, white hands, the convict was unsure at first what sort of demeanour to adopt in front of this aristocrat. One of the white hands held in its delicate grip a broad-nibbed fountain pen. This would be the very instrument which had so often dashed his hopes, the instrument which had determined which course the law must take in William Henry's case. He observed that it was tortoise-shell and the nib appeared to be of solid gold.

"Convict D995, William Henry Kelly," the Chairman spoke, in an equally well-groomed accent, not an Irish accent at all, "the Governor tells me you are an intelligent man, quite the intellectual, in fact."

William Henry felt that most men in authority seemed to have a most annoying habit of making a question sound like a statement and a statement sound like a question, perhaps with the intention of tricking him into speaking out of turn, when his own comparatively lowly status dictated he ought to remain quiet. Therefore he simply nodded.

The Chairman continued, "I see there are a number of petitions and letters on file, including one from the management at Harland and Wolff, where you served your time as a skilled shipwright. One of your foremen has also spoken up for you - a Mr. B'sant?"

William Henry found himself further irritated by the Chairman's swallowing the first syllable and placing undue stress on the final syllable of Johnnie's surname, as *B'sant.* This further persuaded him that MacDermot was not in touch with the common Belfast man. Johnnie Beasant was descended from Huguenots, many of whom had chosen Ulster as a place of refuge from French Catholic persecution. Ulster had adopted them as her own sons. Names like *Beasant, de Crommelin* and *D'Aubin* had been common in Antrim but were nowadays pronounced and written the local way – *de Crommelin* had become *Crumlin, d'Aubin* was now *Dobbin* and Johnnie pronounced his own surname to rhyme with *pheasant.* Of course this Connaught gentleman was unlikely to know that. William Henry resolved however to try to put aside his irritation on this occasion, as his quick temper and sharp tongue had not served him well in the past. He thought it appropriate now to speak however.

"Yes sir. My employers is willin' to have me back at my trade and in fact they need my skills more urgently than ever right now, for the amount of ships as are bein' lost in the war needs to be replaced and quickly ... sir."

William Henry advised the great man that he had built the White Star Line ships, and he reeled off the impressive list of names. He said he was aware that some six thousand of his former colleagues were away fighting, and so there were few skilled men left to turn out the ships which would win the war for Britain. The Chairman seemed to accept this point, but he turned next to William Henry's crime.

"I understand you are here because you killed your wife?"

132

The inflection in his voice let William Henry know this definitely was a question. He recalled from his research that McDermot's wife was a daughter of the aristocrat who occupied Belleek Castle. He guessed McDermot never had to rely on *his* wife to riddle the ashes, light the fire and make the supper. He would have a servant to chastise if these tasks were not done when he came home after a long day's fishing or shooting. He noticed the temperance badge in the Chairman's lapel.

"I had too much drink taken, sir, and so had my wife. The judge and jury thought it was not in my normal character to do such a thing and so the charge of murder was dropped to one of manslaughter. I can assure you, sir that no drop of drink will ever again pass my lips," he vowed, hoping he had struck the right chord.

"If I had a penny for every time I heard that from some miserable wretch's mouth, why I'd be as rich as Croesus!" the Chairman exclaimed sarcastically.

William Henry had never heard of this Croesus, but doubtless he was another Connaught gentleman who had never had to stuff newspaper into his boots to keep the rain out. William Henry saw no point in trying to explain what pressures drove common men to drink.

"I loved my wife above all things," he said, calmly, "and though I can never set things right, it is my earnest intention, if released, to do my bit for the Empire and to prove myself a worthy citizen of Belfast. You have my word on that, sir."

A faint snort of disbelief escaped the Chairman's nose, and he glanced down to peruse William Henry's file further. After a few moments, during which William Henry fully expected him to declare "the law must take its course", the Chairman sat back and looked long and hard at him. As the two men gazed at each other, William Henry felt just a tiny flicker of hope for just a tiny fraction of a second.

"You have served almost seven years of your twelve year sentence," the Chairman said, as though William Henry were unaware of the fact, "well, you know, I am a firm believer that every herring must hang by his own tail. You made your bed, now you must lie on it."

William Henry's fragile hopes now lay dashed on the rocks of the Chairman's sarcasm. He was still harbouring a barely suppressed urge to take a defiant swipe at him, when the Chairman spoke again.

"Why don't you submit another memorial, reminding me of your skills and long service and perhaps I will take another look at your appeal," he said, closing the file and taking out his gold pocket watch to indicate the interview was at an end.

When next William Henry trundled the library trolley along to the infirmary, Thomas gave him a hand dispensing the books. Out of the warder's hearing, Thomas said he had heard William Henry had been up to see the Chairman of the Prisons Board and he was eager to know how he had got on. William Henry told him what the Chairman had said, including his comment about every herring having to hang by its tail. Thomas was aghast.

"What?" he gasped shrilly, "Well the feckin' arsehole! Herring is it, and him wid a face like an oul kipper hisself! I dunno abewt herrings hangin' be the tails, but I'd hang that oul fecker by his neck, so I wud!"

His hysterical tone softened slightly as he patted William Henry on the arm, "Ah, yiz are not too despondent I hope? I don't want to see yew back in here like tha last toim, and you so sick then yew cuddn't walk tha length o' yerself! Don't yew be worryin' about him now. Don't trouble yerself over the likes o' themmins."

The offence of the incident took hold of Thomas again immediately however and he lashed out once again, "Jayzus, an' isn't that the arsacrockery for ya, inbreeds everyone of 'em. Sure, I wuddn't give tuppence for tha lot of 'em, so I wuddn't. Hangin's tew gud for the loikes a them, so it is!"

Thomas realised his diatribe had reached the ears of the warder. In softer tones now, he whispered "Yew look after yerself William Henry now, good man."

Somehow, Thomas's outrage at the Chairman's lofty attitude served to defuse William Henry's own anger. He really liked the medical orderly, who might well be, as William Henry would term him, a little bit of a *Mary-Anne*, but he was a lovely man nevertheless. Even when William Henry had been helpless in Thomas's care, there had never been any funny business, nothing improper. Thomas was a genuinely kind and caring man. He and young Diarmud had certainly knocked some of William Henry's prejudices into a cocked hat. It occurred to William Henry that the inmates of Maryborough, who were exclusively long-term convicts and lifers, were, for the most part, not too bad a bunch of men. Moreover, he never failed to be surprised either at the kindness shown to him by the Governor, an ex military man, of whom he would have expected a harsher and more disciplined approach. In the six years and ten months he had been in Maryborough, he had, if he were honest, been treated decently. He thought back over his time and the men he had worked with in the sewing shop and in the garden and now in the library. He had met some good men and had learned new skills. If he had to remain here for another five years, then perhaps he might bear it after all.

He now acknowledged he had reached a bit of a low ebb a while back. He had been depressed, but he had been right in believing people had been talking about him. He had heard the MO refer to him as 'delusional'. Well maybe he had been so. He now realised however that it was important not to let the Chairman's response to his appeal get him down. He needed to be clear-sighted on his situation. He knew how lucky he was to have good friends on the outside, but he now realised he also had friends on the inside. He now decided that Thomas and Whelan, who had been so kind to him, were each as decent a friend as a man could wish for, and Warder O'Farrell and the Governor had been kinder to him than he deserved. Maybe he wasn't such a bad fellow himself in fact. After all, over four hundred Belfast citizens had vouched for him. He now felt a great deal more positive both about himself and his ability to cope with his situation. He would not let prison life grind him down but would roll with the punches and would make the best of things.

Coming to terms with his situation certainly enabled him to sleep soundly at nights, apart, that was, from the early hours of Thursday the seventh of June. A loud yet distant noise awoke him at around three in the morning. It had sounded like a major explosion. He decided he must have dreamed it however, as he was fairly certain that the rumble of guns from the Western Front could not possibly be heard in the Irish Midlands, and nor was it likely that anyone was blowing anything up this quiet rural backwater. He had willed himself to quickly fall asleep again, as he had to awake refreshed just a few hours later and be ready to draft yet his latest memorial for that pasty-faced patrician, the MacDermot. After breakfast, he took himself down to the school room and sat for a little while, absorbing the sunlight which poured in through the large classroom windows. The carefree blue skies outside made him reflect upon how much his freedom had meant to him thus far and how it had taken him almost seven years to reach acceptance of his fate. He determined that, should this petition also be rejected, he would not allow himself to feel as dejected as before. It would not be the end of the world after all. He tried to focus his thoughts on what he would write. He determined this time to keep his appeal fairly short and as sweet as possible. He first wrote a covering letter for the Chairman:

> *"Honoured Sir,*
> *I beg very respectfully to inform you that, during my interview with you on last Saturday week, I asked you if you would be kind enough to use your influence to try and get my sentence mitigated. You told me that every herring must hang by its own tail. You suggested at the same time that I should write a memorial and state that I was a skilled workman. Well, Honoured Sir, knowing that obedience is better than sacrifice, I have acted according to the instructions that I got. Trusting that you will commend my case to His Excellency's consideration, after being in prison for upwards of seven years, I am, respectfully, your very humble servant, D995, William H. Kelly."*

Next, he completed the usual pro forma, addressed to the Lord Lieutenant:

> *"The petition of William Henry Kelly D995 humbly sheweth: Your Excellency, that Petitioner begs very humbly and respectfully to state that I have been in prison for upwards of seven years and, although all former petitions has not found favour in your sight, yet I continue to entertain hope. Prior to the unfortunate occurrence, of which too much strong drink was the original cause, which placed me in my present circumstances, I served my apprenticeship in Messrs Harland and Wolff's shipyard for upwards of thirty-six years. As this terrible war demands the service of every man throughout the British Empire, both skilled and unskilled, I very humbly appeal to Your Excellency once more. Trusting that you will be prompted by a generous feeling towards me, to take a merciful view of my case, and show your clemency and compassion in allowing me to become an additional unit to the rest of the skilled workmen in Harland and Wolff's yard/elsewhere, who are doing their bit for their king and country, I am your Excellency's very humble servant, D995 William H. Kelly."*

He handed in his latest submission and returned to his work in the library. This time his heart was filled with neither hope nor fear. A fresh batch of used books and out of date periodicals had been donated to the prison and he would busy himself sorting them out, setting aside any which needed repair and identifying any which would not pass the Governor's suitability criteria. Nothing on a prison escape theme, or on any other subject which might implant in the reader any thoughts of riot or revolt, was permitted. Nothing too racy was permitted either, and such publications would be relegated to the 'rejection' box, though William Henry had on occasion caught Whelan perusing some of these, when he thought he was unobserved. William Henry would not challenge him on this however. The man was

135

in for a long stretch and was young enough still to be missing the company of women. William Henry decided he was becoming more tolerant in his old age.

In the latest batch of incoming donations, he found some pamphlets and books. There was a publication entitled *Communist Manifesto*, which had been written back before William Henry was even born. There were a few more recent works also by authors he had never heard of, including Karl Marx and Frederick Engels. One, entitled *Das Kapital* had been translated from the original German. The other was entitled *Socialism: Utopian and Scientific*. The titles gave him an idea that the content would be very theoretical and dry, but he thought he might as well have a leaf through them anyway, especially as there was not much else to take his fancy in the box. There were some references in these publications to some eighteenth century French philosophers, such as Rousseau and Saint-Simon. William Henry had never heard of any of them either, though he searched for and found some of their works in the library also. As he skimmed through the volumes and the pamphlets, he felt some of the ideas expressed seemed clear and intelligible enough.

He settled down to absorb the notions of class antagonism; anarchy in production and the struggle between the proprietors and the wage-earners. He learned than not only in Belfast was there an age-old battle raging between the owners of industry and their workers but that this same war was being fought all over Europe. Conflict did not just exist between nations, but in fact there was a global war going on between the *classes* within every nation. These books questioned the whole *morality* of established principles he had always taken for granted. They suggested that every man was as good as the next, regardless of his class. They challenged the age old acceptance that wealth and resources belonged in the hands of the privileged and moreover they dared to suggest that wealth should be shared out equally. He read about the shifting ambiguity of the middle classes, or *Bourgeois*, as the author called them. He had no clue as to how that word was pronounced, or whether it was German or French or maybe Eyetalian, but the ideas expressed seemed to make perfect sense to him. Furthermore, there was talk in some of the pamphlets of a revolution by the workers of the world. He realised this was dangerous material, seditious, and not what the Governor would allow on the shelves. He would place it in the reject pile. However, he would read a little more of it first.

Over the course of the next week, the most astonishing news was appearing in the press. It seems that, at the very moment when William Henry had been enjoying the sunshine in the prison school room and scratching out his expressions of humility and respect, over in France, General Herbert Plumer's second army had launched a major offensive against the Germans at Messines Ridge. The story made thrilling reading. During the weeks before the battle, British sappers had been digging miles of tunnels beneath the enemy trenches and had laid huge quantities of explosives. These had been detonated at around three o'clock in the morning of the seventh of June and had blown the top off the Ridge itself. Amusingly, General Plumer was reported as having addressed his troops on the eve of battle with the jest that 'we may not change history tomorrow, but we shall certainly change the geography!' By a lucky fluke – lucky for the British, that is - the explosion had

136

occurred right at the changeover time, when the first watch was being relieved by the second watch, and some ten thousand German soldiers had been killed by the explosion alone. Later that day, the British had followed up the explosion with a major attack. It was reported that a further fifteen thousand Germans had succumbed to the subsequent advance attack by nine divisions of infantry, under cover of creeping artillery barrage.

The detonation of so much explosive beneath the enemy lines was hailed as a military masterstroke and it seemed the noise of this - the greatest explosion in the history of warfare - had been heard not only by Lloyd George in Downing Street but also by Government officials in Dublin. William Henry now recalled the noise which had aroused him from sleep in the early hours of the seventh of June, the day he had written his memorial. O'Farrell confirmed that he and many others had heard the same loud noise and that it must have been the destruction of the Messines Ridge that they had heard. William Henry was astonished. He scoured the press for further reports on the incident and on the subsequent fighting, which was now being termed the *Third Battle of Ypres* and was taking place around a place with the rather romantic name of *Passchendaele*. The Germans had been in possession of the Salient – an impregnable enclave in the midst of the British and French troops – ever since nineteen fourteen, so now that it had fallen to the allies, it really looked as though this might be a turning point in the course of the war. He wondered how the French would react, once peace returned to their homeland, to find that a major geographical feature of their landscape had disappeared. He knew he would be pretty angry himself to return to Belfast and find the Cave Hill gone.

Having given up hope of being released in time to contribute his services to the maritime arm of the conflict, William Henry now hoped the war would end soon. He had recently received a letter from his son Billy, and the news from Billy's shipwright clients was that, as well as building ships, Harland and Wolff were now producing aeroplanes for use in aerial reconnaissance and warfare. The men on the Queen's island had been tasked with converting one of the battleships into an aircraft carrier. Immersed in the day's newspaper reports from *The Front*, William Henry received his customary summons to the Governor's office and was almost resentful at being called away. He had lost count of how many times he had been marched up there, in eager anticipation, to view the Chairman's response, and had then emerged dispirited. Well, it no longer mattered. The sharp pen of *The MacDermot* could no longer wound him. Mr Barrows solemnly handed him two sheets of paper. He recognised the arrogant, broad ink strokes of the Chairman of The Prison's Board, in a missive dated the eighth of June nineteen seventeen:

"Lord Lieutenant: The Chairman of the Prison Board had occasion to see this man lately. He has been usefully employed in the prison library. He is an intelligent man, still well able to work and would probably find immediate employment in Harland and Wolff, but, if he serves out his full time, will be less likely to be able to support himself."

He noted the same, familiar, assertive signature of '*McDermot*' at the foot of the note, before turning over to see the next sheet. It was a pro-forma, setting out details of his application for release on license. He recognised the Governor's handwriting:

"Case of: *William H. Kelly D995*   Offence: *Manslaughter*

Sentence: *Twelve years PS from 20.7.10*   Eligible to apply for release from: *20.7.19*

Convict asks for release to take up work at his former employers, Harland & Wolff. He has been nearly seven years in prison. Conduct in prison – very good; health – good; somewhat eccentric. A quiet, intellectual man."

'Eccentric?' he thought, 'me eccentric? What about McDermot – 'the oul kipper', as Thomas had termed him, with his metaphorical herrings hanging by their tails, wasn't he the eccentric one?'

Below the Governor's comment was another entry, but in a tiny and barely legible hand. William Henry had not thought to bring his spectacles with him. He had left them on the library table. He had to ask Mr Barrows to read the rest for him. The Governor's expression gave nothing away:

"The next comment is from the Lord Lieutenant, the Earl of Aberdeen," he explained, "it says 'this convict may now be released on license'."

Barrows broke into a broad smile, "Well, Kelly, that's the news you've been waiting for. I shall be sorry to see you go, of course, but I expect you will be delighted to get back to your work and your family."

Suddenly the Governor was on his feet, shaking his hand, but William Henry could not take it in. The Governor continued to explain about the terms of the license and William Henry heard some of what he was saying. He understood he was not to consort with criminals, nor should he engage in any criminal activity himself, and he would have to report at quarterly intervals to the local constabulary in Belfast, etcetera, etcetera, but the gist of it all was that, on the nineteenth of June, he would be released from prison. He was in shock and barely knew what to say. He thanked the Governor profusely for his support and they shook hands warmly once more, before the warder marched him at the double back to his work. He was stunned. He had wished so long and so earnestly for release and had been disappointed so many times and, now that he was to be granted his liberty, he could not believe it. Whelan was pleased for him, but said he would miss him greatly. Whelan did not like change and had got accustomed to having William Henry around. He wondered who else they would send him.

William Henry scarcely dared close his eyes that night, in case he should awake and find he had dreamed the day's events. He wondered if Belle would be resentful of his release. Maybe she would feel he had not been fully punished. He hoped she would not desert him now. She did not. The very next day, William Henry despatched a letter to Billy, advising him that he was to be released. He understood he would be deposited outside the gates of Maryborough prison, but would be given a free rail pass to exchange at the station for a ticket back to Belfast. He realised this would be short notice, and he had no idea what train he would catch, but he advised Billy that he would be no trouble to anyone and would call at the

Sinclair Seaman's Church Mission, where he hoped the Reverend Manning, to whom he had also written, would find him a bed until he sorted himself out with work and a rented room somewhere. William Henry suspected he might reach Belfast before his letter did. He had no idea however how his return would be received by his children. He had yet to meet Billy's new wife Barbara and his new children, and wee Belle's husband Jack. He felt sad however that he was destined never to meet Jimmy's family, who were living out in Carrickfergus whilst Jimmy was away fighting the war at sea.

In some respects, he was fearful about his return. He wondered if he would be returning as the same man who had left Belfast in nineteen ten. The law might have decided that he was redeemed, but he did not feel he had redeemed himself. As his admired Mark Twain had once expressed it: '*a man cannot be comfortable without his own approval*'. William Henry did not yet have his own approval and therefore would not yet be comfortable. He now learned the value of the advice he had been given seven years earlier about having his clothes returned to his family, for this meant that the prison authorities were now obliged to furnish him with a new outfit. This was not the coarse, broad-striped frieze of the prison garb, but was a reasonably smart suit, tailored of a better fabric, by his former colleagues in the tailoring shop. He noticed the neat seams which had doubtless been finished off on the Hoffman press. He was also given a small canvas bag with some changes of underwear and socks. This was the last time his clothes would be chosen for him.

Although the points system had been abandoned long since, he still had some credit earned in his 'account' and was duly presented with three pounds in cash as the balance of his earnings, plus a two pound prisoners' gratuity, which was to buy him any tools he needed to resume his work. The written request he had submitted to the Governor that he might be allowed to keep his spectacles had been approved and these, plus his pipe, caulker's knife and some small change and other small items which had been in his pockets upon his arrest, now made up the final items of his worldly possessions. He had taken his leave of his fellow library orderly Whelan the day before but, to his regret, he was not permitted to say goodbye to Thomas or to any of his other fellow inmates. After breakfast and his final bath in the prison's bathroom, he donned his new clothes, signed for his cash, his belongings and his travel warrant, and he was escorted to the gates by O'Farrell who shook his hand, wished him well and reminded him in which direction the station lay.

As the gates closed firmly behind him and he looked out at the little town in which he had lived for the past seven years but had never explored, he became nervous. The prospect of venturing abroad without escort, of being able to walk abroad like a free man, was both exhilarating and frightening. He sent off marching at the double for a few hundred yards, then realised that he no longer needed to keep up the urgent prison pace and indeed would probably look a little odd to the townsfolk if he did, so he slowed down to a more leisurely saunter and took the time to glance back at the prison as it shrank behind him. It seemed strange not to have seen the outside of the place he had lived for the past seven years. It had been dark when he had arrived here in nineteen ten, and so he had not seen so much as a glimpse of the town itself before now. Maryborough was just awaking at that time of the morning and folks were beginning to appear to open their shops and go about their business. He passed a small gaggle of school children with their mother and he remembered to raise his new hat to them. So far, things in the outside world did not look greatly altered. Then again, this was rural Ireland, and things changed but slowly in the countryside.

At the station, he exchanged the prison-issued travel warrant for the single ticket, noting the disapproving expression of the ticket clerk, who doubtless felt he should be walking home to Belfast rather than travelling at taxpayers' expense. He found a quiet bench upon the platform and settled down to await the train. Whilst he waited, he looked at the huge sky above him. This was more sky than he had seen in a long time, even from the gardens of the prison. The sun was not yet over the level of the rooftops, yet he knew it was going to be a fine, warm June day. He looked forward to gazing at the northern skies of Belfast. Would he again have the opportunity of seeing them from the top of the shipyard staging? He did not yet know. Would Belfast look different? Would it still feel like home to him?

Eventually, the Great Southern and Western Railways train squealed into the station and he was pleased to see it was not crowded. He chose an empty carriage and found a window seat at what he hoped would be the sunny side of the train. He had nothing to read but then he was happily anticipating a world passing by the window, so he would not be bored. He now realised he had little recollection of his journey down here seven years earlier, but then it had been dark and he had been escorted all the way. Back then, he had not needed to think about his route or where to change trains, and his thoughts had been preoccupied with what had lain ahead of him. He now gazed out at the various stops en route, trying to take in all he could of these places he had never visited: the flat railway town of Portarlington nestling on the river Barrow by the border with County Offaly, and then the major market town of Kildare. He gazed across vast swathes of open green meadows, and, in contrast to his journey down, only curious black and white cows stared back at him. He felt like a tourist. He would not entrust his little canvas back to the string-netting parcel shelf above his head however, lest he fall asleep and awake to find it missing.

At Dublin, he had to alight from the train and find his connection to Belfast. Now, he found himself in crowds. He also found the sights and the sounds of so many people bumbling around him a little unnerving. The hubbub of chatter in the main booking hall and the close proximity of strangers, some of whom bumped against him in their rush to board trains, was overwhelming after the separateness and the absence of chatter in the prison confines. It took him some time to establish where to catch his train to Belfast, for it turned out he had to change not just platforms but stations. He had to ask several people for directions and realised that this was the first time in seven years he had instigated a conversation with anyone. Dubliners seemed friendly enough but all were in a hurry themselves. This was his first visit to the capital, not counting his previous passage through here in handcuffs, and he now had the opportunity of seeing just a little of the city streets between stations. He would not linger however, as he was anxious to reach Belfast and find somewhere to stay.

He was soon in the care of the Great Northern Railway and en route to Belfast. He had thought about buying himself something to eat, as he was now getting hungry, and he had allowed himself a brief look around the station buffet and the confectioners stall, but he was quite shocked to see how much prices had risen in his absence. He was also worried about spending any of his money, since he did not know how long it would have to last him, so he boarded his train. Places he had heard of in historic context now paraded past his train window: Drogheda on the Boyne, scene of the siege of sixteen forty-nine, which he had commemorated every year with whiskey, and Dundalk, the historic market town of County Louth. Soon, he found himself passing through his own birthplace, Dunmurry, and he felt the rising excitement of homecoming. At Lisburn, a man in khaki boarded and entered his compartment. Sitting opposite William Henry to take his last views of his home town, the young man engaged him in conversation. William Henry was delighted to hear again the familiar accent but shocked to learn the soldier was only twenty two, for the deep, dark sockets of his eyes and the furrows of his brow suggested he had seen much more than two decades of life.

"Which outfit are yiz in, son?" William Henry asked, since the badges meant little to him.

The soldier told him he was with the 36th Division. He had been severely wounded at The Somme and, having spent many months in hospital, he had been granted home leave. Now, however, he was returning to the front. William Henry wanted to ask him how it was, but feared that making him recount his experiences would blight the young man's journey. The soldier asked him what he did. Pausing for a second or two, William Henry answered that he was a shipwright. The soldier nodded approvingly and said he understood they needed more ships, after all that had been lost at Jutland. William Henry told him his own son had been in the conflict at Jutland but had come through it, unlike many thousands of his comrades. Asked if it was true that the shipyard workers had received a big pay increase for their war work, William Henry was embarrassed, since he did not know, but nor did he wish to admit he had been sitting out the war in prison. He nodded, feeling guilty on either count. The two fell into silent contemplation. It was a while before the youth spoke again.

"It's nothing but luck, you know," he said, "whether you live or die. I've lost so many good pals over there. I mean, I don't want to die, but I don't want to be the only one who comes back either. D'ye know what I mean?"

William Henry nodded and reassured him that, as he had made it this far, so he would be all right, and anyway the war would be over very soon, for the Americans were in it now, weren't they?

"I don't want to go back" the soldier said softly and William Henry saw the fear and desperation in his eyes but did not know what else to say to comfort him.

"Will ye say a decade of the rosary with me?" the soldier asked.

William Henry didn't want to disappoint the lad by admitting he was not a fellow Catholic, so he said he was a bit rusty on the words, but if the lad kicked the prayers off, he would follow in his head and heart. The soldier removed his hat, knelt, with some difficulty on the carriage floor, closed his eyes and began to pray aloud. William Henry clasped his hands together, bowed his head and said his own prayers. Joining in with the Lord's prayer, he remembered not to add the defining *kingdom, power and glory,* and, of course, he let the lad go solo on each of the *Hail*

*Mary*s. He felt it particularly poignant each time the intercession of the Virgin Mary was invoked 'now and at the hour of our death', and he echoed his support with each 'Amen'.

Soon, they were at Belfast where they would go their separate ways. Before they parted, William Henry pressed one of his pound notes into the lad's hand and bade him use it to buy a few drinks. Moved by this generosity, the soldier smiled and wished him the blessings of God. The older man now noted how handsome a youth he was, despite the lines of terror etched in his pale face. Wishing him the very best of luck, William Henry watched the lad head off for the docks to catch his boat. His heart filled with sorrow for the youth. He now realised however that he could again smell and taste the tang of salt in the air. An old, familiar noise now came to his ears. It was the clangour of steel reverberating around the city, he fancied like Dick Whittington's churchbells, as if to welcome him home.

Part 7 – **THE RED HERRING**

By March of nineteen eighteen, the drone of aircraft in the skies over Belfast was rivalling the industrial sounds from the busy shipyards beneath. So frequent were the test flights of de Haviland flying machines that the shipwrights no longer glanced up to marvel at them. The model-building office at Harland and Wolff, which had seen brilliant and innovative designers challenge the sea gods, had now become an aircraft drawing office. Whilst, over in France, the Germans had commenced a major offensive which was threatening to prove as bloody a campaign as any so far in this seemingly endless war, the British Ministry of Shipping had leased to Harland and Wolff forty-one acres of additional land at the east side of the Musgrave Channel to facilitate ship construction and repair. The one resource which Harland and Wolff could not buy however was skilled tradesmen. A few had been poached from other local shipyards and some from further afield in Scotland, but William Henry now found himself training unskilled men in the application of hydraulic caulking technology to the construction of the new standard merchant ships. Those under his tutelage were labourers and raw boys, all eager to learn the new skills. Pleased to be back in his proper place at last however, he applied himself earnestly and wholeheartedly to his duties.

Belfast's engineering plants were now running flat out, and her linen industry too was working at full production, since linen was the material of choice for covering the aircraft fuselage. The continuing need for her industrial output gave Belfast a renewed sense of self worth. Her citizens, in particular her shipwrights, had keenly felt the importance of their role in the war, despite the Home Rule issue having reared its contentious head once again two years earlier, when the Government had tried, unsuccessfully to sell the Nationalists self-determination in return for accepting conscription in Ireland. The war was no nearer to being won however, for, whilst German Generals now held Paris within their sights, back in Harland and Wolff's new joiner's shop, construction had commenced on a vast, heavy bomber, the Handley Page V1500, which would be capable of reaching Berlin. With his eye as ever to the main chance, Pirrie had also purchased a one hundred and seventy acre farm at Aldergrove, north of Belfast, and had turned it into an aerodrome. His Belfast shipyards, although still desperately short of manpower, were outstripping his Clydeside yards in their production of shipping also, and he realised that, if he were to continue this pace to meet the insatiable demands of war production, increased use of technology was the only way forward.

Pirrie had established joint committees comprising Unions and Management, in which uneasy coalition Johnnie Besant now played a major role. Johnnie had explained to William Henry that, for fear of seeming unpatriotic and unsupportive of their comrades overseas, the unions had been obliged to agree the increased use of semi-skilled and unskilled labour. This concession had been granted in the hope that those skilled shipwrights fortunate enough to return from the war would have their former jobs returned to them. With unions and management in accord, the record losses of merchant shipping were now being met with record production of replacement ships. The wartime working week in the yards, and indeed in most of Britain's industries, was now fifty four hours. This did not concern William Henry, for he felt he had a great deal of catching up to do in terms of contributing to the war effort and, besides, what would he do with leisure time if he had it?

He was now lodging with his sister Lena, in Hallidays Road. The arrangement proved ideal, since they were both now widowed, and so he brought home his pay to supplement her army widow's pension and Lena kept house for them. It was a convenient location for visiting his children and grandchildren, who mostly lived in the little warren of streets between Hallidays Road and North Queen Street. He was surprised to note how little Belfast had changed in his absence. Many of the old terraces, which had been condemned and had appeared to be falling down when last he had seen them, miraculously still stood and were still occupied. Unsurprisingly, in view of the war, there appeared to have been little new development. He now worked until quite late each evening, so he was only in the house each night in time for a late supper and his bed. Nowadays, he would take the tram home along Duncairn Gardens and alight at its junction with Hallidays Road. He avoided the New Lodge Road these days, so he would not have to pass the top of Shandon Street, and nor would he pass by *McCusker's*, the spirit grocers at the junction of Hallidays and the New Lodge, where once he had been a regular customer for their rum. Of course there were two other such spirit sellers along the Hallidays Road nowadays, but he would cross over before he reached them.

He was surprised at the proliferation of cinemas in the city now. He had heard there was a huge and impressive one, the *Lyceum*, built alongside *McCusker's* now, but he had neither been to a picture house nor seen a film, and he no longer had a desire to do so. Simple things amused him now, like seeing the children at their play in the streets along his way. They still swung from the cross bars of the iron lampposts or played their skipping games with a length of old rope tied to a drainpipe, just as his own children had done. He would often stop briefly to chuckle at them and give them a penny or two for sweets. The skipping games were the same and the rhymes they chanted were pretty much the same too. *The Belle of Belfast City* was still popular, he noted, thought it now saddened him to hear it.

Usually after work, he would walk as far as the tram stop with Johnnie, Hughie and the others of the squad, and their talk was of the same issues of contention between men and management as it had been before William Henry went away. The war had made Johnnie's long-held fears a reality. The increased sophistication of hydraulic drilling, riveting and caulking methods now enabled that work, which had hitherto been the preserve of the skilled, mostly Protestant shipwrights, to be carried out by a significantly large cadre of labourers, many of them Catholics. The Scottish shipwrights, who had come over to replace the enlisted men, were sympathetic to the Unionist views of protectionism and elitism. William Henry and Johnnie agreed they themselves had no beef with either Catholics or

144

Scots. Indeed, it was William Henry's long held suspicion that it suited the management to use religious and ethnic differences to divide and rule the workers.

However the more worrying aspect of this issue was, as both men saw it, the erosion of the pay differential between the skilled and unskilled. Before the war, an unskilled man could earn just over half of the skilled man's wage. Now however he earned two thirds of the skilled rate. As desirable as this was for both the unskilled man and for the yard's productivity, William Henry could see this as a potential further cause of distrust, and one which had the potential to drive an even greater wedge into the crevice of the sectarian divide. Since he no longer joined the men in the pub after work, William Henry had only the narrow opportunity of his walk to the tram stop in which to satisfy his longing for a heartfelt exchange of views with Johnnie and the others, but he enjoyed their discussion all the more for that.

It was a delight for William Henry that he could buy himself whichever newspaper he wished and whenever he wished, and it was now his pleasure to have one every day. He would peruse it on the tram, if travelling alone, and continue to read it over his supper. Although he was also pleased to see that the forty shillings he had received for his week's labours back in nineteen ten had now increased to almost sixty shillings, it was clear that the cost of living in Belfast had more than doubled since before the war, and his pay did not go so far as it had back then. For that reason, and of course out of patriotic duty, like most working people, he opted to work overtime whenever it was offered. One Saturday, en route home from work, he bought on impulse two picture postcards to send to his former prison companions, Thomas the hospital wardsman and Michael Whelan in the library. They pictured views of the Lagan and he thought the cards might cheer them up, so on each he wrote the same message: '*The auld herring is swimming in his own familiar river again. Regards, WHK.*'

In France, the Germans were throwing their all into trying to take the vital rail lines at Amiens and from there gain easy access to the channel coast. They had moved war-weary troops across Europe from the Russian front in an effort to achieve this. With a little bolstering from the Americans however, the allied forces were able to meet them head on. Losses on both sides were colossal though, according to press reports. Two hundred and fifty-five thousand allied troops had been killed in the trenches of Northern France that month as against two hundred and thirty-nine thousand Germans. William Henry read the headlines with disappointment and wondered if any of his shipwright comrades would come back alive from the Somme. Worryingly, territory which had been hard won with great loss of life the year before, such as Armentières, Ypres and Messines, was now falling back into German hands. Most alarmingly however, the press reported that the Germans were now only fifteen miles from the principal French channel ports.

Back home, civilian morale was very low. The squads of telegram boys on their cycles, who had become a familiar sight in the Belfast streets over the past three years, continued delivering the small manila envelopes to fearful families who dreaded hearing that knock at the door. Many families received more than one such cruel missive. April saw another hundred and ten thousand allied troops killed in the offensive. Losses of one hundred and thirty seven thousand were reported in May and a further thirty five thousand in June. The figures seemed unreal to William

145

Henry, who had no word of his own son Jimmy. He had not met Jimmy's wife Mary or his three year old son, whom everyone referred to as *just Jimmy*. They lived out on the coast in Carrickfergus near Mary's parents, who had been told William Henry was long dead. He had heard from Billy that Jimmy and Mary now had a second child, a baby daughter, Margaret. Still, there seemed to be no further great battles at sea and so he assumed Jimmy was safe, even though it occurred to him that, should the awful telegram arrive, it would come to his daughter-in-law Mary, and not to him.

Yet another major and bloody land battle was fought at the Marne in July but, just when victory seemed beyond the grasp of the allies, the tide of the war slowly began to turn. An allied counter-offensive, fought mainly on the flanks of the now overstretched German army, began to take effect. By August, the Germans, who, like Harland and Wolff, were fast running out of men, were facing defeat. In November, an armistice was signed and the management of Harland and Wolff announced a two week holiday for all the men.

William Henry had never taken a holiday in his life, and did not have the wherewithal to do so now. However, on impulse, he decided to treat Lena to a day out at the seaside. On the Saturday, they headed off on the train to Carrickfergus where, despite the fact that the days were now shortening; the heavy clouds rolling in across the Atlantic and the sea breezes sharpening into cold gusts, there was nevertheless an atmosphere of relief and relaxation. Many other folks were out walking or sitting chatting along the seafront, and clusters of children were playing happily on the shore. Apart from the absence of young men, it was as if there had never been a war. As William Henry and Lena strolled along the shoreline and took in the views of the dark, Norman castle, he gazed at the young mothers and infants, and he wondered if, somewhere amongst them, were his own grandchildren.

Having persuaded him to stroll, rather than marching along at the double, a habit he seemed to have picked up in prison, Lena watched him with mild concern. She guessed his thoughts and felt sad for him. She wondered if he had really settled back into his own skin again. She could not help but hear him as he talked to himself at nights. The thin walls of their little rented house afforded them little soundproofing and so she could hear him conversing, clearly under the delusion that he was speaking to his Belle. She supposed it was due to the guilt and loneliness. She noticed also that he now had some other odd little habits. He would always leave his working shoes at the same spot, just inside the front door, at a perfect right angle to the wall, and he had bought himself a pair of felt slippers which, when he left for work, were always placed in exactly the same spot, also perfectly angled in relation to the wall. Even more strangely, when he assisted her by laying the supper table, he would sometimes lay out just a knife and spoon, but no fork. He would occasionally take a scrap of bread up to bed with him too, which she presumed was in case he became hungry during the night. She thought however he probably was not the only sixty-two year old man with little oddities of behaviour. As they sat on a bench by the sea and savoured their fish and chips, William Henry was remembering the many times in prison when he would have sold his soul for a paper of fish and chips, and for the freedom to sprinkle on his own salt and vinegar as

146

liberally as he wished. In fact, for him, the taste of fish and chips *was* the taste of freedom.

The rest of the week brought heavy and persistent rain. A break in the showers on the Sunday however afforded William Henry and Lena the opportunity to visit their brother Patrick who lived in Flax Street, up off the Crumlin Road. Patrick worked as a flax dresser at Lyndsay, Thompson and Company's Prospect Mill. The mill was one of the most progressive mills in terms of up to date machinery and processes, although not perhaps very progressive in terms of its staff welfare. Patrick and his family were happy however to be living in one of the cottages opposite the mill which, although small, had an open outlook at the back and a view of the hills from the upstairs. The tram dropped William Henry and Lena off at the Crumlin Road post office and they were about to head back a block towards the bottom end of Flax Street when the tram driver warned them there was flooding up by the mill, so they would be better taking a detour up Hooker Street and along Butler Street. When they arrived at the top of Butler Street, they found a commotion going on.

The River Rosehead, which flowed down the hill in a course parallel to Flax Street and had been culverted to run beneath the houses, was running high, as it did regularly after heavy rains. Usually, the mill owners despatched their workers with hundreds of sandbags to block Flax Street at its corner with Crumlin Street to prevent the flood water flowing into the mill. Unfortunately, this invariably had the effect of diverting the swollen river instead into the little terraced houses in Crumlin Street, ruining what few possessions the residents had.   This being a Sunday and the mill being closed however, it seems the Crumlin Street residents had anticipated this and they had set up their own barricades across Crumlin corner, to divert the water back downhill along the lower part of Flax Street. The mill managers had turned up to see the flood situation and were not happy at this initiative, as the water was now flowing threateningly close to the mill entrance. Voices were raised as more of the residents appeared out on the streets to confront the managers. As William Henry and Lena watched the encounter, squads of police now arrived from the Leopold Street barracks, doubtless summoned by the concerned mill owners. The police began to tear down the Crumlin Street barricades.

William Henry and Lena watched, horrified, as the situation quickly escalated, the residents attempting to maintain the barrage in order to protect their homes and the police beating them back with truncheons. In the clash between desperate and outraged families on one side and overexcited constables on the other, several heads were subjected to blows, not least that of William Henry, who had stepped between a charging constable and a fleeing woman and child. Lena eventually managed to disentangle her brother from the affray and they made their way up Flax Street to Patrick's house, which luckily was just uphill of the flood zone. Patrick, who had been watching the incident from his doorway, was surprised now to recognise his brother emerging from the mêlée and alarmed to see his injured head. He brought them inside, where his wife Eliza and their two daughters tended to the cut on William Henry's head and made some tea.

"My gawd," William Henry exclaimed, "that's not right, setting tha poliss on women and weans, when they're just tryin' ta protect their homes is all!"

147

"Aye, I know," Patrick agreed, "but most of the folks roun' here, the men women and children, work at that mill, and most's Catholics too, so it's natural the Protestant police force would look out for the mill owners' interests. What does poor people's property matter to them? Sure, the floods comes every winter and the poor wee folks gets flooded out every time, so they do. The worst of it is the mill owners can get their own back by layin' off some of the families involved."

"Ye see, that's the problem," William Henry said, his dander up now, "it's all about the unfair ownership of property. Tha Unionist militia o' tha state protects tha property of tha Linen Barons but not that of their workers. See, if that mill wuz owned be tha workers, and not be tha capitalist proprietors, it would be a whole lot fairer, so it would. Why should tha mills, factories and shipyards be in tha hands of a small and wealthy minority? People should be free to reap tha profits of their own labours. If tha profits wuz shared out in a fair way, sure those poor wee folks would be livin' in better houses and their weans would be better fed and better educated. Those profits could go into hospitals and schools, for the benefit of society."

"Ach, don't be talking like that!" Lena chided him, "and don't be tacklin' tha poliss head on again, will ye, or we'll have to be heading for tha hills!"

William Henry smiled at his sister's allusion to the events of sixteen forty-one. It had been a few years since he had heard that phrase.

"Don't let Lord Pirrie hear ye talkin' that way neither, or ye'll be outa yer job!" Patrick warned, as they drank their tea.

Patrick was right to suggest William Henry's increasingly socialist views would not be popular with his employer. Governments and owners of industry all over Europe had observed with alarm the disintegration of three of the world's great empires - those of Russia, Turkey and Austria. As nineteen nineteen now dawned, with the Russian Tsar and his family apparently having been assassinated, the Bolsheviks were gradually turning Russia into a workers' state and there were socialist uprisings also in Vienna and Berlin. In Belfast, a post-war slump in industrial production was fully expected, and yet still the workers in the major industries were held to working a fifty-four hour week. Many in fact worked as much as sixty-five hours, never seeing daylight until Sunday came around. Most owners of industry were reluctant to return to normal pre-war working hours and conditions however. The euphoria caused by the end of hostilities and the imminent demobilisation of the fighting men seemed blighted by this intransigence on the part of the employers and the mood slowly gave way to despondency and unrest.

Johnnie advised the men that the unions in all sectors of industry were pressing for a reduction to a forty-four hour week, as they saw this as the only way of reabsorbing the returning, demobilised servicemen and staving off mass unemployment. The intractable Harland and Wolff management however would only concede a return to the pre-existing forty-seven hour week, and that concession was reached only after protracted negotiation. On Saturday the twenty-fifth of January, some twenty to thirty thousand workers, including William Henry, Johnnie and their comrades, staged a lunchtime march into the city centre, holding aloft banners, optimistically proclaiming: '*44 hours means no unemployment*'. The men then dispersed to their various union halls to vote on the possibility of strike action. A resounding ninety-two percent of the city's workers voted not to accept the forty-seven hour week and, moreover, ninety-seven percent voted for strike action. Since the men of the shipyards were now off duty anyway on this Saturday afternoon, they dispersed to their usual watering holes to discuss the turn of events.

Johnnie led a group of thirty or so of the caulkers to Clancy's capacious saloon bar. William Henry accompanied them, though he made his excuses in advance that he would consume nothing whilst on the premises, and those men who knew him understood. Johnnie explained to the men that, technically, the strike was unofficial, since the Trades Union Council had accepted, despite the results of the lawful ballot, the employers' offer of a forty-seven hour week. However, in no location across the British Isles was this offer deemed acceptable to the workers. In fact, Belfast's demand for a forty-four hour week appeared reasonable, given that workers in Glasgow and elsewhere in the UK were demanding a further reduction to forty hours.

"When will the strike start?" one of the newly employed youths asked.

"Well," Johnnie informed him, "it already has, though the employers may not realise it until Monday. They may be expectin' us all to turn up on Monday mornin', but that won't happen. The good news is that the power workers is all behin' us too. The electricity and gas will be shutting down from this evenin' and when it does, the effects will be obvious to all. The Corporation workers is also comin' out and, even though the rope works and the linen works is not joinin' the strike, they'll have no power from this evenin' and so they won't be able to work."

"What about the power supply to the hospitals?" another asked.

"There's a skeleton staff goin' ta see till it that they gets power all right. Unfortunately, keepin' their supply on means power will be available to some other small businesses who are on the same grid, but we'll have pickets out to persuade them to switch off, if we see them operatin'."

"D'ye think they'll bring in scab labour again, like they did with the dockers' strike that time?" William Henry asked.

Johnnie said he did not see how they could construct ships using *entirely* unskilled outside labour, and he was pleased to see that most of the new men and boys, recruited from the unskilled pool during wartime, had joined them in the strike. However, he was concerned that many of the shipyard apprentices had not come out, and nor had the clerical staff. At this, there was a murmur of disapproval, mainly concerning the less than popular timekeepers, some of whom they termed, derisively, 'toilet keepers'. Johnnie further advised that volunteers would be sought from amongst the more able-bodied members to perform picket duties. He explained that a picket would be established across the Queen's Road to prevent employees – and that meant *all* employees, clerical staff, managers and company directors included – from entering Harland and Wolff. Further pickets were to be posted outside other industrial works, such as the Sirocco works, where the workers had not yet joined the strike.

William Henry rose to his feet, as he would have done in the old days to make a loud point, and indeed he still felt equally passionate, but his passion no longer needed to be driven by alcohol.

"Brothers, is everyone agreed that this is not a Protestant strike, but that it is an action by the united workers of Belfast?" he asked, "can we all be clear that this

149

time aroun' we must not let the employers turn the strike into a Protestant versus Catholic issue? I know I've said it before, and some of yez are sick o' hearin' it, but it remains true that capitalists like Pirrie will seek to end this by dividin' us. We have our Catholic brothers alongside us, just as Catholics and Protestants stood together in tha docks strike of nineteen-oh-seven, and, only if we stick together, will we win the concessions we want. But the employers is frightened of radicalisation and when they see how united we are in our goal, they will try to break that unity."

Most of the men nodded their agreement on this issue, though one of the Scotsmen, Robert Bell, commented that he would be surprised if the Catholics amongst their ranks were willing to strike, given that they would lose their jobs in the yards anyway, with the imminent return from war of the Protestant shipwrights. This caused the Catholics in the group some momentary alarm. Johnnie would have liked to reassure them that this was not so, however, he could not, for he suspected it might be. William Henry was on his feet again:

"Well, that might indeed happen if, when he lads comes back, we're still working a fifty-four hour week, for there won't be enough work to go aroun'. However, it's in everyone's interest right now to achieve a shorter week. That way, when the orders comes in to replace all the lost cargo ships, there'll be enough work for *all* of us here now, Catholics and Protestants, as well as our returning comrades. Don't forget though, and I hate to say it, but a lot of them may not be comin' back. If the management does decide to lay some of us off, there's no sayin' who'll stay and who'll go. That's why we need to stick together and not alienate any of our members, whether Catholic or Protestant, Irish or Scot."

Robert Bell thought he perceived a barb in William Henry's final word, but he realised his own comment had upset a few and the majority of those assembled were now agreeing with William Henry. Johnnie Beasant now added that, although their action was still deemed by the TUC to be an unofficial strike, an official Strike committee had been established, which, in his book, set the official seal on the strike. William Henry offered to buy his squad a round of drinks before he left, but Johnnie said that was not necessary, and everyone would understand. Accordingly, he went home to break the news to Lena.

The absence of the vital power workers had indeed made its mark that very evening. The city was without electricity, so the trams could not run, and the gaslights were out. William Henry had had the foresight to buy a large box of candles on his way home, which pleased his sister, whom he found sitting, baffled, in the dark. On the Sunday, he went along with Johnnie to join an audience of eight thousand men at the Customs House steps where they heard speakers from the Strike Committee. Predictions were made that the city's coal stocks would begin to run low within a week or two. A further strike meeting was held at the City Hall, after which some two thousand workers marched over to the shipyards to conduct a peaceful picket. They chanted and cajoled the apprentices and clerical staff to join them. When peaceful blandishments failed to work however, the pickets forced their way in through the gates, dragged the apprentices out and, with the same ferocity used for throwing in their *bourds* at the end of each shift, they now pelted the offices with stones, breaking many of the windows.

150

"There's no street lights on tha night, Wim Henery," Belle remarked, as she gazed out of his little bedroom window later that night, "is that *your* doin'?"

"Aye Belle, it is," he told her, "for we have the power workers onside now, and tha city cannot function long without electricity or gas. Industry will come to a standstill and the employers'll have to listen to us. It's time tha workin' man, aye an' woman too, had a voice and a choice in how things is run. It's happenin' in other countries and it'll happen here, so it will. The age of working class obedience and every man knowing his place is passin' into history, Belle. Thousands of working men of this city are fightin' a war to preserve the nation as tha sorta place they want to live in. Each man should know his worth and be treated accordingly, so he should. It's time for change, right enough."

Belle shook her head; "'sounds like the spirit of revolution is in the air, alright, but supposin' ye fail, Wim Henery, what then?"

The city was eerily quiet without the drone of heavy industry or the rattle of trams. Belfast was not alone in this however, as most of Britain's industrial centres had similarly ground to a halt. Squads of roaming pickets also broke the windows of any businesses they spotted using electricity. This included the city's main newspapers, which were not fully sympathetic to the men's demands anyway. The strike committee established their own paper, the *Workers' Bulletin*, which William Henry helped to distribute, since he was fully supportive of the strike but would have been unwilling to engage in the strong arm tactics used by some of the pickets. He realised this insupportable action was contrary to TUC recommendations, and sure enough, the Strike Committee responded by appointing its own peaceful pickets to roam the streets accompanied by police officers. The Commissioner of Police now recruited three hundred special constables and placed them on guard duty to protect the major businesses around the city. The Commissioner was however reluctant to cede to the further demands for military intervention, made by Pirrie and other leading employers, who were now alarmed by the increasing radicalisation of Belfast's workforce. Their demands in this regard would be met by a greater authority however.

By the end of the second week of the strike, the winter snow arrived making the silence in the city even eerier than hitherto, and Saturday afternoon saw miserable shoppers walking home through slush-laden and darkened streets. Those disappointed shoppers now found prices beginning to rise and supplies of commodities diminishing. Although some of the unions were paying strike pay to their men, the engineering unions would not. It seemed to William Henry that the strike was hurting the working class families far more than it was concerning the owners of industry. Forty thousand workers were now out on strike in Belfast and a further twenty thousand were laid off because of the strike action. The dockers, carters and railway men had promised the Strike Committee that they too were prepared to withdraw their labour but the Committee kept this fact up their sleeve for the time being, realising that this would prevent many food supplies coming into the city. They did not wish to alienate the working class citizens against the action. However, as it was, the lack of lighting and transport during this bitterly cold spell served to heighten the public's negative perception of the strike. The news from Glasgow was even more disheartening, for the chairman of their strike committee,

151

one Emmanuel Shinwell, had been arrested, and Highland troops had moved into the city. Tanks, machine gun posts and patrols of troops with fixed bayonets now confronted the Scottish strikers.

The Belfast Strike Committee was now losing heart. It did not wish to call out the transport workers as it feared it could not run the city. The return to work by the Scottish strikers did nothing to strengthen the Committee's resolve. What they had hoped would be a short but effective strike, looked set to drag on. The city's three main newspapers now launched bitter attacks against the strikers, calling them *'Bolsheviks, Anarchists and the hirelings of Germany'* and accusing them of trying to set up a *'workers' parliament'*. The press variously accused them of being revolutionaries and supporters of *Sinn Féin*. William Henry bristled to recall how the news of the Easter Uprising back in nineteen sixteen had been displaced, understandably enough, from the front pages by the tragic news of the ensuing Battle of the Somme, and then the British press had cynically manipulated public reaction into accusing the Irish Nationalist rebels of betraying their dead countrymen. Such was the vitriol employed by the British press, that it had turned many Irishmen against the rebels and only the execution of the condemned men, and the sight of one of them disabled and carried to his death in a chair, would restore any sympathy for their sacrifice. The views expressed in the British papers were, William Henry deduced, those of the press barons. Maybe, he thought, revolution was indeed what was needed.

The *Irish News,* alone amongst the Belfast-based press, had been sympathetic to the Belfast strikers' cause, but the effects of the strike had now forced its closure. To the delight of the employers, the Grand Orange Lodge of Belfast now issued a manifesto, declaring the strike to have been instigated by forces other than the workers or employers and demanded that the strikers resume work. William Henry was furious at these thinly veiled attempts to blame the Catholics and *Sinn Féiners* for the industrial action. He vowed never to set foot in an Orange Lodge again. His ire was further aroused when members of the Strike Committee led many of the striking workers in the funeral cortege of George Cuming, who was not only one of Harland and Wolff's directors, but had been deputy Chairman of the wartime Ministry of Munitions which had set the fifty-four hour working week in the first place. It stood to reason that Cuming must have been the driving force behind Harland and Wolff's stance in trying to maintain this into peacetime. William Henry despaired at the fact that the strikers still saw the management as being their *'betters'* and therefore worthy of their respect. How misguided they were; why could they not see beyond such cynical theatrics? Behind this public display however, higher forces were plotting.

Viscount John French, who had been Commander-in-Chief of the British Forces, until relieved of his post by General Haig in December nineteen fifteen, was now C-in-C of the British Home Forces and was therefore also Lord Lieutenant of Ireland. This hot-tempered and antagonistic issuer of confused orders, which orders his war time generals had learned to disregard, and whose direction of the early battles of Neuve Chappelle and Ypres was responsible for the annihilation of the British Expeditionary Force, now sat in Dublin Castle, holding the reins of British power in Ireland. To the disgust of many, not least his own sister, Charlotte

Despard, herself a member of *Sinn Féin*, his was the iron fist which had crushed the Easter rebellion in Dublin three years earlier. Now created, with a bitter irony, First Earl of Ypres, he cast a steely eye over the Belfast industrial dispute before sending the Military Commander for Ireland, General Sir Frederick Shaw to the city. An avowed hater of the Irish, Shaw's arrival in the city gave out a clear message, especially when he promised the Lord Mayor that troops would be assigned to protect both vital installations and any blackleg workers. On the seventh of February, Lord French's view, that the strike was organised by Bolsheviks and *Sinn Féiners*, was published in the press. Now the Defence of the Realm Act, known by the deceptively friendly sounding acronym *DORA*, was extended by the London Government to make it an offence to deprive the community of light, or even to encourage others to do so.

On Valentine's Day therefore, soldiers moved in to occupy both the Belfast gasworks and the electricity stations. Picketing workers were forced back to work at gunpoint. William Henry now knew it was the beginning of the end. On the same day, he and Johnnie attended a mass meeting of strikers in Custom House Square. Charles McKay, Chairman of the Strike Committee reassured the men that the forty-four hour week was "as good as won". Thus encouraged, the men voted to stay out. Johnnie and William Henry were not so sure McKay was right in his assessment. They had been listening to the speeches from a good vantage point, sitting on the balustrade of the adjacent General Post Office steps.

"I wish I had McKay's confidence," Johnnie said, "for we've lost the initiative since the Corporation had the power restored, and, though our pickets is stoppin' the trams leavin' the depôts, sure it's only a matter of time before the army takes on the pickets."

He explained how complicated the negotiations had now become. The Strike Committee had recommended acceptance of a settlement, based on the men returning to work for a fifty-four hour week, to include paid overtime for anything over forty-seven hours, with the promise of further negotiations at a national level later on. The Engineering union had suspended its Belfast and Glasgow union secretaries for engaging in what it now deemed an illegal strike. The Glasgow Strike Committee having collapsed, it appeared that the negotiations now were continuing only between the Belfast Employers' Federation and the shipyard workers' unions. Even if the shipwrights won themselves a shorter working week, the engineers would not benefit from any reduction in *their* hours.

"The Mayor is now callin' upon all loyal citizens of Belfast to offer their services as scab labour," Jim Thompson declared, "he'll have the troops crush us soon enough."

"Aye," agreed Johnnie, "and it doesn't help that Lloyd George is callin' us anarchists and revolutionaries and using terms like '*Prussianism*'. He's doin' his best to associate us with our recent enemies and turn the public against us. He's callin' the strike illegal because the Engineer's union has called it unofficial. How can a strike be illegal or unofficial if all the members voted for it? An' sure the Strike Committee isn't the Union, *we're* the union. They're just our representatives. They shouldn't be makin' decisions without ballotin' the members. Revolutionaries, is it? Well, maybe a revolution is what we need. For this Strike Committee doesn't seem to be very firmly behind us. Why didn't they bring the transport workers out on strike? They're sellin' us out, so they are!"

The others agreed with him - to a point – for, William Henry apart, they weren't so keen on talk of revolution. The Strike Committee proved him right however by next recommending a return to work. Although their recommendation was not popular and was received by the workers with accusations of betrayal, further balloting of the workers now revealed how broken was their morale, when twenty out of the twenty-two separate unions voted to end the strike. All but a fifth of the workforce returned to work the following week, after a month's strike had failed to break the resolve of Government and employers. The troops were then withdrawn and soon even the last pockets of resisting strikers were back at their work. The greatest industrial dispute in the history of Belfast was over.

Reflecting back on the strike, William Henry decided that few of his comrades had been as committed to solidarity as he had. If they had, they might have allowed socialism to replace their traditional sectarian ideology. Now he felt demoralised, and he supposed all of Belfast's workers were too. No-one was any better off now than they would have been had they accepted the employers' original offer, but rather a great number of them were worse off. Belfast workers did not turn out to march on May Day and did not join in the Irish Labour Party's industrial action, since the purpose of this was to show support for self-determination for Ireland. However, the Belfast unions did call upon their members to show their solidarity with the ILP by joining a Trades Council march two days later, on the third of May. This being a Saturday, the workers were more comfortable marching in their own time. Although the press reported that around one hundred thousand workers had taken part in the march, they nevertheless referred ungraciously to the participants as the 'little band of disgruntled red socialists who had taken part in the strike'.

William Henry now consoled himself with his growing family. His son Billy and second wife Barbara now had three children. He was delighted that the boy had been named after himself and the second daughter after his Belle. Seemingly, Billy had forgiven his father's most awful transgression. In keeping with local custom, their first born daughter had been named Ellie, after Barbara's long-deceased mother. William Henry tried to see as many of his grandchildren as possible at the weekends, for they were invariably in bed asleep by the time his still long working day was at an end. Jane's two daughters were growing fast and were fine, healthy girls. Wee belle had a little daughter now, though, tragically, she already had one little girl of three months dead and buried in William Henry's family plot. His beloved Belle now had three weans alongside her for company, their daughter, their granddaughter and Patrick's wee son Hugh. Fortune failed to smile upon their eldest daughter Alice and her husband Henry Anderson, as they seemed destined never to be parents. William Henry looked forward to spending Christmas in the company of his children and so many beautiful grandchildren and, now that he was earning his full wage again, he was saving up for some little gifts for each of them.

If Lord Pirrie harboured any concerns about having a resentful workforce in his shipyards, he gave no sign of this, as he canvassed and won orders for more cargo and passenger ships. Even more new machinery was being installed and the focus was now on diesel powered, rather than coal burning vessels. He now owned engineering works at Finnieston on the Clyde where these engines were developed and was able to obtain supplies of oil and steel from his own producers. The new East Yard in Belfast was fully operational in November and boasted innovations such as portable coffer dams, concrete causeways and electrically operated tower cranes. As part of its war reparations, Germany had ceded a number of her remaining ships to Britain, and now Lord Pirrie had acquired the Danzig-built liner Columbus. Launched in nineteen thirteen for the transatlantic passenger trade, Columbus had never been finished but had been laid up during the war. Harland and Wolff shipwrights were now fitting her out with great luxury for the White Star Line. She would be the replacement for the super liner *Britannic* which had been sunk in the Greek Islands. The original, pre-war plan to name the next White Star Liner *Germanic* was dropped, for obvious reasons. The name *Homeric* was chosen instead. William Henry thought this might be in a fate-appeasing nod to *Britannic*'s final resting place, or perhaps as a tribute to the Greek fishermen who had rescued her crew. He could not wait to see the re-vamped luxury liner sitting in the fitting out wharf, albeit that she would not be as large or as fast as *Titanic* or *Olympic*. For then, he hoped his life would be exactly as it had been back in the old days – in all but one major respect that is.

If things had more or less returned to normal in the shipyards however, it was not so in all areas of Belfast. As expected, the return from war of all but some five hundred of the shipyard men contributed significantly to the growing unemployment in the city. More of the fighting shipwrights had survived than was expected. The same could not be said for Ulstermen in general however, since many thousands had perished. The growing prosperity of Pirrie and his shipbuilding industry was not paralleled in the city in general. In fact the city's unemployed now numbered some fourteen thousand. The Lord Mayor, who had already demonstrated he was no friend to the poor and the working classes, now dismissed out of hand a plea for implementation of the nineteen fourteen act which required local councils to provide free school dinners to the children of its poorest citizens. The Lord Mayor refused to acknowledge that levels of poverty and unemployment in his city warranted this, notwithstanding the many war widows and orphans who now had no source of income save charity. Not every Belfast family was anticipating Christmas with as much eagerness as was William Henry.

December brought him news that his son Jimmy and wife Mary now had another daughter, this time named Alice after Jimmy's eldest sister. William Henry said he would like to meet Jimmy some time, if that were possible. Billy promised he would try to arrange something. The meeting happened much sooner than William Henry could have hoped, for Jimmy had been demobilised from the navy and was coming to Belfast to try to obtain work as a merchant seaman. The following week, to William Henry's joy, he was embracing his elder son in Billy's front parlour. Their father eagerly lapped up Jimmy's stories of his encounters with the enemy, at both ends of the Atlantic, for Jimmy had a great way of making his accounts both gripping and amusing. He had brought more photographs of his wife and children to give to his father. William Henry gazed at them for some time before

155

tucking them carefully into his pocket. He told Jimmy he had not been allowed to have more than four pictures in his prison cell, but now he would have many displayed about his room.

"How was it in prison father?" Jimmy asked, "was it hard?"

"Ach it was bleak and miserable, sure enough," his father said, "and tha loneliness was tha worst bit, and of course I was also worrying about you bein' away in tha war, but the thought of seein' yez all again kep' me going, so it did. And what about your work, son? Billy tells me yer after a job on tha boats."

Jimmy said he was indeed hoping to enlist at the merchant marine office, though he had heard the competition was fierce, with thousands of other demobbed sailors also looking for work. William Henry suggested he call in and see his aunt Lottie, as she had at least one boy working on the Ulster Steamship Company's Head Line ships.

"If it's anythin' like tha shipyards, it'll mebbe help if ye have someone to recommend ye," he advised.

Jimmy said he would go straight over there and hopefully one of his cousins could take him to the company offices the following day, assuming they were not all away at sea. He advised his father that, since he had joined the navy, everyone now called him 'Jim'.

"Ach, well, ye'll always be my wee Jimmy, so ye will," his father said, as he hugged him and wished him the best of luck.

As the new decade was celebrated, William Henry was reminded that he had now been almost ten years without his beloved Belle. He began to wonder how it was that he still went on, working and surviving, so sound in limb and mind, without her. So many times he had wished himself dead so that he could be with her. It must have been with some purpose in mind that God had spared him from being hanged. He now felt he was waiting for something to happen, but he did not know what that would be. Might it be death?

He felt greatly cheered however when the results of the January local elections were announced in the press. Any self-satisfaction the industrial barons had felt at having choked off the strike must now be sticking in their collective craw, he thought, as he read of the increased number of seats the Labour candidates had stolen from the Unionists. Under the new electoral system, with its concept of proportional representation, the three existing Labour seats held by the Belfast Labour Party had now expanded to thirteen. Five of the thirteen successful candidates, including the Shankill's new MP Sam Kyle, had been leaders of the strike. The Independent Labour Party won a further three seats, and the Unionists gained six, reducing their fifty two seats to twenty nine. Traditionally, the membership of Belfast's Labour Party had been almost exclusively upper middle class. Now however an increasing number, William Henry Kelly included, were working class and ten of them, Johnnie Beasant amongst them, were trade Unionists. William Henry thought that the industrialists might have won the battle, but they might not win the war. He wondered if he would live to see the day when Labour would break the Unionist grip on his beloved city. Perhaps it was this hope which kept him going.

Of course others with different political agendas were causing concern to Belfast's industrialists. The Nationalists had won five seats in the city and Sinn Féin another five. Although the men of the yards were unaware of it, first the strike, and now the diminishing power of the Unionist party, were giving Lord Pirrie cause to plan a possible relocation of his shipyards to the British mainland. Outside Ulster of course, the Nationalists had won ninety-one per cent of Irish seats in the previous year's national elections and had immediately announced the birth of an independent Ireland, with its own independent parliament. The Ulster Unionists had not been too impressed to be considered a part of the new nation when they had not been consulted on the issue. William Henry thought this ironic, since the Unionists did not appear to respect ballots. More worryingly of course, Independent Ireland had effectively declared war on the British authorities. For two years now, the Irish Volunteers, now re-named the Irish Republican Army, had been attacking Royal Irish Constabulary barracks, but the violence, hitherto sporadic, was now escalating.

As the fine spring gave way to the warmer days of summer, so Belfast's citizens spent longer on the streets. For several thousand of them, so recently returned from combat and now still unemployed, there was nothing else to occupy them but discussion of the war of independence which was waging in the country, that and their own situation, of course. Lena was not interested in politics and would not engage with William Henry in any talk of how much better their lives might be in a socialist Utopia. Belle was not exactly a willing participant in political discussion either, but her disinterest did not discourage William Henry from sharing with her his hopes and fears.

"Yootopia? Sure if folks cannot live harmoniously in Belfast, how'll they get on any better in your Yootopia?" Belle reasoned, with her usual weary cynicism.

"It's not a place, Belle, it's ... a system, a state of mind," he explained, "a situation where conditions is right for people to live better lives. All men would be equal and every man would have tha right ta work. Th'industries would be in tha hands o' tha people, and tha profits would be shared out equal like. There'd be no bosses. Things'd be run by committees and issues decided by votes an' such."

"Committees? When did committees ever achieve anythin'? Look at yer strike committee," she scoffed, "they collapsed pretty quick, didn't they? All the fine speeches an' marchin' an' banner wavin' and then, as soon as tha bosses and tha police gat thagether, yez were all back te work."

"Ach, that's history now, but we have to work thagether, Belle, like in them Russian co-operatives. We have ta stop bein' side-tracked by sectarian differences. Whilst we're fightin' amongst woorselves tha capitalists is controllin' us. We need to control woor own destiny, so we do. But tha workin' class cannot act alone. We need to get tha *Bourgoys* onside as well," he expostulated.

"What buggers are ye talkin' about?" Bell asked, puzzled.

"Tha ... *Bourgoys* ... tha *Bourgoyzee* - ach, the middle classes, themmins as runs small businesses, tha perfessionals, teachers, doctors, white collar workers an' tha like," he explained.

"Ah, *them* buggers, but, sure people roun' here is too pig-headed to work thagether, Wim Henery," Belle ventured, "they resent each other more than they resent tha bosses. Ye won't get no co-operation roun' here, so ye won't. But you be

157

careful, Wim Henery, for them capitalists won't tolerate yer ideas. They're workin' against ye right now, so they are."

"Ye mebbe right, Belle" William Henry conceded, "but we have to try to make things better, even if it kills us."

It was the annual July holidays. Like many of the city's industries, Harland and Wolff had shut down for the fortnight. Ireland appeared to be rushing towards formal partition of the heavily Protestant northern counties from the mainly Catholic south. In the country areas and the towns of the south and west, bloody conflict still ran on between the flying columns of the IRA and the hit squads of trench-hardened *Black and Tans*, as the temporary recruits to the Royal Irish Constabulary were known. Press and politicians now termed it a war. To some it was a war for independence, to others an uprising. It manifested itself in cowardly attacks by both sides on policemen and civilians alike; in raids and arms seizures at rural police barracks and in assassination incidents and bloody reprisals. Amidst all this unrest and uncertainty however, children still played in the Belfast streets and women still went to the market for their provisions.

With leisure time on his hands once more, William Henry now noticed the extent of the damage the earlier, global conflict had caused to those who had fought and to their families. Almost every street had its quota of maimed and limbless ex-combatants. Many, with obvious mutilations, begged on street corners. Others displayed the terrible physical and mental effects of neurasthenia – a condition resulting from modern warfare and commonly termed 'shell shock'. These were men whose bodies were permanently racked with violent tremors and who threw themselves under the nearest cover at the sudden backfiring of a grocer's van. There were men whose eyes were vacant, whose hearing was destroyed and whose minds were scarred. William Henry thought of the young soldier he had met on the train and wondered if he had survived. The unemployed and the unemployable, many of them festering resentment at those who had been paid overtime during the war, now loitered on street corners. Queues at the workhouse door and at its hospital were longer than could be admitted in a day. The philanthropic heart of the parish relief, never a soft touch, now hardened against the overwhelming tide of supplicants. Incongruously, children now played war games with gruesome military souvenirs their fathers had brought back. Some men had brought back service revolvers.

William Henry spent many hours of his holiday in the free library on Royal Avenue, where he could browse the newspapers and journals and could read novels and political works at his leisure. He followed current affairs with interest. At the library, he discovered something he had not previously seen – London newspapers and editions of journals from further afield, such as the *New York Times*. In the British press, the Limerick Trades and Labour Council's strike, called in response to the imposition of martial law in the county, was reviled as the 'Limerick Soviet'. The rest of the world's press was taking a vehemently anti-British stance however. American and French correspondents spoke of a 'war of reprisals' in which the crown forces were encouraged to murder civilians with impunity. A panoply of crimes, ranging from armed robbery of small businesses to the sacking and destruction of houses and whole villages; from the robbery of businessmen at gunpoint to the kidnapping and execution of civilian suspects, was being carried out by the *Black and Tans* and their officer class, the *Auxiliaries*. The foreign press referred to it as a 'stain on the British character'.

William Henry noted that there were some highly educated correspondents, some of them authors, reporting on the *Anglo-Irish War*. He enjoyed their prose style and their perceptive and intelligent interpretation of the motives of the protagonists of this war. As well travelled and well read men, they viewed the conflict in a European context, defining the attitude of the British Government as being a response to their fears of the class revolution which was manifesting itself all over the continent, and indeed further afield. Strikes were occurring in Australia and America, in Liverpool and Limerick. The protracted and bloody war had changed people, the journalists expostulated. Men had lain down their lives for their countries; families had lost all their sons in order to maintain a society which seemingly did not value their sacrifice. The world would never be the same again. Ordinary men, not just professional soldiers, had stared into the mouth of hell. They had earned the right to be acknowledged and valued, and had lost respect for the privileged classes who had governed and employed them. They now wanted a voice in government. If they now were fearless, the capitalists were afraid. William Henry read, with growing awe, the suggestion that social equality was the common goal, and, moreover, it was one which might now be within man's grasp.

The fervour and defiance of the Orange marchers seemed to increase as the glorious twelfth approached. The beating of the Lambeg drums resonated around the city in the days running up to the annual event, reaching fever pitch on the big day itself. Catholics maintained a low profile in their homes as the Orangemen, their ranks now swelled to pre-war levels by many of the ex-combatants, took possession of Ulster's main streets to celebrate the victory, two hundred and thirty years earlier of the dwarfish Dutch homosexual, the Protestant King William Of Orange, over the egotistical Catholic who would later be deemed by his own Irish troops as *Séamus an Chaca – James the shite*. William Henry acknowledged there was a time when he too would have been out marching in such a ridiculous pageant, but now he ignored the hullaballoo and bigotry and enjoyed the fact that, with all the shenanigans going on out in the streets, he had the library to himself.

During the following week, he was surprised to read that a senior Police officer, Banbridge resident Gerald Smyth, had been assassinated in Cork, for his part in the death of the city's Mayor the previous March. Smyth had been the man credited by the press for giving the *Black and Tans* the green light to kill any Irishman acting suspiciously, even if simply walking along with his hands in his pockets. Smyth's ill-considered instruction and his promise of immunity from disciplinary action, had caused a number of the regular Royal Irish Constabulary officers to resign and some had even joined the IRA. Although aghast at Smyth's arrogant and irresponsible direction, William Henry anticipated that the shooting by the IRA of this unarmed, and indeed one-armed, decorated war hero would be interpreted in some quarters as an attack on Unionism or on the Protestant faith itself. Despite the fact that many thousands of Irish Catholics had fought and died in the Great War, whilst almost two thirds of the Belfast Protestants shipyard workers had not, there existed a perception amongst the latter that the Protestants had fought on behalf of Catholics who had taken their jobs.

159

On the Saturday of Smyth's funeral, William Henry was not greatly surprised to hear of anti-Catholic disturbances in and around Banbridge. He was surprised however, when he turned up at work, to find notices attached to the gates of the shipyard, urging all Unionist and Protestant workers to attend a meeting that lunch time outside the gates of nearby Workman Clark's shipyard.

"What d'ye think that's all about, then?" he asked of Johnnie Beasant.

"I have a bad feelin' about this, William Henry," Johnnie shook his head, "but I think we'd better go and find out what's occurrin'."

William Henry pointed at the notices, "d'ye not think it odd that them's *printed* notices? Tha Workman Clark's offices musta had them printed for whoever is organisin' this meetin'. I smell collusion here."

"Yes, yer right," Johnnie agreed, "and their management wuz implicated in gun runnin' for the UVF back in nineteen thirteen. Clark is a Unionist millionaire. He could be manipulatin' all this, so he could. I don't like it. I don't like it at all."

The speeches were well under way when Johnnie, William Henry and the rest of their squad of caulkers arrived outside Workman Clark's premises. Several thousand men had gathered to hear calls for the expulsion of Catholics from the shipyards. Men who had engaged in a show of solidarity only eighteen months earlier, now demanded also the expulsion of Socialists and Labour party members. One speaker asked for a show of weapons, and a number of men produced service revolvers and held them in the air. Someone even let off a couple of shots into the air.

"Come on," Johnnie urged his men, "we'd better get back to the yards and warn the Catholics, for there's gonna be murder done here tha day!"

Back at Harland and Wolff's yards, Johnnie went to alert the management with a view to getting the gates closed against the expected armed mob, whilst William Henry and the others set about warning their fellow workers what was happening. Huge numbers of Catholic men headed for the gates and many managed to get away, but soon shots were heard and the mob was now in the yards. Suddenly, Johnnie was back at William Henry's side.

"The bastards has locked the gates, but with the mob on the *inside*!" he yelled over the sounds of shouts and shots. To the white-faced young apprentices and the shocked Catholics who were now trapped, he advised: "you'd better try to climb the walls or head for the water. This is serious. Go, now!"

Most of the men took to their heels, but some were stunned into inaction. All around him, William Henry now saw men being man-handled, searched for evidence of their name and religion and beaten. Many of the attackers had now armed themselves with whatever weapons had come to hand, lengths of iron piping, riveter's hammers and of course the eternal *Belfast confetti*.

"Stop this, fer Gawd's sale!" William Henry cried out, as he tried in vain to pull three men away from a young, bloodied apprentice, "this isn't a holy war, it's a class war! Yer just doin' what th'employers wants. This is wrong, wrong, I'm tellin' ye!"

His protests were silenced by a fist in his face. Suddenly he was on the ground and his assailant was kicking him in the stomach and ribs. He turned onto his side and rolled himself into a ball in a vain attempt to make himself a smaller target, but every kick hit home and one got him in the head. The screams and shouts around him appeared to be receding and feared he was losing consciousness. His attacker was shouting abuse about killing all the Socialists too, when Johnnie, his nose and mouth pouring with blood, caught him from behind, swung him around and with one blow, laid him out. Johnnie now had William Henry on his feet and the pair were running along towards the river. Various sharp missiles rained down upon them as they reached the edge of the quay and continued to strike them as they entered the water. After the shock of hitting the perpetually cold Lagan water, they swam blindly, out into mid channel, with no particular direction in mind, other than endeavouring to keep close to each other and escape their attackers.

The two friends eventually found a spot along the river away from the bloodbath which still raged in the yards and where they could clamber out. They paused a while to get their breath back before heading to Johnnie's house in Bryson Street, which was much nearer than William Henry's.

"I'm too old for this sort of caper," William Henry exclaimed when at last they were safe inside Johnnie's house.

"Look, ye'd better get outa them wet clothes, afore ye catch yer death," Johnnie said, "and let me fix yer head, for it's bleedin'."

William Henry declined however, as he wanted to get home as soon as possible to see if Lena was all right. He did not know whether the mob would be roaming the streets once their business in the shipyards was done but even if they dispersed, Lena might have heard about the violent events and be worried for him. He reminded Johnnie that his own young children were out playing and he might want to find them before further violence erupted onto the streets.

William Henry headed across North Queen Street and commenced the long walk along Hillman Street up to Halliday's Road, continually glancing over his shoulder, lest anyone should be following him. Along the way, he saw shopkeepers boarding up their premises and mothers gathering up young children. Word had travelled fast and the city was bracing itself for more trouble. By the time he reached home, William Henry was shivering uncontrollably. He had hoped to get into the house and cleaned up without Lena noticing the state he was in, but she was waiting for him and was shocked at his appearance. Whilst she banked up the fire and boiled water to bathe his wounds, scald the tea and fill him a hot water bottle, he changed into dry clothes and sat in the fireside chair. Lena emptied the pockets of his sodden trousers, putting his pipe, caulker's knife and his loose change into a dish on the table. She noticed a rivet head amongst the coins, and thought that an odd thing for him to be carrying. Still, he was a rather odd man at times, but a likeable one nonetheless, when he wasn't talking politics and revolution. She sensed he did not want to go into detail about what had happened so she sought to reassure him.

"Ach, it'll all blow over in a day or two," she said softly, "you'll see.

The situation did not blow over however. Miraculously, no-one had been killed in the attack, but a couple of dozen had been hospitalised, with more being treated at home, and tensions erupted that very night when the predictable reprisals began. As William Henry took to his bed, still shivering, despite the dry clothing and the coals Lena placed in the grate in his bedroom, shots could be heard around the city. Billy called at the house, having heard of the events from his customers.

161

Lena told him that his father had been roughed up and had a deep wound on his head but would not let her summon a doctor. She said she thought he was suffering from shock also, since no amount of warming would stop him shivering, but both agreed it would be best if he rested, rather than having to re-tell the horror to his son. Whilst William Henry slept, exhausted both mentally and physically, rioting was in full swing around the city. Trams carrying shipyard workers home from their work past the Catholic areas were halted and their passengers attacked. Catholic mobs now roamed the streets and the police were out in force, mounting baton charges into the crowds in an effort to regain control of the city. All afternoon and into late evening, live firing could be heard.

By nightfall the army had been called out in the hope that a short, sharp response might quell the unrest, but the riots continued throughout the night, leaving thirteen dead – seven Catholics and six Protestants, all civilian and all shot by the military. More deaths occurred over the next few days, as did further expulsions of Catholics from the city's engineering works, albeit with a lesser degree of violence than had been experienced in the shipyards. In Bombay Street and Kashmir Road, Catholic families were evicted at gunpoint from their homes, and many of the city's mainly Catholic-owned spirit grocers were destroyed - their stocks of liquor having been drained dry first, of course. But William Henry was unaware of all this. Still feeling the effects of his saturation in the Lagan, he had now taken a chill and was developing a harsh cough. As soon as it was safe to do so, his daughters visited him, bringing soup, and Billy arrived with a red, woollen muffler and a newspaper for his father. Billy was surprised to find his father, still in bed and looking smaller and thinner even than the day he had returned from prison. With some difficulty, William Henry eased himself up in the bed to speak to his son.

"Do you know what's happenin', son?" he wheezed.

"Well," said Billy, "it's been bad, real bad. There's been gangs of men - *enforcers* they calls themselves - from the Belfast Protestant Association, visitin' all the workplaces and making sure there's no Catholics on the premises. The papers says there's mebbe as many as ten or twelve thousand been expelled, but it's not just Catholics. Anyone in the yards who was against the expulsions is bein' called a 'dirty prod' and they've been kicked out too. There's two or three thousand of them expelled. The Catholic women in the mills is out on their ear as well, but in the places that mainly employs Catholics, it's the Protestants that's losing their jobs. I even had the rioters in my place, tryin' to have me outa there cos thought I was a Catholic, but the customers spoke up for me and the mob went away. It's a right mess, so it is. Ach, but it'll sort itself out eventually, so don't you mind right now. You're not well and ye need ta get better."

"No, son," William Henry whispered, "it won't sort itself out. I've lost my job too, for they called me a 'dirty Prod' and chased me out. All the Protestants as wuz away fightin' wants their jobs back, and that's understandable. It's their right. I was holdin' down one of their jobs myself."

"No, ye weren't father," Billy reassured him, "you wuz holdin' yer *own* job, a job ye'd had for thirty five years or more. Ye'll be back there as soon as yer better, so ye will."

162

"No, I won't son," William wheezed heavily and shook his head, "tha war veterans will get their jobs back and there'll be no work for the likes of me. And that's how it should be."

Billy left his father sleeping uneasily and noisily. Over the next few days, William Henry had a steady stream of visits from his sister Lottie and his daughters. His beloved grandchildren trooped in to see him, but his exhaustion would permit him to do little more than smile at them briefly. Johnnie Beasant came to see him, to see how he was and to bid him *au revoir*, for he was going over to Scotland for a while to work at Harland and Wolff's Glasgow yards. He told William Henry that the north Belfast headquarters of the Labour Party had been burned down and several of the Labour Party members were going to Scotland for the time being and had offered to pay his fare. Harland and Wolff had agreed to employ him and other union representatives in their Scottish yards for the time being, just until things settled down. Johnnie guessed the management might be feeling slightly guilty at what had happened but, more likely perhaps, they did not want to give further cause for industrial action. William Henry was very sad to hear of his friend's imminent departure but thanked him for the support and friendship he had shown him over the years. Johnnie reassured him they would be working together again soon. William Henry nodded, though he knew he would never see his good friend again.

"Best of luck t'ye, *Top Hat,*" he said feebly, as Johnnie took his leave of him.

July became August and heavy unseasonal rains beat against the little bedroom window. William Henry remained weak and in his bed. Billy would call in regularly and bring a newspaper, though the news in it was not improved and did not therefore bring cheer to his father. Another of the policemen implicated along with Colonel Smyth in the murder of the mayor of Cork was also assassinated, and riots once more engulfed the city. Yet another round of sectarian shootings and evictions flared up and the news served to depress William Henry still further. The optimism he had felt at the Labour gains from the Unionists in the elections was well and truly quenched, as, out in the streets, neighbour killed neighbour and workers fought each other. He realised now that, though his hopes for recognition and fair pay for the hard-working folk of his beloved city might one day become a reality, he would not live to see that day. Whenever he tried to sit upright in the bed to read, sharp pains would grip his chest, and bronchitis now had him in its grip, worse than ever it had before. Lena did her best to cheer and comfort him also, but to no avail.

"Is there anything I can get ye, William Henry?" she asked him, as she sat with him and they listened to the rain.

"A job, mebbe," her brother joked, "for I have lost mine, so I have."

"I went to enquire about the old age pension for ye thaday, for some of the retired men aroun' here is gettin' five shillin's a week. Mind you, you have to be over seventy. You don't qualify for it yet, as yer only sixty-six, but there's a lotta men lyin' about their ages, so we might swing it for ye yet. Anyway, we'll manage fine on my pension for now, so we will. Ye've no need to worry, sure ye haven't," she reassured him.

"It's not tha money, Lena," he sighed, "it's havin' work that's important. For a man is defined by the work he does. Last month I was a shipwright. I had a

163

job – a skilled job. Today, I have no job. What am I now? Nothin', that's what. A man who loses his job loses everything. It's all over for me, so it is."

Lena did not know what to say to console him. He now started to cough quite violently. She felt his forehead and it was hot and feverish. He was clearly in pain. She decided she would send for the doctor.

The physician listened to William Henry's chest and then went down the stairs to speak with Lena.

"He has considerable pulmonary congestion. We must keep an eye on him in case it should turn into pneumonia. How long has he been like this?"

Lena told the doctor her brother had been worsening ever since his immersion in the Lagan on the day of the riots in the shipyards. The doctor looked grave. He expressed the view that swimming in the bacteria-ridden Lagan was not a suitable activity for a man of sixty-six, though the shock of the attack in the yards might have exacerbated William Henry's condition. He advised Lena to call him again if William Henry seemed to worsen or if he appeared confused or delirious.

"Pneumonia," he explained to a disconcerted Lena, "we call it 'the old man's friend' you know, and in fact, it is a relatively gentle way to go."

During the course of the day, William Henry did indeed appear to be going downhill. Several times as she went about her chores, Lena heard him calling out for Belle. She now found a small boy in the street and sent him over to Carlow Street to summon Billy. Billy arrived with his sisters Jane, Alice and wee Belle. Word had reached William Henry's sister, Lottie and she arrived also.

As his children assembled in the tiny bedroom, the small figure in the crumpled bed now seemed but a tiny shadow of the strong man who had carried them as infants on his shoulders. Jane tried to support her father's head and guide some water past his foamy lips, but the cough racked him still and he had barely the energy to acknowledge their presence. Time slipped slowly by, accompanied by the ticking of the mantel clock. Flickering shadows from the hearth crept across the threadbare bedroom rug and the quiet of evening was punctuated from time to time by far off sounds of the unrest in the streets. Their faces solemn and respectful, his children each took turns to hold his hand as they sat with him for the last time. William Henry's breathing now grew softer and shallower. His eyes opened at last however and he gazed beyond them all to the pale wee lily of a girl who stood by the foot of the bed. He stretched out his hand to her.

"Belle," he smiled.

Lightning Source UK Ltd.
Milton Keynes UK
UKOW050853150212

187336UK00001B/69/P